ZOM  Γ

Discover other titles by Mark Tufo
Visit us at marktufo.com
and http://zombiefallout.blogspot.com/ home of
future webisodes
and find me on FACEBOOK

Edited by:
TW Brown

Cover Art:
Shaed Studios, shaedstudios.com

Dedications:
To my wife, my coffee drinking buddy! I love you!
To Katherine Coynor, beta-reader extraordinaire thank you for all your tireless work.
To the men and women of the armed and uniformed services, thank you for all of your sacrifices.
To Perla Tirado, she's done more work for me than I could ever afford and I appreciate it greatly.
To Pauline Milbourn, the word Super-Fan seems to fit! (Is that technically two words?)

Alright if you're this far into the series you should know this is where it gets a little crazy, on ZF4 I posted on Facebook that if anyone wanted on my dedication page they just needed to post, got a little over a hundred responses, I was floored and honored. So I figured HEY I'm going to do that again for ZF5, well got over seven hundred names that time. As much as I would have liked to do the same here I was afraid I might get in the neighborhood of two thousand names and my editor would most likely have quit.

So I changed it up a bit, mostly had some contests, some involved guessing, some were just for laughs, others were at the right place at the right time and still a bunch others helped out when I asked. I truly cannot and could not ask for a better group of readers if I tried, you guys post funny pictures, or send your well wishes, or sometimes just tell me how much you and your families enjoy my books. I just need you guys to know that EVERY time you contact me, that I'm humbled, honored and thankful.

Dean Window, happy birthday to my wonderful husband love your beloved wife Janice Window & your number 1 son Harry Window, all our love always & forever. Xxxxxx (she asked!)

Adam Trout, Aisha Blevins, Aleks Jimenez, Alethea Baldwin, Alfa Polanco, Alfred Birtz, Allen Gurganus, Amanda Udell, Amber Cichon, Amber R. Johnson, Ami LawLess, Andrew Casavechia, Angela Berube-Gray, Angela Silvers, Angela Slade, Angi Martin, Annabelle Hawkins, Anne Shield, Ash Wheeler, Avon H. Clements, Bailey Hudson, Beth Bryeans, Beth Giglio Hindbaugh, Bob Reiss, Bob Simister, Bobbi Bradshaw, Bonnie Kalbskopf Williams, Bradley Syracuse Evans, Brandon Cook,

Brenda Spears, Brian Anatello, Brian Cantrall, Brian Diemart, Brigitte LaBelle, Brittany Cousin, Carleen Pierce, Carolyn Brady, Carolyn Johnson-Denton, Carrie Dileo, Cassoll Johnson, Catherine K'baum, Cathy Wagner Wallen, Char Hebert Gutierrez, Charles Ryden, Chris Enterline, Chris Harrington, Chris Leeper, Christine Knapik Myers, Christopher Botteri, Christopher Hackett, Christopher M. Moore, Cindy Sawyer, Cindy Warren, Claire Riley, Courtney Nelson, Dan Abildgaard, Dan Kar, Dan Modzik, Dani Holmes Buhrman, Dave House, David Hoffman, David Marble, David McClain, David Quincy, Dawn Raymond, Debbie Harris, Denise Keith, Diana Smallwood, Diane Johnson, Dieter Wheatley, DJ Parris, Donna Moretti, Dustie Marie Naud, Edna Anthony, Eileen Gurska, Elaine Eldridge Fortier, Elina M. Kelley, E'Lisa Gutierrez-Kirkpatrick, Elizabeth Arguelles, Elizabeth McCurry Wilson, Elizabeth McQueen, Elizabeth Rawls, Emily Spahr, Eric Shaw, Fran Mantuano, Franklin Cheesecake Barger, Gabriel Garcia, Gareth Moase, Garrett Elliott, Gerard Kelleher, Gina Greco Dipalo, Glenda Dill-Franklin, Gordon Fellis, Graham Carr, Greg Lose, Haleigh Martin, Hanneke Amahorseye, Heather Knirk, Heidi Rackliff, Holly Grivois Logue, J.D. Hawkins, Jacob Hawkins, James Reamer, Jamie Bray, Jan Luckett, Jane Gomez, Janice Van Campen, Jason Heine, Jason Lenn Webb, Jayson Sacco, Jeanne Tarrant, Jeff Schmitz, Jennifer Balcom, Jennifer Dotson, Jennifer Saucedo, Jennifer Schindler, Jennifer Storm, Jeremy Allen, Jerry Chesson, Jes Kriner, Jess Hale, Jess Lucero, Jesse Gordo, Jessica James, Jessica Morris, Jessica Parker, Joanne Crissey Dixon, Jody Brooks, Joe Hollingshead, Joe McCormick, Joey Whitley, John Hawkins, John Ross, Jordan Morgan, Josh Hurdle, Josie Ribeira, Joy Burke Buchanan, Joy Welch Evans, Julie Jones, Justin Frey, Karen Clarke, Karissa Rothstein, Kathleen Leeson, Kathy Richardson Roberts, Katina Henderson, Katrina Tanner, Kayla Sylskar, Kebby-Mag Sands, Kelly Lasseigne, Kelly McCloskey, Ken Reynolds, Ken Rutledge, Kesha Adams Bayliss, Kevin Aulinskis, Kim Hennessy, Kimberly A Porto Simon, Kory Kollman, Kristina Teems, Kristy Preston Newell, Kurt Eckert, Kyrstie Walker, Larry Davis, Laura Dunn, Laurie Leeper, Lee Close, Levi Martin, Linda Bouyea, Linda Garfield Burns, Lisa Marie Williams, LoLa Simone, Lynda Thomas Guydon, Mandy Hampton Fitch, Mandy Lees, Marcus Ryan Gross, Marcy Young-Salo, Marinda Grindstaff, Mark Chivas, Marty Boren, Mary Grace

Huff, Mary Philo, Matt Landrum, Matt McCarthy, Matthew Whinnett, Maxwell Nathan Frankenstein, Melissa Carver, Melissa Fitzgerald, Melissa Herevia, Melissa Kendrick, Melissa Shipley, Michael de Jager, Michael Martin, Michael Morris, Michael Turner, Michaela Seifert, Michelle Costin, Michelle Di Loreto-Pope, Michelle Harper, Michelle Way, Mike Pittman, Mindy Lenox, Minka An Bob, Misty Wehner Mackey, Neika Frye, Nevin E. Adams, Nick Anthony, Patricia Dzuba Stevens, Patrick Marshall, Paul Erickson, Paul White, Paula Best, Philip Spencer, Rachel Estok, Rachel Fuller DeAmato, Rachel McMillan Koch, Ramon Valdez, Ray Druszkowski, Ray Logan, Rebecca True Wilson, Rita A Livergood, Rob Tolliver, Robert Craig, Robert Wade, Rod Carnahan, Ron Casey, Ryan Matthew Walsh, Ryan MegaGeek Colley Garland, Sakina Pecchillo, Sandy Colella, Sara Bee Lindsay, Sarah Leech, Sarah Mayo, Sarah Olliso Flores, Sarah Pratt, Sarajane Hawkins, Scott Ferland, Scott 'skinner' Sinclair, Sean Marsh, Sean Ward, Shannon Durkin-Wade, Sharon Edelman, Sharon Payne, Shawn Breen, Shawn M Lynch, Sheila Jared, Stacy Clark Williams, Stephanie Dagger, Stephanie Sorensen, Steve Campbell, Steven Conte, Sue Pierpont, Summer Butler Bagley, Suzak Baker, Sydney Lorraine Franklin, Talea Fields, Tammy Craig Williamson, Tanya Dilworth-Cochran, Teri Selix, Terin Barnes, Tez Leaver, Thea Hollis, Thomas Aurand, Tim Root, Tom McCraney, Tom Muscle II, Trenda Lee, Trisha Smith, Tristan Simpson, Truls Fundingsrud, Vicky Bostick, Virginia Marquez, Vix Kirkpatrick, Wanda Guzman, Wes Harding, William Fortner, Willy Williams, Xavier Villalobos, Zach Rocha, Zachary John Francis Allen, Zoe Fletcher

ZF6 is an absolute trip. It takes you from the afterworld to the underworld and then back to Maine. I loved it.

- Katherine Coynor

Table of Contents

PROLOGUE ONE

The blackness was complete within and without the tattered walls which should have housed my soul; I could not see my hand in front of my face. I could not even tell if I was corporeal.

"Michael," an omnipresent voice rang out.

"God?" I answered.

"Some have called me that, others, have used Zeus, Allah, Jehovah, and Buddha."

"Am I dreaming this?"

"I am an eternal being that watches over the affairs of man."

"So God then basically."

"My name, if I had one, matters little. You may use Yoda if that makes you feel more comfortable."

"Oh come on, you're telling me I'm talking to the One God and you're giving me a *Star Wars* reference?"

"I did not like Jar Jar Binks."

"Nobody did," I shot back. "You seem mighty affable for an omnipotent being that could smite me down. Or is it smote?"

An older man of indeterminable age appeared before me at some point. In the last flash of a second, the blackness had been stripped away and replaced by a source of light equivalent to a noonday sun; yet I could see no hint of its origin.

"I didn't really see You like that," I said thoughtfully. "Maybe I did...this is rather confusing."

"Would you rather I appear as this?" The man surged to over forty feet tall; fiery eyes peered down at me and a long flowing beard almost touched the tips of his sandal-clad toes. His voice booming, "I appear as the person that stands before Me expects Me to be."

"No, no the old man thing is way better!" I yelled up. "So if I was a feminist?"

He sighed deeply but was back to the form of the

kindly stranger before I finished my words.

"It has come to My attention that Poena has deemed you as her plaything."

"Just now you figured that out? I thought you knew everything, and I figured he was a she…almost had to be. She's been messing with my life for decades. Maybe if you had skipped a movie or two I wouldn't be in this predicament."

"I think I know exactly why you are in this situation," he said pointing to my mouth.

"Yeah probably right about that," I said sheepishly.

"I will release you from the binding she has placed on you."

"Why now Yoda?" I asked, testing the boundaries—typical stupid-ass Michael Talbot.

He looked at me with a glint of humor in his eyes; like a proud father that wanted nothing more than to scoop his wayward child up and laugh but was required to set an example. Who the hell did he have to answer to?

"Contrary to a lot of fatalistic individuals, I care very, very deeply about the world of man. But there are strict rules laid down by nature herself that do not allow me direct intervention."

"You're God, what can possibly stand in Your way?"

"More than you will ever know."

***

What seemed like an eternity passed as I pondered His words. Maybe it had. Maybe mountains formed, oceans dried, the planet died and was reborn. All I knew was I loved my family and friends and I desperately wanted to be with them. I gulped hard, not sure if I was ready for the answer to my next question or not.

"Am I alive?"

"Do you want to be?"

"God, I had a philosophy professor once tell me the

meaning of life."

God arched an eyebrow and asked, "What was her definition?"

"Life is a bowl of snow."

"Did that make any sense to you, Michael?"

"About as much as Your question."

"Fair enough. You must answer the first question, but I can answer the latter." It was my turn to arch an eyebrow. "The meaning of life? Well that's simple, it is merely LIFE. To live, to breathe, to laugh, to love, to procreate, to exist. It is nothing more and nothing less."

"What about the zombies?"

"They are an abomination created by man. They are not life, they are the antithesis. They destroy everything in their path without the ability or want to create."

"I would very much like to be alive," I begged.

"Then it shall be so."

"It has been an unbelievable honor to talk with You, but I have to ask one more question."

God waited patiently, as He watched me struggle to ask a question that I hoped would not offend Him.

"Am I dreaming this?"

He laughed...heartily, I might add. "Oh, Michael, you are a fun one to watch. Now get off the street and hide. Eliza is coming and she plans on laying waste to the entire city."

"Will I see You again?"

"Get your soul back and we will talk some more."

He placed the heel of his hand against my forehead. I felt as if I were being shot from a cannon. The rush of matter as it streamed by at light speed was disorientating; it wasn't until I picked my head up off of the pavement that I knew where I was.

"I'M BACK!" I screamed triumphantly, then I remembered God's—or my vivid dream's—last words and I tried to get up and make a run for it.

PROLOGUE TWO

The slight woman and the stocky man walked across the parking lot as the sun blazed down. The four truck drivers watched as they approached.

"How stupid do you think they are?" Al, at twenty-eight, the youngest of the group asked.

"I guess we'll see," their self-appointed leader Kong replied.

He had been a decent man when the world still made sense. But these were not normal times; he would, and had done, all it took to survive and even thrive, including some things that were not necessary. Without the possibility of paying for his crimes, he had taken advantage of numerous situations.

Even from across the parking lot he could tell that the woman was beautiful, but there was something else there…something cold, deadly. He involuntarily shivered.

"She's fucking hot!" the third driver, Dom, said. "Can I have her after you, Kong?"

Kong wanted to say he could have her first and that he was getting the hell out of there, but he stayed put against his better judgment. Her beauty only intensified as she approached, but so did his feelings of unease. She stopped no more than ten feet from where the men stood. Kong could tell from the men's posturing that they were feeling differing forms of unease just as he was.

"Are those your trucks?" the woman asked.

"What's it to you?" Dom asked.

Kong noticed the woman's eyebrows furrow.

"I have a proposition," the woman stated.

"I've got your fucking proposition right here!" Dom yelled, grabbing his crotch.

Randy, the fourth—and thus far, silent—driver, spoke with laughter in his voice as his 6 foot 5, 315 pound frame approached the woman, "I'd probably break her in half."

"Let's hear what she has to say," Kong said, placing

his hand on Randy's shoulder.

Randy shrugged it off. "Fuck you, man. I'll listen to what she says after I break a piece of that off. You got a problem with that?" Randy shouted as he pointed at the stocky youth that had come with the woman.

The young man merely smiled sadly. For some reason, that scared the shit out of Kong. Randy's steps began to falter as he got closer to the woman. She did not move a muscle; even her hair seemed unaffected by the wind. Kong noticed that she was somehow above the earthly elements.

"I'm...I'm glad you're not running," Randy said as he started fumbling around with his fly. "I hate when they run. Oh, I catch them...always. It's just that I'm usually sweaty by then, and then I ain't so nice. You know what I mean?" Randy asked with a leer as he pulled his penis free from his pants. "Like what you see?"

The woman, without looking down, reached her hand out.

"Yeah, baby, that's what I'm talking about," Randy said as he looked heavenward in anticipation.

His high pitched screams started shortly after his dismembered member landed with a wet slap on the pavement.

"Are we ready to talk?" the woman asked as she wiped her hand on Randy's shirt before effortlessly pushing him over.

His screams became a crescendo before they started to tail off into sobs of pain. Shock and blood loss were beginning to take their toll.

"Fuck, Kong, she ripped his cock off!" Al was screaming as he began to back up.

Dom was dry-heaving. Only Kong was holding his ground.

"You the leader?" the woman asked Kong as she stepped over Randy who was now wrapped up in the fetal position.

He nodded quickly, wishing that, after he had shot his

infected girlfriend, he had turned the gun on himself. Anything would have been better than staring into those twin pools of death.

"I have a proposition," she stated again.

"And if I refuse?" Kong asked.

The woman looked back at the huddled form of Randy.

"I'm listening," he told her.

And an hour later, when they were done talking, there were some absolute truths. First and foremost, Kong was confident in the fact that he had just made a deal with the devil.

Eliza stepped on Randy's dried husk of manhood as she walked away.

"Where we going to get more truckers?" Al asked Kong.

"I've got an idea about that. Shouldn't really be a problem," he told the younger man.

"Do you really think these work?" Dom asked as he held out the small vial Eliza had given them all.

Kong was absently rubbing his fingers over the vial he now wore around his neck. He didn't know for sure, but he was going to check because, if they didn't, he was going to consider their agreement null and void. Then he was going to go as far west as he could before driving into the ocean.

"Come on, Al, you ride with me," Kong said.

"You want me to leave my rig here?" Al asked.

"Yeah. I just want to check something out, and the quieter we go in, the better."

"Sure," Al answered, but he wasn't comfortable with it at all.

"What do you want me to do?" Dom asked.

"Get rid of Randy's body. We'll be right back," Kong told him.

"You want me to bury the fat fuck? It'll take me hours to dig something deep enough," Dom replied.

"Did I say to bury him? Just get the body out of the

middle of the parking lot. We're going to have dozens of trucks in here. I don't need someone squashing his lard ass all over the place."

Dom lit a cigarette. "Fine, but I'm not touching his pecker."

"Not much to worry about there anyway," Kong said.

Kong and Al drove a few miles until Kong found what he was looking for: a small band of zombies wandering the neighborhood. They were still far off, but the sound of the huge diesel Mack engine was drawing them in like gypsies to a rhinestone festival.

"Hey, Al, can I see that new gun you lifted off that guy the other day?" Kong asked. Al handed him the piece. "She sure is a beaut," Kong said as he looked at the extended barrel Colt .45. "Loaded too," he said as he looked into the cylinder. "Get out." Kong pointed the revolver at Al's forehead.

"What the fuck are you doing, man?" Al said as he put his hands up and licked his lips nervously.

"A test. Get out. I'm not going to say it again."

"Come on, man, we're friends and shit," Al said, sweat popping out all over his face as he looked out the window to the approaching zombies. "Come on, man, you can't really believe this little vial of shit is going to stop them, do you?"

"Well Eliza sure seems to think that it will. If it does, then I have to honor my end of the agreement. I'll be honest, I'm really kind of hoping that it doesn't so I can get the fuck out of here."

"If it doesn't work, Kong, I'm dead."

"Yeah...sucks for you. Get out."

"Kong, man, please? We're friends."

Kong pulled the hammer back on the revolver. "I've known you for two weeks. I've had a sore on the inside of my lip for longer. Don't make me have to clean your brains up out of my truck."

Al hesitated a moment longer as he stared down the

barrel of his own gun. "You're a fucking asshole," he said as he jumped down off the truck and started sprinting for the nearest house.

Kong reached over and shut his passenger door—locking it for good measure—and then proceeded to watch the show. The zombies changed their angle of pursuit as Al crossed the street and went to the first house he could. Kong snickered as Al frantically pulled on the security door. Al first looked back towards the truck to see if Kong was going to help, then went further down the street.

"Should have told the fucker to stand still. My fault," Kong said as he slowly backed the truck up to keep pace with the fleeing Al.

Al had only been a truck driver for five years, but they had been rough years on his body. He ate fast food and drank to excess while on the road and it showed; he was running out of steam by the time he figured he was not going to gain entry in the second house either. The zombies had closed to within twenty feet. Al turned to meet his fate, fists upraised as if that were going to stop the swarm. Then, just as they got within teeth-snapping distance, they stopped.

The closer ones began sniffing the air all around Al.

"Son of a bitch, the shit works," Kong said almost silently as he tucked in the precious vial under his shirt.

Al kept ducking his head and rapidly blinking his eyes as the zombies gathered all around him, the newcomers having to check out his edibility factor. Some lost interest quickly when they realized he wasn't food. A few others lingered, fundamentally knowing that they should be able to eat him but couldn't.

The zombies approached the truck as Kong stepped down. He held his guns up as the zombies got close. His heart was racing, and he killed two that approached a little too close for comfort. He stopped when they seemed to get the same confused look he had seen with the ones around Al. Again the majority lost interest and left. A few smarter ones lingered. Kong thought maybe they were wondering if they could get around whatever spell was holding them back. He gave them a .45 caliber lead injection against any future inquisitiveness.

He approached Al slowly, constantly looking around to make sure none of the zombies were sneaking up on him. He handed Al his weapon back.

"Let's go," Kong said as if nothing had happened.

Al was close to tears. He was leaning over and bringing in heavy breaths as he reached out and grabbed the gun. Standing up straight, he pointed the weapon at Kong. "I should fucking kill you!" he spat.

"Go ahead. I'd fucking deserve it." Kong turned back to his truck.

The .45 was shaking wildly as Al wrestled within himself against the anger, fear, and betrayal. He eventually followed Kong to the big rig, not saying a word as Kong unlocked the door and let him in.

Dom was inside his truck smoking a cigarette when the duo returned. He got out when he saw Al get down.

"What's the matter? You look like shit," Dom said as Al stormed past.

"The vials work," Kong told him. "Time to get some drivers."

"Shit," Dom said, grinding the cigarette under his boot as he realized what had transpired.

CHAPTER ONE

Day one without Talbot

"Ohmigod, ohmigod, ohmigod," Gary kept repeating, as BT shoved him through Mary's front door.

"Where's Josh?" Mary screamed, her eyes wide with terror.

"He's supposed to be here," BT said, moving to the side so that he could shut the door and look out the curtain.

"He's not here!" she screamed. "You left him out there!" She was shrieking now.

Gary was still muttering on the floor where BT had deposited him.

"Oh fuck," BT said silently as he looked through the large, bar-covered picture window of Mary's modest siege home.

"Where is my son?" she screamed, slamming her fists into BT's chest.

BT pointed with the tip of his rifle before he headed back towards the front door.

Josh was, at the most, two steps ahead of the lead zombie whose outstretched hand was nearly close enough to touch his collar.

"Oh my God!" Mary said in unison with Gary.

"The fucking toy, he went back for the fucking toy," BT said as he headed out the front door.

Josh was running for his very existence, but the large remote-control truck he was carrying was impeding his progress. BT did not trust his marksmanship or frayed nerves to start firing at targets so close to a live body, and he couldn't tell Josh to drop down. BT would be able to get the lead zombie and a couple of others, but there were too many of them. Add to that the real danger that the zombies pursuing him and Gary would completely cut the boy off from the house.

"Drop the damn truck!" BT roared.

Josh looked up; wide, white, terror-filled eyes stared back at him.

"Drop the truck, boy!" BT repeated with more force.

BT watched as Josh had an internal struggle within himself. The boy was deciding on whether or not to give up one of the last things his father had given him or forfeit his life. It was close, but Josh finally let go of the toy monster truck. BT figured the boy's father was still looking out for him as the truck caught in between the strides of the zombie closest to Josh. Josh yelped as the zombie's hands reached out and touched him down his back and the bottom of his pants as its legs became tangled in the rubber and plastic causing the zombie to slam chin first into the ground.

The effect was instantaneous as at least another three zombies went down with their leader. Josh was far from out of danger, but BT finally had an opening with which to let lead fly. He lined up a shot and tried to pull the trigger.

"Oh no," he sighed. He was out of bullets.

"Good a day to die as any, maybe even better than most," he said as he ran towards Josh. His hastily drawn up plan was to use himself as a human shield.

"Get out of the way, you lummox!" Mary shouted behind him. She didn't give him much of a chance, though, as she began to shoot. Most weren't head shots, but the bullets were causing enough damage to slow the zombies down.

Gary came up beside her; he was jamming shells in to his rifle. Tears were still streaming down his face as he began to fire. BT was amazed he could hit anything through the waterfall in his eyes. Luckily Gary was focused on the zombies in the front of the house where his bullets would only slam into the undead.

Josh had about another fifty yards to make it to the house, forty before he made it to BT. BT waited like the anchorman in the first ever zombie relay. First prize was life, everything else was death. BT started jogging towards the house as Josh approached, then snatched him up into his huge arms, going full tilt within four strides. Mary was holding the security door open so that he could dive in with his precious cargo. Gary was busy shoving new shells into his rifle.

"Get in the house!" Mary yelled simultaneously to BT and Gary.

Gary was slow to react. BT grabbed him by the front of his jacket and pulled him in alongside. He pushed Josh ahead of himself as he fell to the floor; he didn't want to save the boy from zombies only to crush him under his bulk. BT's chest had no sooner hit the floor when the first zombies crashed up against the security door. Mary was backing up as the house rattled from the multiple impacts.

Gary shut the front door when BT moved his legs.

"What were you thinking!" Mary screamed at Josh, who was full on crying now. "What were you thinking!" she screamed again.

Josh was sobbing so hard that he was hitching and having a difficult time catching his breath. "It...it was from dad," he wailed.

"Was it worth getting killed over?" She was screaming so loudly, and with such force, that her face was turning red and thick, corded veins were bulging from her neck and forehead.

"Mary, he's alive, he's fine," BT said, trying to restore some order in the house.

She wasn't having any of it and turned her wrath on him. "Wasn't it your grand fucking idea to let him go along?"

"Oh I would imagine it was Mike's insidious ramblings that convinced the boy to go out," Mrs. Deneaux added.

"You shut up!" Mary wheeled, pointing her finger at the crone. It seemed no one would be spared Mary's ire. "Where were you when my son was running for his life?"

"Dear, I'm just an old woman. What could I have done?" Mrs. Deneaux asked in return.

"I should have never opened my door. I should have never let any of you into my life." She was crying now.

"It's alright, mom, I'm alright," Josh said, getting up to comfort his mother. She gripped him tightly as if she were afraid to let him go, lest he not be real. She was crying into his shoulder, their roles momentarily reversed. "Mom, we had to let them in, it was the Christian thing to do."

"I almost lost you, Josh. I can't lose you...you're all I have left in the world." She let loose with a full-throated cry.

"I'm here, mom, I'm here," he said as he led her towards the couch.

"Where's Michael?" Mrs. Deneaux asked BT.

BT shook his head almost imperceptibly from side to side. Mrs. Deneaux was careful not to let her joy show. Gary was staring out the living room window, but his eyes did not appear to be focused on anything.

"I didn't even get a chance to bury him," Gary mumbled. "What am I going to tell my dad?" he asked the question, but that was not anything any one had an answer to.

"What now?" Mrs. Deneaux asked BT.

"We head towards Maine," he told her.

"When?" Mary looked up.

BT couldn't tell if she was wondering when they'd be out of her house or how long she had for her and her son to get ready to go.

Gary had understood the meaning behind her question. "Mary, you can't stay here," he said, finally turning back around to face the group. The room darkened as the curtain slid back into place.

"Oh yes we can!" she said with vehemence as she pulled Josh closer. "We're never going out there."

"You know you're going to run out of supplies," he

said calmly, which belied his true countenance.

"We're better off without them," Mrs. Deneaux said. "The boy will just slow us down."

"As opposed to you?" Gary shot back, very much unlike anything that usually came from his mouth.

Mrs. Deneaux shrugged her shoulders and lit up a cigarette in response.

"How dare you!" Mary said to Mrs. Deneaux. "I opened my doors to you, I fed you, I confided in you, then you turn on me?"

"I was trying to help, dearie. You said you didn't want to go and I thought this would help your argument," Mrs. Deneaux said, smiling with her tobacco-stained teeth showing. The smile was much too wide and displayed too many teeth to mean anything but contempt.

"Handle a snake, you're bound to get bitten eventually," BT said to Mary.

"You must be happy now, BT," Mrs. Deneaux said.

"What are you talking about?" he asked her.

"Well, it looks like you're in charge now. With Mike out of the way, you take rightful control," she said, then took a long pull from her cigarette while waiting for BT's response.

BT almost rose to the bait, but he could see the grim glimmer of smugness right under the surface in the woman's face and he'd be damned if he gave her anything remotely similar to a smile.

"Well the age is right," he said.

"What?" Gary asked.

Mrs. Deneaux's eyes narrowed as she waited for his response.

"She could be Eliza's mother," BT said as he went to the side of the house to see how many zombies Josh had brought back with him.

Josh snorted. "That's funny because that would make her like five hundred and fifty years old."

"I remember when spanking your children was an

acceptable form of punishment," Mrs. Deneaux said, turning towards the boy, who shrunk back into the protective embrace of his mother.

"We're leaving in the morning," BT said, coming back into the living room. "Mary, I won't force you, but I really think you should reconsider."

"Michael would have been more persuasive," Mrs. Deneaux said.

"You done?" BT asked her.

"For now," she said taking another drag off her smoke.

"Mary, please," Gary begged. "You're not safe here."

She scoffed at his words. "Oh yeah, I see how *safe* it is out there," she said mockingly, not even willing to move her hand to point, but rather nodding with her chin towards the front door.

CHAPTER TWO

Mike Journal Entry 1

There was not a place on my body that was not screaming in agony. If I dared to look, I would imagine I had third-degree burns over three-quarters of my body. I smelled like barbeque; it was both disgusting and somewhat saliva-inducing at the same time. Where my head had bounced off the pavement a blackened mixture of burnt skin and wet blood slicked the roadway. My neck crinkled like dried old parchment paper as I picked my head up.

My arms were blistering, the surface looking like a dry lake bed with viscous puss running through the crevices. That did not smell nearly as tasty as the flap of meat on the ground. My blue jeans had mostly melted to my body and karma had come full circle. How many times had I given people shit for wearing their clothes so tight from trying to hold in some excess baggage that they looked like they had painted them on? This was like that. If I was so inclined (which I wasn't) to pull the denim material off of me, it would have easily taken all of the skin and most likely a fair portion of muscle mass.

I screamed as I tried to stand, I nearly teetered over not willing to place my burnt palms on the ground and lose anymore of me. The sky darkened as I made it to an almost standing position. My skin was too dried and burnt to allow for full extension, I was hunched over like a man three times my age—which would have been REAL fucking old. I was fighting desperately to hold onto consciousness, but it was flickering like a basement light in a horror movie. My mind was urging me off the street. My body didn't give a shit.

"Maybe I could just take a little break," I said out

loud. Or maybe I thought it. I don't know, but it sounded like a grand idea. "Move!" I urged my charred limbs. Something creaked, groaned, and snapped, I sounded like a new macabre cereal advertisement. *Get your new Meatie-O's fortified with all the vitamins a growing zombie needs*, I sneered as I thought it. It was funny and it gave me the briefest of seconds away from the agony that permeated my entire being.

I shuffled, the melding of my jeans to my skin making any movement difficult. Tears were streaming down my face in earnest; I would have bellowed in pain if I had been able to catch my breath, it was that intense. I imagined being placed in an iron maiden would have been bliss compared to what I was feeling. Still, I moved; the torment of pain seemingly the only thing spurring me on. It was thirty feet to the closest house. It might as well have been the surface of the moon.

But now I heard noise…and not the good kind. A rat the size of a lapdog loped past. It stopped for the briefest of moments, whiskers twitching as it smelled my cooked countenance, but even a warm meal wasn't enough to entice him to stay. It turned to look over its shoulder and bounded off.

I could think of only one thing that would send a rat on its way: zombies.

Would they bother me? Did I have enough strength to turn them away? I barely had enough strength to think the thoughts, so I kept my ambling shuffle in motion. The house now seemed thirty-five feet away. And no, I have no idea how that happened; I'm not a quantum physicist for fuck's sake.

It was countless heartbeats of pain later and I had halved the distance to the house. I was now a good fifty feet away. I could hear the moans of the undead, they sounded far off, but there had to be a lot of them for me to be hearing them this clearly. Instead of the movement causing my burns to limber up, the opposite seemed to be happening. The puss that was oozing from a dozen different places was beginning to congeal which made my previous shuffle feel like a world class sprint. In reality I had another ten feet to the steps—which in and of themselves were going to be a near insurmountable endeavor. I didn't think I was going to make it.

The moaning didn't sound any closer, but it wasn't moving away. I imagined a column of zombies was moving horizontal to my location. I did a silent 'thank you' to the Big Guy and suddenly had a feeling he heard. I was a little awestruck to think that I might have a direct pipeline. I wonder if this was what Moses felt?

I stubbed my toe against the step. At some point I had my eyes shut, trying in vain to block out the blistering nerve endings as they pounded relentlessly. I couldn't even begin to wonder how I was going to get my leg the eight inches up to get onto the first step. I looked at that front door like I was a Japanese tourist who had left his camera behind and the door was the Eighth Wonder of the World. (Is that a stretch? It seemed to work when I thought about it, seems a little different on paper.)

I placed my gnarled hands under my right thigh and pulled up, the toe of my melted boots rubbing up against the backstop. I almost got stuck on the small lip of the stair that jutted out. Fried skin around my knee snapped apart as I over-flexed it. Oily blood flowed freely, but I sighed in relief as my right leg was now one step closer. The next test would be if I had the power to stand completely upright, then I'd be able to drag my left leg up.

I placed the heels of my hands against the railing and, combined with my leg, I was indeed able to get my left foot onto the top of Mount McKinley—or the first step, however you want to interpret that is fine with me. Now I just had to deal with K2 and Mount Everest and I'd be home free. If you've had the opportunity to read my other journals, you'd realize I have a flare for the dramatic, but that doesn't mean what I was feeling wasn't right.

The moans were either increasing in volume or

zombies were getting nearer as I was strategizing the complexities of my climb. I wondered if just falling forward onto the landing itself would be the best course of action; but unless the door was unlocked AND open so I could push it in, I would be fucked. Once I hit the turf, there really didn't seem any sort of chance that I'd be able to get back up.

"This blows," I whispered, as I once again reached behind my right thigh for an assisted lift, but now it was coated in my juices and it was difficult to get any sort of grip, especially since my fingers were curled up like claws.

I jumped when I heard gunshots no more than a street away, then I began to hear human shouting. It was too far to catch the words, but I'm sure it revolved around the zombies and how they needed to stay away from them. Life had become vastly easy in one sense; you really just needed to survive, no shopping lists, errands, chores, meetings, project due dates, all the bullshit of modernity had been stripped away. It was now a one word world. Sure, how you went about that one word was difficult as all hell, but at least you only had to focus on the one thing. That's got to count for something, right?

Yeah, I know it's bullshit. I'd rather be driving to Walmart with the missus shopping for dreaded curtains than this crap. At least at the end of the errands I could have gone home and got my ass thoroughly whomped by Travis in any Wii game we played. Survivalism isn't nearly as much fun in reality as opposed to when you are prepping. I'd hoped and secretly dreamed for this day whilst I prepared for it. It really did seem so simple back in the day, but I've had my fill of death and destruction. Right now I'd gladly take unclogging a plugged toilet in a strangers home, maybe even without rubber gloves than this waking nightmare I now found myself in.

"It worked!" I said maybe a bit too loud under the circumstances. I had been completely able to occupy my mind elsewhere as I climbed up onto the second step. More gun fire and definitely more human sounds, but the latter was more of the screaming variety. It sounded like a woman was being torn to shreds, but I'm testimony to the fact that once your body is being wrenched apart, even the biggest, beefiest males can scream much like a woman; especially if a particularly tender part is being dined on. Images of that poor bastard Cash, with April back in Colorado, rushed to the forefront; that thought alone spurred me onto the top step quicker than anything else had thus far.

I was beginning to hear footfalls, it sounded like wet salmon being slapped across someone's face. They were getting close. I could only hope they weren't necessarily hunting me down.

The remnants of the screen door hung by my feet. I eyed the door handle and then my hooked fingers. I didn't have the hand strength to crush a gnat, so this was going to be interesting, and now I had the added bonus of them being covered in my own gore. I moved closer so that I would not have to stretch my arm, I didn't think I could deal with another part of my anatomy leaking. My feet tangled up in the aluminum runner from the screen door; I was falling forward, but I could not get my arms up to brace myself. My head struck the door first with a solid thud, I was grateful it was not a hollow sound—my head not the door.

I was falling into the house; I hoped that there wasn't anything too destructive on the floor, like protruding nails, broken glass or bacteria-encrusted old chicken. I think I'd take the glass over the chicken, not the nails, but definitely the glass. It was none of the above. I fell into a crinkling mass of tin foil. The noise of the foil was a small distraction as my head bounced off the hard tile entry way. My vision was blackening, and now my fucking head ached to go along with the rest of the shit storm I was going through.

Zombies were still coming and I wasn't much safer than I had been a few moments earlier. I wriggled my body the rest of the way into the house out of sheer necessity. I managed to push the door closed with my left leg, and was able to see strips of tin foil hanging everywhere as I faded to black—pretty much just like the old movies or even the Bugs Bunny cartoons where you see the shrinking black circle go all the way down to a pinprick and wink out. Luckily there was no fat pig telling me 'Th-th-that's all folks!'

CHAPTER THREE

Eliza & Tomas

"Your face is priceless, brother," Eliza exclaimed.

"It is a shame, dear sister, that the only time you show anything remotely similar to a smile is at the expense of others," Tomas replied sadly.

"Come, brother, share in my happiness...*our* victory," she stressed. "With Michael Talbot out of the way, there is now nothing that can stop us. And yet you still pine for him and his family, don't you? We will meet up with his family soon enough, you can say your good-byes then."

"What? I thought we were done with the Talbots, let them be, they have lost their father, what more could you possibly do?"

"You cannot be that naïve, Tomas, can you? Michael has left spawn behind. I will not let them walk this world any longer than necessary, he has two boys who could spread their seed far and wide and even now the girl swells with another. No, they are like vermin. I must snuff them out while I have them at their lowest and most vulnerable. But first things first, I believe that some of his traveling party are still in this city. There is time enough that we can stay and watch the festivities."

"What have you planned, sister?" Tomas asked.

"I am going to wield my full might upon this accursed hovel of humanity."

"Eliza, have you stopped to think what you will do for sustenance once you have wiped out the humans?"

"Relax, brother, I cannot stand the hairless monkeys,

but I respect their ability to adapt and survive. Right now I just want to have some fun."

"Having fun means laughing, being with the ones you love, go-karts."

"I do not know about the go-karts, Tomas, but I will laugh as the humans run fruitlessly for their pathetic lives and you at least love me, is that not enough?"

"I think you're missing the point, Eliza."

"My zombies will be in place soon. Come, let us find a better vantage point that we can watch from. And I'm starving anyway…this will flush some of them out."

Tomas paled.

"And I know that you are hungry, you have not eaten in days."

Tomas could not deny the fact that his gut was twisted in knots as it begged for food. He was repulsed every time he fed, but he could not control himself, the hunger was too great. He could feed off animals in an emergency but it was equivalent to a human sustaining life by eating lettuce.

"I see that you are not disagreeing. Soon, brother, you will be able to drink to your heart's content."

"I curse you for what you have done to me, Eliza."

"You should have stayed home with papa," she sneered, recalling their days in Germany some five hundred years ago.

"You were all I had, Lizzie," Tomas said as he bowed his head.

"It appears that is as true today as it was back then." She laughed, but it had more to do with the irony of her statement than mirth. "This will work," Eliza said as she stood on a small hill that overlooked a vast portion of the town below.

"Oh God," Tomas intoned as he saw the black smudge of zombies that dominated the horizon."

"God, Tomas? Really? You might as well ask for Jesus and that fat man the children seem to worship."

"Santa?"

"I suppose, I never stop to ask questions as I feed, I find it distracting."

"Those are people, Eliza, with hopes and dreams."

"I am a predator, Tomas, I care not for the prey. Does a lion sit in self-doubt about the harm it bestows upon the gazelle?"

"I understand what you are. What *we* are," he corrected when Eliza arched an eyebrow at him. "But what you are doing now is not the natural order of things. Lions don't kill indiscriminately, wiping out everything."

"Spare me the lesson in morality, brother, I care not. I like to watch the humans suffer, it brings me enjoyment. And stop trying to control my herd, I can feel you trying to send messages to them. They will listen only to me."

Tomas looked back at his sister, unsure what to do next. He sat on the grass to watch as the first of the zombies entered the town. His vision alternated between looking at the ground and watching as the zombies advanced, he was caught completely unawares as he sensed something. He wasn't sure what it was, and was fearful to look up at his sister lest he give it away, she was completely fixated on the town below.

Michael? He thought it without transmitting the message, his sister would surely figure out what was going on if he did that, and as of yet he wasn't sure. It was as if he was 'seeing' Michael through the wrong end of a telescope. There wasn't much to hold on to, it was so faint that he thought it was most likely just residual feelings. But still it nagged around the edges of his mind. *It is!* he thought excitedly. *It's probably too faint for Eliza to pick up especially with her so focused on controlling the zombies.*

Tomas began to emit what he could only describe as waves of white noise, much like televisions without a satellite or cable signal.

"I've already told you, brother, you cannot wrest control of the zombies from me. I am in direct communication with them and this static will not disrupt that."

Tomas began to shiver with the effort to broadcast even louder as the signal from Michael grew from imperceptible to miniscule.

"What are you doing, Tomas? You begin to annoy me."

"I thought that I might be able to stop them this way," Tomas lied.

"I already told you this would not work yet you continue."

Tomas could 'feel' Eliza probing through the 'noise' trying to figure out what he was up to. He literally began to vibrate from the effort of expanding so much energy and was unsure how long he would be able to conceal Michael's presence.

Eliza was closing in; she was adept with the workings of the mind after so many millennia of practice.

Tomas urged Mike on, but to where? And to what end? Eventually she would discover that her sworn enemy still yet breathed air, and Tomas could tell that the thread from which Mike's life hung was frayed and would not be able to take much strain. Tomas amped up his concealment just as Eliza was closing in. Just when he felt that all was lost, he lost Michael completely. He rocked backwards, breathing heavily from the mind strain.

"Done now, brother?" Eliza asked clearly confused.

Tomas did not answer. He was still trying to figure out what had just happened.

CHAPTER FOUR

BT & Gary

Gary was having a difficult time sleeping. Every time he shut his eyes, he saw Michael fall over. Sometimes there was only the loud thud of his head reverberating off the ground. But more often than not, Mike would cry out in pain and anguish; first asking for Gary's help, then accusing him of abandoning him. It was not all that hard to stay awake, the town was in the midst of a full-scale zombie invasion. Houses were burning, the sounds of gunfire were rampant as were distant screams.

Gary strode over to the couch and went to shake BT awake.

"I'm not asleep," he said.

"We should get going. Whatever is going on out there is starting to get closer," Gary said. "Plus, the zombies that were around the house have left about ten minutes ago, probably to go and enjoy the fun."

"What? They didn't want to miss out?"

"That would be my guess," Gary answered in all seriousness.

"What about Mary? Will she change her mind?" BT asked Gary, knowing full well that he didn't have an answer either. "We can't leave her here."

"We both know that, BT, but we can't force her either."

"The old bat was right about one thing," BT said.

"What's that?" Gary asked.

"Mike would have somehow convinced them to come

with us."

Gary winced at the name of his brother in the past tense. "You're probably right. I'll talk to her one last time, but I think we should get going while the getting is good," Gary said even as he realized the futility of his words falling on Mary's deaf ears.

BT saw the cherry of the cigarette glow before he realized that Deneaux was standing at the far side of the room. It startled him for a moment because he thought it to be half of a pair of glowing evil eyes.

"Weren't planning on sneaking out in the middle of the night and leaving us here, were you?" Mrs. Deneaux asked as she took another drag. A small raspy cough following her words.

"Any chance that's lung cancer?" BT asked Deneaux as he sat up rubbing his eyes raw. The smoke from the burning town was making its way into the house. It was subtle at the moment, but soon it would be impossible to take a breath that did not result in a coughing fit, and that would be followed soon by asphyxiation.

"You're sounding more like him every minute," Mrs. Deneaux replied dryly.

"From anyone else I would consider that a compliment," BT said as he stood. He walked over to the window and confirmed what Gary had already told him, the zombies had taken a break and were out getting some lunch…most likely fast food. BT's mood soured at his poor joke.

***

"Mary do you have a minute?" Gary asked as he walked into her room.

She had ten candles burning as she tried to keep the dark at bay and was sitting up in her bed. Josh was asleep with his head in her lap while she was absently stroking his hair as she looked at the window across the room. Her gaze slowly swiveled towards him as she came back from whichever distant world she had traveled. "We're all dead." She said with conviction.

"Even Josh?" Gary asked striking out as hard as he dared, she flinched from his words.

Her eyes were vacant as she turned back towards the blackened window.

"You have a real chance if you come with us," Gary nearly begged.

A flicker of anger stretched across her features. "Your brother was a half-vampire, former Marine survivalist, and he fell. What chance do I and Josh have?"

Gary couldn't tell if she had given up or was looking for a real answer from him. Gary could only respond with a lame sounding, "You can't stay here."

He wished he could bolster her argument above and beyond their food stores, but maybe she did have it right. They were alive after so many countless billions had perished; she'd done something right to keep them safe so far. And just because Mike was dead, Gary didn't think Eliza was done with the Talbot clan by any stretch of the imagination.

"We're leaving within the hour." Gary said before he turned to walk out the door. He watched as she blanched from his words. "I hope you come, but I'll understand if you don't."

"Just make sure you lock the door on your way out." And with those words Mary completely shut the door on the topic.

***

BT lifted his chin to Gary as Gary walked in the room, as if to ask 'Well?'

Gary shook his head side to side and looked down.

"We're going to need wheels soon," BT said, trying to plan out there escape.

"Mary has a car in the detached garage," Mrs. Deneaux said. "We could take that."

"No," Gary said forcibly. "She'll need it eventually."

"She's not going anywhere. Poor damn thing has lost her marbles," she said as she spun her cigarette laden hand around the right side of her head, the cherry leaving tracers in the murkiness.

"What is wrong with you?" BT asked. "Gary's right. At some point she's going to realize she needs to get out of here. Her maternal instinct will kick in eventually."

"Let's hope it isn't like that poor lass that lined up her children against the truck like they were targets. That was horrible," she added at the end like an afterthought.

BT shook his head. "I'd trade a thousand of you for Mike."

"But yet here I am," she smiled.

"I'd leave you here to fester in your own corroded soul, but that wouldn't be fair to Mary," BT said. "Ten minutes and we're leaving."

Gary started grabbing their meager possessions and loading the guns. Deneaux continued smoking.

BT kept staring out the window. It was still night time, but the sky was lit up from the blaze of at least a hundred houses. Smoke was drifting lazily across the front lawn.

"Yeah…that's not too fucking eerie," BT said as he watched the swirls of smoke pass by. "A thousand zombies could be hiding on the other side of that mist."

"You say something?" Gary asked as he tried to jam a sixth bullet into a five-bullet cartridge.

"You were the fastest sperm?" Deneaux questioned Gary. "Must not have been much to choose from," she laughed.

Gary stood. "I rue the day I ever met you," he said as he put the backpack Josh had given him on. He strode over to BT to see outside. "Wow, the city is burning."

"Rue?" BT asked as an aside.

"It's all I could come up with."

"I guess it works. You alright?" BT asked seriously.

"No, I've now had two brothers die, neither of which I was able to bury. My father expected me to bring Mike back and I failed."

BT placed his arm around Gary's shoulder. He knew Anthony Talbot had actually demanded that Mike bring Gary back, but he wasn't going to correct him...not now...not ever.

"This is war, Gary. There aren't promises you can always keep. People are going to die, good men are going to die," he added for emphasis.

Gary broke down for a moment, silent tears dropped from his face as his throat constricted.

"Don't you say a fucking word!" BT said, pointing a meaty finger at Mrs. Deneaux.

She placed her hands up as if to say 'I'm innocent.'

Mary was standing where Mrs. Deneaux had been moments earlier.

Gary turned to see her; his heart momentarily lifted when he thought she may have changed her mind.

"My neighbor across the street left his second car. He gave me the keys when he left, said I could have it if I wanted. They're hanging on the peg in the kitchen."

"Mrs. Deneaux said you had a car," BT said.

"I do, but it doesn't run and he knew it," she said.

"You keep it, Mary. I'll give you my father's address, come up there when you have to," Gary said.

"I've already told you we're not leaving. We're *never* leaving."

BT shivered at her use of the word never, it left very little room for doubt.

"You don't know that," Gary intoned. "Things change."

"It's too late anyway," she said in that far away voice.

"Too late for what?" Gary asked as alarm began to spread throughout his body.

"The whelp," Mrs. Deneaux said blandly.

"What did you do?" BT asked. Gary was already heading up the stairs. BT was following.

"Too late," she repeated as she sat down heavily on the couch.

"Josh!" Gary yelled. "Josh!" he yelled again as he ran into Mary's room. The boy was in virtually the same position he had been when he first came up to ask Mary to leave with them. Gary took in the whole scene before him, an open bottle of pills and an empty glass of what appeared to have contained chocolate milk judging by the residue around the lip.

"Josh!" Gary said running to the side of the bed and grabbing the boy.

"What happened?" BT yelled.

"Pills," Gary said, feeling the boy's neck for a pulse. "BT, I can't feel anything." Gary was panicking.

"I know CPR, put him on the floor."

Gary quickly did as BT said. BT had been around enough death to know when the Angel of Darkness had already come and gone. Josh had departed long moments previous, but he still tried for fifteen minutes before his arms and lungs burned from the effort.

"I'll try now! Just show me what to do," Gary pleaded as BT sat up against the wall, his hands tightly clasped together to keep them from shaking.

"It's too late, Gary, he's gone," BT said while lightly smacking the back of his head against the wall.

"What? He can't be. That's impossible. Just show me what to do!" Gary yelled.

Gary started pressing on the boy's chest, mimicking BT's earlier efforts.

"Gary stop," BT said calmly. "Put him on the bed, let him rest in peace."

Mary had at some point come back upstairs and was leaning up against the door frame; heavy tears were dropping. "Don't you see it's for the best," she was telling them.

"You're insane!" Gary said, advancing on the woman who was shrinking back. BT stood quickly and grabbed Gary. "He's the future!" he spat.

"There is no future," she sobbed quietly.

Gary shrugged away from BT who cautiously let him go. Gary brushed past Mary without glancing at her. "I've got to get out of here," he said as he headed down the stairs.

"It's better this way," Mary said pleading her case with BT.

"I'll never agree with you, Mary. You just killed something beautiful in this world. I hope your God forgives you, because I won't," BT said as he left the room, Mary was still sobbing on the hallway floor when the trio departed.

***

"Do you think Mike will show him the way?" Gary asked as they quickly crossed the street to get to Mary's neighbor's garage.

"What makes you think Mike knows the way?" Mrs. Deneaux asked. "It was a joke," she said when both Gary and BT looked at her crossly.

"Good thing you didn't have to survive on your comedic talents, good looks, or disposition," BT said.

"Done?" she asked.

"Shhh," Gary said, holding his hand up. "I thought I heard something." He was pointing into the smoke-enshrouded street. Sounds were simultaneously dampened and enhanced in the density of the choking smog. It was becoming more difficult to pinpoint what they were hearing or where it was coming from.

Gary was having difficulty breathing through the waves of smoke and haze; his eyes beginning to water under the assault. Mrs. Deneaux seemed unfazed as she plowed through another coffin nail. It seemed they had at least protected her from this toxic soup.

She pulled the hammer back on her revolver and spun. She had no sooner brought the barrel up when she let loose a shot. A zombie dropped no more than two feet from where they stood.

"Move!" BT yelled. "I think we're surrounded!"

Another shot rang out from Deneaux's pistol and another zombie fell with a crisp, clean hole drilled through its skull. Gary had his rifle up but hadn't found a target yet.

Deneaux seemed almost precognizant with her shots, Gary was wondering if it was because, with her advanced age, she was so close to death herself, that she could sense its approach.

"Try to act more like your brother and shoot something," Mrs. Deneaux said to Gary as she was shuffling along while dropping the spent shells out of her gun and reloading.

Gary wanted to shoot her to start with but she seemed to be the only one that could spot the zombies around them.

"I can barely tell if I'm going the right way," BT said as he kept them close. The smoke was rolling in like high tide. Mary's neighbor's house was merely an object that appeared somewhat more solid than the surrounding gray smoke.

A small wind kicked up from the super-heated air of the burning town. It was just enough for Gary to catch the nightmare heading their way.

"We need to move faster," Gary said. His eyes, which had seconds earlier been squinting, where now nearly bugging out of his head. Hundreds of zombies were advancing down the street towards them. He didn't get the feeling they had been spotted, but they'd be found just by the sheer number of invaders.

"We go any faster and we'll miss the garage." BT kept his attention focused to the front.

"Any slower and we'll be food," Gary said.

BT turned to look as the small clearing in the smoke rapidly closed. "Shit."

"Back to Mary's?" Deneaux asked.

This was the most scared Gary thought he'd ever seen her, it almost made her seem human, but even reptiles have a strong will to live.

"Closer going forward," BT said, urging them along quicker; the threat of tripping and falling rising with their increase in speed.

"There'll be nothing left here in an hour anyway," Gary said, the loss of Josh affecting him deeply. "I couldn't go back there anyway," he said softly.

"Shit, I'm bleeding," BT cursed.

"You alright?" Gary asked, alarmed that BT may have been bitten.

"Got hung up on thorns," BT answered.

"Really not the time to stop and smell the flowers," Deneaux chortled.

"Are the roses orange or pink?" Gary asked, his back to BT as he scanned the area. The sound of so many moving feet was unsettling.

"Who gives a shit! This is one time I agree with Deneaux."

"If they're orange, they are grandiflora, if they're pink they are climbers," Gary said,

"Gary...come on, man, am I losing you?" BT asked.

"No, the orange ones were on the left side of the house and the garage was right beyond it, the climbers were on the other side."

"I'm not going to ask right now about how you knew the names of the roses, but we'll talk later that's for sure. They're the orange ones by the way," BT said as he skirted around the bush and towards the garage.

"Gary, just start firing," Mrs. Deneaux said to him.

"I can't see anything clear enough," Gary told her.

"Doesn't matter you won't miss," she told him calmly.

Zombies were nearly within reach of grabbing Gary's rifle barrel as he fired. BT had him by the waist and was steering him in the right direction as Gary watched their retreating back. "I'm out!" Gary yelled, thinking that their *end* had finally broken through and found them.

It was then that Deneaux began to fire. She had strategically waited for him to expend his ammo so that she could keep them alive while he reloaded. Gary realized quickly her tactic and began to throw rounds into his magazine. Her shots were more measured than his, but even so, he only had about fifteen seconds before she was out. The signal from his brain to his fingers was getting fouled through the panic of nerves. He dropped at least three of the precious rounds, foregoing precision for haste.

"Gary?" Mrs. Deneaux asked as she was pulling the hammer back on her final shot.

"We're at the garage!" BT said triumphantly.

Deneaux's last shot punctuated the momentous occasion. Phantom zombies raced by in the shadows, some drawn to the sound of the gunfire others heading to unknown destinations. Gary finally drove the full cartridge home as a zombie came out of the murkiness into Mrs. Deneaux's blindside.

He tried to pull the trigger, but it was frozen in place he had yet to chamber a round.

"Duck down!" BT bellowed as he brought his arm up. He shot the heavy caliber hunting rifle one-armed, the weapon not even braced against his shoulder. Even in the desperation of the moment Gary was able to appreciate the strength of the man as the recoil did little more than ripple his shirt.

"Get in!" BT yelled as he physically picked up Deneaux with his free hand and put her in the side door of the garage. Gary was quick to follow along with BT after two more shots.

"Twit," Deneaux said to Gary, her hands shaking as she placed another cigarette to her mouth.

BT propped up a small step ladder against the door as zombies began to run into it.

"I'm sorry," Gary said. "I thought I was ready to shoot."

"You could have got me killed," she spat.

"Would that have been so bad for us?" BT said, making sure his makeshift barricade was going to hold.

Mrs. Deneaux was silent for a moment before she began to cackle.

"Oh no." BT turned around, confident the door would hold. It appeared that the nearby zombies had already departed for greener pastures. Why hunt when a buffet was laid out? Somewhere there were people in much more dire straits than themselves.

"What's the matter?" Gary asked, fearful that something had found another way in or was already laying in wait.

BT pointed towards the car. "Besides the flat tire, it's a lime green Pinto."

"I had a servant that drove one of these," Mrs. Deneaux said.

"Should we see if it starts before we change the tire?" Gary asked. He was afraid the engine noise would attract more zombies.

BT was thinking along the same lines. "Let's change the tire first. It's not like we can go anywhere if it doesn't work, and those zombies will come back if they hear this piece of shit. I bet it idles as loud as a howler monkey."

Gary noticed that the dome light was very dim as he opened the driver side door and popped the hatch to the rear so that he could get to the jack.

"What do you think?" BT asked as Gary placed the jack on the frame of the body.

"Well if this thing isn't so rusted out that it could support its own weight I'll be able to put on that spare tire that is barely better than the one I'm replacing. And once I drop the car back down and the tire seems to have some air pressure, we have to contend with a battery that may or may not give us three engine cranks before it craps out. We might need more than that because of any condensation that may or may not have got into the gas tank," Gary told him.

"And if all of that goes our way?" BT asked further.

"Well, then at that point, the worst of all possible scenarios happens."

"And what's that?" BT asked, thoroughly concerned.

"We find ourselves in a lime green Pinto."

"Should have known I was being set up, you are a Talbot. Do what you can. I'm going to see if there is anything in here that we can potentially use," BT said, clapping him on the shoulder.

Mrs. Deneaux had found a small stool and was flicking her ashes within inches of a red gas can.

"You know that's gas right?" BT asked grabbing the small container.

"A dehydrated ant could piss more than is in that can," she answered as she took a pull from her smoke.

BT unscrewed the top. She was mostly right, there was at most a half gallon of fuel; and by the look and smell of it, it had some motor oil mixed in. "Must be for a weed whacker," he said aloud, Mrs. Deneaux paid him no attention.

"Twit," she said again looking in Gary's direction.

***

Gary had just tightened the last lug nut and was setting the car down when the shed shook. Even the slumbering Deneaux looked up.

"What the hell was that?" BT asked, looking up from the hatch where he was placing anything that could be used as a melee weapon.

Gary quickly dropped the car, and when he was confident the tire would hold, he threw the jack in the back just as the shed again shook. He would have sworn it moved on its slab foundation. Dust and debris began to rain down from the rafters.

"Shit," BT said looking up. Flimsy sheets of plywood held up storage boxes; some labeled, Christmas, Halloween and even one ominously named Bowling. BT didn't want to be anywhere in this garage when those boxes began to fall.

"Get in the car!" BT urged them as the wooden garage door splintered from another assault.

"What's going on?" Gary asked as he stared in horror at the large bay door that was beginning to buckle.

"Pretty sure it's not the cavalry, Gary," BT said pushing him into the car.

"Get that piece of shit started. I'll hold off whatever it is," BT said. His words held more conviction than the tremor in his voice.

Deneaux was already seated in the back of the car.

Gary turned the ignition and was rewarded with—at first—nothing. Then came the slow wind of an under-powered starter, then three loud clicks before Gary turned the key back to off.

"Gary?" BT asked tremulously as the garage door was rapidly becoming wood scraps.

"Trying," Gary said as he pumped the gas and turned the ignition…this time only receiving the loud clicking noise.

"Oh, God," BT said softly as he began to back up.

Gary looked up from the dashboard. "Oh shit," he said as he began to furiously pump the gas in a fervent hope that the friction from the action would somehow send power to the dying battery.

"Shoot it!" the usually reserved Mrs. Deneaux shouted.

The beast struck again, the only thing holding it back now was the thin strips of metal that had been part of the door's support. BT had seemingly forgotten about the firearm in his hands.

"Shoot it!" Deneaux screamed again.

Her shrill voice seemed to awaken something in BT. He raised his rifle and pulled the trigger and the behemoth on the other side barely moved as its head rocked back an inch or two. White bone shone through on its forehead for a moment before it was covered in a brackish black goop.

"Get in the car, BT!" Gary screamed, not even caring that his voice was at least three octaves higher than it normally should be.

"It'll kill us," BT said, not willing to look back at Gary. The beast was pulling the metal strips apart with a dexterity that the zombies had not shown previously.

The car settled down appreciably as BT got in quickly closing his door to the nightmare beyond the too thin glass windshield.

"Please, God, I've always tried to live my life as best I could," Gary said as he again turned the key in the ignition. For a moment there wasn't anything, not even the dead clicking, merely dead silence—that and the grunts and groans of the beast trying to get at them…and then the engine roared to life. Although to say that a four-cylinder Ford Pinto engine was roaring to life would be like saying that Paris Hilton was a fantastic actress (although if you count her night vision adventures she was alright).

The giant zombie was in the garage, it brought its honey-glazed-ham-sized fists down on the hood of the small car. Giant imprints were left behind as it raised its hands up to do more damage. Gary was afraid the monster would drive the hood into the fan blades, then their escape would be over before it ever even started. Gary threw the transmission into drive, and for one long, heart-stopping second, the engine sputtered and threatened to die before the car lurched forward and was immediately stopped as it ran into the zombie's tree trunk-like legs.

"Go, Gary, go!" BT yelled.

"Sounds like Dr. Seuss," Gary said. "Through the zombie, then we're free. Go, Gary, go." Gary pressed gently down on the gas pedal, trying to find a balance between more engine thrust and the car's ability to take the influx of gas without flooding and stalling.

A deep moan came out of the zombie's mouth. Gary

had initially thought the vibrations he felt in his chest were coming from the car until he saw the zombie's throat warbling.

"Gary?" BT pleaded.

"I've got the gas halfway down, we're not moving!" Gary replied excitedly. Smoke was billowing all around the garage from the effort.

"Maybe you should put it all the way to the floor," Mrs. Deneaux said, leaning forward.

"I think I agree with her on this one," BT said, leaning as far back as he could—which wasn't far considering the confines of the small car.

A stiff wind had kicked up, and the roadway was surprisingly clear. Gary was able to notice that more zombies of the traditional variety began to make their way over towards them.

"Now or never bud," BT said noticing the same thing.

The engine popped and sputtered as Gary pressed his foot into the nearly rusted out floor board. The giant zombie had bent down and was now trying to lift the front end of the car off the ground. It appeared to be having some success.

BT quickly, and against his better judgment, rolled down his window and fired twice; one bullet tearing through the right side of the zombie's jowl. Gnashing teeth shown through like a doctor's examination room diorama. The second shot caught it in the forehead an inch or two from the previous wound. The zombie did not fall; but at least it dropped the car and staggered back.

The zombie was still moving backwards when the engine finally had enough thrust to get the transmission moving. The car shot out like a turtle wading through molasses. Gary did his best to avoid the behemoth, but with limited room and the size of the beast, it was easier said than done. The car was rocked to its rivets as it struck the zombie.

BT's head almost made contact with the dashboard. The only thing preventing it was that he was wedged in tighter than a tick on a moose's ass. Gary took a hard left away from the majority of the zombies, but it was still no easy feat avoiding them. He knew the Pinto could not sustain any more damage than it already had; a factory-new Pinto was suspect, and this had seen its best days decades earlier. Gary wouldn't swear to it, but he thought he heard a maniacal laughter emanating from Mary's house as they passed on by.

"Roll up your window," Gary asked BT as he shivered.

CHAPTER FIVE

Mike Journal Entry 2

The sound of a small engine car racing past the house awoke me from my daze, that and the crazy, long-haired bastard that was looking down at me.

"Are you real?" he asked.

"Where the fuck am I?" I asked as I was peering around the room that was covered from floor to ceiling and the ceiling itself in tin foil.

"Hey...hey...hey!" he started. "I'm asking the hyperboles!"

So I know my grasp of the English language is suspect at best, but even I knew that was an incorrect sentence.

"Ask away," I said weakly. I felt marginally better than I had when I fell into the house, but how much better was still in question. If crazy-eyed, long-haired, bearded man attacked right now with more than a plastic spoon I would be done for.

"I'm asking the questions here," he said, trying to establish his authority.

"You said you were asking the hyperboles?"

"Why the fuck would I say that? That makes absolutely no sense," he said, scratching his head. "Why you here? Did they send you?"

"Can I get a drink first?" I asked, my throat felt like it was on fire, which I guess wasn't too far removed from the truth.

"I dance on my bed."

How do these people find me? It's like I have a heavy dose of crazy attractant sprayed all over me. "That's nice," was all I could think to say in return.

"Scotch okay? I don't drink water since the government started putting fluoride in it. It makes you dumb," he said, tapping his finger against his head.

"So how much water did you drink before you realized that?" I asked him.

Bearded Man was already heading into the kitchen; I think he was muttering something about Kelly Clarkson. I could hear the rattle of glasses and then a few of them smashing.

"You alright?" I asked as I tried to sit up.

"Thought I saw bugs," came his reply.

"What's with the tin foil?"

"What tin foil?" he said as he came back into the room holding two large glasses filled to the top with an amber colored liquid I could only hope was scotch and not Pine-Sol.

"Need some help?" he asked as he put the glasses down and extended his hand.

I was grateful for the help, but was afraid to touch him lest my burned flesh slough off in his grip.

"Come on, man, I haven't bitten anyone since that one time in the K-Mart parking lot, and I thought he was an alligator," he said, seeing my hesitation.

"I'm kind of burned bad, and I'm not sure if my skin will stay on."

"You're funny, man! You're dirty as hell, I'll give you that, but you ain't burned. I mean I thought you were when you came in, but the more I looked at you the more convinced I was you were just a dirty bastard."

I looked down at my hands. There seemed to be some residual burn marks, but it was nothing like what I had been looking at when I was in the roadway. I winced as he grabbed my hand, still half-convinced he would fall backwards with a fair portion of human material stuck in his grasp. My body popped and snapped as I stood, but I felt like a caterpillar shedding its old cocoon and becoming a butterfly. Okay…so that really isn't a manly enough metaphor, let's go with a snake shedding its old skin, that works much better and probably a lot closer to the truth considering what I was now. Half, half of what I am. I had to hold onto that other half with everything I had now. I picked up my glass and took a large swallow, the liquid alternating between burning and soothing my throat.

"How did the government know I was here?" Bearded Man asked.

I gripped the edge of a small table as a serious case of vertigo swooned by me. "Whoa, cheap high," I said, harkening back to a reference I had used since my youth whenever I got light-headed from rising too quickly.

"There is nothing cheap about my highs," Bearded Man said indignantly.

I thought I had crazy cornered, shit was I wrong. "No one sent me, definitely not the government. I was trying to get away."

"From her?" he asked.

The swoon struck again, I tried not to let him see it.

Then he moved on. "I once ate a Snickers bar on a dare."

Who the hell doesn't like Snickers bars? I thought, *and who would 'dare' someone to eat one?*

"Can we start again?" I asked.

"When did we finish?" he asked back.

How many gods have I pissed off? I wailed internally.

"My name is Michael Talbot," I said as I extended my hand, thinking he would shake it, then tell me his name. He looked at my proffered hand like it was a claw.

"No way, man," he said.

I understood not shaking hands; he could be a fellow germaphobe. But that didn't make any sense considering that he had just helped me to stand.

"Okay," I said, pulling my hand back in, unconsciously rubbing it against my side. Blue jean material fell way like dried sand. I began to brush my legs. More fried clothing fell to the ground.

"Dude, you're messing with my high man," Bearded Man said as he backed up.

I stopped what I was doing, realizing that if I kept it up I would be naked in front of another man real soon. (Not that there's anything wrong with that, it just isn't my cup of tea. Okay, so tea doesn't seem masculine enough, let's go with lager, yeah it's not my stein of lager, much better).

"Are you melting?" he asked, still backing up.

"Molting more like it." I gulped down my apprehension as I began to ask him my next question. "Do you have any clothes I could borrow?" As it was, I had to wash store bought clothes twice before I would ever wear them, and now I was asking this unkempt stranger if I could borrow some of his stuff.

His eyes glazed for half a second then some lucidity popped in for a quick respite. "Sure I'll be right back."

What the fuck? I mouthed. This guy was insane…I was just hoping not *criminally* insane. I can deal with varying degrees of insanity; I'm a Talbot after all.

He came back a few moments later with a heavy woolen poncho, white socks with yellow stripes—I hadn't seen anything like those since grade school—a pair of pants that looked fashionable during the Nixon era, and some tightie-whities.

I gladly accepted just about everything except the underwear. They could have been brand new, but the mere fact that he had touched them made them soiled in my eyes. And these were far from Inspector Number 5's hands; the elastic waistband was all stretched and worn out and there was a small hole in the seat.

"I was going to toss those soon," he said as he watched me looking at the underwear.

"Well I'm glad you found it in your heart to hold onto them until you bequeathed them to me."

"You're welcome, want some french fries?"

"Thank you and yes." What the hell else could I say?

Who turns down french fries? Plus, I thought it would give me an opportunity to stash the underwear while he went into the other room to gather the mythical fried spuds.

I manically brushed the remainder of my singed digs off of me as Bearded Man made quite a show of preparing our side dish. The poncho which was scratchy actually felt surprisingly wonderful on my new itchy skin; the polyester pants were on the tight side and about two inches too short, but it beat naked any day. I hid the underwear in the poncho's oversized front pocket. I was putting on the socks when he came in with a tray of steaming french fries.

"Who are you?" he asked stopping a few feet from me.

At first I thought he was pulling my leg, but he just kept staring at me. "Michael Talbot remember? You just got me some new clothes? And thank you by the way."

"Oh right, I thought I was imagining you. Whoa french fries!" he exclaimed, like he just realized what he was carrying. He started popping the steaming starch sticks into his mouth. "Mmmmm, these are so good," he said with his eyes closed. He opened them and peered at me for a moment as if he was sifting through his memory trying to figure out who I was again. When he came up with a satisfactory answer, once more he asked if I wanted some.

He put the tray down and I ate some. They actually had some spices on them and were delicious.

"I used to be chef for a five star resort," he said as he watched me obviously enjoying his cuisine.

"These are fantastic," I said as I stuffed some more in my face. Apparently almost dying by fire and meeting God take their toll on one's appetite.

"Nice poncho I've got one just like it, I wish I knew where I'd put it."

"What's your name?" I asked again as I sat down, wanting to get closer to the addictive food. Bearded Man seemed to have forgotten about them completely; this was fine with me, I was famished.

"John the Tripper," he said with a faraway look.

"Excuse me?" I asked almost wrongly swallowing a half chewed potato strip.

"John the Tripper," he reiterated.

I had to ask, but I already knew the answer. "Because you fall over things?"

"What's that got to do with anything?" he asked back.

"You said John the Tripper."

"What?"

"John the Tripper."

"What?"

"Your name."

"What about it?"

"I figured it might mean you fall over things, apparently not though."

"I toured for twelve years with the Grateful Dead," he told me.

"Of course you did. Any chance you filled in some of the down time with some serious karate and weapons training?"

"I watched a Bruce Lee film once, didn't understand it though."

"John the Tripper..."

He said "What?" again before I could finish.

"Shit," I said, rubbing my hand over the top of my head where my hair should have been. "Do you have a mirror?" I asked as I patted down my entire head. I was pretty alarmed at this point.

He pulled open a drawer in the small table that I had used previously to support myself. It was overflowing with handheld mirrors of varying size and shape.

He looked up at me a little sheepishly. "Sometimes I just need to see myself to know that I still exist."

"I can actually relate," I told him as he handed me one. My right eyebrow, along with all of the hair on my head was gone, burnt to a crisp much like my clothes had been, three-quarters of my goatee was gone. I looked pretty sketchy to say the least. I'm not sure if I would have gone close enough to this person in the mirror to drop a quarter in a cup. I looked like I was suffering some serious malady. I just hoped it wasn't catchy.

"Do you have cancer?" he asked as he rubbed my smooth head.

"I hope not, although that would probably be preferable to what ails me," I told him, eyeing the top of my head with the mirror.

"Does shaving your head keep the evil one out?"

I was so intent on trying to find some vestige of hair on my head that I almost missed his comment. Let's be honest, most of what the guy says can't be construed as anything other than crazy and I had just become a Telly Savalas stunt double (Yul Brynner? Does that help as a reference? Okay, how about Doctor Evil.)

"What, John?" I asked finally looking over at him, my neck thankful I had stopped craning it in strange ways.

John the Tripper began to look around wildly. "Who's John?" he asked me.

"You are. That's what you told me."

"My name is John the Tripper."

"That's what I said," I answered, although I hadn't, I had only called him John now that I reflected on it.

"So there's nobody else here?" he asked, the concerned look on his face dissipating.

'Just the voices in your head buddy.' I wanted to tell him, but I was afraid we would get so far off topic that neither of us would be able to recover. "Nobody else, John..." He was about to ask who John was again "...the Tripper." That seemed to appease him. This was going to be a pain in the ass if I had to call him by his full man-given name every time I wanted to talk to him.

"Your hair...did you get rid of it because they were acting like tiny antennas?"

John was giving me a headache. His verbal gymnastics was like watching two highly skilled Chinese

Ping Pong players playing a game hopped up on Red Bull. I couldn't keep up, or maybe more like a sure-footed goat on a Nepali Mountain pass, I couldn't follow his windings.

I shrugged. "John...(his mouth opened)...the Tripper (it closed) I don't know what the hell you're talking about?"

"You're hair, man!" he said all wide-eyed. "Did you shave it off so that she couldn't communicate with you?" And before I could answer he added. "I wished I had thought of that, had to go out about five times to get enough tin foil to wrap the whole house. There are some funky people out there. Did you know that?"

Did he just call zombies 'funky' people? Well that was a different slant for sure. This guy didn't even know we were on the losing end of a zombie apocalypse, I didn't think I had the patience to explain it to him. And for what purpose? John the Tripper seemed to be making his way just fine through his made up world.

"I mean I toured with the Grateful Dead and even Phish for a while. Smelled some truly funked-out hippies, but those people out there..." he said, pointing through his tin foil-covered window, "...there's not enough patchouli in the world to cover up their smell."

"Do you have guns?" I asked him, but the odds were that if he had, he would have converted it into some makeshift bong by now.

In a moment of clear thought he looked at me like I was the one on a twenty-year acid stint. "Do I look like I would own a gun?"

I could hear explosions throughout the city. I would learn later that they were the propane cylinders for heating that were catching fire as the city burned.

I stood and walked over to the window.

"What are you doing, man?" John the Tripper asked, his eyes getting wide.

"I just want to look out the window."

"Hold on!" he yelled, running into the kitchen. He came out with what looked like two tin foil boats, at least until he put one on his head. "Here," he said, thrusting the other one at me.

"What do you want me to do with that?" I asked.

"It scrambles the signal."

"What signal?"

"How have you not heard her?" He tilted his head.

Oh, I heard her plenty, and it was a constant struggle to 'hide' myself from her. I could feel her evil oiliness as she swept by trying to locate prey or predator with her thoughts. "What the hell?" I said as I grabbed the hat and placed it on. Well if I wasn't certifiable before, I had now joined the ranks plunging in with both feet. John the Tripper seemed appeased.

"Okay you can check now," he said with a waving of his hand.

What I saw just about took my breath away. The city looked like you would envision Hell. The sky was lit up a blazing red, dust and ashes moved down the street in tidal waves. "We can't stay here," I said, not able to tear my eyes away from the inferno I was gazing upon.

"*Fire, fire on the mountain,*" John the Tripper sang the Dead tune as he was staring out the window next to me.

"John, you need to get whatever you think is important and we need to get out of here," I said. He was too lost in the vision before him to even take note I had not called him by his proper name.

"*Get up, get out, get out of the door,*" he said still in a sing-song mode.

Good, I thought, *he's on the same page.* At least that is what I thought until I realized he was still singing the song. "John!" I said grabbing him by the shoulders. "We need to get the fuck out of here!" I yelled, small flecks of spittle hitting him in the face, he didn't seem concerned.

"I know that, does John, though?" he asked.

"Probably not. Grab whatever you think is important and can help," I added. Who knew what he thought was important. For all I knew, he would start ripping out the copper piping down in his basement. "Do you have a car?"

"A car? No," he answered, I could physically witness his thought process as he was trying to go through the catalog of his possessions.

My heart sank. It was going to suck trying to get out of the city ahead of the zombies and the fire.

"I've got a van, though."

I almost kissed him, until I began to wonder if maybe he was using it as a planter in the backyard or something equally as useless. "Keys?"

"In the ignition," he said, turning back towards the fire. "I was always losing them and that seemed like the safest place.

"It runs then?" I asked, still keeping my fingers crossed.

"In the garage," he said pointing. "I grew up a few streets away from here before I became a roadie. I loved being on the road, but there was always a part of me that wanted to come home." Tears were forming in his eyes. "I heard that you can never go home, but that isn't true. I did, married my high school sweetheart...she still held a flame for me after all those years I was away. We took some cooking classes because we liked to eat well when we got the eats." He smiled sideways as he reminisced. "Come to find out, I was something of a protégé in the kitchen and ended up teaching the class the following year. Stephanie never got any better, but she attended just to stay close to me." He didn't clarify, but I figured Stephanie was his wife. "We were married for seven of the greatest years of my life."

"I'm sorry, John the Tripper, I am. What happened?"

"She went to Washington."

"What?" I figured she had contracted some rare blood disease and died in his arms.

"She got a job offer. She wanted me to move with her, but I had finally come home and I didn't want to leave again."

I wanted to berate him for letting the love of his life

get away from him, but it was his life to live as he saw fit. Who the hell was I to tell him differently? Shit, I was just some bald guy wearing a poncho and a tin foil hat. I would have been shunned by bums in Detroit. "I'm sorry," was all I could muster."

"For what?" he asked, looking at me. I truly think he forgot the entire thread of the conversation we were just having.

"Ah...nothing. Do you have any shoes I could wear?" I asked as I looked down at my yellow-rimmed tube socks.

"You going somewhere? I sure could use some mushrooms."

"For cooking or eating?"

"Both, what else would I do with them."

"I was thinking you meant the psychedelic kind."

"Oh no, those taste like shit. I make sheet acid."

"Forget I asked. John, I need some shoes if you have them, and you need to go pack some shit up. We need to get out of here."

"Why would I pack shit up?" he asked.

"Figure of speech."

"You make no sense, man," he told me as he headed up his stairs. I really hope it wasn't for a nap.

"Well this is a first," I said to the empty room. "I'm not the craziest one in attendance."

"What size foot do you have?" John the Tripper yelled down.

"Ten!" I yelled back up.

"I'm an eight. Can you fit in those?"

"When I was twelve maybe."

"Well can you or can't you then?" he yelled down.

I think I would be better off with socks rather than trying to cram my feet into a shoe two sizes too small.

"You could wear a pair of Stephanie's that she left behind!"

"I don't think that's going to work."

"She was a women's thirteen!" he added.

"What are they canoes?" I asked softly, I didn't think he would have heard me.

"She had a condition."

"Amazonian?"

"A women's thirteen is about a men's eleven-and-a-half. You want them?"

"Sure, bring some extra socks." Now I just had to get over my phobia of putting on someone else's shoes. Hadn't been bowling in over twenty-five years after I once figured out how many nasty-ass feet those things had been donned on. And that little squirt of disinfectant deodorant that the 'shoe technician' put in there would do little to overwhelm the hardy microbes that must be breeding vigorously in that germ-rich soup of toe fungus and foot jam. How's that sound for appealing? Might as well dip your feet in dirty toilet water.

I was still rubbing the unseen germs off of me when John came back down the stairs. He was carrying an armload of socks and quite possibly the brightest pink sneakers I had ever seen in my life. I mean they looked as if they were potentially battery powered.

"You're kidding right? Please?" I begged.

"I like socks."

"No the sneakers."

"No, Stephanie left a bunch of stuff behind. We're still married. She visits about once every two months…she's late this time though."

My mouth opened, he had once again surprised me. I moved on to something I understood.

"Can you shut those off?" I asked, shielding my eyes from the brightness.

"You're a funny bastard!" he said, handing over the shoes and some socks.

"I wasn't trying to be funny," I said sadly as I went over to the couch to put on my new digs.

John went over to another table in the far corner of the room. He retrieved a large folder that looked thick with paperwork.

"I don't think you're going to need to file taxes any time soon," I said, looking up happily. The sneakers were ugly as hell, but with the added pair of socks, they fit pretty well. Plus, I had the bonus of being able to walk on water if the need arose.

"I've never filed taxes," he said.

"You're kind of my hero right now," I told him as I stood, surprised at how well Stephanie's footwear felt.

"I'm ready to go," he said, heading towards the kitchen.

"That's it? That's all you want to take?" I asked him. "Paperwork?"

"Oh shit, man!" he exclaimed when he turned to me.

"What?" I asked looking around wildly.

"My wife has shoes just like that! How weird is that!"

"Weirder than you know. Let's get out of here."

He led the way into the kitchen which had a door to an attached garage, thank God for small favors. The garage was filled with fine soot that was coming in through a partially broken window, but even that did little to obscure the rainbow painted VW van sitting there.

"Did I really expect anything else?" I told the gods of irony.

"Isn't she a beauty? I bought her brand new back in '92."

I didn't have the heart to tell him they stopped production of his particular model somewhere around the mid-seventies. And beauty was not a word that could be used to describe what rested in his garage. The bright paint did little to hide the various rust holes or the vast number of dings, the van looked like it had been parked on the moon for a few centuries and had suffered a barrage of micro meteor hits.

"It runs?" was all I could ask. It looked too beat up to even be considered a hippie planter.

"Stephanie can't cook worth a shit," he said

conspiratorially. "Don't tell her that," he added as if she were in the next room. "But she has a way with tools like you wouldn't believe."

I was now secretly wondering if perhaps Ship-Sized-Shoe-Stephanie, who couldn't cook but could apparently keep an ancient vehicle finely tuned may or may not be of the feminine persuasion. Again it made absolutely no difference to me, just fodder for my thoughts.

I handed the keys back to John, I wasn't too particularly thrilled with someone of his mental state driving, but it was still his car.

"Oh shit no, man," John the Tripper said, pushing the keys back. "I haven't driven since '88 and I just dosed."

"You're kidding right?"

"Nope."

"Besides thinking that right now was a perfect time to drop acid, why would you buy a car if you don't even drive?"

"The dealer said it fit me."

I shrugged. "It does, but that still doesn't make much sense."

"You feeling anything yet?"

"About what?"

"I put some in your fire water."

CHAPTER SIX

Eliza & Tomas

Tomas sat for a moment longer. His sister turned her gaze back towards the city that was now under attack. He had felt Michael, of that he was one hundred percent sure, but then what? He could not figure it out; it was as if someone had used the Jaws of Life to severe their connection. Tomas was certain that Mike yet lived, because the connection had not faded to black; it had just stopped even as it was increasing in strength. No, something else was happening here. So when his sister suggested they go and join in the fun down below, he was all for it, if only to see whether he could get some clues and possibly feed; he was so hungry.

"Do you smell that, Tomas?" Eliza asked as she tilted her nose up.

"I smell fire and fear," Tomas said morosely.

"Exactly," she answered with a smile. They had just reached the outskirts of the city and were coming in from the west the zombies were pouring in from the north.

"What are you two doing?" a woman shouted from her porch. She was flanked by three malnourished children, all of which were carrying rifles of varying calibers.

"We are just going for a stroll," Eliza answered in a sing-song voice, grabbing Tomas' arm.

"You need to get out of the street!" the woman cried. "There are zombies all over the place!" The woman was dressed in a moo-moo that at one time may have fit, but now billowed in the breeze. Her hair was pulled back tightly, pinching her sagging flesh against her ears.

"Are we truly in danger?" Eliza asked aghast, placing her hand to her breast.

"Is she daft?" the woman asked Tomas.

"Most likely," Tomas said. Eliza shot him a wicked glance.

"Come in here!" the woman screamed.

Eliza started heading towards the door.

"What are you doing?" Tomas asked.

"She's inviting us in for dinner, Tomas. It would be rude of us not to accept."

"They're just children, Eliza," Tomas moaned.

"That's what makes it so special. Come on, Tomas."

He reluctantly followed.

The woman ushered her children in and began to doubt the wisdom of her graciousness as Eliza strode purposefully closer.

"You ain't dangerous or nothing are you?" the woman asked with a quiver in her voice.

"My dear we are your worst nightmare," Eliza said as she crossed over the threshold.

"Please," The mother begged Tomas.

"It's too late," he said softly.

"Don't be shy," Eliza said to the mother as she pulled her in. "Some have said I have no heart, but I offer you this," Eliza told the young mother. "Would you rather I kill you first or your children?"

The woman nearly swooned. Tomas reached out and steadied her.

"Momma, should I shoot her?" the oldest boy asked. He was standing bravely in front of his smaller sister and brother.

"Run, Jacob, run!" the woman screamed.

"Yes, Jacob, run," Eliza mimicked. "I love the taste of adrenaline in blood it gives it a slight tang I find pleasant upon my palate," she said as she swept her tongue across her extended canines.

"Not my babies, please not my babies," the mother

begged.

"Come, come. What would become of them if I left them to their own devices?"

Eliza spun to her right a few inches as a rifle round caught her in the shoulder blade.

"That is how you treat guests?" Eliza said as she traversed the room in the span of an eye blink.

Jacob was six inches off the ground suspended from his neck as Eliza gripped him tightly.

"Please!" the mother sobbed as she fell to her knees.

"Finish her, Tomas," Eliza barked.

"Let us leave, sister."

"Finish her or I will pop this boy's head like an over ripened peach."

Eliza wrapped both her small hands on either side of the Jacob's head. She was applying so much pressure that the boy's eyes were beginning to bulge.

"NO!" the mother shrieked. The small boy and his sister were screaming as they watched the whole encounter from midway up the stairs.

The sound of the oldest boy's skull crushing dominated above all the other din within the room. His face fell in as bone ground against bone, his body twitched spasmodically.

"Jakie!" the little girl screamed as she ran down the stairs. Brain matter leaked through her brother's ear.

The woman collapsed. Eliza, in one fluid motion, let the boy drop to the ground and plucked the little girl up into the air. She plunged her fangs deep into the girl's throat and drank heavily. Urine ran in rivulets from the only remaining sibling.

Tomas was straining against his urges as he watched his sister drink her fill. Her eyes never left him as she pulled the life out of the little girl one drop at a time.

"You must eat, brother," she said to Tomas as she discarded the girl like a used juice box.

The mother was moaning in her unconscious state,

her head resting up against Tomas' leg. The boy watched as Tomas bent down and almost tenderly placed his lips against her neck. The young boy did not move, he did not blink as blood leaked out from around Tomas' mouth and onto the carpet.

Eliza laughed as she climbed the four stairs to the boy; he placed his thumb in his mouth.

"No, Eliza!" Tomas said forcibly as he stood after getting his fill.

"The mother lives, Tomas, I can smell her stench of life from here. You are doing her no favors by allowing her life."

"We have eaten, Eliza, why must you torment them?"

"Two of her whelps are dead and she will be weaker than a newborn for the next two days. My zombies are destroying this entire city. They are not nearly as efficient in their feeding as we are, the pain these two will suffer at their hands will be far worse than the end I offer."

"You don't get it. You could stop *all* off it," Tomas beseeched.

"How did father tolerate one with such a dramatic disposition?"

"I'm done here," Tomas said, heading for the door. He waited in the middle of the roadway for another five minutes before Eliza walked out. She wiped the blood off her mouth with her fingers, then licked them clean.

"Don't be so sad, Tomas, they now live eternally. Come, let us go see what other fun we can have," she said as she grabbed his arm.

CHAPTER SEVEN

BT and Gary

It was long moments before any of them had calmed down enough from their close encounter of the girth kind. The city shone like a dying sun in the rearview mirror.

"That's really the end of them," BT said looking back.

Gary's eyes were wet with remembrance.

Mrs. Deneaux was subdued, but it was more out of self-preservation than from any type of respect. To her, Brian's death was a necessity; he died to save her. Paul was an idiot that shouldn't have made it anyway, and Mike's demise was more of a stroke of good fortune. She realized that he had more than a sneaking suspicion that she was in some way involved in Brian's death as well as Paul's disappearance, and he would have kept pressing the matter. Especially since Paul had been eaten—by cats no less. She smiled as she humored herself with the thought. *Who dies by cats in a zombie apocalypse? That's like dying from a hangnail during a war.*

"Something funny?" BT asked her.

She hadn't realized she'd been displaying her mood on the outside. "I'm just happy to be away from there." she said, recovering smoothly. "I mean safely of course. I am sorry for your loss, Gary," she said as motherly as she could. It sounded more like a pit viper before it struck a field mouse.

Gary did not hear the tone, only the words. "Thank you," he practically sobbed. "I...I don't know how I'm going to tell Tracy, the kids, my father."

"I'll be there with you, Gary, we'll get through it," BT said as he turned to face him.

"It should have been me, BT," Gary sniffed heavily.

"Please tell me you do not plan to cry the entire drive to Maine," Mrs. Deneaux said. When BT turned an evil eye on her she added. "I'm merely looking out for the lad, he won't be able to see the road properly and he will give himself a truly bad headache."

We lose half our number and she survives, the fates are cruel and unjust, BT thought sourly. *I am going to have to watch her carefully.*

Mrs. Deneaux smiled broadly as Gary looked at her through the rearview mirror.

The Pinto may have been the ugliest thing still on the road, but it ran and that counted for a fair amount. They had just crossed over into Virginia on Route 85 almost to the 95 interchange when Gary noticed that the fuel gauge hadn't moved since they'd left Old Fort nearly some two hundred miles ago.

"I think we might have a problem," Gary said.

BT, who had been lost in his own thoughts, sat up. "What's the matter?" he asked looking around. BT thought Mrs. Deneaux might be sleeping but he couldn't tell; the old bat had one eye open.

"Fuel," Gary said pointing to the dash.

"It says we're three-quarters full," BT said moving his head so he could see.

"Yeah…and that's what it said when we left."

"Then maybe you should find a place to get some. Did I really need to point that out?" Mrs. Deneaux said opening her other eye.

"Maybe if we're real lucky some gas will spill on you, and the next time you light a cigarette, the world will find itself a slightly better place," BT said turning to face her.

She lit another cigarette in response.

"Come on, BT, we're all we have left," Gary said,

trying to make peace.

BT wanted to tell him 'And ain't that a shame.' But he could tell the elder Talbot was already hurting enough. He wouldn't swear it on a stack of bibles, but he thought he had seen Deneaux stick her tongue at him as he turned back towards the front. "Bitch," he mumbled.

Gary pulled off the highway. BT made sure his rifle was fully loaded as did Deneaux with her pistol. Gas stations, for some reason, tended to be a hot bed of zombie activity.

"Should we siphon some gas or just find another car?" BT asked as they pulled into the service lot.

"Find another car?" Gary asked. "Really?"

"Oh you can't be serious?" BT asked back. "You like *this* car. This car was a pile of steaming crap when it left the factory. They should have saved the metal and made waste baskets."

"I'm kind of attached to it now," Gary said as he patted the dash board where it instantly cracked as a result of dry rot and ministrations of the driver.

"Yeah she's a beauty," BT said sarcastically.

"Well I think she's a darling little car," Mrs. Deneaux said as she hunted for an ally.

Gary pulled up to a pump.

"What are you doing?" BT asked.

"Getting gas, what does it look like I'm doing?"

"Do you think maybe you can have the attendant check the oil, too?"

"What's the matter with you, BT, they haven't done that in years," Gary told him. "Oh." The light of recognition coming across Gary's visage. "The pumps aren't working, sorry just habit." Gary was about to start the car up.

"Don't worry about it, we'll just find a can and get some gas, let's try to find a screwdriver, too, the last time I siphoned gas, I drank about a quart of it," BT said.

"What's the screwdriver for?" Gary asked.

"Gonna punch a hole in the fuel tank and just let it drain into the can."

"Kind of wasteful isn't it?" Gary asked.

"You plan on coming back this way again?"

"Maybe...if not to bury my brother than at least to say goodbye properly."

"Sorry, man," BT said meaning it. "We'll find a few cans and make sure we get it all."

"Probably should have left the car running," Gary said as they cautiously walked towards the front of the service station.

Mrs. Deneaux exited the car and was leaning with her back against it. She arched her back, her long aristocratic nose fully turned towards the heavens.

The store had been completely ransacked; what wasn't gone off the shelves had been torn into by rats if the droppings were to be believed. *Although they were some industrial-sized rats*, Gary thought.

"I hate this part," Gary said as they made their way over towards the far side of the store. "Okay, I'm going to pull this door open and then get out of the way. You shoot whatever is on the other side." Gary got ready to open the storeroom door.

"Ready when you are," BT said.

Gary pulled hard, his hand slipping off of the handle, the door didn't move. "Shit...it's locked."

BT smiled.

"Should I kick it in?" Gary asked.

"I don't think that'll be necessary," BT said as he twisted the handle and pushed the door open. The door swung effortlessly inwards, BT stepped back, it was too dark inside the small room to see anything.

"I could have done that," Gary said trying to salvage some face.

"I know, it's alright, I won't tell anyone," BT said as he went into the closet after he realized there was nothing in there. He pulled out a mop and bucket. "That'll work...the bucket is for the gas," BT explained.

"I knew that, I just didn't know what the mop was

for."

"Steering wheel," BT said as he pushed the bucket across the floor. "See if you can find something to puncture a tank and either a funnel or something we can make a funnel out of.

Gary came out a few moments later with a broken windshield wiper fluid bottle and a small knife meant more for display—a tourist's memento as opposed to something that could withstand use, but it was all he could find in such short notice and he didn't want to have to stay in there alone any longer than he had to.

"Here let me see," BT asked as he put his hand out for the knife. "Kind of flimsy, but it might work. I'll make the puncture, you just be ready with the bucket. When it's about half full go use it to fill the Pinto and we'll keep doing that until we top it off."

Gary was nodding as he cut the bottom of the windshield fluid bottle off.

BT walked over to the end of the gas station lot; a white Toyota Camry was parked on the grass awaiting a repair that would never be forthcoming. "This will do," he said as he slid under the car. He hoped there was enough gas in it to make it worth their while, he hated being stationary; stationary meant exposed and exposed was not what anybody wanted to be these days.

"That's a nice car," Gary said just as BT was about to try to drive the knife home. "Kind of a damn shame to wreck it."

BT drove the knife blade into the metal. "Dammit!" BT yelled. "Blade snapped, gimme the bucket." BT's right arm was flailing about looking to grab the gas catcher.

"You said the blade broke, what do you need the bucket for?" Gary asked, even as he began to smell gas.

"It made a pencil-sized hole and it's starting to splash around my damn face. Give me the bucket or I'm going to drag you down here with me."

Gary pushed the bucket under.

"This is going to take forever to fill, go see if you can find anything I can use to make this hole bigger.

From BT's vantage point, he could only see the bottom of Gary's legs and when they didn't move away, BT reiterated his request.

"He can't 'cause he gots a nine on his back."

BT started to scoot out from under the car when he heard the unfamiliar voice. "Cuz, I wouldn't do that if I were you."

Another voice said off to his left. "Man ain't chu a big un." Obviously referring to BT.

"Listen," BT said, "we're just trying to get some gas.

"See that's the problem...that's our car." The first voice said.

"See I told you it was a nice car," Gary said.

BT didn't think it mattered which car they had used, any of them would have been a problem with these two men.

"You and your old lady trying to leave our part of town without paying the proper respects?" the man next to Gary said.

"Cuz, you said 'old lady'." And the other one laughed.

"What's so funny? She is an old lady," Gary said to the one holding him at gunpoint.

The man with the gun could not have been much more than twenty, but the scar that ran down the side of his face and the haunted look in his eyes gave him the appearance of someone almost double his age. His partner— who appeared older—acted the younger of the two, taking all of his queues from the man with the 9mm.

BT had a good idea who they were dealing with. He hoped they were wannabe gang bangers as opposed to the real thing, or what remained of their lives wasn't going to be worth much more than the bucket that was filling with the gas.

"You're a funny fuck!" the younger man said, sticking the barrel of the pistol right up against Gary's cheek.

"Wait, wait, he didn't mean anything by it," BT said, wriggling out enough so that he could at least see the two men.

"Who the fuck told you to move!" the scarred man said, now thrusting his pistol down towards BT. "And why is your Uncle Tom ass hanging with these two crackers to begin with?"

"Crackers?" Gary asked. "Is that another term for crazy? Because Mike probably was but I'm not."

"Shut the fuck up before I bust a cap in your ass!" the man yelled.

Gary was about to ask what a cap was, but was headed off at the pass by BT.

"Relax," BT said, holding his hands out.

"Yo, who the fuck you telling to relax?" Scarred said.

"My...it is so hot here." Mrs. Deneaux was fanning herself with what looked like a road map. She approached slowly as if she didn't have a care in the world.

"Shortie, I might need to hit that," the man without the gun said.

"Shit, man, are you serious?" Scarred/Shortie answered. "Wings, that bitch has to be pushing two hundred."

"It's still the first thing I've seen with a pussy in two weeks," Wings said, grabbing his crotch and moving towards Mrs. Deneaux. "Yo, sweet thing, what chu up to?" Wings said getting up close to Mrs. Deneaux.

"Well aren't you just the sweetest thing," she said as she placed the barrel of her revolver up against Wing's forehead.

"Yo, you crazy bitch!" Wings yelled.

"Careful," Mrs. Deneaux said calmly, "you're likely to get my heart fluttering and I haven't taken my pills today. Who knows what could happen at that point, I might just blow your pretty head right from your shoulders."

Wings didn't move except to get his hands up.

"I'll kill your little bitch boyfriends," Shortie said,

looking back to Mrs. Deneaux.

"See if I care," Deneaux said coolly.

"Are you for real?" Shortie asked.

"Help me, Shortie," Wings said as his sweat began to come in contact with the barrel of the pistol.

"Yes, help him, Shortie," Deneaux said. "This gun is getting dreadfully heavy. Maybe if I just shot a round it would be that much lighter.

"No, no, no," Wings stuttered.

Shortie pulled the hammer back on his 9 mm. "I ain't fucking around, bitch, get that piece off my boy's head or I'll kill this white boy."

"I also *ain't* fucking around, homeboy." Mrs. Deneaux smiled, it was difficult to tell if she was making fun of Shortie or truly did not know the appropriate slang; the former seemed more in her character. "Shoot him, he's the brother of the idiot that's wanted me dead for the last month. How much do you think I'm going to miss him?"

"Yo, this bitch is crazy!" Shortie said to the world, Gary nodded in agreement.

"But before you do shoot him, I just want you to know, I will kill, what was your name? Wings...how quaint. Gary will not have hit the ground by the time I put one in your friends head."

"Is this bitch for real?" Shortie asked BT.

"Unfortunately she is," BT said. "Let us get our gas and we'll get out of here."

"I can't now," Shortie said. "You've made me look bad. Blood has to spill here."

Shortie was covered in brain matter before he heard the report. Gary pushed up on Shortie's arm and grabbed the pistol as Mrs. Deneaux leveled her revolver on Shortie.

"Oops," she said, bringing her free hand to her mouth. "I told you it was getting heavy."

Shortie was shaking with fear and rage. "You don't know who you just fucked with!"

BT stood up. "What the fuck did you do that for,

woman?" he asked.

"As much as I think Gary is a twit, I do believe he will play a pivotal role in ensuring my safety. Wings was an impediment."

"What now?" BT asked.

"We kill him," Mrs. Deneaux said evenly.

"Yo, I didn't do nothing. You can't just kill me."

"You did *nothing* because we did not allow you to do anything," Mrs. Deneaux said. "Otherwise, I think that you would have done just as you pleased."

"We can't just shoot him," BT said.

"Sure we can. What do you think will happen if we let him go? He will just go quietly into the night, thankful for the lesson we taught him? No...either he'll follow us and we'll have to deal with him later after maybe he gets a lucky shot off and kills one of us, or this thug has like-minded idiots that will pursue us and finish what they tried."

"She's right," Gary said.

"Don't listen to the crazy bitch," Shortie said. "We was just trying to bust your balls, see if we could get some food or something."

"Self-defense is one thing, but this is cold-blooded murder," BT said. Although, it could be argued that Wing's death was cold-blooded also. "I won't allow you to shoot him."

"Allow? It seems that I have the gun and I can do as I please," Mrs. Deneaux said.

BT stepped in front of her barrel. "Am I just another impediment?" BT asked, looking down at the woman who appeared to be calculating her risk factors if she just planted him in the ground also. She finally withdrew her gun.

"You're almost as big a twit as Gary," she said. BT relaxed.

"Gary, keep an eye on him. We'll let him go when we get our car filled up," BT said.

Gary had Shortie sit up against the Camry as BT made a couple of trips with gas.

"Nice ride," Shortie said sarcastically. "Me and my boys are going to hunt you down for killing Wings."

Gary paled. "You left us no choice."

"I'm going to kill you with a knife," Shortie said looking up at Gary. "One stab to the guts, then I'm going to twist the blade back and forth."

Gary subconsciously placed his left hand over his stomach. Shortie smiled sickly.

"Oh this is ridiculous," Mrs. Deneaux huffed as her shot broke the silence of the day. The round caught Shortie high in the neck.

"What the fuck are you doing?" BT said, dropping the gas container and coming back to Shortie who now had both hands pressed up against his spewing wound.

"Bad shot. I should get my eyes checked. You'll die soon enough," She said to Shortie. "Bleeding out is a relatively easy way to go. Don't worry the panic flows away with the blood." She smiled.

BT physically removed her from her spot. "Why?" he screamed.

"Because it was the right thing to do," she replied as he set her down.

"We've got to get out of here," BT said looking around.

"They're dead. What's the rush?" Mrs. Deneaux asked as she opened her cylinder to drop the two expended cartridges and replace them.

"They were gang bangers," BT said. "And either they'll eventually come looking for these two, or zombies will smell the meat."

"Fair enough," Mrs. Deneaux said as she headed over to the Pinto.

"Do you want to get more gas?" Gary asked, still looking as if he was trying to process all that had just transpired in the last few moments.

"No...well, yes...but not here. We need to get gone. Last time I checked, we had a good solid half a tank that should get us far away from this place," BT said, heading over to the car.

"She's a stone cold killer, BT," Gary said, looking straight into BT's eyes. "She showed absolutely no emotion when she killed Shortie. I mean, not that he wasn't an asshole and probably deserved it for something he had done, but shit...she might as well have been pulling lint from her belly button."

"To have a belly button would mean she was human. I'm not quite convinced of that. Let's get out of here, but we need to keep an eye on her. She wasn't lying when she said she would kill whatever threatened her existence...and that includes you and me."

"And probably, Brian and Paul," Gary added.

"Probably, the devil we know..." BT said.

"I'd rather deal with the one we don't know."

After a sluggish churning of the starter, the car caught and purred like a one-lunged kitty. The smoke hadn't cleared from the group's departure when a gang of men came upon the bodies of their two fallen comrades.

"Get the bikes," the leader said as his long, black leather jacket flapped in the light breeze.

"Cyrus, you know the noise from the bikes draws the zombies."

Cyrus merely looked over at his second in command.

"I'll be right back," he answered.

CHAPTER EIGHT

Mike Journal Entry 3

"Why would you do that?" I asked in alarm. There were times to take acid, most of them revolved around good friends, about twenty-five backwards revolutions of the earth around the sun and some great tunes. None of those things were in attendance right now. "John."

"Who? Whoa I'm seeing trails."

"John the Tripper, we're about to face zombies, man, and you gave me acid. I don't even know how to deal with this right now."

"Relax, man," John the Tripper said, putting his hand on my arm. "It'll happen on its own."

I'd had a few 'bad trips' over the years, one involved a girl and the other was just a low point in my life, felt like the world was crashing down. The key word in my last statement was 'felt' like it was crashing down. How the hell was I going to react now that it really was? I think the years had wizened me enough that I would be able to handle the onslaught of the chemicals to a certain extent, but we were still talking about tripping on acid during the destruction of a city on fire during a zombie invasion, this oughtta be a blast. (Can you see the sarcasm dripping off of the page?)

"We gotta get out of here, man, before this kicks in."

"Before what kicks in, man?" John the Tripper asked as he was staring intently at the webbing between his fingers. "I'm a fucking dolphin," he told me.

"Let's go, Flipper." Then I laughed, my time was running short.

I almost stepped down into the garage when John pulled me back in. I noted apprehensively how easily I almost lost my balance. His face looked drawn out, but his eyes burned bright. "Wait!" he shouted loudly as if we were at a Black Sabbath concert. I'd seen them three times but never with Ozzy, twice with the great one Ronnie James Dio at the helm, and once with Ian Gillian of Deep Purple fame, not that any of this is conducive to the story it's just to show that my thoughts were beginning to stray even more so than usual.

"What's the matter?" I asked, thinking that maybe the cooler was out of beer. For the briefest of seconds I did not even acknowledge the fact that quite possibly he was talking about zombies. I'm not sure if my life had been in greater danger at any one point more so than now just because I was not aware of my surroundings.

"Don't take your hat off...not ever," he said, then the corners of his eyes crinkled up from his infectious smile. "Want a beer?"

"Sure do."

"Well let's go, the cooler is in the van."

When'd he do that? I thought, "Well that's one benefit of the zombie apocalypse...drunk driving isn't a crime anymore."

At some point, John was no longer next to me but had opened the door to his van and was now seated comfortably in the back seat. I walked over and was about to get into the driver's seat when I noticed he wasn't shutting his door.

"You want me to get that?" I asked, looking at him through the rearview mirror. He looked up at me with a startled expression.

"Get what?"

"Right," I said as I got back out and slid his door closed. I shut my door, the dome light went out and the garage suddenly seemed darker by significant degrees since we had started this endeavor. The ash that had been sifting through the numerous structural holes now looked as if it was being pumped in. We were in serious danger of death by smoke inhalation and I had suddenly become fascinated by all the numbers and letters on the dials of the VW's dashboard.

John tapped lightly on my shoulder with a beer, it brought me back. "Thanks," I told him. It was a cold Old Milwaukee in a can, not necessarily my favorite. But I had adopted a new beer credo for the end of times: my new favorite beers were, first, free ones, and secondly, cold ones. John had fulfilled both of those obligations. I popped the tab and was amazed at the feeling of the carbonated bubbles as they bounced off my nose and adhered to the remainder of my moustache and goatee. That first pull of that disgusting beer might as well have been nectar flown down to earth by the gods themselves. I was momentarily in Heaven right up until zombies began to break into John's house.

"Party crashers," John laughed as he pointed behind him. Zombies were at the entrance to John's garage. "Must have left the door unlocked. I do that a lot."

"Shit," I said, praying that when I turned the key in the ignition the van would start; but that would only solve one problem. I truly didn't think that the zombies would be so kind as to open the garage door for me.

The van rocked as the first of our uninvited 'guests' slammed into the side. The van started as John had promised, and it sounded good, but was about as useless as tits on a turtle if we couldn't get out of the garage. Then I busted out laughing over my crappy quip. I mean to the point where my stomach was cramping, the muscles on the side of my face that controlled smiling were in agony because I was smiling so long and so hard, tears were rolling down my face. To compound it, zombies were at my window, biting and gnashing at the glass which just seemed like the funniest fucking thing on the planet at the moment. Somewhere deep, deep down inside, I knew I was in a world of trouble. Weird thing about it was that I just didn't care.

It had been a long time since I had been able to just let loose, and I guess when you're faced with your imminent demise, that's as good a time as any.

"You see his mug?" I said, tears still streaming as I pointed to the nearest zombie. I looked into the rearview mirror and immediately sobered up—if only for a moment. John was playing with something, much like someone else I had loved had been doing so long ago, felt like about forty years, but in reality was only about six months previous.

"What do you have there?" I asked John

John was busy sweeping his hand back and forth. I couldn't tell because the zombies were so loud crashing into things, but I think John was even making airplane noises.

"John the Tripper!" I yelled.

He stopped mid-flight.

"What do you have there, buddy?"

"Who the hell is 'Buddy' and this is a garage door opener that I am pretending is the plane that took me to San Francisco back in '69 to catch the Dead.

My excitement was short-lived as I realized that, without power, the opener was better off as the toy plane…and then the garage door rumbled open. I didn't give a shit how, I dropped the transmission into drive and headed out. I had to go over the lawn to avoid a small contingent of zombies in the driveway.

"Don't hit her azaleas or she'll have a cow. Ran over them once with my Segway. She was pissed for twelve years, three months, and a day-and-a-half."

"So it took her that first part of a half day, twelve years, and three months later to get over it?" I asked. He said it so seriously that I could not doubt how long she was mad; the Segway part though was a little tough to swallow.

"And a day," he answered as he shrugged his shoulders.

"How'd the garage door open, John?" I asked.

He looked up again then past the mirror to the window outside. His hand immediately flew up to his head where he touched the tin foil hat and became comforted. "When'd we get outside?"

"Oh boy," I said as I did a curb check bouncing the

front passenger side wheel off of a curb. I had been so busying studying John's expressions, and then I had been distracted by a particularly interesting smudge on the small mirror—it looked to be a cross of a young Elvis with a touch of Jamie Lee Curtis thrown in there. Can't explain it, it's just what I saw at the time. I nearly rear-ended Johnson's propane truck—I knew the name from the foot high lettering on the rear—but pulled the wheel far enough to avoid that fun little disaster in the making.

"Where we going?" John asked.

"Out of the city first, then we'll decide. I don't think where I want to go is the same place as you," I said, thinking that he was going to want to hook up with his Stephanie. I hoped that wouldn't be the case. First off, because I'd lose my ride. And second, I kind of liked the crazy bastard even if he did dose my ass without me knowing. Setting him loose in this world was the same as signing his death certificate, and I didn't think I'd be able to do that with a clear conscience.

If I had just pointed the damn van north and gone towards home I most likely would have caught up to Gary, BT, and the bitch. There were a couple of plusses to our detour and some minuses.

CHAPTER NINE

Tomas and Eliza

"This reminds me of Northern France during World War One," Eliza said as the city burned around them. She had a faraway look in her eye as if lost in nostalgia.

"I had been following you, Eliza, you were in California around that time."

"Do not presume, brother, to think that I did not realize you were slinking around. I *let* you know where I was, but I would roam the world just to walk among the damned. Almost as an angel of mercy," she mused. "I put vast numbers of their like out of their misery."

"They should have nominated you for sainthood," Tomas said as they strolled down the street, zombies streaming past them heading to wherever they thought they could find a meal.

Eliza stopped for a moment. "That sounded very Michael Talbot-like, maybe you have more of him in you then you realize."

"I wish," was Tomas' reply.

"Tomas, I grow weary of your fondness for the humans. You are no more human than this thing," Eliza said as she grabbed the nearest zombie, picked him up, and thrust it headfirst into the pavement. Its head ruptured from the impact. Tomas turned away.

"You care for nothing, Eliza."

"That, Tomas, is an untruth. I care very deeply for myself and quite possibly a small amount for you. I have not yet decided on that matter."

"I just wanted us to be back together."

"Back in that hell hole you called home?" she spat. "I don't know what fondness you remember about that cesspool in time, but I harbor no such feelings. Father selling me to pay for food may have been the best thing that ever happened in my life. I got away from him, and I was given the chance to live as an immortal. Humanity will pay for all that they have bestowed upon me."

"You're delusional, sister, these people you hunt down have done nothing to you."

"I did not create this plague."

"Yes, but you are taking advantage of it."

"Isn't that the 'human' thing to do?" She smiled.

"You know what I meant." Tomas stopped. He heard a noise off in the distance that sounded out of the ordinary with the cries for help and small explosions that happened from time to time.

"Someone is making an escape attempt," Eliza said as she heard the same sound. The car was heading away from their present location. "It is of little matter," Eliza continued as the sound faded away. "The world grows smaller, and its inhabitants fewer still, we will cross paths eventually, and if it is any of Talbot's hardy followers…we will meet sooner rather than later. It does rather smell like our childhood home though, doesn't it?" Eliza asked, turning her head up to catch a smell of the smoke.

"And after we destroy the Talbots…what then, Eliza?"

Eliza stopped mid stride. "You said 'we', brother. When *we* destroy the Talbots. I think I might have felt a surge of pride for you. Of course, this could still be some sort of ploy on your part, but just too hear the words issued from your mouth gave me a moment of pause."

Tomas smiled wanly.

"Well perhaps, brother, we will celebrate and go on holiday. Visit the pyramids of Giza or the Coliseum in Rome."

"Do you know how to pilot a boat or a plane, Eliza? These humans you are so hell bent on destroying were the true rulers of the planet. You were merely a walking nightmare that stole their dreams."

"Who is in charge now?" she screamed. "While they try to save their pathetic little lives, hiding from everything that goes bump in the day or night, I walk openly in the city streets afraid of nothing or nobody!"

"Yes, you are Lord of all you survey."

"Careful, brother, I don't really *need* you. I find great solace within myself. You are merely at times a distraction."

Tomas' face fell.

Another wicked grin came over Eliza's face. "Tomas, what don't you understand? You once knew me for twelve brief years. I am mid-way through my sixth century on this world, I've changed. I'm not that frightened little girl that father did those vile things to, I am that nightmare you speak of and I have gained a foothold in the waking world. I will not be swayed from my decision to rule the pathetic survivors and to use them as I see fit. I am having fun at this point, the humans will adapt…they always do. They breed like the livestock they are. Those we do not kill today will huddle in the dark and fornicate, making more of their kind. If the Great Black Plague and two World Wars could not curb their existence, than neither will this new plague or myself."

"I curse father for what he did to you and now I curse him for what he didn't do."

"And what exactly is that, Tomas?"

"He should have killed you. In retrospect, that probably would have been the best thing, and you and I would be long dead and buried, together again in the afterlife."

"There you go again with your God. Have you not learned he cares not for his woe begotten children? Look around you, is that not proof enough?" she asked as she turned completely around in the middle of the road with her arms outstretched.

CHAPTER TEN

BT, Gary & Mrs. Deneaux

"Would you mind if I drove?" BT asked.

"Have you seen the size of you? You can carry this thing if you want to," Gary told him.

"No...seriously, I haven't driven in a very long time. Without any traffic on the roadway I should be alright."

"Well doesn't that just make me feel all confident in your abilities," Mrs. Deneaux said. She was silent for a moment as she cocked her head.

Gary pulled over to the shoulder, BT got out to walk around the car as Gary scooted across the seats.

"Do you hear that?" she asked from the back seat, as they got rolling again with BT at the helm.

BT couldn't hear anything over the churning of the Pinto's engine. Gary rolled down his window and stuck his head out much like an over eager Golden retriever; so much so, BT felt the need to grab Gary's jeans by the waist line.

"I'm not going to fall out," Gary told him.

"Not now you're not," BT told him, with one hand on the wheel. "This car is all over the road. Driving this thing is like the *Flight of the Bumblebee*."

"BT, you have culture?" Deneaux asked.

"I don't get it?" Gary asked as he pulled his head in.

"It's part of an opera," BT explained.

"Like the rock opera *Tommy* from The Who?" Gary asked.

"Something like that," BT answered.

Deneaux scoffed.

BT glanced up into the rearview mirror, mostly wishing he hadn't. "Motorcycles."

Gary stuck his head out the window nearly as far as he had the first time. "Coincidence?" Gary asked coming back in.

"You do know you could have just turned around while inside the car and have seen them, right?" Deneaux asked cynically.

"What do you think?" BT asked Gary, ignoring Deneaux's remark.

"Any chance this thing can go faster?" Gary asked, finally heeding Deneaux's advice and looking through the rear windshield.

"I could probably push the pedal through the rusted-out floorboard, but I don't know if that would make it go any faster. Plus, if the CV joints in the front end are gone and I go any faster, we hit a bump and we'll catch air...then we'll be screwed," BT said.

"I think we already are," Gary said, sitting back in his seat making sure that his rifle was fully loaded. "There's seven of them."

"I don't remember seeing zombies in any of the *Mad Max* movies," BT said grimly.

Gary looked over at his friend; Deneaux for once was silent not able to think up a retort.

"Mad Max." BT said again as if that short statement would explain everything.

Gary shrugged his shoulders.

"Come on, man, it was a classic. A post-apocalyptic world? Had a shitload of car chase scenes with motorcycles?"

"Okay," Gary said. "So?"

"There were no zombies in those movies is all I'm saying. How many dangers should we have to face on any given day? We've got zombies, vampires, rednecks and now a biker gang. Enough is enough already!" BT yelled as he slammed his fist down on the steering wheel.

The car pitched hard to the left.

"How about not breaking our ride," Mrs. Deneaux snapped. "Our friends are getting closer."

"You don't say?" BT said sarcastically. "I figured at fifty miles per hour I'd be able to lose them.

"Really?" Gary asked. "How fast do motorcycles go?"

Deneaux rolled down her window. "It came down to you or Shortie, I wonder if I chose correctly." She answered.

"We're not entirely sure if they're the bad guys," Gary said hopefully. The timing was impeccable as his side view mirror blew apart into fragments.

"I guess that solves that dilemma," Mrs. Deneaux said as she stuck her head out the window.

BT hoped a particularly large breeze would catch her and carry her out of the car. At least that was what he was thinking up until her first shot caught one of the rapidly approaching motorcyclists. The motorcycle's front wheel violently cut back and forth until the bike flipped over itself, the rider skidded along the ground and was still. The remaining six, instead of backing off, came up even faster. Gunfire peppered the back of the small car.

Deneaux pulled her head in, a look of smug satisfaction across her features as she along with the other occupants in the car ducked down. Glass shattered, and the sound of metal being punctured dominated above all else.

"Isn't the Pinto the car that used to catch on fire!" Gary yelled.

"They have automatic weapons!" Deneaux yelled. She had tried to poke her head up to get some shots off, but the suppressive fire from their pursuers was too intense. They drove a few more miles like that. The rear end of the car had become so riddled with holes as to become nearly non-existent.

BT knew it was only a matter of time before bullets made their way into the car, then they'd go out much like the infamous Bonnie and Clyde—in a hail of bullets. He began searching for something, anything to help them out of their predicament. The gang was keeping a respectable distance of around twenty-five yards, but it would be sooner rather than later when they became emboldened enough to come alongside and finish them off.

"Hold on!" BT yelled, not really giving anyone enough time to prepare as he took a hard left, never slowing. The car screeched like a white trash woman who'd realized her man had just gotten another woman pregnant. If BT had not been fighting for their lives to hold the car onto the dirt roadway, he would have found great mirth in Deneaux's futile efforts to pull herself away from her door. The car bounced and jostled, a loud twanging signaling the death throes of one or more of the rusted out leaf springs. The wheel whipped back and forth in BT's hands; trees came dangerously close to ending the group's forward momentum.

A large leafy branch struck Gary against the side of the face as he tried to pull back further into the car. Gunfire was still erupting from the bikers, but it had become more sporadic as they fell back, the choking dust of the dirt road having the desired effect. BT did not think the old Ford would be able to take much more of the pounding the surface offered, but his choices were limited at the moment.

"Take the next right!" Mrs. Deneaux shouted.

BT didn't know how she could see anything from her vantage point but he did as she said.

"Now stop!" she practically shrieked.

BT thought she might have seen a tree up ahead, he laid on the brakes which, of all the mechanical things on the car, seemed the least likely to fail. The car came to an abrupt stop just as the roar of motorcycle engines was almost on top of them.

"What now?" Gary asked.

"Quiet," Mrs. Deneaux said through clenched teeth as dust settled all around them. "Take your damned foot off of the brake you're going to give us away." She extracted herself from the car quickly.

"Nice we'll just let them race on by, then we'll get out of here," Gary said enthusiastically.

The first motorcycle raced past the Pinto's detour before Mrs. Deneaux started firing. Gary threw his hands up to his ears, unprepared for the noise of the reports.

"What are you doing, you crazy old fuck?" BT shouted. "They would have driven right past!"

"For what…another hundred yards before they figured we weren't up ahead?" she answered between shots.

After Gary recovered from the initial shock, he opened his door and grabbed his rifle. At least one motorcyclist had met his demise, and the rest still didn't know what was happening through the kicked up dust. Gary fired three shots—the last of which caught the front of the motorcycle or possibly the driver, either way the driver planted his bike into the nearest tree. The gang banger behind him had been following too closely and crashed also. He was not dead, but his cries of pain most likely put him out of this battle.

Then it was quiet as the rest of the gang discovered the ruse. The bikes throttled down from their surge to an idle. The bike that had gone past was now slowly coming back. The roadway was settling and the carnage was visible to all. The man who hit the tree was twisted with his legs bent backwards and up over his head; the world's most flexible gymnast could not have struck that pose.

"Ah fuck, Teets and Dogger are dead," one of the men said.

"Come and get me." The one that had wrecked yelled. "My arm and my leg are busted."

One of the trailing men got off his bike.

"Don't!" the man up ahead yelled. "It's a trap."

"Fuck man it's Deuce. I've got to get him," The first man replied.

"Give me your rifle," Mrs. Deneaux said softly to Gary. The words were barely out of her mouth when she grabbed it from him.

"What are you doing?" he asked as he handed it the rest of the way over.

"I'm giving Deuce's friend a little incentive," she said as she fired a round off that caught the fallen man in his broken arm.

"Oh fuck!" he screamed. He was writhing in agony, the intense pain from his shattered elbow all he could think about. "Help me!" he screamed again. "Get me out of here!"

"Q-ball, I've got to get him, we go way back," the man on the left said.

"Come on, come on," Mrs. Deneaux whispered as she kept her eye to the rifle's aperture.

"You sure are one cold bitch," BT said as he came up alongside her.

"The Viet Cong were famous for this," Deneaux replied.

"What is she talking about?" Gary asked.

"The Viet Cong would wound a soldier and lay in wait until other soldiers would try to rescue him, then they'd kill them all," BT explained. "It was some pretty sick shit."

"That's what's going on here?" Gary asked incredulously.

"Mike understood the value of a well-placed ambush," Deneaux said.

"Not like this," BT said.

"Really?" she asked finally looking up at BT long enough to arch an eyebrow. "Michael knew the aspect of our fair advantage."

"This is murder," BT said.

"How are you so dense?" she asked. "It is our survival or it is theirs, by any means necessary."

"She's right, BT," Gary added. "Mike understood that. There are more than just zombies now. It is a struggle of good versus evil. The zombies have just marked the lines of delineation. Instead of scouring the earth of the scourge of humanity, those same lowlifes have risen to the top and are taking over. While the good people stay hidden protecting themselves and their own, these assholes take whatever they want and destroy whoever they want."

"That man is defenseless." BT pointed to the wailing figure on the roadway.

"And if he wasn't?" Gary challenged.

"That's not the point!" BT said, letting anger begin to inflect his voice. "He's a human being and we're treating him like a zombie."

"You mean like this?" Deneaux asked as she drilled the man's forehead with a shot. His head snapped back and his crying ceased.

"Q-ball they killed Deuce!" the distraught man yelled.

"How would I have missed that, Digger?" Q-Ball yelled. "We didn't want to hurt you," he added.

Deneaux started laughing in response. "Neither did we."

"You've killed six of my men, this isn't over!"

"It could be," Deneaux said. "Just step into the clearing."

"Yo, bitch, what is your problem?" Digger yelled. "That was my friend."

"Well now I gave you a reason to pour some of your forty ounce beer on the ground. Isn't that what you do? Kind of as a homage?" Deneaux cackled.

"I'll fucking kill you!" Digger screamed as he began to run to the clearing, his rifle chattering from the multiple rounds he was expending.

BT shot him before Deneaux had an opportunity. The bullets had come dangerously close to their location.

"And then there were two little Indians," Mrs. Deneaux said cheerily.

"Fuck you all!" Q-ball said as he hopped on his bike and headed down the dirt path. It was moments later and the last remaining man got on his bike and headed back the way they had come.

"Well that was fun," Mrs. Deneaux said as she began to brush broken bits of glass from her hair.

BT was still at a loss for words. Gary was approaching the dead men.

"What are you doing?" BT asked him.

Gary bent over and grabbed the assault weapon.

"Oh," BT said as he came over, "any ammo?"

"Check the bikes. At least one of them had saddle bags." Mrs. Deneaux reloaded her pistol and Gary's rifle. "We've got a problem."

"Huh?" BT asked.

Gary was opening the bike's bags. "Damn, looks like a brass factory in here!"

Mrs. Deneaux pointed to the ground where a spreading pool of liquid was emptying from the bottom of the Pinto.

"Shit," BT said as he ran back to the car.

Mrs. Deneaux was going over to Gary. "Help me lift this bike," she said to him. Him helping turned out to be him lifting it.

Mrs. Deneaux straddled the machine; she held the clutch in and pushed down on the starter. The bike stuttered and died, she pushed again the bike started up. She got off and started to inspect the front end. "It should be fine," she told Gary.

"Fine for what?" he asked her.

"For you or BT. I'm taking Digger's motorcycle," she replied.

"Taking it where?" Gary asked, obviously still confused.

"The Pinto is dead, so unless you want to walk, this is our option."

"I don't know how to drive a motorcycle," Gary replied in alarm.

"First off, one does not 'drive' a bike, they 'ride' it, and you'd better hope BT can, then."

"You'd really leave us then?" BT asked as he came over.

She didn't reply as she went over to Digger's bike

and gave it the once over.

"And you do?" BT asked in reference to her knowing how to ride a bike.

"I belonged to a motorcycle club back in the late sixties," she said with a smile.

"Of course you did," BT responded. "This bike has some front end damage."

"It'll be fine, it's just going to be a bumpy ride for you is all."

"You know how to ride then?" Gary asked BT hopefully.

"I've had experience, I'm not great. With my size and the damage to the front end you should ride with Deneaux."

"Fantastic!" she cackled. "You will be my bitch!"

They grabbed their meager supplies out of the Pinto and stuffed every available pocket and saddle bag with it and started off. Gary was reluctant to wrap his arms around Deneaux, but when she started and he almost pitched off he thought better of his hesitation. Deneaux was laughing madly as they started for the road. BT was cautious on the rough dirt road and was already a few miles behind Deneaux as she was screaming down the highway.

Gary had his head huddled into her back and was holding on for dear, dear life.

CHAPTER ELEVEN

Mike Journal Entry 4

"Got another beer?" I asked John. Drunk was infinitely better than tripping and the quicker I could change my altered states the better. I had long ago stopped staring at the van's gauges. They kept swirling and melting into each other anyway. The roadway wasn't much better, but I still had enough presence of mind to keep watching that...barely.

I almost slammed into a tree when I felt the icy prick of death against the back of my neck, or it was the beer John was handing to the front. "Fuck," I said as I reached back and grabbed the beer. "My hand, John, my hand!" I told him.

"What's the matter with it?" he asked sitting up to take a look.

"Nothing, just put the beer in my hand next time."

"Oh you need a beer?" he asked. "Why didn't you just say something?" He reached in the cooler and placed another freezing can against the back of my neck.

At least this time I was ready for it and I grabbed it quickly. The glow of the burning city in my rearview mirror would have been surreal under normal circumstances. I couldn't get over the sensation that Godzilla was real and he had just laid waste to the entire area. I hoped that Gary, BT, Mary, and Josh had made it out, because from my vantage point, it didn't look like anything had survived.

"Man...you crying?" John asked, he was completely leaning over the seat, mere inches from my face.

"I'm fine," I told him, trying as nonchalant as possible to wipe my tears away.

"Are you out of beer?"

"I'm good," I told him, but we need to find a place to

hole up. I can't keep driving, if that's what you'd even call this."

"There are some cabins a few miles up the road. It's a little bit off the highway, nice and secluded," John said.

John's flashes of lucidity were always welcome. "Just point the way," I told him.

His index finger was up by the side of my face as he was quite literally pointing the way. I thought he might have been joking at first, or maybe he'd only leave it up there for a moment or two, but ten miles later his finger began to bend as we were coming up on our turn. Then straightened back out as we made the left.

"You think it's safe?" I asked him as we pulled up to a small camp ground that had six or seven cabins for rent.

"We never got caught," he answered.

"Who?"

"Me and the wife…we never got caught," he answered.

"And who would have been doing the catching?" I asked.

"That's not the point. Come on," John said as he quickly exited the vehicle.

"Caught doing what?" I asked to his back as I followed. "And that's exactly the point." I was three mother fucking steps away from the van when I realized I didn't have my rifle. I was paranoid, I swear I could see zombies all around, or it was light poles, reality was blurring heavily with hallucinations. I ran quickly back to the van and began to look inside when after a moment I couldn't find what I was looking for, I had completely forgotten. I jumped, hitting my head on the ceiling when right next to my ear, John asked what I was doing.

"I don't remember," I told him.

"That happens to me all the time," he explained, "It was important."

"It always is. If you were meant to have it, it will come back. If not, then you've set it free," he told me prophetically.

"Isn't that love?" I asked.

"We hardly know each other."

"I'm never tripping with you again, John," I told him.

"OH! That's why I feel so funny. Come on we should go inside." He said as he fumbled around with a large key ring he produced from God knew where. The keys themselves were making strange echoing vibrations inside my head as they jangled together.

I looked longingly at the van, wishing I had found or could even remember what I was looking for. But I still followed John to the cabin. I don't know if the drugs were having an effect, but each cabin was painted in some of the most garish colors I had ever seen. The one we were going to was plum purple; the one next to ours—which I was glad we were not going to—was blood red.

"These are some intense colors," I said to John, hoping that I wasn't hallucinating this also.

"I've never noticed," John said, standing on the small porch. "We should probably get in, the funky people are coming."

I didn't know who the 'funky people' were or why I should care, but John seemed to be distressed about it and that was good enough for me. He led me inside. I'd seen closets that were bigger than the cabin, but it had a bed, a small fridge, a television and a chair, pretty much anything a lone man or a couple on a getaway needed.

"I think I know what I forgot," I told John excitedly.

"About what?" he asked. He was looking through the cabin's side window.

"The beer, I forgot to get the beer."

"It's alright, man," John said as he took two strides to get across the room to the small dorm fridge. "They're probably warm but they're wet." He flashed a smile as he opened the door, at least a case worth of Natty Lite was stuffed inside.

Had I not been so fucked up on acid, I would have

gagged at the display, but as it was, they looked like gleaming cans of honey. "Wonderful," I said as a funky person slammed into our door.

"Whoa you think they want one, too?" John said as he went to open the door and ask just that.

"We don't have enough to share," I said selfishly as I grabbed one of the lukewarm god nectars.

"Probably right," he said as he let the door handle go.

"Man they're persistent," I said as I downed the beer in two or three gulps. Even as high as I was, I was more in tune with how disagreeable the sub-par beverage was thonking around in my gut than I was with the zombies that were trying to gain entry. "I really wish I had a gun," I said arbitrarily.

"Are you a fed?" John asked warily.

"What?" I asked as I turned to him, not realizing that I had another beer open and was now pouring it down the front of my poncho.

"You said you wanted a gun, only feds have guns."

I turned back to my beer and with a conscious effort I tilted my hand back up so it would stop soaking me. "Naw, man, I ain't no fed, I just think we need one."

Glass shattered from the side window, at least four or five sets of hands reached through the curtains.

"Whoa that's intense!" John said.

"Zombies!" The word finally found its way through the folds of my convoluted mind and out my mouth. Arms poked through the window and the door looked like it was in danger of giving at any moment. Like a caged animal I looked frantically for a back door, even in my state it would have been extremely difficult to miss something like that in a cabin so small.

"We should get in the basement," John suggested.

Again I spun around like a top on Red Bull. "John there's two windows and a door that leads outside. There's no basement."

"There isn't?" he asked with alarm. "That's bad news

then, we'll have to share our beer with the funky people."

"John the Tripper, they don't want the beer."

"Well that's good," he said as he physically relaxed.

"Not so much," I said softly, the seriousness of the situation was beginning to break through the stranglehold the hallucinogen had on my mind. I grabbed the lamp and pulled the shade off. I started to swing it around to get a feel of the heft of it to see if it could do any damage if it came in contact with a skull, but unless that skull belonged to a squirrel I was going to be in a little bit of trouble.

"Hey, man, that lamp cost twelve dollars. Stephanie is going to be pissed."

"Why would your wife care? And how do you know how much this cost?" I asked him, holding the lamp nearly under his nose, almost in accusation. I didn't know why that seemed like such an important matter, but right now I didn't have anything else to fixate on.

"Stephanie owns these cabins. I'm supposed to manage them but I usually forget," he said sheepishly.

"So does this place have a basement then?" I asked, again doing a pirouette like a drunken ballerina, but I guess that analogy is wrong because the drunken ballerina would still have been more graceful.

"No, man, you told me we didn't," John replied forlornly as he grabbed the lamp from my hand. "It's too bad, too, because I was growing some killer weed down there. I even had a little rhyme, too, 'The Purple cabin leads to the land of enchantment, smurple!'"

"That's how you remember?"

He nodded.

I backed up, and two zombie hands had sought purchase on my poncho. I wrenched myself free.

"We really should get in the basement," he said his eyes wide.

"I couldn't agree more," I told him.

"Why not?"

"Why not what?"

"Why couldn't you agree more?" he asked in seriousness.

"Figure of speech."

"Like an hourglass?" John asked.

"Sure, the basement, John."

"Oh yeah, and you're not the Fed right? Because if I ask...you have to tell me."

"I don't think that's the case anymore, John. But no, I'm not a Fed," I told him as the door began to crack under the zombie assault.

"Good thing." John moved a small throw rug aside. A little hinged trap with a recessed ring for a pull lever looked back up at us. "See, I told you we had a basement," he said triumphantly.

"How big is this thing?" If the size of the trap door was any indication, we were about to be inside an earthen cubby hole, and I for one would rather have taken my chances with the zombies. The thought of lying in the dirt underneath the floorboards as zombies walked above us was sending me into a near state of panic. Zombies walking across our graves; something was fundamentally wrong with the whole picture that was flashing across my mind.

"You prepared to have your mind blown?" John asked me. He pulled on the small ring and the door opened.

I was completely unprepared for what I was looking at. It looked like a rabbit hole, albeit a little bigger, a child could scramble through comfortably enough, it looked *just* big enough for a male. I looked over to John who had a huge grin spread across his face. "No fucking way," I told him. Now all I could picture was being stuck in a tube staring at John's feet as we wasted away.

"I know, right?! Isn't it awesome! We should grab some beer," he said enthusiastically as he hustled over to the fridge and started shoving cans in his pockets.

"John, how deep is that thing?" I asked, taking a step back; fearful that it would suck me in and never let me go. "I have claustrophobia, John!" Fuck the *near* panic, I was in full blown hysteria mode, I would have willingly gone to the zombies at this point rather than deal with the wormhole.

"See you on the other side!" John said as he quite literally dove into the hole. I expected to hear him start screaming that he was stuck or that the giant worm from *Tremors* was chasing his ass.

"Great, Talbot, like you needed another fucking reason to not go into the hole," I said aloud after thinking about the movie that had scared the crap out of me in my youth.

"You coming?" drifted up from the hole. I thought I was imagining it, but then I distinctly heard him tell me to bring more beer. The zombie falling through the window was the last bit of motivation I needed. I screwed up royally and got into the hole feet first. I was death-clinching the small lip of the trap door as I pulled the door shut just as the zombie inside crawled over to me, it's mouth not more than a few inches from my fingers. I was plunged into a darkness a blind person would have sensed.

I could hear the zombie scrambling to its feet. I let go of the lip just as it stepped on the trap door. My fingers were pinched a little bit, but it was nothing compared to the slamming of my heart in my chest. I wasn't moving, John had slithered down the hole like a snake, and I was stuck fast. I tried to wriggle along, but my arms were pinioned above my head, and I didn't have the room to bring them by my sides and help me move.

I wanted to cry. I could feel the walls collapsing on me, breathing was getting difficult. My next option was to push the hatch open and kill the zombie in the cabin, but I knew I'd never get out of the hole quick enough. It would be gnawing on my face as I struggled to get free. Die in the dark or have my face eaten, those were the two choices I was weighing out when John spoke.

"You coming, man?"

"John, I'm stuck!" I screamed. The zombie above me stopped its shuffling. The cabin door finally gave way with a resounding splintering.

"Did you grab more beer?"

"Would you leave me here if I didn't?" I asked, truly concerned.

The zombies above me were having a field day on the cabin; what little possessions were in there were being reduced to rubble. I could hear the planks on the trap door creak every time one or more of them stepped on them and I sincerely hoped they would hold up. I shrieked—yeah dammit, I shrieked—when I felt John's hand wrap around my ankle.

"Did you hear that, man? Sounded like a banshee," he said in all seriousness.

"That's probably what it was then," I said in a near falsetto voice, not yet getting my rampant emotions in check yet.

John was pulling me down the hole. I was trying my best to not eat dirt…I was not succeeding.

"Hi ho, hi ho it's off to work I go!" John was singing at the top of his lungs.

"You're kidding, right?" I asked in response to his song choice. I was being dragged through a tunnel by a tripping madman singing Disney songs…with zombies above me. I couldn't have made this shit up if I tried.

"You ready?" John asked me.

"For…?" I was beginning to ask as I felt myself falling. It seemed like I was suspended in space for hours, free falling through the cosmos, but now that I'm looking back on it, I'm pretty sure that was a side effect of the drugs I was on. The fall was no more than six feet, and I landed awkwardly but softly on some strewn hay.

The cavern—that was what it was—was lit up with some small lanterns that John must have placed here. "Where the…what the hell is this place?" I asked, standing up. I had a good inch or two from the top of my head to the ceiling. I tried my best to not think about it or my claustrophobia would begin to set in again.

"Chateau de Simms." He smiled, his face caked with dirt, I rubbed absently on mine realizing I probably looked much the same. "Come on, come on," he said, grabbing my hand and pulling me further away from the entry hole.

The cavern opened up, the ceiling now a good eight or nine feet from my head, the knot of claustrophobia around my heart began to loosen. The room stretched further out than side to side, maybe twenty-five feet by ten feet. I was having great difficulty with spatial relations and the echoing was completely throwing me off, threatening to give me one hell of a case of vertigo. I could smell a faint scent that harkened back to days of yore.

"Oh, my babies!" John wailed.

"What's the matter?" I asked, looking around wildly.

John sat down heavily by a row of huge potted plants. Correction, huge *Pot* plants. I had only seen plants this size on the news during drug busts.

"They're dying," he said sadly as he caressed some of the sticky buds.

"John the Tripper, I need to wrap my head around this can you start from the beginning?" I asked.

John looked up and over at me, tears threatening to fall from his eyes. "Well, scientists say that the universe was once in an extremely hot and dense state which expanded rapidly..."

"No, man, not that far back."

"Mesozoic then?" he asked clearly confused with my request.

"This cavern, John the Tripper, let's start with this cavern," I clarified, or so I had thought.

"Cave formation begins when rainwater absorbs carbon dioxide as it falls through—"

"Oh fuck, man, you're hurting my head."

"Here smoke some of this," John said, extending his arm, a fairly good sized joint in the palm of his hand. "This will help."

"Like I need more drugs." I said sarcastically rubbing

my temples.

"Exactly," John said as he looked in his hand and seemed surprised at what he found. "Did you give me this?" he asked. He sparked it up before I could respond, even if I wanted to.

I'll admit the sweet smell of the smoke was enticing, but I needed to be closer to reality as opposed to the opposite.

"Man, this is some good shit," John said as he took a sharp inhalation. "Where'd you get it?" he asked as he pulled the joint away and was looking at the burning end. "Colombia maybe?"

"I don't really remember," I told him; that seemed easier than trying to reason with him.

"You got anymore?" he asked, taking another toke.

I shook my head negatively as I began to explore our surroundings. Besides the landing hay and the potted pot plants, there were some tailgating fold-out chairs, a small collapsing table, a bunch of candles and some UV lighting that seemed to run on a cord that went back up the hole we had previously exited from.

At the far end of the cavern was another hole a little bigger than the other, this one looked like you could crawl on hands and knees, but I was in no rush, the mere thought of it got a quickening in my pulse.

"Did you make this place?" I asked John, hoping he would be on a cohesive thought upswing.

"It was here," he said with abbreviation as he took another hit.

"The tunnel from the cabin was here also?"

"No, I did that. I was pretty sure an alien spacecraft had crash landed here in the '40s. So I rented a ground penetrating radar set-up. When it bounced this hole back up, I had to see what it was. Figured the ship would be down here too, it wasn't."

"The previous cabin motel owners—or Stephanie for that matter—didn't care that you dug a hole in the middle of that room?" I asked, pointing back up.

"At first I snuck the dirt out in my pockets in the middle of the night."

"Like *The Great Escape?*" I asked, remembering a World War Two movie my dad and I used to enjoy watching.

"Well I wasn't really trying to escape, but sure," he replied, looking at me like I was the crazy one; and maybe in his skewed reality, that was the truth. "Then, when I got to the cavern, I decided I liked it a lot and I bought the motel...or maybe Stephanie did."

"This is all yours?"

He was smiling again, whether from the weed or being the proud owner I wasn't sure.

"You're fucking loaded aren't you?" I asked. "Like one of those über-rich trust fund babies aren't you!" I said, pointing and laughing at him.

"I had a friend stole two pounds of dope from me, when he sold it, he put all the money into eBay stocks. He felt so guilty he gave me thirty million."

"Dollars? That's unreal."

"What?"

"Wow, you'd never know you were worth that much."

"I'm not anymore."

I figured he had smoked, snorted or swallowed the vast majority of his windfall.

"Stephanie took the profits and rolled it into Google. I think at one time she said two hundred and fifty million."

"Holy shit, John!" I nearly fell on my ass just thinking about the staggering amount. "Why are you still living in that little house in backwoods North Carolina?"

"Where would I go?" he asked in all seriousness.

"Anywhere I suppose."

"Why? It was home."

"Yeah, John the Tripper, I guess you're right. Home is home, that's pretty deep."

"Not really, we're only about twenty feet down."

"I meant the...forget it. Shit two hundred and fifty

million, that's pretty impressive."

"It's only money."

"That's what people who have a lot say. For those that are or were struggling, it takes on a different meaning."

"Want some?"

"I don't think it's worth much anymore."

"Right, the funky people. They've been kinda of fouling everything up."

"Is this place safe?"

"It's deep enough that we don't need the tin foil hats. The funkies can't get here, and the government already removed the spaceship, so they ain't coming back. So yeah…safe as any place can be."

"I need to come down, John. All I'm seeing is tracers, and the reverberation in here is throwing me off. "

"Then you're gonna love this," he said as he snapped some glow sticks.

He started to twirl his arms. The kaleidoscope of colors was mesmerizing. I don't know how long I watched, but the chemical reaction was beginning to peter out when I finally pulled my gaze away.

"Come on sit down," John told me. I had not even known he sat; the colors were still swirling vividly in front of me. "Smoke this." He handed me a pipe that looked suspiciously like a peace pipe.

I took a long drag, the aromatic smoke filling my lungs, the smell of vanilla wafting around our enclosure. "What is this?" I asked, looking at the pipe, realizing that I should probably have asked before taking a hit. With John all bets were off.

"It's a personal blend."

"Your words are not as comforting as I would hope, John."

"North Carolina tobacco, with a smattering of Turkish hashish," he told me as he handed the pipe back.

The sweet-spiced tobacco melded nicely with the tangy tickle of the hash. The buzz was pleasant and rounded the edges of the harsh trip. I was feeling better—not normal, not by a long shot—but at least I didn't feel like I was going to come out of my skin. Although I figured I had already done that once today and that should be enough.

We sat there for an indeterminable amount of time. I found great comfort in John, for a man so out of step with the 'real' world, he was the lord of this domain. I smoked until I couldn't lift my arms any more. We talked some, for the life of me I can't remember anything except the profoundness of it. And then John told me to go to sleep.

CHAPTER TWELVE

Eliza and Tomas

"They are gone or they are dead, Eliza, how much longer must we walk around this dead city?" Tomas asked.

Eliza was about to answer when a woman clutching a bottle of amber liquid stumbled out of her house. "Are you that bitch?" Mary yelled.

"Well, well what do we have here?" Eliza said bemused as she strode over the lawn towards Mary.

Mary's booze-induced bravado barely held up as Eliza stood face-to-face with the woman. But she stood defiant in the face of death. "You are...aren't you? I can smell the stench of death all around you."

"What do you know of me?" Eliza asked Mary out of curiosity.

"You're not smo bad!" Mary slurred, trying to stand up taller, hoping her slight height advantage would somehow intimidate the smaller woman. But what Eliza lacked in size she more than made up for in intimidation.

"Oh, I can assure you that I am," Eliza said.

"That Talbot fellow...he was all petrified of you. I don't see why," Mary said, taking a huge swig of the bourbon she was clutching.

"Where is he?" Tomas asked, suddenly interested in the conversation.

"He's dead!" she shouted, swinging the bottle, some of the fire water sloshing out.

"And you know this for a fact?" Eliza asked, a smirk on her face.

"The big black man and his own brother said so. They're all dead!" she shrieked.

"BT is dead?" Tomas asked saddened.

"I'd imagine," Mary answered.

"You don't know?"

"How the fruck would I know, do I look like a psychic?" she said, taking another swig. "I'm just glad they took the old bat with them."

"Deneaux was with them?" Tomas asked.

"Fucking witch. Now she was scary," Mary replied.

"How long have they been gone?" Tomas asked.

"Who the hell are you?" Mary asked, taking another swig.

"I am her brother."

"Lucky you," Mary said sardonically.

"Did they say where they were going?" Eliza asked.

"Why?" Mary asked suspiciously.

"Why did you not leave with them?" Tomas asked.

"It's not safe out here, not safe at all for my Joshie."

Eliza looked past Mary. "A child perhaps?" Eliza asked.

"He's not in there!" Mary said loudly when she realized she may have said more than she intended.

"So you who thought the world was too dangerous for your spawn, sent him away? Then opened your door to challenge me? How has your kind survived for so long?"

"My *kind*? What are you? I didn't believe any of that horseshit about you being a vampire."

"Well that was your second mistake," Eliza said, effortlessly pushing Mary aside so she could enter the house.

***

Mary began to scream as Josh's body flew down the stairs, to slam against the far wall, then crumple in a heap at the bottom of the stairs.

"The whelp is dead!" Eliza said hotly as she came

down the stairs.

Mary dropped her bottle and fell to the floor to wrap her arms around her son. "He was sleeping!" she screamed. "You'll hurt him!"

Tomas stood in the doorway; he could smell the death on the child and madness upon the mother. Eliza had not done it, he was thankful for small favors.

Eliza stepped over the huddled family and walked past Tomas to get back outside.

Tomas thought there might yet be hope for his sister that she had not killed the mother then he realized quite the opposite was true, she had left the mother alive to mourn over the loss of her son. Her cruelty was not bound by any depths.

CHAPTER THIRTEEN

Maine

Tracy awoke in her bed. *No that's not quite right,* she thought. It was her bed she was using now, then the pain of loss and despair settled upon her like a cloak when she realized the other half of the mattress was cold and empty. But that wasn't quite true either; she could feel the weight of something that was making her gravitate towards the middle. She slowly turned, fearful of what she might find. Henry was sitting up on the bed staring off into space, seeing things only dogs could.

"You miss him, too?" Tracy asked as she stroked the dog's massive face and barrel-shaped chest.

Henry kept looking off into the distance, not acknowledging her ministrations.

"Listen, I know you were always Mike's dog, and I'm so sorry that I yelled at him when he saved you. He loved you, Henry. I love you, too. It's just that I guess he always thought you were our fourth kid, and I didn't see it until recently."

Henry cocked his head to the side like he could hear something very far away. He barked once, which in itself was unusual. His mouth opened wide in what Tracy could only describe as a grin, his heavy tongue lolling about, he finally pulled his gaze back in to register Tracy's existence. He then contentedly lay down and, before finally settling in, let a blast of essence de' Henry waft throughout.

"That's my cue," Tracy said as she threw the covers off and headed for the exit.

Tony was sitting in the living room chair. Ronnie and Tracy had not told him about their suspicions regarding Mike. No matter what she had felt in her heart, she had no proof and did not want to burden the man with it.

"Feeling better, honey?" Tony asked her.

"Surprisingly, I am," she told him, heading over to give him a kiss on the cheek. "What is that smell?" Tracy asked brushing her hand past her nose.

"That Mad Jack guy caught the kitchen on fire. No, no it wasn't that bad," Tony added when he saw alarm on Tracy's face.

"Do you want some tea?" Nancy, Ronnie's wife, asked Tracy as she came into the living room.

Tracy shook her head. "No thank you."

"It's very soothing. It will help to calm your nerves," Nancy added.

"I'm fine, Nancy," Tracy said almost through clenched teeth, apparently Ron had told Nancy and hadn't thought to tell her not to say anything around Tony.

"I'm sure you really need it." Nancy said soothingly.

Tony was closely watching the exchange.

"If I want some tea Nancy I'll come and get some."

"You poor thing," Nancy said, tears welling up in her eyes.

"What's the matter? I may be an old man, but I'm not daft. I've been watching everyone tippie-toe around for the last day. Something is going on and they think the patriarch can't handle it," Tony said angrily.

Tracy swallowed heavily. "Tony, I thought Mike might be dead yesterday, but now I'm not so sure."

Tony paled rapidly, color slowly drained back into the void as he processed Tracy's whole sentence. "What changed?" he asked slowly and cautiously.

"I know this sounds crazy…" She started as she quickly looked over to Nancy. "Henry. Henry changed. I know how strange that sounds, but Henry sensed something yesterday and now he seems to be back to the way he was before. Expectant. He's waiting for his Mike to come home."

Tony was scratching the top of his head; a gesture Tracy had noticed Mike do when he was having trouble wrapping his mind around something. "So Henry told you Mike died and has now been what? Reborn?"

"I...I can't explain it completely, Tony. That damn dog and Mike share something. Henry knew, absolutely knew something bad had happened to Mike and now something incredible has."

"So you believe in your heart of hearts that Mike is alright?" Tony asked, now tears threatening the man's visage.

"I do," she said through the tears. *Because I want to*, she thought. *Because the alternative would be unbearable.*

"I think I need to make more tea," Nancy said, running out of the room.

It was a half hour later when the entire group found themselves sitting on the deck at the Talbot compound: Tony with Carol, Tracy's mom they had become something sort of an item although they denied it to everyone that asked. Ron, Nancy, their children—Meredith, Melissa, and Mark. Tracy, with Nicole, Justin and Travis. Mad Jack, who seemed perturbed that he had been disturbed from his work. There was Angel, Sty, and Angel's brother Ryan and Dizz from the gas station in Massachusetts. Perla, who had been Jack O'Donnell's fiancée, she had yet to pull completely out of her stupor upon his loss. And Cindy Martell, Brian Wamsley's significant other.

"Something's changed," Ron said to the group. Except for Justin, he was the only one standing. "We can all almost feel it in the air."

"It's heavy," Perla said with her head hung low. Cindy wrapped her arms around her friend.

"All the more reason I should still be working," Mad Jack said more to himself than the group.

"In due time, MJ," Ron said. "We had good reason to believe that Michael died yesterday." Even MJ who was usually off in his own world responded with a gasp. Cries of 'are you sure?' and 'I can't believe it!' were all dominated by one small girl,

"The funny man is dead?" she asked, then she started to cry uncontrollably.

"Oh, honey," Nancy said, pulling the small girl to her.

"Okay…hold on," Ron said, putting his hands up. "We're now not so sure," he said quickly glancing over to Tracy.

"What about Brian?" Cindy asked with concern. If Mike had been in danger, then it only followed that they all had been.

"We…we don't know," Tracy answered.

"Have they radioed in and you're not telling us?" Cindy asked as she stood.

"No, we haven't heard anything in days," Ron said, giving back-up to Tracy.

"Then how or why would you think something happened to Mike?" Cindy asked.

Henry picked that opportune moment to saunter onto the deck and lay down in the middle of the throng.

"Him." Tracy pointed to the dog.

"Him?" Cindy sneered. "You scare the shit out of all of us on something the dog did? Did he come out and tell you Mike was dead…oh and then miraculously he was reborn like Jesus Christ!" she shrieked.

"Listen, we're all a little stressed out right now, I just wanted to get everyone together to—" Ron was cut off.

"Don't you give me that stressed out bullshit," Cindy was screaming. "My fiancé is out there and I don't know if he's dead or alive or worse. The sitting here not knowing, what do you know about stress?"

Ron was straining to hold back his own anger. "I *still* have a daughter out there, or did you forget that. I know all too well the pain of loss. If you someday have a child, I hope to God that you NEVER experience the pain I suffer every fucking minute of every fucking day."

Nancy was full on crying. "Anybody want some tea?"

she asked, not waiting for an answer as she exited the room hastily.

"I'm so sorry." Cindy said as the heated wind fell from her sails. "You're right we're all stressed."

Ron waited a moment to make sure that Cindy wouldn't flare up again. "Listen, I'm not one for spirituality, superstition, supernatural or paranormal, that's just not the way I was raised and it's not part of my belief system. And now that I've got that quantifier out of the way, I truly believe something happened to Mike…and for whatever reason, he's back. Mike's resurrection means something and it means something big. I've got to believe he's heading here."

"And so is the shit storm," Travis said.

"No swearing," Tracy told him absently.

"This is still all conjecture though right?" Perla asked. She was afraid.

"Yes," Ron said, "no matter what the truth, or what we are feeling, I think that we need to be prepared sooner rather than later and that we need to redouble our efforts no matter what they may be. From gathering or storing food, to setting up our defenses, to the hundred other things we need to have done to survive an all out attack. And I want to double up on guard duty." That brought a fresh round of moans. "Except for Mad Jack, Nicole, and Angel…we'll all be taking extra shifts."

"I can guard!" Angel said defiantly.

"I know, honey, but you already have a job," Tracy told her.

"I take care of the aminals, pretty lady!" she said proudly.

"And Henry loves you for it," Tracy told her. She looked over to Justin and noticed he was rubbing at his wound where the zombie had scratched him. He was trying to be sly, but it looked like it was itching him something fierce. Her heart froze when it looked like storm clouds swept across his vision. *Mike, wherever you are, hurry up,* she thought.

"I can take an extra shift, Uncle Ronny," Nicole said sleepily. She wasn't quite showing yet but her energy level had dropped considerably.

"No, you need your rest and Mad Jack needs to finish his devices," Ron told her.

"What's the matter with her?" Mad Jack asked, finally realizing he was supposed to be interacting with others.

"I'm pregnant," Nicole laughed.

"How'd that happen?" Mad Jack asked.

"Did he really just ask that?" Travis asked his mother.

Mad Jack's face flushed. "Sorry, you might want to stay away from my stuff while I'm doing experiments."

"Is it dangerous?" Nicole asked, clutching her midsection.

"It shouldn't be, but no sense in risking it."

"I'll keep that in mind. I'm going to lie back down," Nicole told the crowd.

"I'll check on you in a little while, honey," Tracy told her.

"Is she going to start waddling soon?" Travis asked.

"I heard that, baby brother." Nicole shouted.

"Alright, let's get back to work. What ever Mike has going on, I'm sure it's important and we should be ready for him," Ron said before dismissing the group.

CHAPTER FOURTEEN

Mike Journal Entry 5

"Oh, man, pass me a joint," I told John as I sat up. "I don't know which hurts more, my body from sleeping on the ground or my head from the acid and beer."

"You should have slept on a cot," John said, looking down at me from his Army-Navy surplus green canvas cot.

"I didn't know I had the option," I told him. I didn't know how long I had slept, but it was long enough that I was no longer tripping and that was fine by me.

"You should have asked," he said as he swung his legs over and reached into a little bag to produce a pre-spun joint.

"John, how would I know to ask? Should I just randomly throw questions out there and see which ones stick?"

John's eyebrows were knitted together as he thought on my words.

"Okay…for instance, do you have a helicopter?" I asked him.

"Of course."

"Wait, what? Are you kidding me?"

"Why would I do that? Kid, I mean. I have a Safari two-seater kit helicopter."

"Okay I'm going to try and hit the pertinent points all in one shot. First, does it work?"

"Yup."

"Second, can you fly it?"

"Yup."

"Wait…real quick…so you don't have a license to drive your van, but you have whatever license it takes to fly a helicopter?"

"A lot more people on the roadways than in the air," he answered.

"Got me there. On to the bonus round where the right answers are worth double."

"Excellent I love the bonus round," John said excitedly. "So how many points are we talking about?"

"The sky's the limit!" I said, going along with his madness.

He paused for a moment. "I get it! Because it flies!"

"That'll work, hey, John the Tripper, can I shorten your name up to Trip?"

"Is this still the bonus round?"

"Added bonus maybe."

John's lip started to quiver a bit.

"You alright, man?" I asked him.

"That's what my wife calls me. I miss her, man."

"I'm sorry. I didn't mean to bring up any bad feelings."

"Naw, it's cool," he told me. "You can call me Trip, it helps me to remember."

"She's not really in Washington is she, Trip?"

"No." He buried his face in his hands. "It's worse."

"We've all lost people we love, Trip. There's no shame in showing it," I said, standing so that I could rub his shoulder.

"She's in Philly," he sobbed.

"Trip, what the hell are you talking about?"

"My wife, she's not in Washington she's in Philly." His wails started anew.

"I'm confused, man," I told him.

"The City of Brotherly Love, how can you not know about it?"

"I know about Philly, and I'm not sure why that's such bad news. It's actually good because she's that much closer."

"She is? I figured Philly was another country, you

know 'PA' for Panama."

"It's more like 'PA' for Pennsylvania." I hastily drew a rough representation of the United States and the states in question. John's face was beginning to register the new information. I desperately wanted to get home, but his wife was not entirely out of the way and I would feel better if he had company. I shuddered thinking of him stopping to ask some 'funkies' for directions.

"Want to go get her?"

"More than anything, followed closely by seeing Jerry Garcia."

I didn't tell him that our odds were better of seeing Jerry than his wife. "Let's do it then, back to the helicopter."

"Bonus round," he sniffed.

"Bonus round," I echoed. "Can we get to it, or is it in Philly or D.C., too?" I asked, trying for some levity.

"Asheville Regional Airport, it's about twenty-five miles from here."

"So not Philly then, that's good."

"What'd I win?" he asked expectantly.

"An all expenses paid trip to Rocky's hometown."

"The squirrel?"

"What? No not Rocky and Bullwinkle. Rocky the boxer."

John was slowly shaking his head from side to side.

"Sylvester Stallone, famous series of movies."

"Never heard of them."

"How about the home of the Cheesesteak?"

"Who puts cheese on a steak?"

"You're killing me. The City of Brotherly love, man, we're going to go get your wife."

"Wow, that's awesome! What a great prize to win!" he said, clapping his hands.

I had to admit, it was nice to not be the craziest person in a group, but I wasn't really sure what footing that left us on…if any. "We're going to need another car. Any chance you got one waiting somewhere?"

"No, and it's not much fun going out the other side."

"So that hole does lead out then?" I asked, pointing to the other side of the cavern.

"It longer and narrower than the one we came in from."

"You're kidding, right?" But I already knew the answer. John wasn't much of a kidder. Right now, asking the 'funkies' to move seemed like a better option. "Maybe we could widen it," I said.

"It's carved through rock, that one's natural."

I was already starting to breathe heavily and we weren't even in the damn thing yet. "Trip, I don't know. I have this thing about tight places."

"It's just like being born." He smiled.

"I don't remember what it was like to be born, Trip."

"You don't? I thought everyone did. Well it's just like it! No sense in thinking about it… you ready?"

"Not fucking really," I said, starting to work on a world class panic attack.

"It'll be fun," he said as he went over to a large plastic storage bin. He pulled out a small drum-shaped container.

At first I couldn't register what he was doing; my legs were bobbing up and down so fast I couldn't focus on anything. Then he started to grab big handfuls of the white substance and starting at his tin foil hat, began to apply liberal amounts over his whole body.

"Can you get my back?" John asked me.

"What are you doing?" I asked.

"Lard, it simulates the fluids in the placenta."

"I think you're taking this a little too far," I told him.

"First time I went through there I almost got stuck. As it was, it took me four hours to get through. It goes by a lot quicker with the lard."

"Trip, I can't be in that hole for four hours! I'm bigger than you, how am I going to fit? Just go, get your wife, I'll stay here until the zombies leave and go back up through the cabin."

"That's probably a good idea."

Relief flowed through my system, but co-mingled with it was despair. I would be alone.

"Let's have one last lunch together," John said as he wiped his hands clean of the heavy lubricant and dipped back into his storage bin; he grabbed a couple of MRE's and some chemical packets to heat them up. Within a few minutes, my packet of corned beef and hash was piping hot. I grabbed the closed (and sealed) packet from him before he had a chance to open it.

"If you don't stir it around some it of stays cold." He said as he popped a soda and handed it to me.

"I'll do it," I said with a shudder, his hands getting entirely too close to my food, even if there was nuclear safe material between him and the sustenance. "Thank you."

"You're welcome." He grabbed his food, stirred it around, and began to eat heartily.

There was a comfort to the food, not in the taste mind you, that was more like rat stew, but it was the breaking of bread with a friend.

"Want some hot sauce?" he asked.

"No, I'm almost done."

"Good stuff?"

"Edible," I answered honestly. "I'm going to miss you, John the Tripper."

"I wouldn't worry about that too much." John took longer than normal to eat his meal, almost savoring every morsel; even stopping for long moments to examine his Spork.

"Man, I'm tired." I yawned.

"I bet," John said. "Want some crackers?" he asked, splitting the packet open.

"No, and why would you bet that?"

"Valiums have that effect on people."

"What?" I tried to ask with excitement, but I just couldn't get enough adrenaline flowing.

"I put a few in your pop."

"Dude, you have got to stop drugging me without at least taking me out for dinner," I said sleepily.

He grabbed my now empty can and shook it in front of my face.

"Right," I replied. "So now what?"

"I'm going to wait until the pills kick in completely, then I'm going to take off that awesome poncho you've got and cover you in lard, then I'm going to drag you through the birth canal," he said as he popped a handful of crackers into his mouth.

"I'm scared, Trip," I admitted.

"No need to be, yet. Wait until we're in the helicopter...then you'll have good reason."

"Fucking swell," I told him.

We sat there a few more minutes as he poured a mini bottle of Tabasco over the last couple of crackers and washed them down with some red Kool-Aid-looking drink.

"Wouldn't that be awesome if the Kool-Aid man just came and knocked a hole in the wall for us?" I asked John, looking longingly at the spot I sincerely hoped that would happen.

"Does this Kool-Aid man have anything to do with Rocky Stallone?" John asked.

"Where are you from, Trip? Those are national *r*icons."

"Up," he said and motioned. "You just slurred. I think we're ready."

"I'm scared, buddy," I repeated as I got up and started to pull the poncho over my head, and then I couldn't remember in which direction I needed to pull to get it over my head.

"No *problema*, your life is in my hands." He laughed as he finally got the heavy material off of me.

John dropped about a pound of the lard on the top of my head smashing my hat down onto my head; it felt like a damn runny ostrich egg as he spread it around my face and shoulders.

"I'm not really liking the way this feels, John. Things will stick to me."

"Naw, man, this to help from sticking," he said as he slathered copious amounts of the white goo on my ass.

Wow! I'm looking back at the words I'm writing and I'm having a hard time deciding whether to keep them there, this is starting to sound like a porno. If I had a bigger eraser I'd rub those words out. Yes I could keep going in that vein, as a guy it's actually pretty easy. But since my wife will probably one day see this journal, I'm going to swing it back.

"I don't really like people touching me, Trip."

"What? Put your hands over your head," was all he said.

I complied, any more lard and he could have shot me through a straw. He patted down my legs better than any cop frisking I had ever had. I was afraid to move, so sure that I was going to stick to myself. I don't even like the sticky feel of humidity—this was excruciating. I almost wanted to go through the damn hole now just so I could get this shit off of me.

"Okay, now do me," John said as he put his hands over his head. He waited a few moments before turning around. "You said you didn't like people touching *you*."

"It goes both ways."

"It's this or four hours in the hole." He smiled.

"Fuck," I said as I grabbed a giant handful of the lard. "This is so gross, why didn't you use vegetable oil?"

"Wore off too quick." After a few more moments, John seemed pleased with his new uniform of rendered animal fat. He grabbed some rope and made a harness for me securing it together with a mountaineer's clasp. He then did the same to himself, then tied us together with about a fifteen foot length of what I considered to be entirely too thin rope.

"This gonna hold? It looks like dental floss. Or maybe a super model's thong."

"I'd trust my life to this rope," he told me.

"What about mine?"

"You'll be fine, man, I won't leave you."

"I'm more concerned you might forget."

"You ready?" he asked as he tugged hard on our connections. My body was so loose I almost fell over. "You look like you're going to fall asleep. I'm sorry, we're going to have to leave your poncho behind...that's some rocking duds."

"Maybe someday we can come back and get it," I said, then took a big breath.

"Small breaths, okay?"

"Does hyperventilating count?"

He smacked my chest twice. "When I tell you to put your hands over your head, do it okay? And just relax. I've got this. Do you know what day it is?"

I shook my head from side to side. "No idea, does it matter?"

"About what?" he asked as he checked his gear again.

Panic started to force the corned beef back up. But then I pictured myself with the vomit sticking to my thick white coating and I thought better of it. I swallowed it back down. Without another word, John climbed into the hole. *Not so bad*, I thought as I got in.

We had gone maybe ten to fifteen feet on our hands and knees and I was actually doing alright, of course I think a big piece to that puzzle were the 'mother's little helpers' that John had placed in my lunch.

Right up until John told me it was 'wiggle time.'

"It gets fun now!" John shouted.

"I don't think my idea of fun equals the same thing as yours, Trip."

"You do know I was being sarcastic don't you?"

"I didn't, and that's a damn shame considering I'm the self-appointed king of it."

"You don't need to put your hands over your head yet. Soon though," he said as I heard him pulling away.

I traveled another couple of feet, I felt like I was on

the inside of a bottle and now I was coming up to the bottleneck. The circumference of the hole I was about to 'wriggle' through seemed to halve itself. Valium-induced state of calm or not, my phobia was threatening to break through the chemical-induced calmness, with a vengeance.

I would have had great difficulty fitting a sheet of paper on either side of my shoulders. I was already beginning to rub off a fair amount of the animal fat. The rope pulled taut as I was frozen at the mouth. My hand was on my carabiner, I still had time. I could back up and return to the relative spaciousness of the small cavern. A *putrid* of zombies (seemed like a good name for a pack of them) was a far better option than slow suffocation by tons of dirt.

"You coming?" John asked as he pulled on our connection.

"I was thinking about going back and making some cookies." It was all I could think to say.

"There's cookies?" John asked.

I thought I could hear him coming back. "No, just fucking around. I'm coming, I guess."

"You shouldn't mess around with cookies," John mumbled as our connection again got tight. He started to drag me, and if I didn't drop down, I was going to bang my forehead on a low hanging rock.

My shoulders were beginning to scrape, I could feel the friction begin to tear into me. When I took particularly big intakes of air because I didn't feel like I was getting enough my chest would also rub against the rocks.

"Man this is harder than I remember," John said up ahead of me.

"Everything alright?" I asked cautiously.

"Whoa who was that, man?" John asked. I could tell that he turned his head because some light from the small headlamp he was wearing was shining on a small curve up ahead.

"It's me, John," I told him in a near falsetto voice, trying my best to not succumb to my fear.

"I don't know no Mejon? What are you doing down here?" he asked me.

"This is sarcasm right? Because I'm already almost freaking out, Trip."

"Are you from the government? Because I have my medicinal marijuana card. I'm allowed to have up to forty-five plants. No wait maybe that's only supposed to be three. Now I'm still working on getting my Medicinal LSD card, but that should be happening soon, I put a petition in to the governor."

John's delusions were going to send me right over the edge—at least I wouldn't have far to fall. That was of very little solace.

"John the Tripper, I am not with the government, I'm Michael Talbot, remember? We've been together for like two days now." I said in short, staccato bursts of speech.

I didn't hear anything for long moments except the sound of dripping water off in the distance. "You the dude with the rocking poncho?"

"Yeah, yeah that's me, man. They call me Poncho Via."

"Weird name, what're you doing here?"

"Waiting in line for Dead tickets, John." I couldn't help it; sarcasm is my last line of defense in stressful situations.

"You got your wrist strap?"

"I do I'll show it to you when we get out of here."

"Okay," he answered, and then started moving forward again.

I began to crawl as fast as I could to try and keep up so that he would not question the drag on his momentum again. I needed to be out of this particular experience.

John didn't say anything or give any type of warning as I came up on another shrinking of the tunnel. Although to call it more than a gopher hole at the moment was a stretch. There was still a couple of feet of slack in the rope, but a decision was fast approaching. I felt that to do anything that would distract from John's task at hand would be detrimental to my rapidly fracturing psyche. I placed my hands inside the hole ahead of my body, and with my feet paddling like a landlocked fish, I wedged myself tightly in the opening. I tried to gain purchase with my hands; but where they were in front of me I had no leverage to use. I tried to hook my feet around something…anything…to pull myself back. It was useless, and worse yet, I was beginning to feel hopeless.

The rope pulled tight, first against my chest, then it pulled up on my chin and across the left side of my face. It felt like it was digging in for the long haul. I tried to move my head off to the side, but there just wasn't enough room. I strained my neck muscles to keep my head as high as possible so the rope wouldn't abrade against my eye. I could hear John's labored breathing as he was trying to pull me through. My senses were so torqued up that I could hear the rope as it was stretched and minute tears began to form. I was certain the line was going to snap and I would be 'the one that got away.'

Then it did tear but not the rope, my shirt at the shoulders tore—as did my skin. At least seven layers of skin in depth, because I could feel blood start to run down my shoulder and back in small rivulets. Tears of pain were beginning to form in the corners of my eyes as John strained to pull me free. The pain was excruciating, I felt like I was melding with the rock to become some new igneous-tissue hybrid.

"Ahhhh!!!" John screamed. It mirrored my own reaction perfectly. We were past the widest part in my shoulders, but we were far from through. John was pulling for all he was worth. His aggressive spelunking was shaking small rocks free from their moorings, and with a slight decline behind him, the only way they were going was towards me. From this angle, they looked like boulders. I moved my hands so they angled like a bulldozer blade in an attempt to stop them from smacking into my face. They were easily big enough to cause some damage and possibly break a few teeth if they caught me in the mouth.

"Shouldn't have eaten that lunch," John strained to say.

I had to imagine he was talking about me, but there still was a significant possibility he had completely forgotten I was behind him. I would be up shit creek if he undid his harness and just kept going. Between the lard, sweat, blood, and John's extreme exertions, I finally came free like a long awaited turd from a constipated man's ass. Graphic and gross I know, but I'd be lying if I said that wasn't exactly what went through my mind. I was exhausted and I hadn't done much more than worry about what was happening.

After some labored breathing, John finally asked me how I was doing.

"Not so good," was my honest response.

"Got about another twenty feet to go from where you're at."

"Any chance you're definition of feet is somewhat shorter than the American standard?"

"That's kind of funny. Was that supposed to be?"

"That was the intention."

"Don't lose your bracelet or you have no proof how long you've been in line. That happened to me once, but my friend Scooter was able to get me a ticket."

For a moment I was too wrapped up in my neurosis to grasp what the hell he was talking about, then it dawned on me he was referencing my earlier sarcastic comment. That'd teach me for being a wise-ass. "How you doing, Trip?"

"I'm a little tired, Ponch. Probably shouldn't have taken the rest of those valiums."

"What? You took them, too?" I asked in a panic.

"Yeah, this shit makes me nervous too, brother. Maybe I'll just take a small nap."

"No, no, no," I said rapidly. "No naps, you can rest when we get out of here."

"I'm really tired."

"I can't stay in here much longer." I started to

scramble for thoughts and then it hit. "We'll miss the show, man."

"Oh shit, the show. I don't want to miss that! What if they play *Fire on the Mountain*!"

John redoubled his efforts and along we crept, I was starting to push a fairly significant amount of rocks ahead of me soon I would have created an impenetrable wall. A couple would occasionally slip past and catch. One stuck fast in the small of my back, the pain was excruciating as it was forced down onto my spine. Just when I didn't think I could take it anymore, a small rise in the rocks allowed it to move down where it got neatly stuck between my ass cheeks.

"Great it's not bad enough the whole world has gone to hell, but now I'm being rock raped."

"I see daylight! Hey, man, where's the show again?"

"Shit!" I said through gritted teeth as the sharp rock finally rolled off me and down the back of my legs.

"Where?" John asked again.

"Where do you want it to be?" I asked as another rock tumbled over my makeshift plow, that one drew blood as it nicked the top of my forehead. But at least it had the graciousness to keep on going.

"Red Rocks would be nice."

My heart panged at the remembrance of the place I had been to so many times before. "Yes it would, Red Rocks it is, Trip."

"Fuck yeah, I haven't been there since '78!" he replied, adding, "I'm out." With so little inflection I hadn't even put the pieces together. "Hey, Poncho, wait…that's not your name."

"Don't worry about it, you're close enough."

"It gets a little tighter, then you're free."

"Tighter than the last place I got stuck?" I asked. One does not understand the full magnitude of a claustrophobic's biggest fear until you are living it. I was packed in so tight that I could not take a full breath, I could not move forward or backwards.

"Yup, definitely tighter."

"Just get me out," I begged.

"Uh-oh," he said, then didn't say anything else.

"John...John the Tripper? Trip!" I was yelling as loud as I could with the limited amount of oxygen I had to work with.

"Shhh, man, there's some freaky people around, and it looks like they want to cut in the line."

"Zombies, there's zombies? Of course there is," I said quietly so that only I could hear. "Get me out of here, man, and I'll help you hold our spot." I could smell the stench of zombie as it wafted down the shaft. My vision was dimming around the edges. I was in real danger of blacking out. Who knows, maybe that would be better.

I could hear some scuffling up ahead and John must have forgotten we were tethered as I was pulled quickly ahead six inches; my cheek bled as it was raked against a rock. The hole I was in was narrowing even more the further up I went. I had to turn my head to the side to be able to fit through. Then, as I was about halfway through the narrow gap, my movement stopped. My head was canted to the side and the valium had completely worked through my system. I was fucked and in a full on panic. Terror ripped through my body as I lay immobile. My neck was starting to scream in protest at the direction it was forced to be in. My shoulders were on fire and my chest was shuddering while I tried to pull in more air. A sardine had more room in its final tin resting place than I had.

"John, help me, man," I said on the verge of tears. Nothing. "Please," I begged.

I began to jerkily move forward, it didn't feel right, but at this point I didn't care if zombies had improved their motor skills and were now reeling me in like a hooked tuna. My ass was lodged in the tunnel, but at least I could now move my head and finally see the light at the end. Actually, I could see a small sliver of sky—which was comforting—yet I could not move to get any closer. From the tips of my fingers to the lip of the edge couldn't have been more than six feet—or the way I was stuck, thirty miles.

"Get your own tickets!" I heard John screaming from a distance.

We were no longer tied together. If he were to die, or more likely forget I ever existed, I would surely die here. "Pussy," I said aloud. "You talking to me? I'm fucking cracking up, that's what I get for hanging with John too long. Aren't you like half Drac now? More like a quarter and what's that got to do with anything?" Right now it had everything to do with everything. "You're strong, Talbot, stronger than you should be. Fucking dig deep, Marine!" I screamed.

I pulled my arms in so that I could start to toss the rocks in front of me out of the hole. After a few missed attempts, I had them all out. Just that added bit of space comforted me, that or I had finally decided to pull my fate out of the hands of a man aptly named John the Tripper. I turned my hands outward, and with my finger tips, sought to seek purchase on the solid ground ahead of me. Simultaneously, I placed my feet against the wall and then I pulled or pushed as the case may be. Nothing! I was straining; every muscle I could use in the fight to freedom was being exerted to its maximum. Still nothing…then a sliver. I moved no more than a hair's width, but I fucking moved! I redoubled my efforts.

Pebbles scrabbled past as I wiggled, writhed, and shook my way forward. I hadn't moved more than six inches and I was bathed in a sweat that had a hard time finding a release from my lard-caked body. I felt at least one fingernail rip free from its moorings, I didn't stop to mourn its loss, and I pressed on. Occasionally I could hear John's screams, but the rush of blood through my ears made it difficult to ascertain how near or how far away he was.

My entire body was through the small channel. It wasn't exactly voluminous where I was, but comparatively speaking, it was the damned Grand Canyon. Okay, maybe more like Brice Canyon, but a canyon nonetheless. My finger tips were at the edge, I gripped it and heaved. I fell out like a bowling bowl from the bottom of a defective carrying bag (with a solid thunk if the analogy wasn't clear enough).

I stayed on the ground for a moment, reveling in my victory. I had completely torn off the fingernail on my left index finger. The rest would take expert ministrations from a team of Asian pedicurists to get back to something acceptable and I didn't give one shit. I stood up and winced as I placed my hands over my head—this time to shout, "I'm free!"

John was at least a hundred yards away he was backpedaling as two deaders with outstretched arms were almost within grasp. I couldn't tell from this distance what it was, but something tripped the Tripper and down he went. The zombies were nearly upon him.

I ripped off my tin foil hat and as I screamed it, I thought it. "COME TO ME!"

   ***

"What was that?" Tomas asked, wincing as he reached up and placed his hands against his head.

Eliza turned to the west in the direction the summons had come. She wiped her hand across the bottom of her nose and was surprised to see a droplet of blood.

"The game is afoot," was all she said.

   ***

The zombies did not hesitate as they turned away from John and made a straight line right for me. I walked out to meet them as they got closer.

"Stop," I ordered them as I grabbed each of the sides of their heads in my palms and drove their skulls together. The impact shattered the bone and echoed throughout the small valley we found ourselves in. They fell in a heap like the lovers that they appeared to have been once upon a time. "The hat, man, put the hat back on!" John was shouting as he ran closer.

I was screaming to the heavens; anger, pride and satisfaction were warring with each other to become the dominate feeling. I turned and walked a few steps back towards the cavern opening, then fell to my knees. John raced past me and then came running back he hastily put my cap back on, making sure not to snap my face with the rubber band.

***

"He's gone," Tomas said. He was trying to stand back up having gone down after the scream. It had taken him a moment to realize who or what had shredded through his mind.

"Not for good I think," Eliza said as she watched her brother struggling to get back up.

"Is that not reason enough to stay away and let him have his corner of the world, Eliza?" Tomas said as he finally got to his feet. He was shaking, but he felt sturdy enough.

"He grows stronger."

"He was dead. How is this possible?" Tomas asked his sister.

"What about that bullshit you preach about no direct intervention?" Eliza yelled to the sky.

"Eliza?"

"Don't you dare, Tomas! This changes nothing. If anything, it makes our ultimate destination that much more important. You should have let him die on that roof. I would have honored the agreement I made, at least for a little while. His family would have been safe, maybe for a generation, their lives flash by so quickly anyway."

***

"Where's your poncho?" John asked me as he placed his hand on my shoulder. "You look like shit, bad trip?" As he sat down next to me, he pulled a crisp white joint from somewhere. Even more impressive was the lighter. He lit it up and took a grand toke before handing it to me.

The birds chirped in the distance, a slight breeze blew from east to west across my body, the sun shone brightly upon my face, an ant walked across my size thirteen women's shoes. I grabbed the bone, looked at it for a moment, and took a big hit, bathing myself in its calming smoke.

"Thank you for that," I said to John as I exhaled.

"Nice mellow shit, huh?" John asked with a smile as he took the marijuana cigarette back.

"That too," I told him as I let the buzz wash over my mind. "But I meant that." I pointed to the sliver-sized opening in the small mound directly in front of us.

"I don't know what you're talking about," John said as he took the rolled paper almost down to the halfway point.

I had a sneaking suspicion that he did, especially with the sideways smile he was wearing when he handed the joint back, but I guess that also could be attributed to the fact that we were now both stoned. What can I say, I'm a cheap date. We stayed there a while longer, me on my knees, John sitting Indian style (right, right, Native American style). Although I don't really know if it's still necessary to keep up with political correctness in this new age of man.

"Candy?" John asked as he split a peanut butter cup in two.

I ate it before he had even put his half in his mouth. "Rorry. Stress makes me hungry," I told him."

"Did you get the tickets?" he asked as he savored his half.

I shook my head.

"That's alright. Maybe we can catch them next time. We should head for the airport," he said as he arose, he extended a hand to help me up.

The events of the day had impaired me far worse than I had imagined. My legs began to instantly cramp and every scrape and bruise I had on my body was letting itself be known. We had twenty miles to traverse and I didn't think I could make it twenty yards; this was compounded with the fact that, because of the weed, I was even thinking slower.

"Man I'm tired," John said, echoing my thoughts. "Do you have a car?"

"Let's go see," I told him as we headed away from the motel that couldn't have been more than a quarter mile, then I realized we were still in a bit of a lurch. My 'broadcast' for the zombies to come to me had been reached by anything within a certain range and then I realized they weren't moving. I stopped to laugh, my gut started to hurt I was letting go so deeply. John had no idea why I was laughing, but he was not one to shy away from a good time, he joined in the merriment.

"What's so funny, man?" John asked as he started wiping tears away from his face.

It was a few more minutes before I could compose myself enough to speak. "You see the zombies...I mean funkies?"

"Yeah, man," he answered, looking over to the motel. "Hey, what's the matter with them? They look frozen."

I was laughing full tilt again. "They're not moving because I told them not to."

"They're very well behaved," he said in all seriousness.

"Don't you see, man? We didn't need to go through the damned cavern, Trip." John was looking at me strangely. "Forget it, it's over now. I hope I can forget it as quickly as you can. Let's go get your van."

"Oh yeah, I forgot that was here."

We headed back to the motel. I wanted to kill the zombies, but it somehow seemed cruel to kill something defenseless. I know, I know, that's an asinine thought; they wouldn't think twice if the roles were reversed. I also had

John to think about. He had to check each and every one of the frozen bastards out as we walked by. I know he wouldn't have approved of my slaughtering them, and what he thought mattered, even if he would have forgotten by dinner.

He kept waving his hands in front of their faces. The only thing that moved on the zombies was their eyes and it was unnerving. Their eyes followed us like those of paintings in a haunted mansion. There were at least twenty or thirty zombies in the parking lot all oriented towards where I had called them from. And at least another half dozen were inside the cabin having not yet found an exit by the time my 'stop' command had been issued. I had never before controlled so many zombies at once, I was unsure if it was something I would even be able to do again. The range of emotions I had been feeling when I did it would be difficult to match.

"They're like mannequins," John said, waving his hand dangerously close to one of the zombie's mouths.

"Maybe don't get so close," I told him.

"Are they playing some sort of game?"

"Not one that I want to play."

"Me neither," John said as he took one final glance behind him before getting into his van.

I don't know if to this very day you could go down to North Carolina and see those zombies standing there but they hadn't moved when I finally lost them in my rearview mirror.

"Want a beer?" John asked, reaching in to the backseat and opening the cooler.

"Sounds about perfect." I told him.

CHAPTER FIFTEEN

BT, Gary and Mrs. D

Gary chanced a look back as Deneaux rocketed down the roadway. "I can't see BT!" he yelled in an attempt to get past the whipping of the wind.

"I haven't had this much fun in decades!" Mrs. Deneaux yelled back. "I guess I could use a cigarette, though." She opened the throttle up a little bit more. Gary looked over her shoulder and realized they were nearing a hundred and ten miles an hour. He gripped her bony waist a little bit tighter.

She laughed for a few moments and let the bike begin to coast down to a stop. BT was barely a dot on the horizon as Mrs. Deneaux was finishing her smoke.

"Aren't cigarettes just like potato chips?" Gary asked her.

"What?" she said as she ground the stub out under her heel.

"Nobody can have just one."

"Miss your friend?" she asked as she effortlessly produced another smoke.

"I'll tell you what I don't miss."

She looked over at him.

"I don't miss going a hundred and ten miles per hour."

"You must have sucked your mama's teets too long," she said as she took a puff from her cigarette.

"I was bottle fed," he replied, not able to think of anything else to say.

She 'hurumphed' and looked back to the open road that they needed to travel.

BT pulled up a few minutes later. He had a death grip on his handlebars and looked like a crash test dummy due to sitting so rigid in his seat.

"She's fucking nuts," Gary said to BT. "Please let me ride with you?"

"Did she almost crash?" BT asked, slowly getting off his bike.

Gary shook his head with a questioning look.

"I almost dumped twice. You're better off with her."

"She's trying to beat the speed of sound, BT."

"Is this love fest over?" Deneaux asked, throwing her butt to the side of the road. "We've got a lot of miles to roll and it looks like we might get some weather."

"Can we maybe find something with four wheels?" Gary asked.

"And miss out on all this fun?" BT added as he rubbed blood back into his arms.

"We can find something for you two ladies, but I'm keeping this ride. Let's go, bitch," Mrs. Deneaux said to Gary.

"I don't really appreciate that," he said as he walked over towards her.

"It's just an expression." She smiled.

"Could you maybe at least keep me in sight this time?" BT asked as he reluctantly hopped back on his bike.

"I need gas," was her reply as she started the bike up.

"How far is Maine from here?" Gary asked.

"Gotta be close to seven hundred miles," BT told him. "And then another hundred and fifty or so to get to Ron's."

"At top speed we could make it in six and a half hours," Deneaux said, staring at Gary trying to gauge his reaction.

Gary had no desire to do the math and figure out how fast they would be traveling. He once again wrapped his arms around her waist, fearful he might break her in half, then he would be 'ghost' riding a 'murder cycle'. And that wouldn't do…not at all.

Somewhat true to her word, Deneaux kept her speed down to a semi-suicidal rate somewhere in the mid-seventies. BT was sort of keeping pace as he pushed his bike to a speed right outside his comfort zone of sixty.

"Fucking old bat," he said as another bug slammed into the side of his face. "Who in their right mind would want to ride one of these things?" *Shit Mike must have been a world class rider.* BT grinned at the thought. "I miss you, man," BT said, stealing a quick glance upwards. "I hope you made it there."

Deneaux would slow down as they approached cars on the side of the road, Gary checked out more than a few, looking for ones that weren't battle damaged or had gas and keys handy. It was the only thing keeping them from losing BT again.

"Stop stalling or I'll smoke while I'm riding," Deneaux threatened.

"I'm not stalling, I'm looking carefully," Gary told her.

"I see you repeatedly looking back for your boyfriend. He'll catch up. Come on, I think I see a traffic jam up ahead, I'm sure there'll be something that you two girly men will be able to use, maybe a mini-van or a Prius."

"Fine," Gary said reluctantly.

Within a few minutes they were up by a snarl of cars that was L.A. worthy.

"What happened?" Gary asked as he got slowly off the bike.

A snarky comment was on Deneaux's lips, but even she was lost in the devastation that was Route 22.

Even with the motorcycles it was going to be difficult to get around the carnage. Mrs. Deneaux brought the bike to halt at the outer-most edge of the debris field. She stood up to get a better view, shielding her eyes as she tried her best to see the end. She was not successful.

Gary got off the back; his legs were weak partly from Deneaux's excessive speed, but mostly from the devastation in front of them. "It must go for miles," he said flatly.

"I would think you'd be able to find a car that would suit your needs in there." Deneaux motioned with her hand as she grabbed a cigarette from her saddle bag.

"This doesn't affect you?" Gary asked incredulously.

"What? I'm smoking a cigarette aren't I?"

"These were people with hopes and dreams."

"What would you like me to say, Gary? I don't have any words of comfort for you, I didn't know them."

"And if you did?"

"Probably still wouldn't care." She took another drag. "You're going in there?" she asked as Gary stepped closer to the disaster.

"Yes."

"Then you might want to take your rifle off your back."

Gary's hands were trembling as he pulled on the sling to take the gun off his shoulder.

"Is the safety off?"

"Of course it is!" he said hotly. He quietly moved the selector button to 'OFF' hoping Deneaux didn't hear. Gary was twenty or so feet into the wreckage when he began to hear the comforting roar of BT's bike approaching.

A few moments later, BT shut his bike down and dismounted. "Wait up, Gary, I'll come with you."

"He has been." Mrs. Deneaux said.

"What?" BT said as he took his rifle out of the special side mount built into the bike.

"If he went any slower, I'd be able to watch him age."

BT checked his magazine and quickly caught up to Gary. "What the hell happened here?" BT asked Gary as they walked past a burned out pick-up truck.

"I don't know, but whatever it was it involved the military. I've seen a few dead soldiers around."

It was difficult to get an accurate picture of what had happened. What had not been burned to a crisp had been devoured by zombies and/or animals; and what was left after that had been picked through by survivors. The only thing that could be easily discerned was that a great battle had been waged here. Thousands of zombies littered the far side of the road, the highway itself, and the beltway between the east and west routes. Not including the ones that were interspersed with the cars on this side of the roadway. Between dead bodies, zombies, and twisted metal, there was not a whole lot of room left for the trio to continue their journey.

"I don't like this at all, Gary," BT said as he stood up from the car he was looking inside. He tried his best to not think of the empty child seat.

"Should we go back and find another route?"

"And that's a problem, we go back and we run the risk of running back into Q-Ball and a few of his best friends. I look at that and all I can see is ambush. That would be all your brother's fault by the way."

Gary smiled. "So I guess we're going forward?"

"The devil we don't know in this case is better than the one we do know."

"Should we keep looking for a car?"

"Won't do any good if we find one here."

"You're right," Gary said. They couldn't take two steps without dodging something; anything less than a city plow would only get mired in the devastation.

"Let's go back. I want to be clear of this place before nightfall," BT said.

Two shots from Deneaux's direction hastened their pace.

"Sorry," Deneaux said a little unnerved. "I was enjoying the sun and dozed off a bit. A zombie grabbed my ankle. If it had bit first I'd be a zombie waiting to happen."

A soldier zombie with crushed legs had crawled over to Deneaux; its outstretched hand had sought purchase on her leg before she put two rounds through its skull. BT still hadn't made up his mind if he would have been upset or not if the zombie had succeeded in its mission.

"We need to go," BT said.

"No words of consolation?" Deneaux asked.

"For the dead soldier?" BT asked.

"I like you more and more every day," Deneaux said as she kick-started her bike.

"Zombies!" Gary yelled. Speeders were sprinting out of the woods across the highway.

"Which way, hot shot?" Deneaux asked BT.

"Forward," he said as he ran for his bike. "Company bringing up the rear."

"Fuck me," Gary said as he looked down the roadway in the direction they had come. A legion of motorcycles were coming their way, and he was fairly certain they weren't heading to Sturgis. "Q-Ball?" He asked as BT's bike roared to life.

"A good a guess as any. Get on Deneaux's bike, that's your best shot," BT said.

"Are you sure?" Gary asked.

"Get on or I'm leaving," Deneaux said as she stowed her cigarettes.

BT nodded tersely.

Gary hopped on.

"Hold on tight, when I lean you lean. Understand?" Deneaux asked Gary.

Gary merely shook his head as the bike took off. Zombies were within fifty yards and vengeful gangsters were less than a half mile away. BT was rapidly falling behind as Deneaux expertly weaved her way in and out of the traffic. BT looked more like a blind man trying to make his way through an unknown and unseen obstacle course.

"Stop the bike," Gary said. After a couple of hundred yards he repeated his request. She didn't acquiesce.

"Deneaux, stop the fucking bike!" he yelled.

"Why?"

"BT isn't going to make it."

"What do you think we should do? Join him?"

"I know you won't, but I'm going to help him."

"Your funeral," she said as she stopped just long enough for him to get off. She sped away without looking back.

"Bitch," he said quietly.

Deneaux flipped him the bird.

"No way, there's no way she heard me." He turned to get in position to cover BT's approach.

The zombies were sprinting to catch up, but the gang was motorized. "It's almost going to be a tie," Gary said, not really knowing which group he should start to sight in on. It seemed that the zombies were having the same problem. BT was who they had been focused on; but the bigger, louder (more food) group was coming into their killing grounds. The majority of the zombies peeled off their pursuit of BT and headed to the new dinner buffet.

Q-Ball was so fixated on exacting his revenge he was blind to the new threat, but not all of his gang were. A fair number slowed and either turned around or waited on the periphery. Q-Ball was close enough to BT that he pulled his sidearm out of his holster and rested it on his handle bars. Gary had opted for the zombies to BT's left because his avenue of escape was being threatened. What the biker's did wouldn't matter if BT couldn't make it to Gary to begin with.

BT had the luck of the angels on his side when Q-Ball's shot whined off the top of BT's handlebars. BT presented a much larger target, and as such, should have been the one to catch the round. As it was, BT almost crashed as his front wheel shook violently—his great strength the only thing keeping the bike upright. Gary turned his attention to Q-Ball when he heard the round.

Gary's gut wrenched as he sighted in on a human being, but Q-Ball had gained more ground on his friend and the odds that he would miss again had been greatly reduced.

"Forgive me, Father, for I have sinned…" he said as

he pulled the trigger.

A geyser of blood erupted from Q-Ball's throat. The bike fell and slid along the ground, it slammed into at least five zombies, destroying their bodies as it went. However, there were plenty more where they came from as they descended on the dying biker. Gary imagined he could hear the gurgled screams for help as the zombies tore him apart. BT had surged ahead of the lead zombies who now turned their attention back to the gang that suddenly found themselves leaderless and cut off from retreat.

Gunfire blazed as BT pulled up to Gary. "Where's Deneaux?"

"She took off," Gary replied.

"Thank you, Gary."

"It was you or him," Gary said, looking a little worse for the wear.

"I'd have to say you chose wisely, come on, man, hop on."

Gary looked at what remained of the motorcycle seat and was not convinced that an anemic spider monkey would be able to fit. Still, he hopped on, half his ass hanging over the rear fender. The gang would not last long and the zombies were always hungry. *Always fucking hungry*, he thought dourly.

They had traveled a couple of miles at the most when they could no longer hear gunfire.

"Do you think it's over?" Gary asked. He didn't have to yell, the traffic was so thick the bike was barely moving.

"Doesn't matter, whichever side won will still be coming for us," BT said, dodging an engine block that looked like it had been ejected from its former location by a rocket launcher.

"What the hell happened here?" Gary asked, looking around.

"Not sure, but I bet it has something to do with that." BT took his hand off the handle bars for a moment to point before quickly putting it back.

"Checkpoint ahead, be prepared to stop and have your vehicle searched," Gary read the sign. "Well, leave it to the military to really foul things up."

"I don't think your brother could have said it any more eloquently."

"There it is," Gary said, pointing past BT's face; although how BT could have possibly missed the hastily erected gates replete with razor wire, gun turrets, and the standard deuce-and-a-half military trucks was anybody's guess.

"So the US military in all its infinite wisdom backs up traffic for days and the zombies swoop in thinking this is the world's largest food court," BT said.

"And then they start firing on everything, living and dead, trying to contain the virus," Gary finished. "These people start firing at the zombies and the military…bad news."

BT merely nodded. "Almost out of here." The closer they got to the front, the worse the devastation. Large divots of earth where mortars, grenades and rockets had hit were removed. Finding a viable way around was becoming its own hazard.

"I'm getting off," Gary told BT.

"You can walk faster than I'm going anyway."

"Not that I'm not appreciative, BT, but I'd rather find another ride."

"Fuck it." BT got off the bike. He shut it off and put the kick stand down. "I'll leave it here just in case, but there has to be something up closer than we can take."

"I hope so," Gary said. He wasn't holding out hope, though; it looked like the cars here had been used for target practice. Large caliber machinegun rounds were ripped through most of them. People, plastic, wood, and steel were shredded along with the occasional zombie. "It doesn't really look like they cared what they were shooting at," Gary said as he did the Holy Trinity on his chest. BT remained silent, the anger inside of him threatening to boil over.

A large horn blat stopped them both in their tracks, followed immediately by a cackle and the roar of a diesel engine turning over. BT and Gary broke into a trot to see what Mrs. Deneaux was up to now. She beeped the horn a few more times for good measure.

"Fuck, woman, the whole world is going to know where we're at!" BT yelled as they got to within hailing distance.

"Too late, fuckwad!" she screamed as she leaned her head out the window and pointed behind the duo. Scores of speeders were streaming towards Gary and BT.

"I guess the bikers lost," Gary said as he broke into a sprint, followed immediately by BT who quickly outpaced him.

"Your brother was right," BT said over his shoulder. "You are slow."

"Funny, don't make me shoot you," Gary huffed.

A puff of black smoke belched from the deuce's exhaust stack.

"Is she leaving?" Gary cried, trying to find another gear he did not possess. Barring any unfortunate mishap he felt safe in the assumption that he could make it ahead of the lead zombies, but anything past where the truck was now and he was food.

"Fucking bitch," BT said as he surged forward, finding that gear that Gary found so elusive.

Gary had not felt so alone since a junior high dance when his girlfriend Maureen O'Connell had started to dance with his then best friend Pat McDonough. He had not talked to either one since. "Weird thought," Gary mumbled as he plodded on, gaining on the truck but losing ground with the zombies.

The truck, which was facing the traffic jam, was now backing up; Deneaux cut the wheel to the right, then started to swing the truck around. She had it facing away as she backed up to its earlier spot.

BT had caught up and jumped onto the runner on the

driver's side. "Move your skinny ass over!" he yelled.

"I hope you can drive one of these better than the motorcycle," she quipped as she placed the truck in park and did as she was told.

"Getting in the back!" Gary yelled as he hoisted himself up and in. He pulled the small tailgate closed and quickly placed the left side locking pin in place. He was not thrilled with his choice of riding spots as the zombies were close enough to shake hands with. "GO, GO, GO!" he screamed.

Gary scrambled back down the narrow truck bed. He got his rifle ready and shot the first zombie as it came up and into the truck. The truck lurched into gear and stalled. Deneaux was cackling wildly, zombies were slamming full tilt into the truck; a few were trying to get in through the back.

"Oh please get this truck moving," Gary entreated as he began to fire at a multitude of targets. The truck rumbled back to life; more gunfire erupted as Deneaux was shooting at zombies that were coming up on to the sides of the truck.

"Any day," she said calmly to BT, referring to him getting the truck in gear.

Gary had pushed back as far as he could, his back resting against the cool metal of the front of the transport. At least three zombies were having varying degrees of success trying to get in as BT hesitantly got the behemoth truck rolling. It was a good two hundred yards of traveling time before they began to outpace the fast zombies. A baker's dozen of them had latched on to the truck and were making their way as best they could to their targets.

Somehow, a zombie had climbed on top of the truck and Gary could see it trying to rip through the heavy canvas, but he had more immediate problems. The first zombie that had come in was still alive; the bullet had traveled alongside its head and not quite killed it. Two others were dead, and one was holding on to the tailgate for dear unlife. Gary was completely out of ammo.

He frantically felt around his pockets looking for any spare ordinance, remembering that he had left it in Deneaux's saddle bags. A tear above him brought his attention that way as he saw a finger poke through a small hole.

"Time is running out," Gary said as he stood, stooping to stay out of reach. He moved to the rear of the truck, taking careful stock of the dazed and hopefully dying zombie. The zombie on the tailgate snarled and snapped its teeth as Gary approached. Its feet were bouncing along wildly on the asphalt as it clung to the tailgate. Gary couldn't help but smile when he thought the zombie looked suspiciously like Michael Flatley. The moment passed quickly as he brought the butt of his weapon down heavily on the fingers of the zombie.

Nothing, not so much as a whimper, as Gary used crushing force to dislodge the zombie's hands. The zombie was still trying to pull itself into the truck. Gary repeatedly smashed the hands until there was nothing more than shredded skin holding the zombie to the truck; inertia and gravity did the rest as the fingers separated away from the body. The zombie tumbled down the roadway, once it came to a full stop it immediately got up and started running again towards the truck.

"You have got to be kidding me?" Gary asked, just then he heard the telltale sound of canvas tearing followed immediately by a heavy thud as the zombie fell through the hole it had made. "This is insane!" Gary yelled as he rushed over to the zombie and began to drive the butt of his rifle into its skull before it had a chance to regain its legs.

The zombie thrashed wildly back and forth as Gary caved in its head. The pile of bone-infused meat on the floor by his feet did not resemble anything even remotely human, but the twitching wedding band laden left hand would be something that haunted him.

"I think I'm going to throw up," Gary said as he dropped his rifle and lurched to the rear of the truck reluctant to add his bile to the ever expanding pool of human-like matter already there.

He was hanging his head over the lip of the tailgate trying to pull in as much fresh air as was possible, which was not easy considering he was directly in the flow pattern of the truck's exhaust. That was still better than the zombies. The truck was moving and the shooting had subsided, Gary felt they must be out of immediate danger right until he felt something bite down on his ankle. Denim and leather the only things that separated him from certain death, Gary jumped up and scooted down to the front of the truck on the bench seat used for troop transportation using the butt of his rifle as a make-shift paddle, he didn't stop until his rifle butt plunged into the mashed head of the zombie that had dropped from the ceiling. For reasons he still can't fathom, he pulled his gun up and towards his face so that he could see what was stuck there. He vomited as the gray-black gelatinous ooze dripped from the stock and onto his lap.

The zombie that had been dazed and laying on the floor was now making its way to an oblivious Gary. At some point the truck had stopped and BT had come around the back.

"Gary, you alright?" BT was yelling as he did so.

Gary's retching was the only response.

The zombie's hand had gripped the bottom of Gary's boot and was pulling itself closer. Gary was cognizant of the approaching danger but was unable to respond.

"Fuck, man!" BT said as he grabbed the back of the zombie's legs and was now pulling the zombie and Gary towards him.

Deneaux shot the zombie in the head point blank as BT pulled it free from the truck. Gary was staring at the whole exchange not really registering anything.

"He looks bit," Mrs. Deneaux said as she leveled the gun on Gary.

"He's not fucking bitten. Put the damn gun down," BT told her. "Right, Gary?" BT asked.

Gary slightly shifted his gaze so he could look at BT.

"Come on, man," BT motioned. "You can sit up front with us."

"He's covered in vomit and brain, he stinks to high Heaven."

BT looked crossly at Mrs. Deneaux.

"Fine," she said, "but I'm smoking more."

"I wouldn't think that was even possible," BT answered. He extended his hand for Gary who slowly took it. "You alright?" BT asked again.

Gary got down off the truck; he walked a few feet away to the grassy median and deposited a little more stomach sauce. He vigorously wiped as much stain of humanity off himself as he could with the overgrown weeds, and when he felt somewhat decent, he climbed up into the cab without uttering so much as a word.

"I guess he's ready to go," Mrs. Deneaux said as she got in behind him.

BT looked once behind the truck and noticed the zombies were far behind but that they were still following.

A few more miles passed underneath their tires.

"I miss you. Mike," BT said almost silently as they passed out of North Carolina and into Virginia.

"Me too," Gary said even quieter. The first words he had uttered in an hour.

CHAPTER SIXTEEN

Mike Journal Entry 6

I honestly thought John was full of shit, right until we pulled up to the gates of the municipal airport. He made me take a right towards one of the smaller hangars; once we stopped, he grabbed the keys out of the ignition and walked over to the hangar where he opened up a door to the corrugated steel building.

It was darker inside, but the windows high up in the building let in sufficient light. There it was, a helicopter that wasn't much bigger than some of the ones I'd seen hobby enthusiasts remote pilot. John went over to it and began to lock the props in place—they had been folded in for storage.

"I'll be honest, John, this seemed like a much better idea when we were underground." I was having serious reservations. Here was a guy that said he couldn't get his shit together enough to drive a van, but could apparently pilot a toy helicopter.

"It's perfectly safe," John told me as he almost took off the top of his head with the blade, by walking into it. "Help me wheel it out."

Me helping ended up, me doing, as he went over to the large hangar door and began to pull it open. It was surprisingly easy to move, but I don't know why I would be expecting anything else from a helicopter made from spare Erector Set parts. I pushed it some twenty feet away from the building thinking that was plenty of clearance, then I went another fifty.

"You see the checklist?" John asked me.

I shook my head.

"Doesn't matter," he told me as he climbed in.

"Trip, I beg to differ. They have those checklists for a reason, like for checking the fuel level or ice on the wings or shit, man, like a bunch of other stuff." I was stalling, because all of a sudden, the tunnel looked welcoming. Well not really…but at this point it was like splitting very fine hairs.

"No time to go through the list anyway," John said as he powered the copter on. "Might want to duck and get in." The blades began to whir to life. He tapped lightly on his instrument panel. "Hey do you know what that one checks?" he asked.

"I have no fucking idea, Trip, except it looks like it's in the red." I had been in the middle of getting in and was now in the middle of getting out.

"I wouldn't," John said to me, never looking past his instruments.

"Huh?" I asked. I should have known better.

He pointed back and to the right of our present location, zombies were flooding in our direction.

"Oh shit!" I said as I saw the swarm. "How long until we're airborne?"

"I don't know, man, I've never seen the reason to time it. Sure could go for a little Mary Jane."

"Task at hand first, buddy, task at hand," I said to him, trying to gauge how much time we had before we were engaged with the zombies. "More than half a minute?" I asked, trying to press him for information he didn't have.

"Time is just something the man made to keep us all in line," he said as he pressed more buttons on his console.

"Trip, I understand your frustration with the mythical *man.*"

"Oh, he isn't mythical."

"Okay, sorry, but we may need to ditch the copter."

"Almost there," he said.

"The zombies or being in the air?"

He didn't elaborate. I started to get back out.

"Where you going?" John asked.

I had sarcasm all lined up, but I knew John wouldn't

catch it and I didn't have time for an explanation.

"Zombies, Trip, I have to slow them down."

"Whoa," he said as he looked back. "Where'd they come from?"

I didn't have the heart to tell him he was the one that had pointed them out to me.

"You should make them into mannequins."

"What?" I asked looking at the approaching horde and the blades that were lazily spinning, more from the breeze it appeared than any mechanical function.

"Like at the motel."

Why in the hell was I having John the Tripper tell me how to get out of situations? This was like having a dog (not Henry) help me with algebra. (Who am I kidding? The dog could probably do it better.)

I no sooner took my tin foil hat off, when my head was blinded with white noise to the point where I was placing my hands over my ears in a desperate attempt to keep the noise out. On the periphery of my vision I could hear John telling me to put the hat back on, but it wasn't registering as a cognitive thought. I was hearing the words, but could not associate them with a meaning. I was falling out of the copter. John grabbed me and placed the hat back in place; blissful, beautiful silence filled the void of confusion. That was ultimately replaced with the slap of feet on pavement, and with that thought came the realization that we were still under attack. John was busy reaching over me and putting on the flight harness so that I wouldn't swoon out again.

The blades of the copter had picked up speed, we weren't moving yet, though. And the zombies were a football throw away and not an Eli Manning heaving toss it up type of pass, but more the workings of something I'd let loose. I undid my buckle.

"Where you going, man? We're almost up," John said.

"No time, my friend. I just want to say thank you."

John's eyebrows were pulled tight as he tried to figure out what I was talking about. The blades of the copter reached terminal velocity as the small craft bucked forward. "You should get in," he said as he placed his hand over the yolk.

I took one quick glance at the zombies, confident in the fact that we weren't going to make it and still I jumped in the craft, my weight pushing it back down. It made another hop when the lead zombie ran headfirst into the spinning blade—blood sprayed in a complete three-sixty around the craft as the zombie's force pushed us forward.

"How many more of those can we take?" I asked John as another zombie ran into the tail; the smaller rear rotor caught it underneath the chin and split its head in two from bottom to top. Why I felt the need to watch was beyond me. I hadn't thought that there was anything left on the planet which could gross me out. I was woefully wrong.

The copter was being pushed forward from the assault; blood and brain matter was falling like a soft rain all around us. If a zombie came from the side, I was fairly certain it would knock us over. At that point I was hoping for death by scalping. The bottom of my stomach dropped out as we briefly popped into the air. John was stirring the yolk like he was churning butter.

"Hold on!" John whooped. He was laughing crazily.

I didn't have time to stripe my pants as we once again popped up, this time a good five feet. But we had a stowaway and she was threatening to pull us back down to her brethren. John made the necessary correction to keep us level even with our hitcher, but her added weight was keeping us dangerously close to terra firma. Actually, now that I'm thinking about it, she was probably doing us a favor.

John had turned the helicopter around and we were now heading back towards the majority of zombies and the hangar. I was gripping my seat hard enough to make my hands hurt. John had tears running down his face he was laughing so hard. Our unwanted passenger's feet were slamming off the faces and heads of the zombies below us. I was involuntarily pulling my legs closer to my body. All it would take would be a zombie with enough dexterity to reach up and grab our clinger and we would plummet like a kamikaze. John was just thinking this was the funniest thing since just about ever.

"The hangar," I said softly, pointing at the giant looming metallic structure.

"That might be a problem," John said, taking one of his hands off the controls to wipe his eyes. I was eyeing the stick and wondering when he would take the other hand off of it.

We went through the large hangar door, my breath caught in my throat. I was so scared, I was having trouble breathing. I was beginning to wonder if it was possible to choke on air. John was rapidly flying to the other end of the hangar where the door was not—and I REPEAT not—open. We had lost a little of our hard fought altitude and our zombie flight attendant got one of her feet caught up in what looked like arc welder cables, but I was too busy caressing my terror to take much notice. The nose of the copter dipped down and then shot forward and up as we lost our only other passenger. It looked like it was going to be pretty close as to which part of the hangar was going to be our ultimate demise. The far side or the ceiling…I was actually rooting for the ceiling at least that way I wouldn't see it coming.

Then at the point where we couldn't fit Calista Flockhart between our rotor and the wall we stopped. We were hovering perfectly still like the world's biggest hummingbird.

"Whoa you did awesome, man!" John said to me excitedly.

Well if he was talking about hyperventilating and damn near crapping my pants, then yes I had done one hell of a job. "You should probably get us out of here," I said to him as I watched zombies start to come into the hangar and we were close enough to the wall that we would be peeling paint soon.

"Right! Off to see the wizard!"

"Fuck I'd take flying monkeys right now."

"Monkeys don't fly, man," John said, looking over at me.

I waited until we were out of the hangar before I began to speak, I didn't want him to have any huge revelations while we were confined like that. "You know, *Wizard of Oz*, Wicked Witch of the West, Dorothy all that shit?"

He was still looking over at me like I had lost my damn mind. No wonder psychiatrists were batty as shit. How could you not catch some crazy when you were around it all day?

"All I know is that monkeys don't fly," he said as he set his jaw. He looked like I had just insulted his mother. The one thing I could be certain of, though, was that he'd forget soon enough. "So where we headed?" he asked after a few moments of silence.

"Your wife, Trip."

"Oh yeah," he said as he brought his hand to his forehead.

We were a couple of hundred feet off the ground and I was not at all comfortable with the machine I was riding in. It felt as safe as a flying blender. The view, however, gave me an appreciation of the new world we found ourselves in. The roads were deserted and devoid of all human activity…scratch that…all forms of life. The zombies had proved that, in a bind, they will hunt down anything, and with the absence of food they would even go into a stasis. We had long since got past the airport and I had to hope the zombies had forgotten about us. My heart panged as I realized we were heading in a northerly route only with a slant to the east.

I was going to make it home. I just didn't know when and what was I going to tell my father about Gary. He had entrusted me with my brother's safety and I had failed miserably, I could only hope that BT had picked up the torch I had dropped. Conversation was difficult over the chopping of the air, but after the day we had been having—well at least that I was having—I wasn't sure how much if any that John remembered or what his particular take on it could be. For all I knew he probably thought this was a big amusement park ride.

"How much longer?" I shouted. I was expecting the standard, 'time is the enemy of man' or 'til when?' or something equally as inane so I was surprised when he answered in all business tone.

"We'll be there before nightfall."

I hoped so, because now I had another huge fear, when the sun went down, there would be absolutely no manmade markers to help guide us in.

We flew in silence (conversational silence, the chopper was loud as hell) for a few hours. My body ached to flush out the adrenaline high I had been on since this morning had started. The human body is not meant to be juiced up for that long. I had burned through vast stores of the drug and did not think I would be able to manufacture a new supply for quite some time.

Then I looked over at my pilot.

I sat and looked at John's face for a while, worry which had not been there earlier (and Lord knows it should have been) was now creasing his forehead. I desperately wanted to tell him everything would be alright, but how the hell would I know? I did it anyway because that's what people do. We want to believe that everything is alright and maybe by voicing it, we hope to somehow influence the fates. But they don't give a shit, the fates I mean. No matter what we want, what we hope, what we wish for…with one fell swoop, fate will come in and smash it like a man dressed in a Godzilla suit will do on a miniaturized city set.

"You think?" John asked solemnly.

I had already tempted catastrophe once, I wouldn't do it twice, I avoided answering. "What's that blinking red light,

Trip?" I asked, pointing to his instrument panel.

"Oil pressure," he said as easily as if he was talking about the weather.

"Is that important?" I asked, because it seemed important, but he appeared so completely easy going about it.

"Oh...extremely," he answered without elaborating.

"Trip, John, John the Tripper."

He finally looked over at me.

"We're not going to make it there any faster if we're dead."

"You think I should land?"

"You tell me."

And he did, by pitching the copter down at a steep angle. I was thinking we were already in crash mode as my balls sought residency in my lower belly. An alarm over our head began to blare, either from our rapid descent or the oil pressure.

"Wonder how long that thing has been going off?" John asked as he toggled the switch back to 'silent' mode. "Coming in hot!" he shouted.

"What the fuck does that mean?!"

"Hold on."

Like that needed to be voiced, might as well have said 'Evacuate your bladder now!' We were probably still a good thirty or forty feet up when the blades seized. One second they were whirring along and the next it sounded like someone had thrown rocks inside a dryer, then they just stopped, not even lazily spinning, just complete stoppage. We went from 'Coming in hot' to 'Sinking stone' in a matter of milliseconds. John was able to do some piloting magic to get us to coast a bit, it wasn't much, but I think it was just enough. My spine felt like it compressed to half its length when we slammed into the ground. What air I had been holding onto because I couldn't breathe was punched out of me from the impact. The undercarriage of the copter had completely caved in on itself. The glass bubble we were sitting in had shattered much like a car windshield.

Then we were airborne again as the chopper bounced, my guesstimate later would be somewhere in the eight or nine foot range, but I didn't even realize it was happening at the time. Except for the list to my side, I almost stuck my hand out to the side to brace for impact. I'm glad I was too petrified to peel them away from my seat I would have shattered my arm in a dozen places. The glass shell completely dissolved as we again became earth bound. I was completely on my side strapped in to the seat; my face was mere inches from the grass. An ant carrying what looked like a cricket leg walked right under my watchful gaze. The only noise was the knocking of the cooling engine, the slamming of my blood through my arteries and John the Tripper moaning.

I scrambled with my harness and finally found the release button I fell the rest of the way to the ground. My body ached, I felt like a giant baby had used me as a rattle. I couldn't get my equilibrium to come back to center for long moments. When I could finally get my feet underneath me with some semblance of balance I went back to the copter, blood was pouring from John's head.

"Fuck," I said as I cradled him in one arm and released his harness with the other. I put him as gently to the ground as I could. "John, you alright?" I asked as I gingerly moved his tin foil hat and his hair to the side to assess what kind of damage he had incurred.

He started to move his hand up to his head. At first I figured to hold his aching head, but it was actually to put his hat back on. The cut was on the top of his forehead right below the hairline. The pale white of his skull shone through dully as blood filled in the void. His skull looked intact and his head was bleeding like all head wounds do: profusely. But he was in no danger. He'd have a killer headache, but I figured he had enough self-medication to take care of that anyway.

I would have taken my shirt off and used it as a bandage, but between the dirt and my earlier vomit, he was more likely to catch a staph infection and die from my ministrations than anything from the head wound. I started rooting around in our destroyed flying machine until I found what I was looking for, a small first aid kit tucked under the pilot's seat. Although, on further reflection, I had to wonder what the makers of this craft were thinking when they put that there. I mean really, would you be in this little flying beer can and realize you needed a Band-Aid or what? That this little pack of bandages was really going to come in handy during a crash?

Then, yup, it dawned on me…it was coming in handy during a full scale crash. I did a small 'hat's off' gesture to the brilliant engineers.

"Oh, flying monkeys…I get it," John said as I had propped him up against the wreckage and was finishing dressing his wound.

"We should get going," I told him. The noise of the crash was going to attract attention, whether zombie or human didn't matter, both were to be feared equally. "Can you walk?"

"Been doing it since I was a baby, I don't know why that would change now."

I helped him up. He wobbled for a moment. "Nice! Cheap buzz. My head is killing me."

"I can't imagine why." I looked one last time at the copter; it now resembled something more along the lines of what some modern artist would make with scrap metal. God had again shown his hand, we should not have survived that crash. "Listen, I'm starting to understand that whole 'I am your instrument' thing," I said to the heavens. "But is there any chance I could get some upgrades? Like maybe laser beam eyes, or the ability to fly? No, wait, I take that last one back. How about some wicked strong telekinesis so I could push things out of my way."

A slight breeze that sounded awfully close to a slight sigh wisped past us.

"Who are you talking to?" John asked as he was

fishing around in his pockets to light the joint he now had in his mouth. "That's much better," he said with a sloppy smile as he took a big hit from the herbal medication.

"Do you mind?" I asked as I reached over. We walked away from that field, I was happy to be alive. I had survived being under the ground and then being above it. I was content to be right where I was for the moment.

CHAPTER SEVENTEEN

Maine

"Mom, the baby kicked!" Nicole said excitedly. She had been sitting on the couch pretending to read a story, but in reality she had been daydreaming about Brendon and what could have been.

Tracy was in the kitchen washing up. She had just come in from the garden in the back. When she was confident her hands were clean and dry enough, she went over to feel her daughter's belly. Nicole shifted her mother's hand around to the 'sweet' spot.

"There! Did you feel that?" Nicole asked, her cheeks flushed with excitement.

Tracy was about to respond when a dirty, sweat-riddled Justin walked in. "Wow, when'd you get so big?" he asked his sister as he brought his bottle of water up to his lips.

"Justin!" Tracy exclaimed. "You can't say stuff like that."

"Why not? She's like double her size."

"Mom," Nicole wailed on the verge of tears.

"Even I know better than that," Travis said, coming in after his brother. "That's like poking a killer whale."

"Mom!" Nicole wailed again.

"Why are you boys in the house?" Tracy said, standing up and facing them.

"Lunch, and Uncle Ronnie didn't want us around while they were laying the explosives. He said we were distracting," Travis explained.

"You should see some of the stuff that Mad Jack's got planned, it's pretty impressive." Justin said already forgetting he had barbed his sister.

"Almost seems like a waste...haven't seen a zombie in at least two weeks," Travis said in response.

"Oh, they're coming," Justin said as he absently rubbed his head.

"You know something we all should?" Tracy asked her son, all too aware of the connection he had shared with Eliza.

"Don't worry, mom, she isn't there anymore. (*Mostly*) It's a feeling I keep getting."

"I hope you're wrong," Nicole told her brother as she protectively wrapped her arms around her burgeoning belly.

"Me too." He shuddered in response.

"I'm starving, is there anymore of that venison Aunt Nancy cooked up last night?" Travis asked.

I love teenagers, Tracy thought. *What other creature on the planet could forgo just about everything else for the sake of filling its belly?* Then she thought of her husband and laughed, he could do the same thing. She ached for his return. There were unfathomable depths that yearned to have him back by her side, the warmth of his touch, his humor in the face of evil, his protection of the family, his loyalty to his friends. She could not imagine walking through the world without him by her side. She wanted to believe with all her being that he was still alive, that it would take more than death itself to rip him from her side. But until she had true proof, the sound of his voice, or his hand on her cheek she could only go with Henry and his connection to Mike. It had some comfort value, because somehow, the dog seemed to know. She still longed for more, though.

"Mom? I'm hungry remember," Travis goaded her.

"You know you are eighteen and completely capable of getting your own meal, right?" she replied.

"What fun would that be?" Travis asked, leading the way back into the kitchen.

"You alright, sister?" Justin asked Nicole.

"I miss Brendan, and I'm not sure if I believe dad is still alive like mom...and I miss him so much. I'm as big as a tractor trailer and my ankles are killing me. Other than that, not so good."

Justin, in an unfamiliar role, went over to his sister and gave her hug.

"It's that bad?" Nicole asked him.

"What do you mean?" he asked as he pulled back.

"You picking on me I'm used to, you offering comfort...not so much."

"I don't know about dad either, sis. And if he isn't coming back, then maybe it's time for me to maybe step up and be the man of the family."

Nicole's first reaction was to snort out in laughter, but his serious tone and the nature of the topic did not warrant it. This was serious business they were dealing with, and she was more than a little pleased that some of her father was bleeding out of her brother.

"Thank you, Justin," she said tenderly.

"For what?" he asked, thinking she might be setting him up for something.

"Just for being there." Then she did laugh a little as his chest puffed out.

"I can keep us safe," he told her. "Or I'll die trying."

"Just stick to the safe part, brother, the baby is going to need his uncles."

"I know I don't say it often, Nicole, but I love you. Brendan was my friend, and I miss him, too. I'll do whatever I need to so that we all stay safe."

"Thank you, baby brother. I love you, too."

"Now move your fat ass over so I can sit down."

"There's the Justin, I know and love."

Travis came in carrying some plates loaded with sandwiches and bread.

"Thanks, man," Justin said to his brother.

"These are mine, go get your own," Travis said as he

sat down across from his siblings.

"Travis!" Tracy called from the kitchen.

"Fine," he said as he stuffed a handful of the chips from Justin's plate into his mouth before handing it over.

CHAPTER EIGHTEEN

D, G & BT

"I'm running low on cigarettes," Deneaux said.

"Good, because I don't know how much longer I had before black lung kicked in," BT said as he drove the big truck down the near empty highway.

"We need to stop for fuel and clothes for Gary anyway," Mrs. Deneaux pleaded.

"What's wrong with my clothes?" Gary asked.

"Please, I've smelled dumps on hot summer days that are pleasantly aromatic compared to you," she told him.

"I can't imagine you ever going to a dump," BT said to her.

"I've had reason," she replied flatly.

"I don't even want to know," BT said.

"I wouldn't tell you anyway. All I know is that if I run out of cigarettes I plan on making your life a living hell," she told him.

BT laughed. "Ah, as if I'm living the dream right now."

"I do kind of smell bad," Gary said, pulling his shirt up to his nose.

"I know you do, buddy. I just didn't want to give her the satisfaction." BT paused before speaking again. "I hate pulling off the highway, all the shit happens when we do."

"Beats walking," Gary said.

"Barely."

"We're coming up on some gas stations," Mrs. Deneaux said with some excitement as she pointed to the blue information highway sign.

"Everyone locked and loaded?" BT asked as he got over to the right lane and put his blinker on. "Habit," he said aloud when he noticed Gary and Mrs. Deneaux looking at him. BT got to the bottom of the exit ramp; there were two stations to the right and one to the left. "Any preference?" he asked the group.

"More chance of supplies with the two stations," Deneaux said.

"And more chances people have been there," Gary answered.

BT put his blinker on, signaling his intention of going left. "Sorry, it's difficult to break a twenty-year old habit." BT stayed on the roadway, with the truck idling as they looked closely at the gas station.

"It's definitely had visitors," Gary said, looking over Deneaux's shoulder.

"Would you mind not getting too close?" she asked him with no small measure of venom in her voice. She had smoked her last cigarette over five minutes previous and she was already feeling the effects of withdrawal—whether real or imagined—it didn't matter. She was getting as angry as a republican at a tree hugging ceremony. "You just going to sit here?" she asked BT, not hiding her hostility. Before he could even answer, she had opened her door and was climbing down. When her feet hit the ground she pulled the revolver from its harness.

"I feel sorry for whatever poor bastard gets in her way," BT said.

"I think I see some t-shirts." Gary peered into the store's smashed front windows. The gas station was more of the variety store that just happened to sell gas than an outright petrol server. It was resplendent with cheap souvenirs made in China reminding travelers that they had visited the great state of Virginia. Gary climbed down also.

BT swung the truck into the station. When he shut it off, it was the quiet more than anything that unnerved him. It just wasn't a natural silence. "Gary. Diesel?" he asked when he got the other man's attention.

Gary pointed to the large side tank on the truck, outlined in crisp yellow letters was the word 'diesel.'

"Yeah you can kiss my ass, too," BT said as he went over to the underground filling tanks. *Maybe we should just steal a damn fuel truck*, he thought as he pulled the small metal disc up. Then he remembered the old Mel Gibson movie *Road Warrior* and rethought his plan. "Yeah that didn't work out so well either."

BT walked into the store. It looked a lot more intact than he would have expected. Not perfect, but there were still some supplies left and at least half of the shelving was still up. Gary had found a five gallon jug of water and a bar of soap. He placed the water carefully on top of one of the remaining standing shelves. He then stripped off most of his clothes before popping the top on the water. BT turned away quickly when he realized Gary's tightie-whities were going to be see-through as soon as they got wet.

Deneaux was rummaging in the back of the clerk counter. "They only have fucking menthol!" she fumed. "Do I look black!" she was full-on shouting now.

"That's kind of racist don't you think?" BT asked.

"It's not racist if it's the truth," she said looking up. "Why you black people like to smoke them is beyond me."

"First off, I don't smoke."

"Oh I was just using generalizations. Help me find something for a more civilized palate."

BT walked away. He went into the service bay looking for something that would help him get some gas out of the ground. *I wonder?* he thought as he unscrewed a hand pump from a fifty gallon drum of what appeared to be waste oil. He found a large-throated hose that screwed on to the assembly. "Glad no one else thought of this," he said, going out the garage door instead of going back past Gary and the vitriol spewing Deneaux.

He silently cursed himself when he walked past the

window and looked in. Gary had thought better of keeping the underwear on and was now completely unclothed except for his untied boots.

"Well there's something I'll never be able to unsee," BT said, heading towards the tank.

He dropped the hose into it and then unfurled the rest so that he was sitting at the tank of the truck before he started pumping. He was twenty cranks in and was about to call his idea a 'flub' when he felt the diesel pulsing through the line.

"Sweet!" He said as he quickly got the spigot into the tank opening.

After a few moments, Gary came out wearing a pink 'Virginia is for Lover's' t-shirt and a pair of surfer shorts.

"Nice duds," BT told him.

"Better than what I had on."

BT could only agree.

"I'm gonna grab anything I think we can use," Gary said. "Do you need anything?"

"Deneaux still going nuts in there?" BT asked between hand cranks.

"She seems to have calmed down since she started smoking. She keeps saying something about black people and their uncouth tastes. I'm going to grab some cleaning stuff, too, and see if I can get the back of the truck clean enough to get back into."

"You're going to leave me alone up front with Deneaux?"

Gary shrugged and headed back into the store. "Better you than me."

BT pumped as fast as he could, he was waiting for something to happen; Zombies, gangs, rednecks, evangelists, or even rogue cats. It was unnatural to be in one place for so long and have absolutely nothing happen. He wasn't complaining...he was just vigilant.

Deneaux was shuttling small plastic bags full of smokes to the truck. Gary had found a dolly and two five gallon jugs which he was using liberally to get rid of the majority of gore in the back of the vehicle. When BT had finally finished topping off the tanks, he went to the back of the truck to put the hose and pump up. Gary was in the back sweeping the human debris onto the ground. BT could not help notice—although he wished he hadn't—that the ground behind the truck looked like the world's largest afterbirth. He skirted around the worst of it and handed the hose up to Gary.

"You alright?" BT asked.

"Fine," Gary said through tight lips.

"This seem strange to you?" BT asked Gary.

"Which part?"

"The part where we're not under attack."

"Helps break up the monotony of survival."

BT walked away. He could imagine Mike having delivered that line, although it would have been more dry pan and less serious. He could not shake the feeling that this was too easy. Nothing they had done since the zombies had come was easy and he just couldn't fathom why, now of all times, they were getting a break. It was welcome to say the least, and he hated to look a gift horse in the mouth—not that he had ever received one—but he understood the saying.

If this is a trap they sure are taking their time springing it, he thought as he again walked around the truck looking for signs of trouble.

Deneaux was now shuttling some food and bottles of soda that she was able to recover. "Going to eat well tonight." She held up a can of macaroni and cheese. She was smiling around a cigarette. "These really aren't so bad once you get used to them. Maybe you colored folks are on to something," she said as she took another puff of her menthol smoke.

"I told you already, I don't smoke and menthols aren't a 'colored' thing," BT said angrily.

"I'm sure you don't eat watermelon either." She laughed as she threw her booty into the cab.

"You old bat, who doesn't eat watermelon?" BT

asked.

"I love watermelon," Gary said behind the canvas.

"See?" BT said, pointing towards Gary.

"Coloreds and white trash…I guess they're close enough to be the same," she said as she was trying to reason out this new information.

"I can't believe that you even associate with us." BT said to her.

"Zombies make strange bedfellows." She laughed at her own take on the old cliché.

"Could we not mention Deneaux and beds while I'm in the back of this nasty truck cleaning up?" Gary nearly gagged.

"Let's finish up here. I haven't seen so much as a fly, but this place gives me the willies. I'm ready to go," BT said, extracting himself completely from the conversation.

Deneaux made one more trip into the store. She thoroughly searched every nook and cranny lest any pack of cigarettes go unsmoked. Gary poured the remaining water in the jug onto the bed of the truck, the bigger pieces of anatomy had already been pushed to the ground. All that was left was to sluice out the remaining blood which drained down the open tailgate. The pink fluid looked more like something that would be dispensed at a Sonic restaurant than the diluted remains of life-giving blood.

"I'm ready when you are, BT," Gary said as he tossed the red-stained broom out the back of the truck. He shut the tailgate and laid down on the hard wooden bench as BT pulled out of the station.

BT still couldn't get over the fact that they had got just about everything they needed and hadn't had to fight even a mad mosquito to do it. He shuddered when he finally came to the realization of why.

"Calm before the storm," he said prophetically.

CHAPTER NINETEEN

Mike Journal Entry 7

"Any idea where we are?" I asked John as we sat at the end of a tree line. I was looking at a single-wide trailer not ten yards from our location. I didn't see any signs of life, but even before zombies, walking up on a trailer unannounced was a good way to get shot or at least yelled at by a two-fist, bearded hag. Or quite possibly you could end up on *Cops*.

"Weren't we just up in the air?" John asked me as he looked to the tops of the trees.

"We crashed about two miles ago," I replied to him, not taking my eyes off the back windows.

"Why do all the houses look the same?" John asked, trying to stand. I pulled him back down.

"We're in a trailer park. White trash capital of the world by the looks of it," I told him as I looked at no less than five Chevys on blocks. Sixteen clotheslines, replete with wife beater t-shirts and—I kid you not—used, washed, disposable diapers. The diapers smelled and looked relatively new; well, as new as a used diaper can anyway.

"Maybe we should go somewhere else," John said.

It was one of the few lucid things he had said since I'd met him and I would have heeded his advice if I saw anywhere else even remotely close. But it was getting dark and I didn't want to be out any longer than I needed. Between the two of us, all we could offer in the way of defense was some marijuana. So unless our adversary stopped and smoked the majority of John's offering, then immediately fell asleep where we could throttle him out of the picture, we were in a little bit of a pinch.

"Let me think," I said as I sat with my back to the trailer leaning up against a relatively large oak.

"You do that, I'm going to light a fattie."

A small bird, maybe a sparrow, was a couple of branches over me. It was looking down, his head bobbing as he kept us in his line of sight, probably curious as to what we were. Not many of us running around anymore—at least not the living kind.

"Do I smell nuggets?" a voice drifted out from the trailer, the bird looked in that direction then alit from its spot.

John got up before I could stop him. "Not only is this nugget…it is coated with a proprietary blend of hashish oils."

I fully expected John to be blown back towards me riddled with buck shot.

"Well then come on inside," the voice said with a distinctive Southern lilt.

I swore I could hear toe-strummed banjos playing in the background.

"My name is Luke," a gap-toothed smiling man in his mid-thirties told us as he held his door wide open. The mullet he sported harkened back to the early '80s, much like his felt paintings on the walls. There was a whale, an Indian, and of course, what trailer wouldn't be complete without a smiling tassel-laden portrait of Elvis smack dab in the center. "That there is my wife Mirabelle," Luke said as he closed the door behind us.

Mirabelle looked the part of an older Sissy Spacek minus any good looks and make-up. But she was smiling almost as broadly as Luke and somehow that put me at ease. John seemed perfectly content with our new surroundings. A black dog roughly the size of a standard pony walked over to me, took one passing sniff, and got up on the couch.

"Hercules, we have guests now…get off the couch," Mirabelle said to the dog.

Hercules looked over at me and growled. I'd had freight trains pass me by that produced less tremble. He did, however, get off the couch.

"Sit, sit." Mirabelle motioned.

I kept looking over at Hercules who was mean-mugging me.

"What about him?" I asked Mirabelle.

"Hercules? Oh, he's fine. He's just a big old teddy bear." She laughed.

If by teddy bear she meant, psychotic, rabid grizzly then we were in agreement, I thought.

I sat, Hercules growled again—or a fissure had opened up in the earth—I figured both would sound the same.

Luke and John were sitting at the small kitchen table, alternating hits on a Jamaica envious-sized bone.

"Wowee, that'll make your toes curl and slap a turtle!" Luke said as he leaned back in his chair.

"That's good stuff, right? Got it from that guy over there," John said, pointing at me.

"Mister, you want a hit? 'Sidering it's yours and all," Luke asked.

"I'm good," I told him.

"You want some possum pie?" Mirabelle asked me from the kitchen.

I thought about taking a couple of hits from John's weed, thinking that would be the only way I would get strong enough munchies to actually try possum pie.

"It's not really possum," she said when she saw my face. "We ain't been able to find them since the zombies came."

My stomach was roiling a bit. I tried my best to cover up its gurgling sound. I changed the subject away from food in the hopes I wouldn't have to pretend I was on some hillbilly version of *Fear Factor*. "Thank you for taking us in."

"It's what God-fearing people do," Mirabelle said. "They help other God-fearing people. Are you God-fearing folk?" she asked.

"Um I don't really fear him *per se*. Is a healthy

respect okay?" I asked back.

She thought about it for a moment. "I s'pose that'll do. What brings you folks around this way?"

"We're trying to get to John's wife in Philly, then I'm trying to get home," I told her.

"Without weapons?" she asked astutely.

"We've had a few hardships along the way."

"Fell out of the damn sky!" John shouted after taking another hit.

"Get outta here?" Luke asked incredulously.

"Unfortunately it's the truth," I told Mirabelle.

"What is?" John asked.

"You been dealing with him long?" she asked me.

"Long enough."

"And he hasn't got you kilt yet?"

"I figure the score is about even. Every time he tries to kill me, he saves me."

"Hey, Poncho, Luke wants to know if you have any of this killer weed you can sell him?" John asked me as he started to laugh.

"Fresh out, man, check your pockets. I gave you the last of my stuff," I said as I shrugged to Mirabelle.

"Whoa, man!" John said as he pulled baggies of stuff out of his many pockets. "Thanks, Poncho!"

"Any time," I told him. "Have you been here the entire time?" I asked Mirabelle, wondering how a trailer could possibly hold up to a zombie invasion.

"We have." She looked at me a little guiltily. "Our neighbors all either left, were turned, or were kilt. We've been foraging from their stuff."

"There's no shame in that."

"Man what's with the diapers?" John asked Luke.

"Smell of shit keeps the zombies away. They think it's more of them and don't want anything to do with us," Luke answered.

"That's brilliant," I said.

"We noticed when the zombies were attacking our

neighbors that none really came around here, and the only thing we could think was different was Hercules," Mirabelle said.

"The dog's shits are the size of bread loaves, and I ain't talking those normal sized ones either, I mean those fat-sliced Texas toast ones."

I didn't want to tell him that the Texas-sized toast referred to the individual size of the slice not the loaf itself, but I got the visual anyway.

"The dog laid those monsters around the yard like land mines and the zombies really just kind of ignored us. It was Mirabelle's idea to string some diapers up around the yard as an added precaution."

She blushed a little, well that answered that question—they didn't have a child. Better off in this new world...and then I panged for my daughter and my grandbaby that was on the way. It was a horrible time and place in our history to have a baby, but I also couldn't wait to wrap my arms around the infant and the new hope he or she would deliver.

"You guys ever thought to look for a more secure location?" I asked.

"Why, mister?" Luke asked.

"This is home," Mirabelle said. "It ain't much, but it's what we know. Our neighbors left us just about everything we need and more."

"Cept for a little of the green," Luke said, swinging a baggie back and forth in front of his face. "And since Belle found Jesus I don't need to share."

Mirabelle threw a dishtowel at Luke's head which he had no hopes of dodging. "I didn't 'find' Jesus, he was there all along, waiting for me to 'see' him," she said to her wayward husband. "He's a little rough around the edges, but he treats me good and I love him."

"My wife would probably say the same thing." I smiled at her.

"You haven't been home in a while then?" she asked.

"Seems like a lifetime ago," I answered vaguely.

"How bad is it?" she asked.

"You were right to stay here, there's not much good left," I answered honestly.

"You're welcome to stay here as long as you'd like. You could both even have your own trailer if you wanted," Mirabelle said.

I got the feeling she was lonely and frightened, and I couldn't fault her on either count. "The offer is very much appreciated, but I have to get home. I have a wife, kids, friends, and a dog I need to get back to." Hercules perked up when I said dog. "You could come with us." The range of emotions from hope to despair ran across her face, it was like looking at those posters that show pictures of the human face and all the different internal feelings we can emote. "I'll tell you what, do you have paper and a pen?"

She handed me what I needed.

"Here is our address and a rough map. If you ever have to leave here or just want a new start, you come our way. There probably won't be possum pie, but we'll treat you like you're one of our own."

"Thank you." She sobbed a little clutching the piece of paper close to her breast like it was the Word of God. "We can get you a car and some guns."

"We can't take those things from you," I told her.

"We have more of both than we could ever use."

"Really?"

"Come on, I'll show you. Luke, we'll be right back I'm going to get Poncho some supplies."

"Mike," I said.

"What?" she asked.

"My name is Mike. John gave me a poncho to wear when we first met and that's kind of stuck in his head."

"That's funny. I thought it was a weird name for a Yankee," she said.

"I prefer Bostonian."

"Yankee...Bostonian...same thing isn't it?"

"Not really."

She laughed again. "Come on, Herc," she said to the pony hybrid.

He didn't need the summons when he saw Mirabelle heading for the door, he was already up and waiting. We walked a couple of trailers over, one of them had a small steel garage that housed two cars.

"We checked 'em all out these were the two best."

There was a beautiful Ford Thunderbird; looked like someone had poured a lot of money into its restoration. Its beauty was so overpowering that I barely noticed the thing sitting next to it.

"Wow!" I said as I ran my hand down its side.

"That's kind of the one we decided to keep," Mirabelle said. "But this was the second best one," she said proudly.

A lime green Gremlin stared back at me like some hideous engineering experiment gone wrong. "I can't catch a break," I muttered. The thing assailed my vision, even more so because it was next to such a marvel of perfection. It was the old standard just like high school girls; the pretty ones would surround themselves with the Plain Janes who would invariably make them look that much better. It did seem that this was having the opposite effect, though; the beautiful car was making the ugly one that much uglier—all the bubbled glass, and lime green color, the thick set of its body—it almost made me want the Terrible Teal machine back. "It's wonderful," I told her thickly, careful not to touch it.

"Full tank, too," she said proudly.

"This was really the second best car in the complex?" I asked, hoping against hope.

"By miles," she said.

Hercules walked next to me. He lifted his leg and proceeded to piss a small river coming off the small car's front tire and past my shoes.

"He doesn't much like that car," she told me. "I think it had more to do with the old owner. She always yelled at him."

"No, I think it has to do with the car," I said as I patted him on his head.

"Come on, let's get you some guns." I hoped this was going to cheer me up. We headed back towards her home. She pulled a small key ring out of her pocket. "These are yours now."

"Thank you." And I meant it. The car might have been uglier than bloated, blue, bull balls, but it was ours, and if it was a necessary evil that got me back to my family that much quicker, then I would suffer through it. I just hoped I didn't run into anyone I knew along the way.

She opened the lid up to a good-sized plastic bin more commonly used to house gardening equipment. There were a good ten or twelve guns in there with a decent amount of ammo. Most of it looked to be of the .22 caliber variety.

"You keep these out here?" I asked her. She nodded. "What if something happens?"

"The Lord will provide."

"Mirabelle, there's nothing wrong with your faith, but remember…he helps those that help themselves. There's a lot wrong with the world today and we can't afford to lose more good folks to the oncoming evil." I didn't seem to be winning her over with my argument. "Okay, wait new tactic. You said the Lord would provide, right?"

She nodded again.

"Well didn't he provide these then?"

"I'm not sure that's what that proverb pertains to."

"Listen, Mirabelle, I'm not going to tell you how to live your lives, you both look like you've made it through better than I have so far. You just need to know that the evil that walks this earth is not merely relegated to zombies. And crap-filled diapers aren't going to stop them, more than likely it will alert them to the fact that someone is around."

"I'll think about it," she said. "I'm just not a fan of guns."

"Fair enough. I'm going to take two…a rifle and a

pistol."

"What about your friend?"

"He's much better off without one. I'm afraid he would think it was a squirt gun and blow his lips off trying to get a drink of water."

Mirabelle laughed.

There was a 7.62 caliber semi-automatic that looked Chinese built; I really wanted to take that one as it was by far the best thing in that box, but I kept digging. I ended up with a twelve-gauge shotgun from the Depression Era. It was a single-shot breech load and well taken care of, but unless we were taking on slow deer, it was not the optimal weapon of choice. I added to that a nine-inch barreled .32 caliber revolver. I'd never even heard of the manufacturer. All I could think was that someone had watched *Dirty Harry* with Clint Eastwood and wanted to own the same gun. That same person then went down to the local gun store, and when they realized how much a .44 magnum cost, they opted out for the lesser imitation model.

There was a box of twenty-five rounds for the shottie, and maybe thirty-five to forty rounds for the .32. I thanked Mirabelle profusely, she waved my gestures away.

"It's the least we could do," she said.

"I really hope you take me up on my offer," I told her as I held her door open. Hercules scooted in after her. I looked out once for any signs of danger and closed the door after me when I didn't notice anything.

Luke and John were in the midst of some epic laughing and hadn't realized we had returned. Probably didn't even know we had ever left.

"You want to see the spare bedroom?" Mirabelle asked. "You look like you're asleep on your feet."

"I'd love to," I said as I followed her down the narrow corridor.

"Can I ask you something?" she asked as she led me into the small room dominated by a queen-sized bed that looked like a small slice of heaven just now.

"Sure." I hoped she would make it quick.

"Do you want take a shower first?" She looked me up and down and then over to her clean bedding.

There I was, I had a myriad of scrapes that had dried blood on them, and some remnants of animal lard that were caked with dirt. "That'd probably be for the best," I told her as I looked longingly at the bed. "Is that what you wanted to ask me? Don't get me wrong I'm surprised you let us in at all now that I'm thinking about it."

"Luke let you in," she answered.

"Well I guess there's that."

"What's with the hat?"

Where do I go with that? Do I tell her that I can talk to vampires with it off? Maybe after the shower and eight hours of sleep.

"John wanted me to wear it. He gets very agitated if I take it off, and since we're traveling together I figured it was best to appease him."

I might have bought some time with that, but I figured her next question was going to be why John wanted the hats on in the first place. I didn't have answers that would make us sound sane or not completely mollify her. "I'm going to take that shower now."

Her eyes still held a question, but she let it drop as she led me to the small bathroom with the shower enclosure. I stripped down, making sure the hat stayed on. I cut a ridiculous figure with that piece of tin foil on my head. My facial hair, eyebrow and hair (from what I could see) were beginning to fill in quicker than I would have expected. Was it only three days since I'd lost my best friend? My body was as hard as it had ever been in the Marines, and it was in direct contrast to the quiver of my chin and lips as anguish flooded my system. I was just now realizing I had yet to grieve my loss. I wailed as silently as was possible; my mirror image cried with me as I placed my hand against the cool glass surface.

"You alright?" Mirabelle asked with concern outside

the door.

"I'm...I'm sorry," I said as I wiped the offending moisture from my face.

"I have your shower," she told me.

I had no idea what she meant. I moved to the side so that when I opened the door she couldn't see my bare ass. I didn't want to wrap a towel around myself and get the thing encrusted before I even had the chance to use it. Mirabelle handed me a solar shower bag usually reserved for campers or folks holding onto existence during a zombie apocalypse.

"There's a hook in the shower where you hang it from," she said, looking down at the industrial carpeting. "If you toss your clothes out here, I'll get them as clean as I can."

"You don't need to do that."

"I know...you alright?" she asked again, bringing her eyes up.

"I...I just lost someone dear to me recently, I'm sorry."

"No need to be. Are you going to shower with that on?" she asked pointing to my hat.

"No," I assured her, although I didn't take it off. I bent over and grabbed my clothing, thankful that I was about to wash off. If I looked half as bad as my clothes, I thought I might be sick.

Mirabelle looked reluctant to touch them as well. "Umm, there's a lot of clothes around these trailers. What size do you wear?"

I gave her rough dimensions. I wasn't really sure anymore, especially after all the weight I had lost. Seemed kind of ironic that I had lost pounds in the physical realm and gained them all back in the spiritual in the form of pain.

"Time heals all wounds," Mirabelle told me, obviously seeing the hurt I was in.

Normally I would tend to agree with that phrase, but the zombies had a way of repeatedly opening fresh wounds and never allowing the last one to completely heal up. I nodded my head at the right moment and let her believe her platitude.

"Thank you," I told her as I closed the door. She was pointing to her head to let me know I still had the tin foil hat on. I hung the bag, looked to be about two-and-a-half gallons of fairly warm water up on the hook. I opened the spigot and got a good dosing. I'm not going to lie, I was more than a little concerned. There was more lard on me than I had originally figured. I looked up at the bag that now looked entirely too small. I quickly closed the valve, went head-to-toe lathering with the soap twice. I had no sooner finished my second go round when I paused. If we were going to be attacked by zombies, I was as sure as the purity of the soap I was using (99.4% by the way) that it would happen NOW.

I was thinking about that first night the zombies came when my shower was interrupted—how I had *actually* hoped for that very event. FUCKING HOPED! I'd lost a brother, a best friend, a niece, and dozens of others that I cared for in one way or another, and it was far from over. The odds were still greatly stacked against me, and I still had more on the betting line than I was prepared to wager. I turned the flow of water back on, most of the dirt, blood, and lard was removed as the water ran out; the pain…well, that remained.

A soft knock came at the door. "I found some clothes that might fit. I left them on the chair by your bed."

"Thank you, Mirabelle," I told her. I dried off, wrapped the towel around myself and went to bed.

CHAPTER TWENTY

G, BT and D

The group had to stop one more time for gas. BT picked a gas station right before they had turned on to the Massachusetts turnpike. The station was of the old traditional variety; no Slush Puppies, no hot dogs, candy bars, or rows upon rows of gourmet coffee dispensers. There were no aspirins, feminine hygiene products, or even newspapers. There was a counter where a person stood to take your cash or run your card through an old handheld device to imprint an image of your card. Checks were not welcome, neither was American Express; and if you wanted the proprietor's gun, you would have to pry it from his cold dead hands—at least according to the bumper sticker adhered to the side of the counter.

The station looked like it had last seen upgrades at around the time of the Nixon administration and that was just fine with him, it would draw less attention that way. The truck rolled up, Gary morosely hopped down from the back. BT figured that the closer they got to Maine, the worse his friend was going to become. Mrs. Deneaux stayed in the cab; she at least kept a watch out for anything directly in front of her.

"Getting some gas," BT said as he got into the back and grabbed his hose and pump.

"This'll be the last fill up before we get back home," Gary said more as a statement of fact. "My father is going to blame me for this."

BT stopped what he was doing for a moment, not

liking the added time to their stop but it was necessary.

"Gary, listen to me, no one is going to blame you for this."

"Not even Tracy?" Gary asked with red-rimmed eyes.

"Especially Tracy. Everyone including Mike knew the risks. Every time we open a door there is the chance we will dance with death. I miss your brother more than you can know, and I don't blame you for what happened. You did all that you could...we all did. We go forward, Gary, we make those responsible pay."

"When does it stop?"

"When we're in a box, until then..." BT left the comment hanging. He opened the hatch to the tank and began to fill the tanks.

Gary made a few circuits around the station. When he was confident there was nothing to be overly concerned about except for a skunk that was going through some trash he stopped.

"Want a cigarette?" Mrs. Deneaux asked Gary.

BT had watched her get down out of the truck and go behind the station to do whatever is was that reptiles do. A few moments later she had come back to where Gary was sitting.

"Do you mind?" BT asked.

"Quit your bitching. It's diesel and not as flammable as gas," she said as she stuck the cigarette she had offered into her mouth and lit it up.

Within a few minutes they were ready to go; Deneaux up in the cab with BT and Gary sitting on the bench in back. He was leaning up against the canvas, his gaze peering through the hole up top that the zombie had fallen through. The truck got off to a slow start, then jerked to a stop.

"Sorry!" BT yelled in the cab loud enough for Gary to hear. "Skunk walked in front of the truck!"

"Run the creature over next time. You made me crush a cigarette on the dashboard," Deneaux seethed.

As the truck passed, Gary watched the skunk waddle off. It seemed to be doing fairly well given the circumstances. Gary wondered if a skunk crossing one's path meant anything. When he was certain it didn't, he returned his gaze skyward. As they crossed into New Hampshire, Gary's feelings of trepidation grew tangible. He could taste it on his tongue, he could feel the weight of it on his chest, and he did not know how he was going to face those he loved the most.

After another half hour or so, the truck came to a stop.

"What's up?" Gary asked.

"Bladder break!" BT yelled back.

Gary got back down, riding in the back of the seemingly shock-less truck on a pine bench was not doing his spleen any favors and he welcomed the chance to stretch and pop. They had just crossed the Maine state line and Gary felt like his knees might buckle under the added weight of guilt.

Mrs. Deneaux was staring at the sign and the surrounding forest of trees when she commented on the state's motto. "Maine, the way life should be. For who? Chipmunks? I certainly wouldn't want my life to be like this. Looks like the land that time forgot."

"That's the point," Gary said morosely.

"Like the dark ages?" she asked.

"More like the fifties," he told her.

"The fifties weren't all they were cracked up to be. People were still assholes…there was just not twenty-four hour news that catered to the insanity like we have today."

"It's more the idea of the time, I suppose," BT said, defending Gary who looked like a whipped dog.

"One thing that was more in the open than today was racism. I wouldn't think you'd be in such a hurry to revisit those times," she said to BT offhandedly.

"You must miss that?" BT asked sarcastically.

"At least there wasn't all this phony politically correct bullshit. You knew where people stood."

"Yeah, in a circle with hoods on watching crosses burn," he said heatedly.

She scoffed at him, "Are we done here or do you need to tinkle some more?"

At some point, Gary just left the argument and got back on the bench. The truck pulled away moments later, Gary struggled for breaths as dismay and disquiet warred within him.

CHAPTER TWENTY-ONE

Tracy Journal Entry

The day my world crashed in on itself. It was late afternoon and I had finished most of my daily duties. Who knew surviving could be so labor intensive? I was sitting on Ron's deck with Tony and we were enjoying a cup of coffee together. It was the only time of the day I felt at peace, because when the night set in so did my fears. I was looking out over the pond enjoying the silence with Mike's dad when he abruptly stood.

"You hear that?" he asked me.

I thought this strange because he was notoriously hard of hearing, so I did not know the odds of him hearing something before me. (Although I had secretly suspected that his hardness of hearing might more be contributed to selective listening.) Then I heard it, a moment later it was confirmed.

"Truck coming!" Mark, Ron's son, said from his guard station in a turret some thirty feet off the ground. "Military truck," he clarified.

Whoever hadn't heard the truck outright had most definitely heard his warning cry. People streamed out the front door of the house as Tony and I went back in through the back door and out the front to stand on the lawn with everyone else.

"Halt!" Mark shouted as he pointed his rifle down at the truck.

Ron came out from the woods on the passenger side. Tony had his rifle up and pointed squarely at the truck. I did not see Travis and Justin until later. They were in the woods far enough back to not be seen, but close enough and with good enough firing angles to take out anybody on the driver's side.

The large military truck came to a stop.

"Hands!" Mark shouted. "Identify yourself!"

I could see arms the size of heavy tree limbs poke out the side window. My heart leapt. It was BT—it had to be—they were back! And as if to prove my point, the passenger side door opened and Mrs. Deneaux got out. She was her normal pleasant self.

"Oh for the love of God, who else do you think we are? Who else would come down to the middle of damn nowhere?" she said as she lit up another cigarette.

"BT?" That you?" Travis said as he made his way out of the woods, putting his rifle back up.

"Good to see you again, boy," BT said with genuine sincerity as he opened his door and hopped down, extending his hand for Travis to shake it.

"Where's dad?" Travis asked, looking around the bulk of the man as if Mike were hiding.

Even from thirty yards away I could see the tight-lipped, imperceptible shake of BT's head. I felt like someone had pulled a heavy weighted veil over my entire body, the pressure nearly sending me to my knees. I was cognizant enough to see Gary come from the back of the truck and thought that surely Mike was right behind him.

Gary's head was down. He walked past Ron and Justin, who had converged to give their greetings. He was walking towards me and Tony; I felt myself wanting to turn and run into the house. If he could not catch me, he could not tell me. Tony stood stoically, but I could see his white knuckled grip on his rifle. Instead of slinging it across his shoulder, he kept it across his chest. Maybe that was his barrier against the encroaching news.

Gary was ten feet from the both of us when he spoke. Tears were streaming from his eyes. "I'm so sorry," he said.

It was difficult to discern who the apology was directed to, but it didn't really matter.

"No," Tony said, shaking his head. "NO! I cannot lose another child!" he yelled, the force of which stopped Gary in his tracks still some five feet away.

"I did everything I could, dad," Gary moaned.

"NO!" Tony said, taking one hand off the rifle to point an accusatory finger at his son.

Tony did what I had hoped to do and retreated back into the house. I stepped forward and hugged Gary. He sobbed long and hard against my shoulder, it was difficult to figure out who was holding who up.

And even enveloped within my mourning, I was able to hear the rest of the miserable little drama as it unfolded. Erin (Paul's wife) and Perla had been out on the pond fishing when the truck had rolled in. Cindy (Brian's fiancée) had gone down to tell them someone was coming. The trio came up from the side of the house. Erin saw me with Gary. She took a few steps forward and saw BT and Travis, and then Deneaux by herself. "Paul?" she asked of anyone that would listen.

Gary sobbed even harder if that were possible. That was all the information I needed in regards to Paul's fate.

"Paul!" Erin screamed, running towards the truck. She did a complete circle around the entire vehicle. "Paul!" she screamed again.

"Really, don't you think he would have responded by now if he were here?" Deneaux answered.

"What…what are you talking about?" Erin asked. "When are the rest of them coming home?"

"This is it, sweetie," Deneaux said without any soothing effect.

Cindy had waited behind. Her hands had been to her mouth as she waited for Erin to do her route around the truck. When she realized no one else was getting out, she turned and headed back the way she came. Perla was right behind her.

BT was now coming my way. Travis seemed to stagger off, lost in his own grief. Ron had a set to his jaw that would have cracked diamonds and Justin seemed to be somewhere in the middle of emotions—from stalwart to stricken.

His arms opened up and he swallowed me and Gary up. His sobs were added to our own. Erin was screaming incoherently. I did not know it then, but she had gone insane at that moment. Something inside of her mind snapped. Two nights later she would walk out of the house to never be heard from again. I hoped that whatever end she found was a quick and peaceful one.

It was a few hours later and everyone except for Deneaux and Erin were in the living room. BT related the majority of the events as they had unfolded. It sounded as if we were receiving the heavily edited version. That was fine with me, I didn't need the details. As it was, it felt like I was walking through the world through a fog; the only thing that kept me grounded was Henry. The dog seemed completely unaffected by all the emotions that were in that room. He knew something that none of us did, and since he was the only one that offered hope. I decided to throw my lot in with his.

Gary would not pick his gaze up off the floor. He wouldn't look Tony or me in the eyes. I don't believe Tony blamed him, and I certainly didn't, but Gary blamed himself and that was a bigger burden then he was prepared to carry. It was difficult to see someone who was always so upbeat and positive that far down in the abyss.

Nicole had slept through the group's initial homecoming, but she was inconsolable as she sat there, her head was in my lap. I was absently stroking her hair as I tried to listen. It was almost impossible, though, as I felt as if I were underwater. I had to believe Talbot was still alive.

What was the alternative?

And the damn dog, he knew something…and he wasn't telling.

CHAPTER TWENTY-TWO

Mike Journal Entry 8

"Hand-cut jean shorts and a white tank top," I said as I picked up the clothes that Mirabelle had found for me. I shook my head. I'd had as much luck with clothes lately as I had with cars—which pretty much meant none at all. The only thing I could say positively about the shorts was that they fit well around my waist. Whoever had cut them looked like they had severe palsy. The hem went up and down like a cross-eyed orangutan had gone at them. Add to that the fact that they they were way too short. Someone was apparently very fond of showing off their inner thighs; the white material of the pockets hung a few inches below the frayed line of the shorts.

The shirt was a couple of sizes too small. It was something that, a few months ago, I would not have been comfortable wearing as it would have showed all my years of soft living. Now it displayed the hard starkness of definition. At this very moment, I longed for my poncho.

"You look good," Mirabelle said as I came down the hallway. "Want some breakfast?" she asked.

I was self-conscious about my new digs, but in Mirabelle's world I fit right in. "Sure what do you have?" I was hoping for a three-egg cheese omelet, with a side of bacon or maple breakfast sausage, maybe an English muffin or some toast slathered in butter, a pile of hash browns and a pancake or two would be divine and a giant glass of orange juice to wash it all down with.

"Ring Dings and Kool-Aid." She smiled back.

My heart and stomach sank at the prospect of eating the syrupy sweet snack. "What flavor Kool-Aid?"

"Cherry."

"Of course," I responded dourly. I'd had an aversion to cherry flavored anything since around the age of six when I realized that every nasty tasting medicinal concoction back in my youth was cherry flavored. Cherry flavored cough drops, cough syrup, and nasal decongestant, maybe even the suppositories were cherry flavored. I don't know. Even passing by fresh cherries in the produce section of a supermarket was cause for my gag reflex to start the process of producing excessive jets of saliva while my stomach began to perform its Olympic gymnastics routine.

I grabbed the Ring Ding from her hand but left the Kool-Aid alone. I went to sit at the small kitchen table. Luke and John had passed out on the couch. They were sleeping nearly sitting up, their heads were touching keeping them propped there.

"Cute," I said pointing to them, melted chocolate now on the tips of my fingers.

"They stayed up all night." Mirabelle said as she cleaned up after 'preparing' breakfast.

"John," I said. No response, although I really wasn't expecting any. This time I got up and put my hand on his shoulder. I gave him a gentle shake as I spoke his name.

"I smell Ring Dings!" Luke said excitedly. "Mirabelle when'd you pull off that small miracle?" he asked as he got up quickly from the couch. John fell all the way over. "Man my head hurts," Luke said, rubbing the connecting spot where he had spent the night as a temporary Siamese twin.

"I saved them for a special occasion," Mirabelle smiled.

"And Kool-Aid? Is it our anniversary?" Luke asked earnestly.

"No it's for our guests."

He seemed relieved that he had not forgotten something he shouldn't have and extremely excited that he was the beneficiary of the bounty.

"Ring Dings are his favorite," Mirabelle said over

Luke's plastic crinkling noise to get to the snack. "I got that," I told her. "John." I shook his shoulder with a little more vigor. I wanted to put as many miles as possible under our belt today and maybe find some antacids. The Ring Ding was already wreaking havoc on a system that hadn't seen much in the way of 'real' food in a bit.

"Steph, I left the toaster in the pool," John said as I shook him again.

"I hope it wasn't plugged in," Luke snorted.

Knowing John the way I did, I was pretty certain it had been.

"Oh, man, my head hurts," John said as he sat up rubbing his head in the opposite same spot as Luke.

"Weird, man, mine too!" Luke said as he looked around Mirabelle trying to locate the Ring Ding box, that was now nowhere in sight. "Hey, baby, I'm still a little hungry," he said trying to maneuver around her.

"Not a chance."

"You know how angry I get when I'm hungry." He placed his hands over his head. He was shaking them around crazily, hopping from one foot to the other. Mirabelle was laughing.

She kissed him quickly. "No."

I felt guilty that I had eaten one of this man's favorite treats and especially now that they were a finite commodity. I slowly pushed the wrapper into my exposed pockets, hoping that he would not hear the tell tale snack noise.

"Dude, those are some ugly shorts," John said, his face was just about thigh level.

I stepped back. "Yeah well, the Gap was closed."

"I think you look fine," Mirabelle said, coming to my aid.

"Looks normal enough to me," Luke echoed.

The second stop after the antacids would be for new clothes. The probability that I could die at any moment was high and I sure as shit wasn't going to go out looking like this.

"You about ready to rock and roll?" I asked John seeing if he was ready to go.

"No music yet, man," John said, putting his hands on his ears.

"I was actually talking about getting ready to leave, buddy."

"Are you sure?" Mirabelle and Luke asked at about the same time.

"Who the hell is Buddy?" John asked me.

"Okay, let's start from the beginning. John the Tripper, sometimes known as John or Trip, we need to leave soon so that we can find your wife."

"Right, right," he agreed as he grasped at the elusive clarity. "And where is she again?" he asked, looking up at me, once again letting the slippery thoughts slide through his fingers.

"Maybe this will help you remember, honey," Mirabelle said as she walked over and placed a Ring Ding in his hands.

"He gets one but I don't?" Luke asked as he stared longingly at the one sitting untouched in John's hands. Mirabelle put her hand on his chest when she realized that he was going to make a move for it.

"Don't you dare," she warned.

"I don't like apples," John said as he turned the package over in his hands. He then opened it up and popped the entire offering into his mouth. His teeth were coated in a chocolate substance as he over-exaggerated his chews.

Mirabelle grabbed him a drink of Kool-Aid when she realized he was having difficulty with his breakfast.

"Breakfast of champions, Bruce Jenner would be rolling over in his grave (or maybe not, he could still be alive or a zombie)," I mumbled as he washed it down with the vile liquid.

"My wife's in Philly, and she works at a hotel in downtown."

We had at least something to go on. It sure beat

driving around until John recognized something. It was like the sugar acted as a direct infusion to his cognitive thought processes. That was something I would keep in mind. When we stopped for antacids I would add Snickers onto the list of things I needed to get. "Is that downtown?"

"Yes, and why are you wearing Daisy Dukes?" he asked.

"Do they make my ass look fat?" I asked back, trying to deflect the question.

"I'd rather not know," was his diplomatic answer. "Are you ready to go?"

"You're going out like that?"

"I don't have much choice."

"Yeah...then I'm ready whenever you are," he told me.

I made sure that Luke and Mirabelle realized how open the invitation to Maine was. They seemed somewhat interested, but I couldn't imagine them actually leaving their homestead any time soon. Unless, of course, Luke's wife could no longer wrangle up Ding Dongs or whatever the chocolate-like treats he liked were called.

Luke and John embraced and cried like they were brothers or friends who had known each other for decades. "I'm going to miss you, man," John said as he wiped his face.

"Besides Mirabelle here, you're the best person I've ever met," Luke said, trying unsuccessfully to mask his own water works.

They hugged again. Both men's shoulders were bobbing. I didn't know if I should feel jealous or not. I think if I walked out the door and never saw John again he would merely forget he had ever met me. After another ten minutes of them making excuses not to part, we were seated in the Gremlin. John had his hand pressed up against the glass as we passed by Luke's and Mirabelle's. I waved. Their kindness had been like a small hiker's cabin amidst a raging blizzard. I would not soon forget the reprieve, and I did not think John ever would.

"You alright, bud...Trip?"

"He was a kindred spirit," John said, finally looking through the front windshield as opposed to the rear.

"Maybe after you get your wife, you can go back. It's not that far." He seemed to perk up after that.

"Do you think Stephanie would want to?" he asked earnestly.

My first thought was to say 'how the fuck would I know?' "If she sees how important it is to you, then I'm sure she'll want to." Although, in all honesty, I thought the odds were much slimmer than that. Odds that I figured her to be alive were about ten percent; odds that we'd find her in addition to her being well at about one percent. Odds that we found her alive and well AND she would want to hunt down her husband's long lost friend from yesterday? I figured that to be an unimaginably small number, the type that scientists used when they were trying to figure out the weight of atoms.

John, in contrast to his earlier mood, seemed completely upbeat. He must not have received my odds sheet from Vegas yet. *Beside wearing too short shorts and a tight wife beater t-shirt, plus driving in a lime green Gremlin, the day was going exceedingly well.* I knew I had cosmically cursed myself the moment I had the thought. Nothing changes the fates quicker than telling the universe that everything is going great! Might as well flip a cop off doing ninety with a bottle of tequila in your lap and marijuana cigarette hanging out of your mouth. That's about how quickly our day went from 'wicked pissah' to 'what the fuck?'

CHAPTER TWENTY-THREE

Eliza & Tomas

"You ready, Tomas?" Eliza asked as she headed for their vehicle.

Tomas stared back at the city as the last few fires sputtered on. There wasn't much left at this point that could keep it going. He turned to catch up with her. "I am, Lizzie. I just want this to all be over."

"Are we still on the same side, brother?" Eliza asked as she sat down.

"I will not raise my hand up against you, if that is what you mean," he told her as he walked around the front of the black glassed Dodge.

"When Michael Talbot's family are begging for my mercy, you will not help them?" she mused. "I find that somewhat difficult to believe."

"You believe what you want, Eliza. I have not lied to you." What he failed to elaborate on was that he would also not lift a finger to help her if the tables were somehow turned.

"I think we are in for some fun in Maine. Maybe not as much as the Black Plague, but certainly something to rival it."

Tomas had finally come to the realization of who—and more importantly *what*—his sister had become. No amount of reasoning, pleading, begging, or crying would change that. She had become a monster to rival anything ever produced in the pages of a book or on the cells of a film. He only had two hopes left; one was that, once she had destroyed

Talbot's family, the hatred that burned so deeply within her would be extinguished. Or that the resourceful Talbots were able to gain the upper hand and destroy his sister. Either way would almost be a relief.

Tomas turned the car around and got back onto the highway; the restocked tractor trailer convoy packed full of speeders and a new, deadly surprise followed suit. Once the initial attack had subsided, a fair portion of Eliza's human familiars had returned, those were bolstered by her new henchman leader Kong and his trucker friends. She had drained a few of the deserters dry for their actions. The men that were following Eliza knew they had made a deal with the devil, but when you're faced with hell, options are limited. Eliza could barely contain her excitement, her black eyes shined brightly as Tomas drove on.

CHAPTER TWENTY-FOUR

Maine

It was early evening and Mrs. Deneaux was sitting on the deck overlooking the pond. Her gaze had that far away look as she reflected back on her life.

"Beautiful out here isn't it?" Tracy asked as she came out the sliding door. She was holding a steaming cup of tea, hoping that it would somehow drive the cold in her soul away.

"I've seen prettier," Mrs. Deneaux said as she took a drag.

Tracy looked past the comment. "I just wanted to say thank you."

Mrs. Deneaux looked over to the woman suspiciously. "For what?"

"BT told us all what you did. He said they probably wouldn't have made it if not for you. I just wanted to thank you for bringing my brother-in-law and friend back."

Mrs. Deneaux's eyes narrowed. "Do you know why I did it?"

"I would imagine because their well being meant something to you," Tracy replied not sure of the basis to Deneaux's question.

"I did it because I stood a better chance of surviving with them than without them. Not because I have any personal affinity for either one. I think your brother-in-law is a dolt personally, and BT was just your husband's lackey. Without Mike directing him, he is as unsure of himself as an eighteen-year-old virgin with a hooker. Now Michael I miss, that was a man that could get out of a jam, smart enough to know what to do and dumb enough to do it himself." She laughed at her wit.

Tracy was aghast.

"Oh don't look so surprised, dearie, self-preservation is a pretty strong motivator."

"At the expense of all others?" Tracy asked.

"Who should be more important to me than me?"

"And you can live with yourself like that?"

"Quite comfortably," Deneaux answered. She turned back to the pond as a lone loon landed and made an other-worldly cry. Deneaux took another drag from her cigarette. "Are we done talking?" she asked. Tracy had already gone back in.

"Fun isn't she?" BT asked as Tracy fumed past.

She stopped to respond. "You didn't at some point think killing her and dropping her on the side of the roadway was a good idea?"

"Every couple of miles, but she never put the damn pistol away," he responded truthfully.

"How's Gary doing?" Tracy asked, trying to take her mind off of Deneaux.

"He's pretty torn up. He thinks he alone is responsible for Mike's death."

"That's ridiculous, Mike is...was a grown man." Tracy swallowed hard as she made the adjustment from present to past tense.

"He can't help it, as his big brother he feels like he should have been able to protect him."

"I'll talk to him," Tracy said.

"That'll do him some good, I think," BT replied.

"Do you think it's over, BT?" Tracy asked, her eyes pleading for some hope. "Will my children, will my grandchild be able to live in a world in recovery?"

BT wanted to, no, needed to give her the answer she so desperately sought. He could not find it, though, and remained silent.

Cindy who had been seated in the room, her eyes red from crying, looked at the two of them. "We're all dead. There is no hope for us. All day long we prepare for the zombies. We are trying so hard to keep them out never realizing that in so doing we are preventing ourselves from being able to leave. And I'm sorry, but this isn't the Garden of Eden, I don't want to spend all eternity here. The zombies do not die on their own unless we kill them…they will ALWAYS be out there!" She shouted. "How can we possibly defeat that? Even if we somehow keep them from coming in, what have we gained?"

Tracy wanted to argue with her that, as long as they were alive, they had a chance; she just didn't have it in her. She was sadder in life than she could ever remember being and she could not see a way to a better place. The survivors on the planet were quickly gravitating to two distinct groups. There were the Cindys; they were defeated and merely marking time until the end. On the far side of the spectrum were the Deneauxs: the ultra-survivors that would do all in their power to stay alive no matter who they had to crush in order to get there.

Mike had treaded the line in between, firmly holding on to the belief that they could somehow not only survive but win, without sacrificing who he was. With his passing, so too did that dream seem to have evaporated. If not for her children, Tracy thought she might find a way to visit Mike sooner.

***

"I was wondering when you would find me," Gary said to his sister-in-law.

"It wasn't easy," Tracy said. She had spent the last ten minutes hunting him down only to find him at the end of Ron's driveway.

He turned towards her, his eyes shot through with red. Tracy thought that he probably hadn't slept since they got back. "I'm so sorry, Tracy," he started.

"For what?" she asked wholeheartedly.

"Mike."

"Stop it, just stop the 'woe is me', Gary. I heard what happened. How could you possibly blame yourself?"

"I left him behind."

Tracy pressed on, even though she faltered for a moment as she thought about Mike dropping to his knees in the middle of the roadway. "Didn't he pretty much beg you to leave?"

"Yes," Gary said, looking down at his feet.

"And what if you hadn't?" she asked. She waited for long seconds, Gary did not answer. "You'd both be dead. That's what would have happened. BT would have had to come here and tell your father that he lost two sons!" she said heatedly.

"I wished it were me." Tears now flowing freely.

"That's always the case, isn't it? We'd always like to take the place of the one we lost, and I don't think it is nearly as selfless an act as we would have ourselves believe."

"What?" Gary said, looking up from his shoes to Tracy's hard set of features.

"Taking the place of someone we love. It's not all we think it is, any of us would do it in a heartbeat. Oh, I guess partly because we'd like that other person to be safe, but you know what the bigger part of the equation is?" Gary was looking at her wonderingly. "It's so we're not left behind to harbor the guilt, the what-ifs, and the pain of moving on without the person we love. How much easier would it be to just be in the void of death? No feelings, no pain, no remorse, and especially no guilt," she said as she propped Gary's dropping face with her hand.

"He was my brother," Gary sobbed.

"He was my everything," Tracy said solemnly. "And I hold not one shred of blame against you Gary...not one. So if I don't, you shouldn't either. Do you understand?"

He nodded. "Thank you, Tracy. Mike was a lucky

man."

"I like to think so."

Gary walked away. Tracy thought his spirits may have been improved. She couldn't truly tell, though, because she was sobbing.

***

Justin had been watching the exchange between his mother and his uncle from the window in the living room. He was still having a difficult time coming to grips that his father had passed; and now, whether he wanted it or not, he was now the man of the house. It was not a responsibility he felt he was quite ready for or one in which he felt qualified. Especially since he had just recently started to hear the siren call of Eliza in the deepest recesses of his mind.

She was tugging on the folds of his being. At first it was so subtle that he thought it was merely an echo of possession, but he could no longer deny it, whatever was happening was increasing. It had gone from a ghost feeling to a feathery light touch and he was not of the ilk to believe it would subside.

"Easter Evans was a sham," he said aloud as he absently rubbed his forehead, referring back to the man in Virginia that had supposedly exercised his demons. "She was just biding her time. She made it look like she was gone, and now she's going to use me to kill the rest of my family. Well I'm not going to fucking let her!" His thoughts were not nearly as convinced.

Travis had been by the entrance to the living room about to tell his brother that their Uncle Ron needed their help with one of the fences. He had wondered who Justin was talking to, and when he peeked in and realized it was only himself, he had for some reason not let himself be known. Travis had noticed that his instincts had been amped up since the zombies came and he was heeding their advice now to not be seen.

Eliza's back, Travis thought as Justin was talking. He was wondering how long Justin would take to come to that realization and if he would ever tell the rest of the group. He quickly left when Justin stopped speaking. *Fuck, fuck, fuck,* he thought. At least as long as he didn't say it aloud his mother couldn't berate him for it.

***

"Would you believe me if I told you I don't have a shred of evidence but that I know Eliza is on her way?" Travis said to his uncle who was seated on his small backhoe.

"No evidence?" Ron asked.

"Not so much as a napkin with a lipstick stain."

"And you're sure of it?"

"I am, Uncle Ron."

"Any chance you could tell me why you believe that?"

"I could, but I have my reasons not to right now." *Basically I want to see how long it takes my brother to raise the flag. The longer it takes him to warn us the less I'm going to trust him.*

Ron held his nephew's gaze for a few moments, looking for any seeds of doubt in the young man's face, when he was satisfied there were none he spoke. "How long?"

"Not as long as we want. Other than that, I don't have any answers."

"Not very forthcoming are you?" Ron asked. "Fine, we'll play this your way for now, but eventually we'll have to talk. Where's your brother?"

"Damn I knew I forgot to do something."

***

"You alright, dad?" Lyndsey asked her father.

He was standing in his living room holding a portrait of his family they had taken at Sears. His wife Mary had dragged him out because they were having a sale on the pictures. It had taken over an hour to get his four boys still enough to get proper clothes on them and get their hair combed, but that still paled to the two hours his princess Lyndsey had taken primping her eight-year-old self.

He turned to his daughter with the $4.99 portrait in his hand. "When I look at this picture, I can only see black exes where I should see your mom, Glenn, and Mike's faces."

"Oh, dad," Lyndsey said as she came in to be next to her father.

"And I can't help but wonder who the next black ex will descend on. It is against the nature of the universe for a parent to watch their children die, yet two of mine have passed and I have not even been able to bury either one. Where is the justice in that?"

Lyndsey had a myriad of platitudes, 'It'll be okay, we'll make it, hang on, live to fight another day' but they were just hollow words. They had no meaning beyond the airwaves they pushed with the sound of them. She did what she could to console her father.

CHAPTER TWENTY-FIVE

Mike Journal Entry 9

"What the fuck is that?" I asked, but not really to John. He was sleeping, and hard if the line of drool extending down his chin was to be used as an indicator. Down off the highway was a truck rest area, replete with a service station and greasy spoon restaurant. That was not the interesting part. Had I known just how close I was to Eliza, I would have just whipped a U-turn and headed to parts unknown. The truck stop was full, I mean packed with trucks.

The owners of this particular spot had probably never seen so many customers at any one time, and my bet was they weren't even around to enjoy it anymore. The place was bustling, and for some unfathomable reason I *had* to see why—never quite understood that need in me to be exposed to unnecessary risks. I pulled the car off the highway and down a slight embankment that was actually a little steeper than I had figured. I looked to my right and back up the incline wondering if the Gremlin was going to have enough power or traction to get us back on the roadway.

"One issue at a time," I told my non-multitasking self. I then looked over at John, 'take him?' or 'don't take him?' I ran through the question a good half dozen times, the majority of reasons why I would take him revolved around the fact of leaving someone sleeping by the side of the road was just kind of shitty. And if he awoke, would he know what was going on? Or where he was? If he started ambling around, I'd never find him. Taking him into a possible hostile situation was no bargain either.

"Fuck," I moaned, there was no good answer unless I just started the car back up and drove off, no harm, no foul. I got out of the car quietly, making sure I pocketed the keys; John driving off without me would not be good. A gust of wind pulled the door from my hand, the door slammed shut. I silently cursed and peeked my head in through the window. John hadn't stirred, if anything, it looked like he had settled down even more.

"Last chance, Talbot," I said aloud. Although the moment I pulled over, I had made my mind up. "Why do you do this shit? Who else is gonna? Comforting," I said, finishing my dialog off.

I walked down the rest of the embankment, then went through a couple of feet of sparse scrub brush and came to a six-foot high wooden fence. "I hate fences." I said, thinking about the jump down from the top that was going to cause some serious pain in my football, Marine Corps damaged knees. I was pleasantly surprised when I landed on the other side and was not rewarded with the all familiar twinge of cartilage and ligaments past their prime. I attributed it to the lost weight, somehow subconsciously avoiding the fact that I was now enhanced. Not sure how I kept forgetting that, I guess it was a fail-safe system.

I came out behind the service station effectively blocked from all the truckers who were out front. Things sounded normal enough; there was laughter and banter among them, but I still was not feeling secure enough to just stroll on up, especially how I was dressed.

"Shit, I look like a male prostitute," I said, looking down at my outfit. "Wonderful, a pair of roller skates and I'd be perfect."

I thought about blending in, but not like this. Then I was dealt a hand that I had to take advantage of.

"I'll be right back," one of the men yelled. "I'm gonna take a piss."

It sounded like he was coming up the far side of the building. I slowly moved along the length of the building to the side I heard the man calling from. I quickly peeked my head around the corner; luckily he had his head down as he was approaching me while diligently working on opening his fly.

"Must really have to go," I said.

He was approaching a small blue dumpster about midway along the wall. He turned with his back to me so that he could urinate on the trash collector. It was twenty feet from me to him, then what? He hadn't done anything that necessitated me killing him.

"Act first, think later," I said as I started running towards him. He either had a sixth sense, or I wasn't as stealthy as I had hoped. He turned when I was no more than a few feet away, as he turned warm urine traveled up my leg it was almost enough to stop me in my tracks.

"What the fuck, man?" he said, one hand still holding his penis, the other coming up in a defensive gesture.

I caught him with a right cross that I'm fairly certain cracked his jaw. His eyes rolled back into his head and he collapsed. I swear I would have caught him as he was going down, but he was still pissing. Luckily he crumbled more than falling forward or backward so the impact as his head hit the ground wasn't quite as traumatic. At this point I still felt like shit, the man hadn't done anything more than need to relieve himself at an inopportune time. Who knew I might have just smacked the shit out of a sainted brain surgeon. Odds were that I hadn't, but still.

He had one leg bent back behind him, but for the most part he was lying on his back. His penis was still doing what he had been in the act of before I so rudely interrupted. It looked like one of those old bubblers from my youth in school, the ones that were always running before we figured out that wasting a precious commodity like water wasn't such a good idea. Although, even way back then, before the germ-a-phobia truly set in, I would never have drank anything that rusty looking. I wasn't thrilled that he was getting all his clothes, which I needed, wet.

"Fuck, dude, when's the last time you took a pit stop?" I asked him as he just kept going and going. It was looking like he had downed two huge Slurpees and a carafe of coffee. I couldn't wait any longer or he would completely soak his clothes. I quickly pulled his shirt over his head, undid his boots, and pulled his pants down, thankful that he had already done the majority of the work.

I took a couple of deep breaths as I assessed just how sopped his clothes were. And still he was going, I was wondering if he had somehow sprung a leak. I knew I was stalling, how much of a rush would you be in to put on someone else's piss soaked clothes? Yeah didn't think so. I still had to get moving, a dumpster pretty much screamed, PEE HERE, to a man. Soon, someone else would come, and for a second that sounded like a good idea, but this time I would knock his ass out *before* he started to go.

"Shit," I mumbled. I could hear voices, I couldn't tell if they were getting closer but I couldn't risk it. My snake-draining buddy seemed to finally be closing in on empty. I waited a few seconds more as the normally shaken droplets made their way down his side, then I unceremoniously picked him up under his shoulders and dumped him into the trash. I was happy there were at least a few bags at the bottom; somewhat so he wouldn't get hurt further, but mostly so his body wouldn't make a large 'bonging' sound as he hit bottom.

The man's shirt was the traditional gas station attendant blue button down, it even had his name embroidered on it—that was actually not a good thing for me. What were the odds that there were two 'Horatios' in this convoy? And I'm sorry, but who the fuck names their kid Horatio? His childhood must have been a blast. I put his shirt on, not buttoning it for exactly three reasons. First, because I hoped that leaving it open would obscure his name; second, because the bottom front of it was soaked and this way I could keep it mostly off myself; and third, but far from least, I was betting that Horatio's nickname was 'Stretch.' I couldn't have buttoned the thing up if I had wanted to. There was a good four inches of gap between button hole and button. I looked down at the pants; my guess was they were going to be as equally ill-fitting. It was sort of a blessing, because as long as they stayed unbuttoned it kept the majority of wet material off of me, but what were the fucking odds that I would waylay a six-foot-two man that had the waist and chest of a twelve-year-old girl? I thought about pulling him out of the dumpster so I could smack him one more time. He was actually making me regret giving up my jean shorts. I was as low on body fat as I had ever been in my life, yet this man's pants still made me feel like I needed to join Jenny Craig. I knew I was in for a world class struggle when I felt them tugging on my calves.

By the time I pulled them up over my ass, I had lost enough circulation in my lower extremities to be of concern. I could only take air in small, measured doses. The zipper moved maybe one or two teeth up and that was it, the gap between the button and button hole for the pants could not be bridged. I had a couple of things going for me, apparently 'Stretch' had also been losing weight and these pants were 'pre' zombie invasion. He had, at some point, needed to get a belt and luckily it was more my sized as opposed to his. The belt would hide a fair amount of my skin showing, plus, his shirt had that front part that hangs down so you can tuck them in. I have no idea what that's called but as long as no Marilyn Monroe-type breezes started, I might be alright. Although running was out of the question, I felt like Morticia from the Addams Family.

You want to know what the kicker was? This was how I figured out that God has a sense of humor. The guy had a baseball cap which was great, I didn't dare take off my Eliza-screening tin foil hat, but I couldn't imagine walking out in the midst of all those truckers wearing it either. I grabbed the guy's cap, even more reluctant to put it on than the urine-infused clothes—the familiar, dreaded, loathed, hated 'NY' logo of the New York Yankees stared back at me with contempt. This was about the last straw; I almost said 'fuck it.' There ain't nothing worth donning that thing. The only thing that wasn't small on Stretch was his damn hat, the guy had a head the size of a watermelon, and of course he had a non-adjustable, fitted hat, why wouldn't he? At least it would safely cover the foil, and the foil would act as a barrier to whatever diseases a Yankee fan was apt to carry.

"Forgive me, Ted," I said, alluding to the Great One, Ted Williams, as I pulled the damn thing over my head. Odds were, if I looked hard enough, Bucky 'Fucking' Dent probably signed it. The only thing that saved the whole thing was his boots; I could finally rid myself of Stephanie-the-Amazonian woman's shoes. He had boots that, while a little bigger than I needed at ten-and-a-half, would still suit me nicely.

"Here goes nothing," I said as I stepped out from behind the dumpster. A big man easily double my size was heading my way, his clothes would have made it look like I was swimming in them. It still would have been preferable. He did not look at me as he walked past, that's a traditional male custom, if we are within a few moments of grasping our members we do not make eye contact with males of our species. Not entirely sure why; maybe it has something to do with a small dose of homophobia or, more than likely, it's just an intimate moment of sweet release that we do not wish to share with others.

I rounded the corner of the gas station and realized that I'd never had need to worry. There were so many truckers that it was easy to get lost in the crowd. *Now what genius?* I berated myself. I was there for some reason. I just had no clue what for. I circled around, catching snippets of conversations, but never really joining any of them.

"...then she said that it smelled like shit on Astroturf and I...."

"...hauling nuclear waste and dumping it on the south side of the Grand C..."

"...some eyeliner and panty hose it feels great..."

What? The guy looked like a professional wrestler and he was telling a group of five other men. I must have missed a fair amount of that conversation. I was glad I had slowed down enough to listen a little bit to the Randy Savage lookalike. I had changed direction just enough until I came upon what had to be Horatio's rig. I'd love to say that it was because of my extraordinary detective skills, but the giant, red rig had Horatio's Highway Haulers emblazoned in two-foot high lettering across the entire trailer—even I couldn't have missed it. I walked up to it as if I owned it, which according to the keys that were jabbing me through my front pocket only confirmed that suspicion.

"What are the odds his last name, MY last name is Hornblower?" I asked. It was worse: Heimerdinger. "You're kidding right?" I asked as I ran my hand over the pin striping. Horatio 'Slight' Heimerdinger. How many times can a kid get beat up? I hoped he didn't have a riding partner as I stepped up on to the running board and opened the door. Well, I had to give it to 'Slight', he ran a tidy ship. I looked around the entire cab. It was gorgeous, then it dawned on me that I really should take it...Horatio would want me to.

"Who are you?" a voice asked tremulously, I almost fell backwards out the door.

"Department of Transportation," I said, recovering quickly. "Doing a vehicle inspection, I'll only be a moment."

"Where's Slight?" the female voice asked.

"Umm cursory dumpster inspection," I answered. It was all I could think of on short notice.

"Why are you wearing his clothes?"

I was starting to get a little flustered that I had been so blatantly caught. I did the only thing I knew how to do, I went on the offensive. I was turning towards the sleeper portion of the cab as I was talking. "Is there a reason why you feel the need to ask so many damn questions?" Then I gasped. A young woman, more like a girl was handcuffed to a handhold. "Shit...are you alright?" I asked going back towards her. I stopped when she flinched.

"Who are you?" She asked.

"I guess I'm the guy that's coming to save you. Do

you know where the key is for those things?" I asked, pointing to her restrictive jewelry.

She was eyeing me distrustfully. "How do I know that?"

"Do you think I would be willingly wearing clothes that were three full sizes too small?"

"The cuff key is on his key ring," she told me.

"This key ring?" I said as I tried to fish them out of my pocket, but the pants were so tight that I couldn't even fit two fingers in to try and pull them out.

"You might want to hurry."

"I'm trying, it's like they're super glued in place."

"Horatio is on his way back."

"Are you precognitive?" I asked.

"What? No." She thrust her chin towards the front windshield. Horatio was surrounded by three or four other truckers. He was trying to talk, but his shattered jaw was making it difficult. However, his slender legs seemed to work just fine as a growing throng was heading our way.

"Turn away," I told the girl, she again eyed me suspiciously but did as I asked. I undid my belt and rolled the top of my pants down so that I could get to the pocket. I ripped the pocket completely free and the keys plopped into my hand. I quickly rolled the pants back up as best I could and fumbled around until I got her cuffs off.

She rubbed her raw wrists. I saw her looking at the passenger door.

"I won't stop you. Would you have a chance out there?"

She shook her head 'no'. "You a trucker?" she asked.

"I've driven before."

"On a scale of one to ten, ten meaning you could qualify as an *Ice Road Trucker* and one meaning you like to pull on the horn, how would you rate your skill level?"

"Six maybe seven," I stretched.

She looked at me long and hard.

"Four."

"Really?"

"Three and a half."

"Move over," she told me.

"What are you like fifteen?"

"Twenty and I've had my CDL for two years."

I moved over.

Horatio and his growing throng started moving a little quicker when they noticed the twin stacks on his rig begin to blow smoke as my new traveling partner started the engine. I had no clue how she was going to get the truck out of the massive parking lot. I would have had a hard time with my jeep. There were people, gear, and trucks all over the place. She really didn't care as she turned the big wheel and began to navigate us out of there taking out the occasional cooler or grill, a tent or two and maybe a few small cars, it was too difficult to tell as I kept my hand over my face a fair amount of the time.

"Well I could have done that," I told her as she smashed a small Geo against the front of one of the trucks.

She gave me the finger.

I heard a shot or two and ducked down accordingly. My driver never did.

"Warning shots," she sneered. "They wouldn't dare shoot me."

"And me?" I asked.

"You'd probably be better off ducking."

"Who are you?"

"I don't think you want to know."

"Are you an IRS agent?" I asked her.

"What? What's the matter with you?" she asked. The cab was bouncing around with the truck hitting its fair share of things as we approached the exit.

"Are they going to chase us?" I asked as I looked in the side mirror.

"Oh, I would imagine to the ends of the earth."

I turned to look at her.

"Glad you got involved?" she asked, looking over

quickly and smiling.

I smiled back weakly.

"Oh they'll chase me, mister."

"Mike," I told her.

She paused for a moment and stole a quick glance at me before she spoke again. "Okay, Mike, they'll chase me...but not yet. You're safe for the moment. I'll drop you off when it's safe and you can go about your merry little way."

"Who will chase you exactly?" I asked, a pit of suspicion beginning to form in my stomach.

"Listen, the less you know, the better off you are," she said to me.

"Wow, that's usually my line."

She again looked over at me—this time a little longer as we had finally found our way out of the station. She was right; we did not have any company...at least for the time being.

"Listen, I came here with someone, I left him sleeping by the side of the road."

She looked at me incredulously. "He's sleeping while you're navigating your way through enemy territory looking like your blind momma dressed you?"

"Once you meet him you'll understand."

I directed her to where John was. He was still snoozing deeply when we pulled up. The girl—I guess young woman—helped me to put him up in the cab and finally the sleeper in the back. The truckers at the rest stop were watching us but none were in pursuit. I could only think of one person (I mean *thing*) that could put that much fear into people that they wouldn't even act.

I went with the direct approach. "What's your involvement with Eliza?"

The truck which had just started rolling came to a quick halt. "Did you hear the trucker's talking about her?"

So my suspicion was confirmed. I could have done without that little affirmation. "Let's just say I've had my own encounters with her."

"Mike…as in Michael Talbot?" she asked. "Well, I can see by your reaction I got that right. She believes you're dead."

"Oh, if I had a nickel for every time someone thought I was dead, I'd have a quarter."

"You really are Mike?"

"One and the same."

She looked disappointed. "I expected more," she said as she got the truck rolling again.

'Well fuck you, too!' I wanted to say. "Who just got your ass out of that jam?" I asked in defense.

"Me."

"Okay, you drove. Who gave you the ability to do that?"

"You're right, I'm sorry, let's start over. My name is Azile," she said as she stuck her hand out for me to shake. I gave it a couple of pumps before she had to use it to shift gears. "We heading to Maine?"

"Are all those trucks heading there?"

She nodded tersely.

"Shit, Philly first."

"Are you sure?"

"I promised John back there that I'd look for his wife."

"You love your family?" she asked.

"What kind of question is that?" I asked hotly.

"Eliza and her band of idiots are heading there soon. I would think that you would want to do all in your power to get there first and help them."

"I promised John. Philly is on the way, she's there or she isn't."

"You know what the odds of her being alive are."

"I do, that still doesn't negate the promise I made to him."

"Is your moral compass always stuck tight in the upright position?"

"Yeah, it's a character flaw for sure."

"Fine, we'll do it your way."

"Are we going as fast as this rig can go?" I asked Azile.

"As much as I want to push it."

"That'll have to do." I held the offending Yankees hat out my window. I was hoping the wind would shred it, no such luck. Now I had to hope that, as I released it into the wild, that a pack of hyenas would stumble across it, tear it up and eat it and then crap it out over an active geyser, or volcano—either would work in this scenario. Then I pulled my hand with the cap back in. As much as I dreaded the hat, it still beat out the tin-foil, not by much mind you, but it was close. "Shit," I muttered as I put the damn thing back on.

We had been driving a couple of hours. Azile and I had not spoken at all. The concern I felt for my family was placing a giant pit in my stomach. I was delaying getting to them on nothing more than the pipedream of a man who had long ago lost the majority of his reasoning abilities to a wide variety of recreational drug use. We were passing a fair number of abandoned cars, and more than once, I thought about telling Azile to let me off so that I could get one and go.

I kept turning around to the slumbering form of John. He may have tried to kill me a couple of times, but he saved me a couple of times too. I owed it to him to keep the promise I had given. And I didn't trust Azile to do it, there was something about the woman I could not put my finger on. She played a part in the drama for sure, but whether it was a cameo, supporting, or starring role was yet to be determined. I thought I had enough of a bead on her that if I left her to her own devices she would kick John out shortly after I left and would then be on her *own* merry little way to parts unknown.

I could hear John moving about behind us. He sat up and stretched. "When'd we put a bed in the Gremlin, Mike?" he asked, looking over at me. "And who's the girl?" he stage-whispered.

"Her name is Azile and we're in a tractor trailer now," I told him. I was concerned it might freak him out a little, I needn't have been. He scooted up so that he was sitting at the edge of the bed almost between me and Azile.

"This is much better than the car," he said, never once asking how our driver came into the picture or how we came to be in the truck.

"We're about an hour out of Philadelphia," I told him. He didn't say anything, but his hands wrapped tight around the lip of the bed. "It'll be alright, Trip, we'll find her."

Azile chose that very moment to let loose with a heavy sigh as if the whole event was an exercise in futility.

I shot her a glance that she completely ignored.

"What are we hauling?" John asked, possibly as a way to avoid Azile's negativity if he noticed at all.

"I honestly don't know," I said, looking over to Azile.

"Don't look at me, I've been a prisoner for longer than I can remember."

I thought that was a strange response but I didn't ask for her to elaborate. Now I was really curious as to what we were hauling also.

The truck began to slow down and finally came to a halt.

"Go check," Azile said to me.

I had my hand on the door and had just opened it, I could hear John coming up behind me, he was curious too.

"Relax, I won't leave without you." She said smiling.

"That really doesn't make me feel any better. If you were the type of person to leave us stranded, you sure wouldn't care about a little lie to make it happen," I told her.

"You're probably right," she said as she looked at her side view mirror. "Why don't you go check before someone decides to see who we are?"

"Wow, man, she's a mean one. Where'd you find her?" John asked me as he stepped down.

"You do know you're less than six feet from her," I

told him.

"Do you think she heard me?" John asked in all seriousness; in response, Azile bleated the horn.

"Probably not," I told him.

"Good," he said as we walked to the back of the rig.

I kept looking for something to hold onto if she did decide to leave. There wasn't anything I would trust life or limb to. I stared long and hard at those rear doors. I was remembering what Eliza liked to put in her trucks.

"What're we doing out here?" John asked.

That was about all the catalyst I needed to get moving. I placed my hand on the latch, John had moved closer. "Hey, Trip, why don't you move back a little. If any of the funky people are in here, run back up to the cab."

"What are you going to do?" he asked as he took a couple of steps backwards.

"I'll be right behind you." I was thinking we were safe, I didn't hear anything moving back there…unless they were packed so tightly that they couldn't move which meant they would start spilling out the moment I opened the door. But the bigger piece that had me pretty convinced we were safe was I didn't smell anything either. If there were that many zombies this close, the stink would have had a physical presence.

"Ready?" I asked John.

"Hurry up back there, will you!" Azile shouted.

I pulled the latch upwards and pulled the door back.

"Holy shit!" I yelled.

CHAPTER TWENTY-SIX

Eliza and Tomas

"What do you mean she's gone?" Eliza asked.

Her man in charge of the convoy was a three hundred pound bruiser that went by the handle 'Kong'. The last time he had been as scared as he was now, he had been seven and had accidentally lit his garage on fire. His mother had sent him to his room, telling him that he would have to deal with his father. Kong's father was a coal miner and did not suffer stupidity from anyone.

Kong—known better as Buddy back in his early years—had cried for five hours straight waiting for his dad to come home, and with good reason. Mr. Reynolds had laid down a belt whipping that on occasion still made Kong wince. Right now, he thought he'd be lucky if the worst of what he had to deal with was an ass whipping as he looked into the pitiless eyes of Eliza.

He took a quick breath before he spoke. "She got some help. A man came and broke the driver's jaw, took his clothes and his truck."

"Did anyone get a good look at this man?" Tomas asked.

Kong liked Tomas more than Eliza, but it was by only a matter of degrees. Like how one prefers a pit viper over a black mamba. "No. Horatio, the driver, was relieving himself when he got jumped."

"Bring him to me," Eliza said, seemingly bored with the proceedings.

Kong had been attempting to shield Horatio. His ploy

was only going to get him so far. "Eliza, my mistress, Horatio is a good driver and they're hard to find right now."

"I merely wish to ask him a question or two," Eliza replied.

Eliza was not that good of an actress. Kong knew the lie for what it was. He motioned for the men that had been caring for Horatio to bring him forward.

Horatio shuffled forward; he had never met Eliza, but he knew enough about her to be concerned. His eyes had already blackened and his jaw had puffed to nearly double its size giving him a cartoonish appearance.

Horatio had planned to stay strong, but one look at his employer and he had dropped his head.

Eliza reached out and grabbed his shattered jaw in her hand. Kong made as if to move and help the driver, then thought better of it as Eliza turned a questioning gaze on him. He wisely placed his hands down by his sides. Horatio was screaming in pain, as much as a man with a broken jaw can.

Tears rippled down his face and coated Eliza's hand, yet she did not yield her prize. "What did the man that did this to you look like?" she asked softly.

"Mmmfff..." Horatio sobbed.

"Mistress, he cannot speak." He almost added 'with your hand clamped over his face' but decided to leave that part to the wayside.

"Perhaps you should get a pen and paper," Tomas added.

Kong motioned for one of his men to get them. Eliza did not let go until the man returned some moments later. Horatio had to be held up as he nearly collapsed to his knees. His color took on the hue of old, yellowed parchment paper.

"Write quickly," Tomas prodded as Horatio tried to gather himself up and move past the majority of the pain.

'I'm sorry.' Horatio scribbled quickly, a child cresting on Red Bull would have written with less jitter.

Kong watched as the cold in Eliza's eyes turned to heat. "Description, Horatio. What did the man look like?" he asked his driver.

'Medium build....strong...shorts, tight shirt. Skin was pinkish like he'd been burned. Patchy facial hair, missing an eyebrow.' He wrote diligently. He pushed the pain a little further back. 'Tin foil hat.'

Tomas laughed at the last part.

"Something funny, brother?" Eliza asked.

"Michael Talbot is alive and apparently well, sister."

"HOW COULD HE KNOW?" she screamed. "He stops here and takes the most important truck...how could he know?"

"Do you still doubt divine intervention?" Tomas asked.

Kong had doubted his alliance with Eliza from the first day, and now, if the other side was the one God favored, he had chosen poorly.

"This changes nothing!" she raged.

"This changes everything," Tomas replied.

"Mistress?" Kong asked.

"I want the trucks ready to leave within the next three days," she said turning to walk off.

He would lose a good ten percent of his fleet due to maintenance issues if they left that soon, but he would not cross Eliza. "And what of Horatio?" No sooner had he asked the question than he wished that he could retract it. She would have forgotten if he had just left it alone. Tomas bowed his head for a fraction of a second.

Eliza spun back. "No truck, no need for a driver," she said as she again gripped his jaw.

She clenched her hand tight until Horatio's teeth started to pop from his mouth. The bones in his jaw liquefied as she ground them together. Horatio had long since passed out as she made sure nothing structurally was left on the bottom part of his mouth. When she let go, he fell to the ground heavily. Kong had to turn away; the sight of Horatio's caved-in face was not something he would soon forget.

There was a widening circle around Eliza, Tomas, Kong, and the dying Horatio. Those that had been curious as to how it would all play out now wanted nothing to do with it.

"Do not fail me again," Eliza said to Kong.

He nodded.

Eliza and Tomas were heading back towards their car.

"The tinfoil is ingenious, don't you think?" Tomas asked, goading his sister.

"Why will he not die, Tomas? You know him better than I."

"I have known for a long time, sister, the man's importance in this battle. I cannot begin to understand God's design." For the first time, Tomas thought he saw doubt creep into Eliza.

"Do you know how it turns out?" she asked.

His heart ached. This was the closest to *his* 'Lizzie' he had seen in nearly five centuries, and still he thought she might be acting for his benefit.

"I am but a player in this game, Eliza."

"I am *not* a player," she said defiantly. "I make the rules."

"Then someone is changing the game."

"We'll see about that."

Tomas was not happy with the set of Eliza's jaw. She had something in mind, and it did not sit well with him. "Where are we going?" he asked as he started the car.

"Drive, I'll let you know when we have arrived."

***

"Eliza, it has been hours. Perhaps if you told me where we were going?" Tomas asked.

"I go to seek counsel. If Jehovah has broken covenant, then I will offer his counterpart the same transgression."

Tomas brought the car to a screeching halt. "What

you do now is beyond reprehension, Eliza. But even you cannot think involving the Dark One would benefit anyone…least of all the person making the bargain."

"I merely wish to talk with the Fork-tongued One. No agreement will be struck."

"Eliza, no!" Tomas begged.

"Just drive, the sooner we get to New Orleans, the sooner I can go and kill Michael Talbot AGAIN!"

CHAPTER TWENTY-SEVEN

Mike Journal Entry 10

"Rune stones, man!" John said as he jumped on the back.

"What?" I asked. I hadn't even seen the stones, and considering they were the size of a man, that was not easy to do. My eyes were transfixed on the green military boxes. I ran back to the cab of the truck and grabbed the crowbar I had seen resting under the seat. I can guarantee anyone that is reading this journal that they would have been hard pressed to find any kid in any country during any Christmas throughout the ages that was more excited to open a box than I was that day.

"M-240s and M-16s," I mumbled, possibly drooling on myself as I placed the crowbar in a slight opening.

It was too much to hope that the markings on the box matched the contents. John was a few feet away rubbing the rocks, he was muttering something. Azile was alternating between watching our backs and checking out the contents.

"Holy fucking shit," I said as the top popped free.

"What is that?" John asked, taking a second to look over.

"John, what I'm holding here is an M-240 machinegun. It'll shoot in the neighborhood of a hundred to two hundred rounds a minute without blinking and six-fifty a minute if I really want to put the pedal to the metal!" I answered as I hefted the twenty-five pound block of death metal out of the container.

"That's good then?" John asked.

"What?" I asked him incredulously. "Okay, let's put this in terms you'll understand. I feel about finding this like you would if this crate was full of prime California bud."

"There's weed in there?" John asked, pushing me to the side. He was mighty disappointed when he realized that wasn't the case. "Why would you lie to me, man?" he asked with pleading eyes, like maybe I had stashed the find before telling him.

"I was just comparing how I feel about finding this to how you would feel finding some weed."

"Not cool, man." He returned to the Rune stones, I suppose for solace.

"Bullets?" Azile asked.

"Shit," I said. I had been so enamored with the machinegun that I completely forgot about the rounds. Without them, this just became a very heavy club.

"There's a box next to him that says 5.56," Azile said, pointing to the left of John.

"No good, this takes 7.62. That'll work for the M-16s, though," I said, looking deeper into the truck. "This must be their rolling armory…and now it's ours. Well if this doesn't help to change the tide, I don't know what will." Nobody was listening, but I was still talking. This was too big a find to keep bottled up inside. We now had a machinegun and about two dozen M-16s.

"Just use more of them," John replied in all seriousness.

"That'd kind of be like me telling you to just smoke more of the marijuana plant stalk," I told him.

"The plant stalk doesn't have any THC. You could smoke it all day long and not get high," he said. "I've tried."

"Same thing…sort of…with the bullets," I said as I pulled a tarp to the side. There were three more stones making a total of five and two beautiful crates marked 'disintegrating metallic split-linked belt (M13 links), 7.62 in a ratio of 3 rounds to 1 tracer.' "I think I'm going to need some time alone," I told John and Azile as I gently stroked the box. Azile laughed, which was nice, it was the first time I'd seen any emotion out of her, that didn't somehow revolve around anger. John started to walk out of the truck. "I was kidding, man," I told him.

"Wait! Are you sure those are rune stones?" I asked John.

"We should get going," Azile motioned.

"Sure, you can tell by the markings," he said as he ran his hand across the raised etchings.

Azile was getting down from the truck. "Hold on," I told her. She momentarily eyed the doors, maybe figuring if she could close and lock them before I could run to the end. She either figured she couldn't get it done, or that it wasn't such a good idea in the first place. "What part do you play in this?" I asked her point blank.

"I was a prisoner," she told me flatly.

"I gathered that much on my own," I told her. At first I just figured she was a plaything for a demented, perverted truck driver, but she didn't have the feel of 'victim' on her. "There's more here," I stated as I began to wonder. Her name which was unique began to stick in my head. "How do you spell your name?"

"What's that got to do with anything?" she shot back.

"Humor me."

"Is she going to tell jokes now?" John asked.

"Azile!" I snarled. John and Azile jumped.

"A-Z-I-L-E," she said as she put her head down.

I rocked on my feet, John thankfully caught me.

"What's the matter, man? That wasn't even funny." John asked as he propped me back up.

"There's more going on here than you're telling. You just happen to have the same name as Eliza only in reverse?" I asked.

"Whoa, that's freaky. Who's Eliza?" John asked.

"My father knew her," she said, looking back at me defiantly.

"Let's start at the beginning," I said.

"Well, scientists believe that the entire universe—"

"John! Her, not you," I said.

"That's just it, Ponch, the beginning is the same for all of us. That's what makes us all connected," he said proudly.

"My mother was five months pregnant with me when Eliza turned my father. According to my mother, my father visited her once in those last four months and told her that the only way she could protect me was to name me Azile. My mother was so petrified that she believed him completely. She said she had never seen someone so soulless…that was….until I was seven."

"Eliza," I said.

"She and my father came to visit. Eliza killed my mother as my father watched, then she grabbed me." Azile flipped her hair over to show two long-healed, puckered wounds on her neck. "She had just sunk her teeth into me when something in my father, some vestige of humanity showed itself and he begged her not to kill me…that I was even named after her. She backhanded my father so hard that he slid across the floor of the kitchen."

***

"What is your name, child?" Eliza said as she stroked the young girl's hair.

"Azile," the girl said holding her chin high. Her mother was dead—a small pool of blood by her neck. Her father (in biological terms only) was groaning, his back up against the far wall in the kitchen.

"Azile! How rich!" Eliza said delightfully. "Perhaps I should let you live, if for no other reason than to see what happens.

Azile did not understand the monster's words. She could see beyond the veneer of the beautiful woman to the cruelty and horror that lay beneath. The twisted, gnarled thing shrank away from that gaze.

"Well if you are not to die, then it shall be your father," Eliza said as she strode over to Azile's father. She looked back, waiting for some sort of response. Azile stood defiantly, the only person she cared for in life already dead; her father meant nothing to her. She watched as Eliza ripped the man's throat open. His gurgled cries for help went unheeded.

"I believe we shall meet again," Eliza said as she patted the girl's head and left.

***

"I saw her for what she was and she let me live because of it…because of the horror of it," Azile said as she covered her face.

"I'm sorry for everything you've gone through." I hopped down off the truck.

"But?" she asked looking up at me.

"You tell me."

"Group hug," John said, climbing down off the trailer.

I acquiesced, because if I didn't, he would have gone on about it for hours.

"After Eliza killed my mother, I vowed revenge. I knew she was something out of a faerie tale, so that's what I decided I must become to defeat her."

"A unicorn?" John asked, looking on her head for the horn.

We both stopped to look at him.

"A witch," she stated. "I studied the Wiccan ways of white light."

"So you're more like Glinda the Good Witch?" John asked.

"Glinda wasn't so good," I said off-handedly. "I'm just saying, she was happy when Dorothy killed the other witch. She basically told Dorothy to take property that wasn't hers and then sent her off on a mission to kill another witch that she was enemies with. If she was such a good witch why didn't she do it herself?"

John and Azile were not giving me flattering looks.

"That's merely my take," I said, trying my best to extradite myself from my comment.

"Since my mother's murder," Azile continued, "my life has been devoted to stopping Eliza."

I nodded in agreement. "What happened?"

"How did I become locked in that truck you mean?"

"That's as good a thing to explain as any."

"I've been searching for Eliza for thirteen years now. Always practicing my art, always getting stronger when that ultimate day would come and I could exact my revenge."

I looked at her questioningly.

"Yeah, it didn't work out quite as well as I'd hoped. I got my CDL a couple of years ago because it would give me a chance to drive around the country. I could sense her presence, almost like a whiff of ghost perfume in a haunted house. The stink of her was all over that truck stop."

"So you had joined up in the hopes of getting a glimpse?" I asked.

"Oh, it was more than hoping for a glimpse. I had a sacrificial knife, supposedly belonged to an Ute Shaman. She came to see how Kong—what kind of fucking name is that?" she asked as an aside, "was doing. She had a small circle of drivers around her, and I circled around so I was coming up behind her. I had that blade out and was going to drive it between her shoulder blades."

"I don't think that would have worked."

"Maybe, maybe not, but it would have made me feel better."

"I'm with you on that. I think your knife is back there," I said, pointing to the back of the truck.

"Are you sure?" she said, her eyes getting big.

"Beside the stones—which we'll get to—there was something wrapped up in leather roughly the size of a butcher knife."

"And you didn't think to tell me?" she asked hotly.

"Umm, let me think...ultimate weapon of destruction,

or a small item wrapped in dirty leather. Wow, how could I have been so stupid?"

Azile was already running into the back of the truck. "That's it!" she yelled excitedly. She unwrapped it quickly and held it up. I wouldn't have been overly surprised if bolts of lightning rained down from the heavens. I even took a quick glance skyward to see if there were any threatening clouds.

"So how'd you go from would be assassin to captive?"

"Bitch knew I was there all along. Apparently we share a connection because of the bite."

John pulled out a medium-sized, folded up piece of tin foil and feverishly began to fashion it into a hat.

"What is he doing?" she asked me when John tried to put it on her head.

"Save us all, you'll understand once it's on."

"I really don't want to belong to the lithium league," she said as she fended John off.

"Try it for a second."

She allowed John to place the hat on her head. Instantly, her expression changed from disbelief to bewilderment to relief. She quickly removed it, then placed it back on. "How?"

"No clue. John could probably tell you."

He shrugged his shoulders. "Beats me, saw it on a television show once when I was a kid."

"I guess I should have figured as much," I said aloud.

"For some reason, she didn't kill me. She took the stones out of my trailer and had Kong put them in Horatio's truck, then Kong made Horatio handcuff me to his bedrail."

I was staring at her.

"No, no, he was actually fairly decent as far as murdering thugs go. Never once tried to have his way with me, apparently even scum have certain platitudes they won't stoop below. But who knows, some of them were getting a little antsy. I'm sure if given the chance a few of them would have. Luckily I'd only been there a couple of days before you came along."

"I haven't figured all this shit out...not by a long shot. But there's something more going on here. There was a half dozen different ways we could have left this morning and why I felt so compelled to check out that truck stop I'm still not sure. Then Horatio needing to take a piss just then. I find his truck and you. People win the lottery with smaller odds."

"You should play the lottery," John said. "If your luck is that good, you're bound to win something."

"Well let's hold on to that and hope it extends to finding your wife."

"Azile is married to a woman? How very progressive," John said.

"Your wife, John."

"Oh, well then let's get going," he said. "Where is she again?"

CHAPTER TWENTY-EIGHT

Eliza and Tomas

Eliza and Tomas walked among the gravestones of the long interred residents of the Rue Morgue, as calm in their surroundings as new parents would be in their infant's bedroom. Eliza strode with a purpose, Tomas kept up if only to try and keep her from her own insanity.

"There it is," Eliza said with an edge of excitement as she gazed upon the mortuary doorway.

"Abaddon?" Tomas asked, looking at the name engraved at the top of the tomb.

"It means 'The Destroyer'," Eliza said as she pulled the rusted gate open.

"The evilness of this place surpasses even you, Eliza. I beg of you one last time, let us be gone from this place."

"It does have a certain charm doesn't it?" she asked as a large cobweb bathed her face and head much like a wedding veil.

Eliza took the candles from Tomas. She placed them in the form of a pentagram. Latin verse flowed from her mouth as she began her incantations. She stopped long enough to open one eye. "You may want to be in the center with me," she told her brother. He reluctantly got in the circle. "Do not step out of here, no matter what the Deceiver says. Do you understand me, Tomas?" Eliza asked.

Tomas nodded his head. He had been close to God once and did not want to taint that experience with what he was about to bear witness to.

"Tomas, answer me. I am about to complete my

invocation."

Tomas nodded numbly.

"Good," Eliza said as she started back up.

The air got heavy with the smell of burnt cordite and sulfur. The room took on a dull reddish glow as the walls themselves seemed to burn with the light.

"Eliza my pet, why do you call me forward?" a voice borne along the vocal chords of a thousand snakes issued forth.

"I have never been your pet."

The snake hissed in laughter. "You are evil borne from evil, you have *always* been my pet."

"I seek advice," Eliza said, changing the subject from something she did not want to hear.

"When did I become a psychologist? You want advice, I will give it to you, but not freely. Give me willingly what lies between your breasts."

Eliza clutched at the blood stone she wore. "Jehovah has broken covenant."

"What?" The snake roared. The walls glowed brighter.

"He is directly helping a human," Eliza said.

"You have proof of this?" An image of a snake head appeared and hovered close to the edge of the protective circle.

Eliza laid out every detail she thought led to divine intervention up to and including his death and rebirth.

"This is all very interesting, and I would not put it past him, but I fail to see how this affects me?"

"He has broken the laws of nature and you *fail* to see how this affects you?" Eliza asked with vehemence.

"I loathe the zombies, my child."

Eliza winced at his use of 'my child.' He sounded too much like a father she had spent five centuries trying to forget.

"They are dim-witted and dull, they are not easily led astray. I have never had so much fun as when I twist a

Catholic priest into a world of perversion. To twist God's *messengers*, ahh, now those are the moments I yearn for. This human creature which He loves so much is so fallible I would have thought he would have scrapped the entire failed experiment of them by now." The snake head turned into a priest regaled in a black suit with a white collar, his eyelids half closed as he enjoyed some unseen sexual ministrations. "This might be one time where I would be on His side."

Eliza was beside herself. "You cannot be serious?"

"If He is trying to turn the tide so that man can once again be the dominant species, then yes. Before His creation came into being, I only controlled the lower animals—snakes, spiders, rats and cats. Man is so malleable and will do almost anything to anyone to get ahead. They are so wrapped up in themselves that they fail to realize just how little time they will walk the earth. And an eternity in my domain? Well that's just a bonus for me. He gets so upset when He loses one of His children to me."

"This was a waste of time," Eliza said as she prepared to revoke her incantation.

"You desire this Michael Talbot and his family to stay safe?" the priest asked Tomas.

"More than anything." Tomas spoke up.

"I can make that happen."

"I have no soul with which to bargain, Great Deceiver," Tomas said.

"Purgatory is a realm in which I have full access."

"He lies," Eliza said. "He can only go there if given permission."

The priest hissed. "Yes…with your permission I can retrieve your soul and we can make a bargain."

Tomas was looking like he was weighing his options.

"You cannot be serious, Tomas. You would give up eternity for a mortal and his family?"

"You will have a seat next to mine," the priest said. As he waved his hand, an image of Tomas sitting next to him atop the tortured souls of the damned showed on the far wall.

"You are a fool, Tomas!" Eliza shouted.

"Is he, my daughter?" The priest turned into Eliza's father. "I offer him true immortality, to rule alongside me."

"We are immortal, Deceiver!" Eliza spat.

"Ah, now you lie, my child. To be immortal implies that you do not have the ability to die…which I most assuredly guarantee you that you do. I have waited patiently for you to join me. I have set aside such wondrous things for the two of us. If He is helping to facilitate that, then I may have to thank Him." Eliza's father turned back into the form of the priest.

The echoes of the Destroyer's laughter could still be heard as Eliza recanted her invocation.

"Did that go as planned, dear sister?" Tomas asked as he stepped out of the tomb. Her response was icy silence as they got back in the car.

CHAPTER TWENTY-NINE

Mike Journal Entry 11

Azile drove the truck like the pro she was, getting us through some rough patches of choked traffic jams mostly unscathed. We saw the occasional zombie, but with food so scarce, they were going to stasis mode more and more. We only had one run in of any sort while we were on the road: two motorcyclists who looked like they'd seen better days rolled up alongside us.

One pulled out a large caliber pistol and waved it around, making sure that I saw it. I started laughing my ass off as I raised my M-240. He veered off so hard that I thought he was going to flip his bike. I saw him waving his partner off as they both stopped.

"What'd they want?" Azile asked with some concern.

"I guess they just wanted to say hi," I told her.

"You do know that the M-16 is a much easier weapon to handle don't you?" she asked.

"Don't take this away from me, Azile. When am I ever going to be able to walk around with a machinegun again?" I asked her back.

"Have it your way," she replied.

"Just like Burger King," John said. "Although that's not always the case. I once asked them for McDonald's french fries with my Whopper, because their fries taste like used socks and the kid behind the counter called me a hippie and maybe if I didn't have tin foil on my head that I would realize what burger joint I was in. I knew where I was," John said as if he needed to defend himself to us. "BK has better hamburgers and Mickey Ds has better french fries. Is it too much to ask to have the both of them together?"

I nodded in agreement. I couldn't even remember how many times I'd had that exact thought. I sincerely hoped there weren't too many more thoughts John and I shared in common.

"Did you ask for extra pickles?"

"Pickles give you whooping cough. Everybody knows that," he informed me.

I looked over to Azile for confirmation to see if he was speaking the truth, she shook her head slightly.

It was a couple of hours later when Azile spoke, at some point I had dozed off. "Now what?" she asked as she reached across John and shook my shoulder.

I brought the machinegun up rapidly only to notice that the truck was idling and I was looking at the 'Welcome to Philadelphia' sign.

"John…what now, buddy?" I asked him. He was staring at the sign also, although I wasn't sure if he was cognitively registering it.

"We get Stephanie!" he said excitedly.

"Philly is a pretty big place, Trip, any idea where we should start?" I asked him.

"Are you kidding me?" Azile shot out. "The stoner doesn't even know which direction to go? How are we going to find her? We can't waste our time on a wild goose chase!" Her voice was raising and I think she was approaching flip-out.

"Azile…Azile," I said more forcibly when she didn't listen the first time.

John's eyes were wet. "I know she's still alive," he said with dejection.

"I know, we'll find her," I told him, giving Azile a healthy dose of stink eye over his shoulder.

"We don't have time for this, Mike," she told me much more softly. "Your family is in danger."

"So is his," I told her.

"Eliza will get away," she said resting her head on the steering wheel.

"You haven't met the Talbots yet, they're not just going to roll over and allow her to do as she wants. We've got some time."

"If you say so, chief," Azile surrendered. "Where to then?"

"She owns the Courtyard in downtown Philadelphia," John stated.

"You mean works there?" Azile asked for clarification.

"No, John and the missus are loaded. If he says 'own' he means it."

"Let's start there. Do you have an address?" she asked him.

"To where?" John asked her back.

"The hotel."

"You think she's there?" John asked against hope.

"You got a better place to start…I'm all ears," Azile told him.

"Your ears are actually quite small," he told her as he looked at the side of her head.

"What?" she asked.

"And she called me the stoner."

"It's an expression. John." I tried to head off the next five minutes of explanations.

"It's a stupid one," he mumbled.

"Do you know your way around Philly?" I asked Azile.

"Do you?" she shot back.

"You're the truck driver." I said it as if that meant she should know the entire United States.

"I'm sorry, I'm just a little on edge. Eliza has me wound up," she explained.

"That's fine, I've known her for a lot less time and she has me in knots. John gave me the address. Twenty-one North Juniper Street."

She gave me the look that it was still a long shot. I sympathized, I did, but we were still going to give it a go.

"Check the glove box, Horatio had an Atlas," Azile said, pointing to the dash. Not sure if I could have missed it even if I looked through John's eyes. Damn thing was the size of an overhead compartment on an airplane—and not one of those little shuttle crafts either.

Traffic got thicker the closer we got to downtown, but like nearly everywhere else, the virus had hit so suddenly and with such force that most folks were caught completely off-guard. A couple of times, the truck bounced as Azile had to push her way through a particularly nasty snarl and the resulting noise would invariably bring a zombie or two to check out the noise.

"I wonder how many sleepers are in the city?" Azile asked, looking up at some of the huge skyscrapers

I shuddered thinking about them. "You've run into them, too?"

"Bathroom break." She blushed. "Found a gas station, walked in and I saw a big mass of them. I figured they had been killed and stacked. Didn't think too much about it...I mean, the stink was horrendous, but I had to go so bad even that didn't matter at the moment. Felt a little bad for the next passer-by when I realized the water didn't flush when I was done. That was the least of my problems, though, I heard stuff going on in the next room...figured it was rats. I'm not a fan of rats, but they don't scare me, so I peeked my head in and I saw zombie after zombie peeling itself away from that congealed mass of whatever it was."

"They are creating some sort of secretion that keeps them safe while they are in hibernation. I would imagine it also has some nutrients involved," John said, glassy eyed.

"I don't know how he does it," I said aloud to Azile's question before she could voice it. I pulled out the atlas and first found Pennsylvania and then checked out the Philadelphia insert. "It looks like we're about three or so miles away," I said as I got my orientation within the city. "You've got a left coming up."

"Mike, I don't really like this," Azile said as she was

swiveling her head back and forth.

And I couldn't really put my finger on it, but I wasn't a fan of the city either—and not just because they were Phillies AND Eagles fans here and in its heyday the city had been anything BUT the city of brotherly love. Philadelphians couldn't stand outsiders…or themselves for that matter. It was claustrophobic; the streets were getting smaller and narrower the closer to the center we got. It was a shortcoming of all major cities on the eastern seaboard, they had been settled at a time when horses and carts dominated and those paths were made from the natural game trails of the deer and Indians before them. They were never built with the thought of a semi driving around.

"It does feel like it's closing in," I said as I put the muzzle of the gun on the frame of the truck door.

She looked over and nodded, her eyes big, she looked a lot like the scared kid that she was. "We could get in a lot of trouble real quickly, and with the noise this rig makes, I think that will happen sooner rather than later." Almost on cue, air released from the drums letting out a large squelching sound.

Then it began, zombies just started to pour into the street. One moment the intersection ahead of us had an overturned cab and a burned minivan, and the next it was filling rapidly with running zombies that were coming out of the buildings on both sides.

"Shoot them, Mike," Azile said with an edge to her voice. The truck was slowing down.

"I can't really shoot it straight ahead unless I take out the windshield."

"Don't do that!" she shouted as if I were truly contemplating it—although I kind of was. "Stick it out the window!"

"I won't be able to hold it steady enough. It's a machinegun and it's got a ton of kick."

"Would the M-16 have been a better choice now?" she asked sarcastically.

"Do all women get together in a big annual rally and figure out how they can bust our balls better?" I asked as I pulled the muzzle in and quickly rolled the windows up before our guests arrived.

"Oh this is bad," John said as he looked like he finally realized what was happening. "Is there a parade? This is really going to delay us getting to Stephanie's hotel."

If we can get there at all, buddy, I thought.

"A fucking parade, are you kidding me?" Azile said as the first zombie slammed into the truck's grille.

"See any floats?" John asked as he craned his head around.

"Not one of those kinds of parades, John," I told him as I was trying to figure out how to best use my heavy paperweight.

"Must be a demonstration, they look kind of pissed. They mad about Viet Nam?" he asked me solemnly.

"That's probably it," I told him.

"Why do you coddle him like that?" Azile asked hotly. "He needs to know what's going on or he's going to get us killed!"

"Hey, John, I'm going to talk about you as if you're not here, you okay with that?" I asked as I put my hand on his shoulder and looked into his eyes. He nodded in reply. "On some level he knows exactly what's going on," I said, looking up from John to Azile while I left my hand on John's shoulder. "This is his way of dealing with it. Who am I to tell him it's wrong? Hell, I wish I were with him, his is an infinitely better world. And this man that 'will get us killed' like you said, has saved my life twice!" I accidently on purpose left out the part about me having to rescue him because he thought a couple of zombies were line jumpers for Grateful Dead concert tickets, but what she didn't know wouldn't hurt her. "This is also the same guy who figured out how to block out Eliza's mind transmissions."

"Fine," issued forth reluctantly from Azile's mouth, but it was not difficult to see that she was not happy about it.

John was reaching over me heading for the door.

"Where you going, buddy?" I asked him.

"Philly cheese steak, I'm starving."

"Yeah I'm hungry, too, but I'm not thinking this is the best time."

"No, no, it's the best time. All the street cart vendors come out for the parades."

"See!" Azile said, throwing her hands up in the air.

"What's your solution, Azile? Are you tough enough on the inside to sacrifice him?" I shot back.

"If he ever puts my life in danger I'll—"

"Stop!" I told her. "Don't say something you'll regret or force me into a decision I don't want to make."

She turned to face forward; the set of her jaw told me she was straining to hold back a litany of words best left out of this journal.

The truck was starting to jostle around as an increasing number of zombies made our acquaintance and still more were coming. I know it's wrong, I'm not so far removed from reality to know my thoughts aren't politically correct, but the image I got of all those zombies around the truck was of those late night commercials that beg for money. You know the ones where the Red Cross truck pulls up into the village and the people all run to the truck for their allotment of food? Unfortunately, in this case, we were the food.

"Can you drive forward?" I asked Azile.

"This is a truck not a tank," she replied as we looked over the expanding sea of dead.

"You guys need to find something to wad up and stick in your ears."

"Fireworks?" John asked. I thought I might have caught a glint of fear in his eyes, but it was quickly replaced with a stoned countenance.

"Close enough," I told him as I pulled back the charging mechanism.

"What are you doing?" Azile asked.

"I am going to destroy these motherfuckers." I took off my hat under the severe protests of John.

"Listen, bud, I just need you keep the line of firecrackers straight as I set them off. Can you do that?"

"Sure, man, but you should still keep your hat on."

"I'm fine for the moment." And I was. The white noise was replaced by an eerie silence in my head. Eliza was nowhere around, at least not in broadcasting mode. I 'pushed' the closest zombies away from the running board and opened the door. The nearest ones were straining against invisible bonds, their teeth gnashing at the empty air like Doberman Pinschers trying to find a meaty thigh. And did I tell you how much Dobies scare the shit out of me?

When I was eight, I had a friend in my neighborhood that had two of them. To get to his door to knock, you first had to go through the gauntlet. The walkway was up against the house, and the dogs were chained on the right hand side, their saliva dripping muzzles could *just* reach the edge of the walkway. I would walk with my back up against the house with my arms outstretched as if I were walking on a six inch ledge forty stories up. Those dogs would be snarling and snapping; long lengths of saliva would be pouring out of their muzzles as they strained against their chains to get at me. The leather on their collars the only thing holding them back from my certain death.

I shuddered thinking of those damn dogs and pushed a little harder against the closest zombies, I wanted them as far back as possible. It didn't seem to me that they were heeding my 'advice' quite as well as I would have hoped, but I had other things on my mind, so the dividing of my thoughts may have had something to do with. I placed the barrel of the machinegun in the crux of the window frame and the truck body. I pulled the trigger and nearly flung myself off the truck.

"Umm, Trip, maybe come over here and grab my belt," I said before I dared shoot again. I was thankful when my instruction did not lead to a four minute explanation.

When I felt he had a good grasp, I let loose with a torrent of hell.

Aiming wasn't even necessary, annihilation surged from that barrel. Zombies liquefied as the steel-jacketed 7.62 rounds would slam into first one zombie and then into his mates behind him—maybe as many as three deep before the bullet was finally sated with death. As I looked over the multitude of zombies that day, there were all kinds from all races. Men, women, children…fuck, even babies. Some were black, some white, Hispanic, Asian, there were medical workers in scrubs, cops, construction crews, some McDonald's workers (hopefully Becka was in there—see journal number two), my point being, no one escaped this plague. It's that, in my memory, I choose to believe that ALL zombies resemble Durgan: white, male, asshole. That's how I can sleep at night. I just need to pretend that every former human I destroyed that day resembled that one particular asshole. It was that and only that thought that kept me on the good side of the sanity line.

Watching what that large caliber round can do when it strikes a five-year-old girl is not something that is conducive to my already thinly spread mental health. My zombies are ALWAYS big goons who are deserving of that bullet. That is all I am saying. Zombies fell like wheat to a Harvester, and wasn't that what I was doing? Harvesting the dead? The bullets slammed into them, the sound almost louder than the percussion of the rounds being expended. The ones that weren't neatly cut in half were pushed back as if the thumb of God had pressed them in the abdomen. Heads disintegrated into a spray of blood, brain, and bone, to mist down on their brethren like a bloody spring rain. But there would be no bumper crop rising from the resultant moisture.

"Where are they going?" John asked over the din of the gun.

It was time for a break anyway, the belt was getting low on rounds, the barrel wasn't glowing quite yet, but it was thinking about it. Something strange was happening, zombies were still being attracted to the noise, but they were moving away from my firing zone; well…at least the ones that still could.

Azile's mouth was hanging slightly agape. I don't know all she'd been witness to since this started, but it may have been safe to say it was nothing quite on this scale.

I leaned my head in so she could see my face. "Drive, girl, before they figure out I'm not firing."

She might have been in a bit of shock. It didn't stop her from getting the truck in gear, though. She slammed both feet on the brake, almost sending me once again off the truck, when she ran over the first fallen zombie. She was frozen, her feet were pressed solid on the brake, and her arms were locked straight out in front of her. Her back may as well have been adhered to her seat.

"Shit," I said.

"You have to go number two too?" John asked.

I didn't even have time to respond to that. "Hold this," I said to John as I handed him the machinegun. "Do *not* touch the barrel." And before I completely lost my mind, I removed the remaining rounds.

I had not even finished climbing over him when John screamed in pain. "That's fucking hot!"

"I told you not touch the barrel," I said as I got between him and Azile.

"That's the barrel?" he asked.

"Azile, you alright?" I asked gently. She didn't even acknowledge my presence. "Plan B it is," I said aloud as I watched the zombies stop their evacuation, they weren't yet coming back.

I grabbed Azile's right hand and pried her white-knuckled fingers from the steering wheel; the left came off a lot easier. I then reached down and pushed up on the back of her knees so her legs would bend. Then I stood up over the gear box and physically slid her over to my previous spot.

"Here goes nothing," I said as I restarted the stalled truck. She still hadn't moved on her own or even looked over at me.

The truck bucked wildly as I threw it into what I thought was first gear (it wasn't). I had to stick my hand out to keep Azile from slamming off the dash.

"Buckle her in, John."

"You said hold this and don't touch the barrel. How many more things do you think I can do?"

"One more?" I asked hopefully.

"Okay, fair enough."

John effortlessly got the belt around her and secured her in. I started the truck again, hoping for better results.

"John, one more thing and I promise that's it."

There was no need for the precursor statement, he had already forgotten about our previous conversation and was looking at me expectantly.

"Put your seat belt on."

"Seat belts are just a way for the insurance companies to impose their will upon the people."

"I don't fucking care, put it on."

Thankfully he did. I again engaged the truck into gear, the bucking was much less severe. I must have been somewhat closer to first this time around. I was so intent on watching my hand on the gears and making sure I was giving adequate gas to the engine, I at first could not figure out why we were thrashing around so violently. I thought I had been doing everything right, then it finally dawned on me as I looked through the windshield, I was driving over the fallen bodies of hundreds of zombies.

The bucking had been so much better, it hid a majority of the bone splintering sounds of tires crushing human skeletons. Occasionally I would see matter spray off to my left, coating the curb and sometimes nearby buildings. No matter how much I tried, I could not convince myself that I was running over garbage-sized bags of ketchup, unless the condiment now came packed with meat. Chunks of the spray dripped down from whatever it hit; lamp posts, mailboxes, cafe furniture, even nearby zombies, though they didn't seem to care too much.

Azile had the right state of mind for this: catatonic.

John was diligently studying the machinegun. A hundred more feet of the sausage grinding and we would be free—free physically, never mentally. This would be something we all took with us for the long haul.

"Just babies," Azile muttered.

I wanted her to shut the fuck up, like yesterday. The zombies to our side fell in step with the truck, some tried to get in, the rest were content to follow for now, most likely waiting until we became an easier target.

"Take a right up here," John said, never looking up from the gun.

I did it. I didn't even ask. I didn't know if it took us any closer to our destination, all I did know was that it would take the zombie skid line out of my rearview mirror. And that...well that was fine by me.

"Left up here," John said, again not looking up.

"Buddy, I appreciate the directions, but are you sure?" I asked. He didn't even question my calling him buddy. There were zombies outside the truck and apparently inside too. He didn't answer, so I took the turn. Right, left, straight. Didn't matter much; I had no clue where I was going.

"It's up on the left about another mile," John said.

"You sure you've never been here?"

He finally did look up this time. "I think I'd know where I've been or not been."

"Just asking."

Then there it was: a Brown Stone Hotel in downtown Philadelphia. At one time it was probably a pretty nice place. Ornate windows looked into a Victorian themed lobby adorned with marble floors and ceilings. Now, however, it looked exactly like what you would expect a building in a war zone to look like. Bullet holes pock marked the marble in a hundred different places. Furniture was burned or stained a brownish red color. (*Don't dwell, don't dwell*—I said the little mantra over and over.) Zombies that had been milling around inside came out when we rolled up. My first impression was that nobody was alive in there. How could they be? Then it dawned on me. Zombies only hang around when food is available.

"Hey, fucktard!" Someone shouted from above. "Yeah, you, fucktard!" the guy said as I craned my neck to look up the hotel. "Why don't you get that big zombie dinner bell outta here!"

"We're looking for someone!" I yelled up.

"Do I look like the fucking white pages, get the fuck outta here!" he yelled back, this time he showed the muzzle of hunting rifle to move his point along.

"Give me the damn gun," I said to John as I pulled my head back in the window. John carefully handed it over the slowly awakening Azile. "Two can play that game, ass wad!" I yelled up as I stuck the formidable machinegun up and out my window.

"Oh shit!" He pulled his head back in. "We don't want any trouble! Loud noise brings zombies, that's all I'm saying," he answered, not showing himself.

"You just let us know if you have someone up there. If you don't we'll be on our way." I was about to ask if John's wife was up there, but I didn't know her last name. I looked over to John, his eyes were closed and his fingers were crossed. I was really hoping this went well, but I wasn't counting on it. Let's face it everyone knew the city's nickname about brotherly love was a misnomer. New Yorkers feared this place.

"John, what's your last name?" I asked, embarrassed that I had either forgotten it or that I had never thought to ask. Tracy told me I had the social graces of a goat, now I believed her.

Again I was surprised when he didn't start in on some diatribe about how last names were a way for the government to keep us in check.

"Stephenson," he said quickly.

"Okay," I told him as I poked my head back out. Now I had my fingers crossed. "I'm looking for Stephanie Stephenson!" I shouted up.

There was nothing for long moments. I was about to yell back up; the street was starting to get crowded and I wanted to get out of here before I opened up again with the M-240.

Had I not been sitting, I would have had to find a seat when the ass wad from above answered. "Who wants to know?" he asked.

"Do I look like a process server, you idiot?" I yelled up. "Her husband is here."

A pause but much shorter this time. "John, John is here?" a woman asked.

I was about to respond, but that was before the wind was knocked out of me by John crawling over my lap. "Stephanie, I let the sour cream expire!" he shouted.

"John, you silly, silly man. I have missed you so much," she said, tears were dropping from her handsome face. She was pretty in a feminine, lumber jack sort of way. Her meaty forearms hung out as if she hoped she would be able to scoop her man up. "I don't know who you are, mister," Stephanie said, obviously talking to me. "But thank you from the bottom of my heart."

John didn't quite catch the connection when he responded. "I was afraid you might not remember me, you missed you're last scheduled visit."

"I would never forget you, my sweetheart. I was thanking the man that brought you to me."

"Who? Ponch? Yeah he's a good guy. He had shoes just like yours."

"John, man, you're really pressing on some places that are making me uncomfortable." He didn't move.

"Ponch?" Stephanie asked.

"It's actually Mike, and you're welcome. Your husband is a...unique man he's saved my life more than once."

"Thank you, Mike."

"Okay, this has got to be snap decision time. We don't have much time until this place is flooded with zombies. Either you guys need to come down here and travel with us, or I need to know how to get John up to you."

"Hold on," Stephanie said, going back into the room.

"John, what do you want to do?" I asked him.

"With what?" he asked back. He was looking at me less than three inches from my face, my personal space was getting severely violated.

"The general consensus is to stay put," Stephanie echoed down. "But I'm doing whatever John wants me to."

"I'm not sure he gets the gravity of the situation, Stephanie, this is probably your call," I told her.

"Hi, Steph!" John yelled up.

"Hi, baby," she said softly, throwing him kisses.

"We have food here for months, we have guns, and we're relatively safe. Why don't you all come up?" Stephanie said.

I'll admit I was pleasantly surprised when I didn't hear a bunch of protestations from behind her.

"Make sure he brings that damn gun with him," was the only thing I heard from behind her.

"I think John should go up with you. Nobody deserves to go where I am."

"Mike, there's plenty of room for you and the girl," she said as she shielded her eyes so she could see into the cab.

"I'm coming, Stephanie!" John said as he started to climb out of the truck.

"Hold on, buddy," I said as I pulled him back in.

"I've been meaning to ask you who this buddy guy is."

"We'll circle around to that. Just hold on for a second. Azile you back with us?" I asked as I focused my attention on the girl.

"Mostly," she mumbled.

"They're offering sanctuary here. My suggestion to you is to take it."

"Will Eliza be here?"

"Not anytime soon, and never if I have any say in it," I told her honestly.

"I'm going with you then."

"I don't think that's the wisest choice you could make, but I'd love to have you because I can't stand driving this kidney killer."

She actually had the corner of one lip pull up in a sliver of a smile.

"It's just going to be, John," I told Stephanie.

"How close can you get to the side of the building?" she asked, pointing to her right. The hotel ended and abutted up to an alleyway. "Right at the edge of the alleyway is the fire escape, the truck should be just the right height."

Except for a couple of lampposts and a mailbox, I thought I could get pretty close.

"Move," Azile said as she watched me guesstimating how I was gonna go about getting the truck in position. I figured I could make it in about a twelve or thirteen point turn.

"Thank you," I told her as I moved a reluctant John back to his seat, then crawled over Azile.

Surprisingly, the street poles broke away with not too much effort on the truck's part. The mail box, on the other hand, seemed to have twenty-foot-deep pylons set into the earth's mantle. Black smoke poured from the twin smoke stacks as the truck strained against the blue box. The truck thrummed and vibrated as the box failed to yield.

"Fuck this," Azile said as she threw the truck in reverse.

"Seat belt, man," John said to me.

"Yeah good move," I said as I quickly strapped myself in.

Azile took out more than a few zombies as she backed up a good hundred feet or so. The real fun, however, began when the truck started to move forward. She was whipping through the gears, and I wouldn't doubt if we hit that box doing forty. I wouldn't know I was too busy holding on for dear life to give the odometer a second glance. Cable bills, vacation postcards, and birthday cards blew in the wind as Azile destroyed that box.

"Air mail!" John yelled.

"Fuck me," I said as I quickly undid my belt and John's. Azile had the truck within five feet of the black metal fire escape. "Let's go," I told John as I leaned across him, first checking out his rearview mirror, then opening his door. We had a window of opportunity; Azile had cleared a decent sized path.

John started to get out of the truck by stepping down. I grabbed him and pointed up.

"Right," he told me as he stepped on his seat and onto the roof of the cab. "Nice view," he said to me as I joined him.

I didn't agree. I was looking back the way we had come. It looked like a casting call for *Thriller* coming down the roadway. There was a couple of feet separating the truck from the trailer and the trailer was maybe a foot and half taller than the truck itself. It was not that an imposing of a gap, so I was completely confused when John was looking at it like he was attempting to jump over the Grand Canyon on a moped.

This was the same guy that didn't mind tunnels much wider than a snake's asshole and flew a helicopter that looked like it came out of a cereal box. "John, we've got to get moving. Just follow me okay?" I stepped up and over the gap, no harder than if I was going to stand on a chair, and not those stupid office chairs with wheels on the bottom of them either.

He missed, his right foot hovered in the air came forward, caught the lip of the trailer and began to slide down the front of it. I reached over and grabbed one of his flailing arms and manhandled him onto the trailer.

"Any chance you want to move this along?" Azile asked, poking her head out. She was seeing the same sight I was.

"Working on it," I told her. If John thought the gap to the trailer was the Grand Canyon, then the distance to the fire escape might as well have been the *Valles Marineris* trench on Mars. I don't know the exact dimensions; I just know it dwarves the Grand Canyon. Maybe it would have been better off if I had just used terrestrial examples, like from the truck to the trailer looked like Snake River Canyon and to the fire escape looked like the Grand Canyon, but would that make any more sense? Who really knows how big the damn crossing is on the Snake River? Even Evel Kneivel couldn't do it in his stupid rocket motor cycle.

"John, you can do this?" I told him.

"Do what?" he asked, all wide eyed.

"You can do this, honey!" Stephanie said as she started rushing down the escape.

Ohmigosh! I thought, *she was a big-boned woman.* Not fat…not at all. Just maybe like as a child she had been separated from her Amazonian tribe and come to live in Philadelphia with us lesser human beings. I was under the impression she could have, and should have been a comic book super hero. For a moment, I saw exactly what John did in her. She was statuesque, almost a demi-god.

"Just remember your support group," she said as she was now standing on the escape directly across from us.

"Support group?" I asked her.

"He's afraid of heights," she informed me.

"What about that gyroscope he called a helicopter?"

"Small heights frighten him."

"Is there even such a thing?" I asked John.

He shrugged his shoulders.

"Listen, John, you're going to need to get to the end of the trailer and get a running start, then curve over right about here," I said, pointing to where I was standing for just this reference. "Then you're going to need to jump like your life depends on it…because it does. You got all that."

He was nodding 'yes' as he was looking feverishly at his Stephanie.

"Mike, goddammit, hurry up," Azile said.

"Honey, we're running out of time," Stephanie urged.

I should have known how poorly this was going to go just by how closely John nearly walked right off the back of the trailer.

"He has spatial issues," Stephanie said to me after she took in a great gasp of air at his near blunder.

"What? Wait. John, hold on!" I said, but he was already barreling down the trailer. "Fuck." He was making the turn and coming right towards me, then he missed, he flat out missed launching himself. My mind and my body were racing; John was hanging in the air like Wile E. Coyote in that moment before he plummets to the ground.

Luckily I had already been in movement as John was going by; I had one hand on his belt as one managed to get a grip of a fair amount of shirt material around his shoulder. I tossed him much like one would a midget down a bowling alley. (I mean if you're in to that kind of thing, I'm merely using it as a descriptor.)

As he was arcing towards his wife, I was pin-wheeling my arms violently to keep my balance. I watched as John's outstretched hands failed to grasp onto the metal railing, Stephanie plucked him out of the air like a little girl chasing airborne dandelions. I had just regained my balance as Stephanie gave me a questioning look. I had snagged her husband and tossed him five feet with no more difficulty than if he had been baby-sized—not that I'm advocating throwing babies.

"Momentum," I lied to her.

She accepted my explanation. "Thank you so much," she said as she hugged her weeping husband tightly.

"I never thought I'd see you again," he told her. "I brought you something." He extracted himself from her and showed her a giant Rasta-joint that I had no idea where he could have had it on his body and kept it so pristine.

"Honey, you know I don't smoke," she said as she kissed him fiercely.

"More for me and Ponch then," he said turning back. "You coming, man?"

"This is where we part, my friend. It has been both an honor and a trip to have made your acquaintance," I told him, I was sure going to miss him.

Azile's horn blast negated nearly every part of John's response, but I caught something about meeting again. I hoped so as I quickly climbed back down the truck and in. Azile quickly pulled away. I stared out my window as I wiped an errant tear away from my eye.

"You alright?" Azile asked after we had left the bulk of the zombies behind.

"Yeah I just hate leaving friends behind," I told her.

"You'll see him again," she said really not even thinking about how her words were just placating platitudes.

I looked over at her.

"Sorry," she said. "Just seemed like the right thing to say."

"It's alright, you were just trying to make me feel better," I told her as I dragged my hand across my face. I rolled down my window and maneuvered my face so I could see it in the mirror; I was pleasantly surprised to see some facial hair making a comeback.

"You looked like you checked out there for a minute. Are you alright?" I asked her as I pulled my head back in.

"I...I've just never seen it that bad I guess. I was already on the road when the invasion hit. Hardly would have even known it happened on the open roadway. The real first clue I got was obviously the radio news reports, then the lack of them. And still I thought it might be some elaborate hoax until I noticed just how little traffic was on the highways. There was just no way that many people could be involved in something like that."

"Just count yourself lucky. It was no bargain on my

end. I would have much rather preferred a newscast letting me know what was going on as opposed to living it."

She prodded me for more information, which I reluctantly gave out in bits and pieces. The vast majority of my recent memories were still sticky, pus-oozing sores, and I had no desire to peel back the scabs to see if they smelled of rot or not. After a few hours of the sanitized, abridged version, she realized she wasn't getting much more and let me stew in everything she had made me stir up again.

I was not sad to see the Pennsylvania state sign become a distant milestone as we cruised into the Garden State. It was a damn shame that it took a zombie apocalypse to make the state not smell like a fermented garbage pail.

The beauty of youth, I thought concerning Azile. She'd been through a lot in the last few days—maybe as much as me—plus she was driving and looked like she could go at it for days. I was fading fast; the mile markers were putting me into a trance. I knew she carried a severe hatred for all things Eliza, but did it burn so bright inside of her that she couldn't rest?

"Are you sure about this, Azile? I know I asked before, but if you just helped me to find a new ride and turned this rig around there's a decent chance you could have some sort of life somewhere."

She didn't say anything for nearly a mile. "I had no life before, and I can't imagine finding one now. When Eliza killed my mother, the state awarded me to my uncle."

I told her I was sorry when I figured where this might be going.

When she understood the origins of my apology she spoke. "No, no it's nothing like that. It's just that he was twenty-four and had absolutely no desire to take care of a kid. He was always decent to me, never did anything inappropriate. No...probably my biggest complaint was that he just didn't know what to do. There I was this emotional wreck, crying all the time, looking for comfort, and he would leave me alone. He just didn't know how to handle it." She looked over at me to gauge my reaction.

"Raising kids is hard when you're planning for it. Being thrown into the mix without a clue has got to be brutal," I told her.

"He tried. He bought me more stuffed animals than he could afford, and that was another thing, he worked at a video store and was barely paying his bills before I got there. He had a one bedroom apartment and he gave me the bedroom when I moved in. He tried, he really did, but we both knew I was a burden. He didn't bring dates home or go out with his friends that much either. He was always afraid to leave me by myself which was kind of funny, because he always left me alone in his room while he sat on the couch." She finished with a faraway look in her eyes.

"Where is he now?" I asked.

"Bonneview Memorial Cemetery. The night I turned eighteen he went out and celebrated with his friends. He wrapped his twelve-year-old Honda around a tree six houses down from his apartment. Funny thing is…I heard it. I was laying in bed thinking about my mother and how much I missed her when the explosion of metal and glass crashing into oak shook my window. I didn't know it was him, but I did. Does that make sense?"

I nodded.

"On some level I knew it was my uncle, he had finally won his freedom I guess."

"Do you blame yourself for it?" I asked.

"I did…for a while, but it didn't make sense to. Everything traced back to Eliza. She killed my mother, my father, and my uncle and she should have killed me. In a way, I guess she did. There are parts of me that will never function properly, starved of nurturing as they were. Is that too dramatic?"

"Not at all, if that's what you feel."

"So back to your original question, Eliza's death is the only reason I hold on to this life. Until I kill her, I don't think I can find peace. So yeah, I'm sure I want to come with you."

"Fair enough. Most people I have this discussion with don't normally have as much insider knowledge about Eliza as you do. I'm glad you're coming if only so I don't have to drive this thing."

"I think it was your driving more than anything that got me out of my stupor."

"Great, another smart ass, just what the world needs." She stuck her tongue out the side of her mouth at me.

"What's your family like?" She sounded genuinely curious, or she might have just wanted to while away the time as she drove. It wasn't like she could turn the radio on and listen to *America's Top Forty*.

That side thought hurt a little more than I wanted it to; I'd loved music since I was a kid and my parents had bought me a Realistic transistor radio. I think the first song I ever listened to on it was *While My Guitar Gently Weeps*, the Beatles version. I knew I was hooked from that moment. Music had been a constant component of my life, from the hundred or so concerts I'd attended, to listening to it while I worked—my desk job and my construction one—during the commutes to and from work or errands. It would be safe to say that I listened to more music on average per day than I watched television. And now my life had another little void in it where music once filled it.

"Mike?"

"Sorry I have a tendency to lose focus every once in a while."

"Your family?" she asked again after waiting a polite amount of time for me to continue.

"Yup, sorry, completely spaced it. Well let's start with my dad, Tony. He's a World War Two vet, saw a lot of action. Sometimes he's as tough as nails, and at other times you can see he's on the edge. Wait…not the edge…that sounds wrong. I don't mean of breaking down or anything like that. If you look long and hard at him when he's quiet, you can see what his stint in the war did to him. It fundamentally changed him, and at times I think it's a daily vigilance for him to have it not affect him. My mom passed a couple of years ago. I miss her, but she was far from the easiest person to love. She had great difficulty expressing concern for anything that did not revolve around her.

"Then there's my oldest brother Ron. He's all that a big brother should be, always looking out for his siblings— sometimes more than we would care for, but always appreciated. I know he's kind of grooming himself to become patriarch of the family as our dad passes the torch, but I'm not sure if he's relishing it right now. The stress of keeping your family safe weighs heavy. He's married to Nancy, great lady, she can make a can of beets into a soufflé. Don't ask me how, it's like fucking magic."

Azile snorted.

"They have four kids, Melanie, Meredith, Melissa and Mark. Melanie hasn't been heard from since after the first day of the invasion. Ron went and looked for her once, and so did Meredith—both times almost compounding the disaster. Then there's my brother Gary, he's a twin with my brother Glenn who again we haven't heard from since the start. I have my reasons to believe he's since passed. Gary is the free spirit of the group. Of all the people I've ever met in my life, he's easily the most comfortable in his own skin and some of that passes off to you when you're around him. There's my sister Lyndsey. She could easily make cheerleading an occupation. She's not that crazy bubbly 'rah! Rah!' crap. She just genuinely enjoys life and lets everyone know about it. She's married to Steve, kind of a reserved man, almost as quiet as my sister is talkative. They have a son Jesse, good kid, always willing to lend a hand.

"Then there's my wife Tracy, the love of my life," I said with what I imagine was a faraway stare. "I cannot wait to hold her in my arms. This time I will never let go. She is my strength and the reason I continue on when all seems lost."

"She sounds very special. You're lucky."

"She is and I am, and she lets me know it at every opportunity."

"That's funny, do you have kids?" she asked.

I let out an involuntary gasp of air, just thinking of my kids knocked the air out of my solar plexus. *Why the fuck did I risk my life on this journey when I should have been with them?*

"I do," I continued when I thought I had composed myself enough. "My oldest, Nicole, is pregnant. Her fiancé Brendan died saving my stupid ass from another of my hair-brained ideas. I guess that's not entirely fair, he had been bitten before he came…long story that I have no desire to revisit. My daughter reminds me so much of my wife. I hope that someday she's able to raise a family with a man that is deserving of her. My middle son Justin is a good kid, hell of a shot, he would do anything for anybody, he's had a tough go during this whole thing."

"How so?"

"He was scratched by a zombie."

"He lived? I'm sorry was that callous?"

"That's alright, and yes, he's alive. It was touch and go for a while, and a lot of the time he had to battle constantly to hold onto himself. Eliza invaded his thoughts and sometimes he didn't even know which team he was playing for. Then my youngest, Travis, it's hard for me to see him any older than the seven-year-old boy that he was when we would build Lego castles together. But that boy has got me out of more scrapes than I care to count. Sometimes I'm afraid this world is going to harden him to a brittle shell of himself and at other times the scared boy shows through. Well that's the condensed version of my family," I told her as I wrapped up. I really didn't want to dwell on it anymore. I still had to contend with telling my father that I had no idea where Gary was. Last I had seen him he was alive, and that was at the point in which I was going to stop pondering his fate. There was no way BT would let anything happen to him.

My thoughts turned sour instantly as I began to think of the loss of my lifelong friend Paul. I had always considered him my fourth brother and his death was a tangible hurt. I could touch it, it had so much presence. How I was going to walk in that house and tell his wife Erin was beyond me, the tears cascading down my face would be all she needed to know as I hugged her. There would never be a reason why I would tell her *how* he had met his fate. And what of Cindy and Perla? They would always hold me responsible for what happened to their significant others; no matter that I had nearly begged them *not* to come with me. Much like I had asked Azile, maybe I should just kick her out of the truck, or better yet, maybe I should just hop out. No, that wouldn't work. She knew where the convoy was going.

I was still thinking as the uncaring sun began its descent on the horizon. It had shined when the earth was nothing more than a caustic stew of magma. It had shined down for hundreds of millions of years as dinosaurs ruled. It had heralded in the dawn of man and it would once again rise on our plunge into extinction. Zombies would be the dominant predator for a while, but if the tree huggers thought the average man was an earth destroyer, they would change that tune after the stripping of life the zombies incurred. As horrible a beast as they were, why they weren't cannibals was beyond me. Did they have that modicum of a moral compass? I sat up quickly when that thought came to my head.

"What?" Azile asked. It looked like I had taken her out of a state of road hypnosis.

"You look half asleep."

"I'm fine," she replied while also stifling a yawn.

"It's not going to do us any good if you crash. Find a good spot. I'll take the first shift while you get some sleep."

She looked like she was going to protest, but that was right before her next yawn. "Sounds good. We're going to need some diesel soon, too."

"I hate gas stations."

"We'll worry about it in the morning."

"Oh I can guarantee I'll worry about it all night," I told her as she pulled off the highway. It looked like some sort of industrial park and she found the oldest, dilapidated piece of corrugated crap to park behind. Seemed perfect for what we wanted, but on the flip side, it looked like the setting for ninety percent of every horror movie. It was four stories of scrap metal; meth heads would have avoided the thing it was so far gone—even they had standards. Sleep would not easily be forthcoming.

It wasn't three minutes after the engine noise stopped echoing through the abandoned building when I heard the rhythmic breathing of Azile. I'm glad she pulled over when she did. There was a slice of moon in the otherwise cloudless night; the stars were beginning to make themselves known, although I did not think they would honor my wish. My gaze alternated between the brilliance of the night sky and that damned building. The broken windows with panes of glass hanging out of them looked like eager jagged teeth that wanted nothing more than to kill what was left inside of me. I heard a bottle skitter along a concrete floor somewhere within the structure. I peered at the windows, willing myself to evolve a few millennia further when man could finally see in the dark. It wasn't working. Then I fell into the trap that every—and I mean EVERY—person in movies, literature, and real life situations fall into.

I waited and expected more noise, another hint or clue to what had made the original sound. When it was not forthcoming I tried my best to rationalize it away, reasoning that it was most likely a rat, or the wind, or even a ghost. But never once thinking that it was truly what it was, something out to kill us. Wouldn't something with nefarious reasons that had just given itself away with some blundering move, immediately try to become a black hole of sound? Unmoving, ultra-cautious? It only made sense.

How many times have you been in bed, and in the middle of the night you had been awoken by an unexplainable sound? You sit up rapidly; your heart is crashing against your breast plate. You struggle to adjust your vision to your surroundings. Alert for danger from any quarter, ears trying to pick up the minutest of sounds. When you realize that the threat is not immediate, you begin to relax, starting to find rational causes: the over-stacked dishes in the sink toppling, the dog knocking over the trash can, maybe even a particularly heavy gust of wind causing the drapes to push over a lamp. Never once believing it to be the man right outside your bedroom door holding an eight-inch curved blade, but he's patient, he knows he should have been more careful when he knocked the family picture off the small table in the hallway.

He'll wait until he hears your soft snores before he slowly turns the handle on your bedroom door, when he hits that creaking floorboard right next to your bed, it'll be to late as you catch a glimpse of the steel glinting in the sliver of moonlight shining through your window as the blade is drilled into your neck, severing you carotid artery. Screams will escape you as he places his gloved hand over your mouth. Thoughts of your children in their rooms will fleet through your mind as your life slides away.

I sat up, there was a malevolent force in that building, and it was staring at me I could feel it's gaze upon me like a physical presence. I brought the M-240 up to rest on the windowsill. I would light that fucking building up like the Times Square Christmas tree if given half a reason. Azile was young enough that she probably wouldn't have a heart attack when that first round went down range.

"Show yourself, fucker," I whispered. I was calm, mostly. I was hoping I wasn't making any mind phantoms. There were enough demons and monsters running around without the need for me to create mythical ones.

"Mike?" Azile asked.

I jumped. Thankfully my finger was not on the trigger or I would have certainly blown off fifty or sixty rounds before I knew what I was doing.

"What's going on?" she asked as she saw the gun in the ready position.

"I heard a noise in there," I said pointing. It sounded a lot weaker when it was verbalized, and I didn't tell her about my *feeling*.

Now she was listening. After a while she spoke. "Probably just the wind."

"And wouldn't that be what they wanted us to think?" I asked her before I truly thought about my word choice. Oh boy, my paranoia was on high alert that fine evening.

"Who, Mike? Do you see something?" she asked as she was peering over my shoulder.

"I don't *see* anything. Something sees us, though. I can feel it."

***

"Do you think he sees us, Dave?" the dark haired man asked nervously.

"I don't think so Greg," Dave said, putting his night vision scope down. "But I swear he keeps looking right at us."

"Why don't you just shoot him?" Greg asked.

"First, because Kirk hasn't told me to...second, because it's not an easy shot...and mostly because of that fucking gun he has. If I miss, he'll punch holes through this piece of shit building. A lot of fucking holes," Dave said, again picking up his scope and looking at the barrel of the death dealing machine. "I can guarantee one thing, though, Kirk is going to want that gun."

"You saw the gun. You should tell him," Greg stated nervously.

Their leader Kirk was a scary, solitary, psychotic man, who ruled more by abject fear than through any true leadership qualities. The last person that had left their group had been hunted down mercilessly. When caught, Kirk had ordered him to be hung upside down and whipped until foot long strips of skin scraped against the ground as he swung back and forth on the chain that secured his ankles. Dave shuddered as the man had screamed for mercy that wasn't ever going to come. And what had made it worse was the man was Dave's friend, and he had done nothing to protect him.

Dave had convinced himself that it wasn't so bad under Kirk's regime. They were safe, they ate every day, and as long as they did exactly as they were told, there was nothing to fear. That wasn't always the truth; sometimes Kirk forgot what orders he issued, or if the outcome wasn't to his design, someone would pay. But for the most part, if you did what you were told you were safe. Dave's friend Bill had begged him to leave with him. Dave had refused, not because he didn't want to go but because he was petrified of what Kirk would do.

When Bill had come up missing during morning roll call, Dave had not even hesitated when asked where he was or where he might have gone. In fact, it was Dave that had to deal a significant amount of punishment to his 'friend.'

"We're friends, Dave. Don't do this," Bill had begged. "We grew up together for Christ's sake. Dave, stop this!" Bill had screamed as he was hoisted in the air.

"Five lashes," Kirk ordered.

"Five lashes? That's it?" Dave asked, hoping that his friend would someday be able to forgive him.

"Yes, five lashes from you. And hit him like you mean it or I'll make you do it again," Kirk said.

Bill screamed as Dave whipped him across the back.

Kirk said, "Zero. Hit him harder or I won't count them."

Dave reared back and struck again. Bill writhed in agony, screams, tears, and blood coming from his body.

"Better…one," Kirk counted. "Continue."

Dave delivered four more brutal blows. Angry wet, oozing welts as thick as breakfast sausages criss-crossed Bill's back. His body heaved as he sobbed.

"It's over, buddy, it's over. I'm so sorry," Bill said as he headed over to the chain release.

"What are you doing?" Kirk asked.

"Letting him down," Dave said with a confused look on his face. "You said five lashes."

"Yeah and your five lashes are done, I meant five lashes from each of us." Kirk said sweeping his hand across the twenty-eight-person populace.

"You'll kill him," Dave stated.

"No shit. Hand the whip to Chad," Kirk stated as he went back to playing his Nintendo DS, the beeps and whistles the game produced doing little to drown out Bill's whimpers and groans.

By the time the whip made it all the way to Kirk, Bill had come to the last link in his chain of life. Dave was amazed Bill had anything left, but when Kirk began to whip his face, he managed three more screams as his eye was torn free from its facial moorings and his lips were flayed off. The affect was grotesque as his face began to slough away. More than one person in the group had to walk away. Dave didn't, though, because Kirk was watching him intently as he finished his friend off.

    ***

"Let me see the scope," Kirk said as he came up next to Dave, startling him out of his memory.

"Jumpy?" Kirk asked as he grabbed the night vision glasses.

"Sorry, the guy in that truck sort of scares me."

"More than me?" Kirk asked smiling. "Just busting your balls," Kirk said as he looked through the scope. "Holy shit, did you see that gun?"

"I did. That's why I had Greg get you."

"Well go get it then."

"Wait...the gun...by myself? How?"

"Relax, you take shit too seriously," Kirk said

smiling. "Just busting your balls again."

"Ha ha," Dave laughed insincerely, hoping Kirk didn't pick up on it.

"Hey, dipshit!" Kirk yelled.

Dave was about to ask 'Him?' when Greg called out 'Yeah?' from behind them.

"Go release the zombies," Kirk said.

Greg raced away.

Those fucking zombies, Dave thought. They gave him the willies just thinking about them and that they housed them in the same building had been one of the reasons he had a major loss in sleep.

***

"Something's going on," Azile said in my ear.

Not sure how she thought I could miss the loud metallic clanging in the otherwise still night.

"Sounds like a security door rolling up," Azile said. "They had them at the loading docks where I worked."

"Not good, not good," I said as I charged the weapon. A heavy cloud chose that exact moment to cross over our small source of light. The moon was completely blanketed as we both heard the sounds of metal scraping along pavement. Sparks were shooting up from the ground as what we later learned were chains being dragged along. We couldn't see what was dragging them, but it was clear they were headed in our direction and fast.

"Shoot!" Azile begged.

"I can't see anything. Get us out of here!"

Using the sparks as an indicator, whatever was coming had halved their distance and were not slowing. Without being able to see what was coming I could not shoot I was ninety-nine percent sure what it was, but not a hundred.

I heard the whir as the truck tried to catch. "Azile, now would be a good time."

"Won't start," she said as she pumped the gas and

messed with the stick shift.

The cloud cover passed, my nightmare was revealed as hundreds of zombies raced toward the truck. Bullets and tracers lit up the night as I hammered them into the oblivion they so rightfully deserved.

***

"Fuck," Dave said as he watched the hellfire issue from the truck. He was glad he hadn't taken a shot. He would have never got a second one off if he had missed, and he was no marksman.

"He's killing my pets!" Kirk shouted. "Kill him!" he shouted at Dave.

"I don't have a shot."

"Make one or you'll be running out there."

Dave lined up a shot. His crosshairs dancing wildly as he made the attempt. The shot went wide blasting through the windshield.

***

"Fuck!" I shouted as the windshield blasted out away from me. I had caught the muzzle flash from my peripheral vision and swung the M240 in the general direction. Bullets slammed into and through the thin aluminum shell of the building.

***

Bullets danced over the heads of Dave and Kirk as they dropped for cover.

"That might have been a bad idea." Kirk was smiling again. Broken glass, debris and dust were still raining down on them long after the bullets had ceased their attempt at ending their lives. Kirk didn't get back up to look out the windows until the gun started up again and thankfully not in their direction.

***

I was not egotistical enough to think that I had killed the threat from the third story window, but I imagine I had put the fear of whatever deity he believed in into his heart, and as long as he embraced that fear, I'd be fine. "How's it going, Azile? I'm running a little low on ammo."

"I'm trying, stop yelling at me!" she screamed back.

***

"Recall the zombies!" Kirk yelled as he raced down to the first floor.

Dave stayed where he was. Recalling the zombies meant putting out some of their prisoners as bait and he didn't want to be part of it. "I should have left with Bill," he said softly.

"You say something?" Greg asked.

"What'd you hear?" Dave asked.

"Something about you wishing you'd left. I'm going to have to tell Kirk."

"Tell him this for me," Dave said as he put a round in Greg's chest. Dave ran to the opposite end of the building and down the two flights.

"What the fuck is going on out there?" Len asked as Dave nearly plowed into him.

Len had the unenviable task of guarding the door that was located the furthest from the action.

"Armageddon, Len, I'm getting out of here."

"You know the rules, Dave, nobody in…and especially nobody out."

"Len, just let me go. Or, better yet, come with me."

Len actually did think about it for a moment. "Shit, Dave, I'd like to, but you saw what he did to Bill. I can't go through that."

"Just let me go, Len."

"I can't. There's one way out from the back of this building, who do you think he's going to blame?"

"Just say you didn't see anything."

"But I did and I'm a horrible liar."

"Fuck, Len, I'm sorry" Dave said as he shot Len in the midsection.

Len fell back into the door as he placed his hands over the wound. "That fucking hurts, Dave," Len said as he slid down the door.

"I'm sorry, man." Dave grabbed Len's legs to move him out of the way.

"Not as sorry as you're going to be," Len said as he pulled his .38 Special from his holster. He drilled a hole in the top of Dave's head. The smell of expended rounds and burnt brains dominated the small enclave. Dave was dead before he could form the thought.

"Asshole. Who does that to their friend?" Len said, referring to Dave's whipping of Bill. He lifted his shirt and his bulletproof vest; a fist-sized bruise was already forming on his stomach. "That's gonna hurt," Len said as he slowly worked himself back up into a standing position. He opened the door quickly, making sure nothing was out there. His plan was to drag Dave out so that he wouldn't bleed all over his guard station and then a new thought formed in his mind.

"Fuck it." He ran for the tree line.

***

I had maybe fifteen rounds left when the zombies stopped coming. Fifteen rounds to a machinegun is like eating one potato chip; it's not enough.

"You stopped shooting, Mike, are you out of ammo," Azile said, checking under the dash for potential truck starting problems.

"The zombies are heading back in," I said, trying to figure out what was going on.

"Why?" Azile asked, and that was immediately followed by the screams of the reasons 'why.'

"They're using people to bring them back." I put my head down on the butt stock of my gun.

"What?" Azile asked in surprise, then she figured it out. "Shoot the zombies!"

"I would," I told her sadly, "but I don't have enough rounds, and I don't know exactly where the people are. I'd just as likely kill them as save them."

"This can't be happening." Azile frantically pumped the gas pedal and turned the ignition.

Oh, it most assuredly is, I thought as I heard the screams of the eaten.

A few moments later, when the hordes had been retrieved and the cries of the lures had died down, we could hear the doors that housed the zombies being lowered.

"What is this newest nightmare?" I asked in preparation for round two.

"Hello, travelers!" a voice shouted from the shadows. "My name is Kirk and I am the captain of this facility."

"Like Captain Kirk?" I asked Azile.

"Who's Captain Kirk?" she asked as she shrugged her shoulders.

"Where's Spock! I want to talk to Spock!" I yelled.

There was some muttering, then Kirk spoke back up. "There is no Spock here. Perhaps we can come to an agreement."

"You mean since your first attack was unsuccessful in killing us, you want to go to a diplomatic approach?" I asked dripping in sarcasm.

"The release of my pets was unfortunate."

"Pets?" Azile and I asked each other.

"Someone here misunderstood my orders," Kirk added.

"Was he one of the ones you fed to your pets?" I asked.

"No, no, they were prisoners of war."

I wanted to tell him that the war was against the zombies, killing each other off wasn't doing anybody any good; he didn't seem like the reasoning type. Spock would have been a much better negotiator.

"And if we don't come to an agreement?" I asked, leaving the question hanging.

"Well then, I would consider that an act of aggression," he stated simply.

"Azile, what are the odds you can get out of the cab and grab another box of ammo without being seen?"

"I'd have to crawl out the window so the cab light doesn't come on."

"Shit," I said as I caught movement in my rearview mirror, "they're trying to come up behind us. I hope I sound convincing," I told Azile, then I yelled to Kirk, "My rear observer just told me that you have people attempting to come up behind us. If they don't stop now I will level your building."

There was a long pause. "Let's be civilized about this."

"I've been nothing but, you're the one that sent your pets to kill us, then fed them dinner. And now, while we are in the midst of negotiations, you send men to try and waylay us. I will consider that an act of aggression." I opened up the breech so that I could make as much sound as I could 're-loading' my weapon.

"Okay, hold on," Kirk's voice said with an edge. "My men are returning."

"We'll talk more when my observation post confirms this. He says they haven't moved yet. Azile, you need to move. Sooner or later he's going to figure my ruse out."

Azile rolled her window down and slid effortlessly through the opening. She peeked up. "Once I roll the back door up, the cab light will come on."

"Okay, I'll improvise. Make sure you grab the box that says 7.62."

"I know guns," she muttered.

"They're not quite gone yet!" I yelled.

"Patience," Kirk yelled back.

"Oh I'm patient but you see my gun here she isn't."

The dome light came on, startling the hell out of me. I pulled the trigger and let a controlled three-round burst issue forth from my gun. That would get any 'lookie loos' diving for cover. The echo of my firing was just dying down as the light clicked off.

"Sorry...mosquito!" I shouted.

"I've got a girl" someone said triumphantly behind me. I heard some scuffling.

It seemed that my rear observation post had failed me. I put the weapon down and exited the truck as quickly as I could. Azile was struggling in a man's arms. Her legs were kicking uselessly in the air as he had lifted her up against him and was pulling her back to the building.

I ran at him, he had been looking back towards the building. When he finally turned forward and saw me, I was within ten feet.

He put Azile up as a human shield. "Wait...you don't even have a gun."

I kept coming at him. Azile pulled her head to the left as I brought a punch from somewhere off in right field. Azile's attacker was not able to do much more than watch as my fist made contact with his face. I had struck him so hard, bones cracked. At first, I was certain the snapping bones had been my knuckles. It was difficult to tell in the moonlight, but I was certain that his face was indented; it was a nauseating sight.

His nose had been pushed flat and his right cheek bone was non-existent. He fell backwards to the ground, the back of his head slamming off the pavement. The cavity in his face was soon filled in with a rush of blood.

"Jonas," Kirk called out, "you still got her?"

I could hear blood pounding in my ears, fury had taken root. "That would be a negative!" I yelled as I grabbed Jonas by his shins. I screamed in rage as I tossed his body a good fifteen feet, more of his frame splintered as he landed with a crushing blow.

Azile was watching me, possibly thankful, possibly warily. "How?" was her one word question.

I wasn't entirely sure if she meant, *how* did I cave his face in or *how* did I throw a two hundred-something pound man fifteen feet. More likely both. My chest was heaving from the adrenaline, not the effort, no, that had come easy enough.

"Shit, Kirk, he just killed Jonas!" someone yelled from one of the higher stories.

We were in the open and had nothing to shield us.

"NO!" Kirk screamed just as I heard the doors open back up.

Zombies were streaming towards us. "RUN!" I yelled to Azile as if she needed any prodding. I mostly meant for her to run away, but in the confusion she headed back to our haven, our not operating haven.

I ran to the back of the truck to retrieve the fallen ammo box. I quickly turned to head back to the passenger side door and realized I wouldn't make it—or maybe I would. I started swinging the box like it was a Louisville Slugger and my team was down by three, bases loaded, two outs, and bottom of the ninth. I figured if I was going for cliché, I might as well go all the way. The lead zombie met the full fury of a twenty-five pound ammunition box as it completely caved its skull in. He hadn't hit the ground before I drove it into Kirk's next pet.

Brain matter shot out the tops of heads like sleeves of Mentos dropped in a gallon container of Diet Pepsi. I was covered in the viscera, and still they came. My arms were beginning to burn from the effort.

"My pets!" Kirk screamed from a doorway. Some saw their 'master' and turned to express their gratitude; most stayed behind thinking I would eventually let one in. More than once I nearly lost my grip on the box handle as viscous blood coated everything. "Get more prisoners!" Kirk screamed as he headed back in.

They might be his pets, but he knew enough to realize that they bit. More screaming ensued as the damned witnessed their fate bearing down on them. I would have chased the retreating zombies down, but I was exhausted and exposed. It was only a matter of time before someone shot my ass.

"He fucking killed like twenty zombies with...with his bare hands," the man that had informed Kirk of Jonas' passing yelled.

To be fair, it wasn't my bare hands. Now my chest was heaving from the exertion, I moved quickly to the truck and pulled myself up with no small amount of difficulty.

"Mike?"

"Later," I said breathlessly. "Help me...lift the gun." My arms were jelly-filled rope. Azile did her best to help me while also not getting too close; I was beyond gross. I loaded the new belt in. "Keep the ammo straight," I told Azile as she got up behind me, reaching to my left to hold the ammo up. "This'll...be...loud," I breathed out heavily, looking back at her.

"I'm fine," she returned.

"Friend!" Kirk yelled.

"Friend this, motherfucker!" I unleashed hell's fury in multiple 7.62 projectiles. Screams of terror echoed throughout the building as I tried to tear it down. Bullets whined as they struck home, some ricocheting inside and doing more damage as they careened off of poles or beams. I was indiscriminately doling out death. I hoped the prisoners were tucked away safe but even if that wasn't the case, I had to believe I was giving them the escape they had longed for. Kirk didn't seem like a benevolent captor. The building's groans of protestations were the only sounds once I dry fired.

"Mike?" Azile asked again.

"I'm fine," I told her through gritted teeth. At least as fine as a mass murderer can be.

Azile did the only think she could think to do, she

tried the truck again. Of course this time it started without a hitch.

CHAPTER THIRTY

Eliza and Tomas

Kong was underneath the hood of yet another truck trying his best to hold up his end of the bargain with Eliza, when one of his men tapped him on the shoulder.

"Fucking what?" Kong asked heatedly.

"She's back," his helper answered nervously.

Kong turned, the black tinted window, late model Chevy Camaro idled on the far side of the lot. The car was pointed directly at him; he knew better than to wave her over to him. He jumped off his work bench and walked over. He wiped the grease and now-forming sweat off his hands as he did so. Her window lowered as he approached. He could not fathom how someone so beautiful could be so cruel, and on top of that, she seemed particularly pissed off. He noted that his end of the conversation was going to consist of a bunch of head nods and yesses at all the appropriate times.

"We will leave within the hour," she told him, never even looking over at his face as he bent over to look in.

He had ten great reasons why that couldn't happen. "As you wish, mistress," was his reply.

Her window rolled up.

Now he had the unenviable task of figuring out how to make it happen. "Wrench!" Tank shouted for his helper. "Are all the trucks topped off with fuel?"

"You know the answer to that," Wrench told him, getting back to switching out the water pump in the truck they had been working on.

"Shit," Kong said. Eliza was a day earlier than she

had told him she was going to be. They had completely sucked the diesel tanks dry at the truck stop. He was going to send a fair number of trucks to a nearby station to top off, now he had no time. "Wrench, stop what you're doing." Wrench looked up. "Any truck not making the journey or has less than half a tank of fuel needs to have its fuel siphoned."

"Kong that is NOT going to go over well with those truckers."

"Not much of a choice. Get an armed escort if you have to. She wants to leave in less than hour."

Kong was happy when Wrench didn't say the traditional 'Ain't gonna happen'; there was no sense to it. They had all thrown the dice when they opted to work for Eliza. Although 'work for' might be somewhat liberal, 'indentured servant' was probably a better fit.

The smell of diesel wafted across the parking lot as men in a hurry took diesel from one truck to place in others—more than a fair amount landing on the ground—and still Eliza sat in her car. Kong doubted she was watching any of the activity going on around her.

***

Exactly fifty-eight minutes later, the last of the trucks pulled out of the parking lot, seventeen trucks stood as lone sentinels.

Kong pulled up alongside Eliza's car. "Five of the drivers of the seventeen trucks sitting are not going," Kong said as he pointed back to a small group of men standing in a loose circle.

Eliza rolled her window back up. Kong hurriedly put his truck in gear, wishing to get as far away from what he expected to happen as soon as possible. He had made sure to double check with the men, strongly urging them to rethink their stance, they hadn't yielded. He saw Eliza's car rolling towards the men in his rearview mirror before he turned and lost sight.

***

Eliza stepped out, her black leather high heeled boot cracking into the gravel of the parking lot. "I will require my vials back," Eliza stated as she approached the men.

Detrick, one of the first drivers to come on with Kong spoke up. "See. Mistress," he said, taking his Mack Trucks hat off and wringing it in his hands, "we sort of felt like maybe we had earned them with all the hard work we've done for you."

"Is Michael Talbot and his family dead?" Eliza asked arching an eyebrow.

"Well, and that's another thing, this Talbot family and his kin…they haven't done anything to us. Isn't that right?" he asked the other four men who looked like they would all rather be receiving hot lava enemas at the moment than being under the scrutiny of Eliza's gaze.

"Is it not enough that they have wronged me?" she asked almost sweetly.

"We don't have to take this shit from an itty bitty little girl," one of the newer drivers, Lonnie, stated. "My rig is a fucking paperweight now just because I didn't have a full tank of gas. I've given all I'm going to give, and if this stupid vial does half of what all you scared fucks says it does, I will consider it payment for my fuel. Now you're all bowing to this?" he asked pointing to Eliza.

Tommy was shaking his head back and forth as he watched the exchange. Eliza was wearing a bemused smile.

"Mistress, he's new. He doesn't know what he's talking about and doesn't speak for all of us," Detrick replied.

"Fuck you, man," Lonnie said. "We were just having this conversation before she came over, and if I remember correctly, you said something about how you'd like to bend her over your fender." Detrick looked like he'd swallowed a living fish, his body was quivering. "In fact, I'm not so sure this vial is adequate payment." Lonnie approached Eliza and broke into her personal space. He was looking down at her threateningly. "Look, even her pussy brother's not coming to her aid." He pointed to the Chevy.

"Don't, Lonnie," Detrick said, at first stepping closer, but then stepping back when Eliza looked over to him.

"Why? She's so fine, maybe Lonnie junior can put a smile on that frozen face," Lonnie said with a leer.

"Would men be able to think at all if they didn't have their manhood?" Eliza asked Detrick. "You pull that scrawny little worm out that you call 'Lonnie Jr.' and I will tear it from your body."

Lonnie faltered for a moment. "Come on, guys, we can all have her," he said, all of a sudden feeling like he needed back up.

"Mistress, we just want to go on our way, your fight is not ours," Detrick said, handing her his vial back.

The three other men who had been hanging back followed suit with Detrick.

"Fine, you bunch of women!" Lonnie yelled at the group. "It's your lucky day," he said, pointing to Eliza, "but I'm keeping the damned vial." He turned and began to walk away.

"I get the vial back, Detrick, or none of you leave this parking lot alive," Eliza told him coolly.

Detrick had seen enough of her work to know that this was no idle threat. "Stop him," he told the other three.

It was a minor scuffle, but within a minute, Lonnie's vial was sitting in the palm of Eliza's hand.

"We're free to go now?" Detrick asked.

Eliza didn't answer as she headed back to the car.

"You're truly letting them go?" Tomas asked incredulously. His question was answered before the reverberations in the air flow stopped. A group of a dozen or so speeders came through a row of hedges some fifty yards away from the departing men.

It was Detrick who noticed them first. He alerted the

rest of the group and then looked back to Eliza's car before he started running in the opposite direction.

"Let's go," Eliza told Tomas.

"You could have let them live," Tomas said to her as he watched three zombies drag down Lonnie.

The rest of the zombies stopped until they were gently urged to keep chasing down their victims by Eliza.

"You do know at some point you will need humans to repopulate so that you can feed, right?" Tomas asked Eliza.

"Yes, but this is so much more fun than merely letting them go," Eliza replied.

Tomas sped up to catch the convoy as they were heading down the highway.

CHAPTER THIRTY-ONE

Mike Journal Entry 12

We traveled for a few miles. I didn't say too much, only grunting when we came across a small river. I had Azile stop so that I could clean up. I got behind the truck and stripped down, hoping that I could find something to replace my crusted clothes. It wasn't going to happen. I hopped in, the river was about as warm as I was expecting it to be, which meant I was taking in small sharp breathes as the ice cold daggers of water rolled over my body. I had the clothes I was using secured under a rock a few feet down stream from me.

"I'm washing up in a river in New Jersey," I said as got down as low as I could. The water was only about two feet deep, so I was nearly in the prone position. Chunks of debris were flowing off of me, I chose to ignore them. I spent at least twenty minutes cleaning myself and another ten getting my clothes into somewhat respectable condition. Well this wasn't a Tide commercial, and my whites were never going to be clean again. I was not thrilled with the idea of putting them back on wet and probably would have waited until they were dry if I was still with John, but I didn't think it was fair to expose Azile to that kind of trauma. I laughed at my thought.

"You know I'm not a prude," Azile told me when I squished onto my seat.

"Well I didn't, but I am," I told her back.

"You're going to catch your death of cold like that."

"Wouldn't that be nice if that was how I had to worry about dying?" I asked her, looking wistfully out the window.

"I guess it would be," she said as she got the truck

moving.

***

"Oh what now!" Azile said as she slammed her fist off the dashboard; the truck was losing power. "Whatever was wrong last night, I think is showing up again."

"Can't you fix it?" I asked her, my mood had not rebounded quite yet.

"Do I look like a master mechanic?" she asked.

I looked over at her. "I thought all truckers were. Isn't that part of the job?"

"Have you used a stove?"

"What kind of question is that? And yes, to answer it, I have."

"Does that make you a master chef? How about that writing in your journal?"

"I get it, I get it. And yes, I've written a lot in my journal…and 'no' that doesn't make me a literary genius."

We were finally back in Massachusetts; we had made decent time down the Mass Pike and had just got onto 495 which skirted around Boston. My fear had been getting back on route 95 and potentially running into Eliza on the open road. That hadn't worked out so well the first time and I was in no mood to revisit it, although right now that didn't look like it was going to be a problem.

"Any ideas?" Azile asked as she manhandled the now dead truck to the side of the road.

"We could wait for a good Samaritan," I told her.

She looked over, trying to ascertain if I was serious, then she smiled. "What about Triple-A?"

"That's the spirit, let's get armed up."

"I hate what this world's become," she said as she pushed rounds into her magazines. "I'm more than likely going to need these today," she said, rattling her rounds, "than this." She pulled a pen out of her pocket.

"That's a nice pen."

"You want it?"

"Sure."

"At least someone will use it." She handed it over. I spent a few more moments taking a look at it before I stuck it in the middle of my rolled up journal, once again wrapping my thoughts and words in a plastic bag and securing it with a rubber band. My present life necessitated this action, I'd lost more than one journal to blood and gore.

"Shit." Azile shielded her eyes from the sun as she looked up and down the roadway.

"Keep a look out, I'm going to ditch this stuff." Odds were, a family in desperate need of rifles and food was not going to stumble across this truck. The sure bet was a renegade band of some sort of desperados, and with God's innate sense of humor I could almost guarantee that these would be used against me.

"Just light the damn truck on fire," Azile said as I was about halfway through emptying the rig.

That did seem way easier, and the groove I was wearing in the ground as I hauled the stuff to the tree line was getting pretty noticeable anyway. "This royally sucks," I told Azile as I strategically placed the ammunition, my beautiful M-240 and a crate of M-16's in the back of the truck.

"You say something?" Azile asked peeking her head from around a tree.

I motioned her with a frantic hand waving to hide. I pulled the pin on the grenade I was holding, tossed it into the rear of the truck, and ran. I had just made it to the large tree Azile was hiding behind when the grenade blew; it was a millisecond later when the concussion from the explosion of the grenade and ammunition struck.

Heat from the fire was causing rounds to cook off and randomly fire in all directions.

"Didn't really think this out, did you?" Azile asked.

"I rarely do."

It was a lot like waiting for microwave popcorn to

finish. There were hundreds of 'pops' from the majority of the rounds, then they began to decrease until it was down to the occasional release. This batch, though, we didn't care if it burned completely. We waited a full ten minutes after the final explosion before we ventured forth. I guess I shouldn't have been surprised when I noticed bark missing on the tree we had been using for cover, but it still came as a shock to see so much damage to our 'protector.'

"Thank you," I told it as I placed my hand against its trunk. I'm glad it wasn't an Ent; it would have kicked our ass. (Lord of the Rings reference).

I cautiously walked back to the smoking destroyed ruins of Horatio's truck dismayed to see my M-240 twisted and destroyed.

"You need a minute?" Azile asked, putting her hand on my shoulder.

"I'll be alright," I sniffed.

"Now?"

"Now we walk at least for a little while. That blast is going to attract some attention." I had no idea how prophetic my words were going to be, and from what quarter we were going to receive help. Some shit just can't be made up.

CHAPTER THIRTY-TWO

The Start of the End - Maine

It was twilight and Travis was walking on the raised deck for his shift of guard duty. Nobody had seen much more than a wayward raccoon in days. His eyes were scanning the horizon but not focusing on anything other than how the early evening air had a bite to it. He felt it long before he saw it; the pressure treated boards under his feet were vibrating, at first so subtly he thought he might be having a muscle spasm. That changed when he watched the small deck table start to move from the thrum. The movement was quickly transferred into the house.

Ron ran up to the railing. "I guess it's time," he said, heading in as quickly as he had come out.

Travis was still trying to process the information when the majority of the Talbot compound residents came outside.

"Ron, we can't...the entire system isn't ready," Mad Jack was pleading.

"No real choice," Ron said.

"What is it?" Perla asked, her eyes wide.

"Has anyone seen Erin?" Tracy asked. "I checked the entire house and the garden, she wouldn't have left the grounds would she?"

Tony was coming from the rear of the house. He looked up at everyone on the deck. "Back gate was open."

The words were foreboding to Tracy. She had known how distraught Erin had been over Paul's passing but she didn't think she would do anything quite that foolish as to leave the security of the compound.

"We have to go look for her," she begged. No one heard her with a half a dozen conversations going on. "Ron," she grabbed his forearm, "I think Erin has left, we need to find her."

"She's as thick as her husband. Not to fret it's Darwinism at work," Deneaux said.

"Ron, I've got to find her," Tracy said with alarm.

"Absolutely not. We have no idea what's coming, but it's not good. Erin put herself at risk I will not put others out there also. Besides once we arm our defenses getting back will be near impossible."

Tracy ran over the deck to the backyard to see if Erin was still in shouting distance.

"Grab the ammo," Tony said to Travis. "Station it every ten feet along the deck."

"Ammo is a last resort, dad," Ron stressed.

"Hurry up then," Tony told Travis with a smile. The defenses they had built looked formidable, but every fortress was pregnable.

Travis turned and headed back in. He noticed Justin in the shadows of the darkened living room. His lips were moving but no words were emanating forth. "Justin?" Travis asked nervously.

"She's fucking back, brother." Justin shivered. Travis walked over cautiously to his brother. "Relax, I can see the concern on your face. I haven't gone to the dark side yet."

"No?" Travis asked. "How long have you known they were coming?" he asked before going to fulfill his grandfather's orders.

Justin was caught off guard. *Long enough*, he thought.

Tracy was frantically calling out Erin's name. The only thing answering back was the chirp of crickets that were beginning to still with the approach of multiple diesel engines.

***

Erin heard the ragged screams calling her name, but the peace the woods offered her pulled too deeply. That and the half bottle of valiums she had taken were all she wanted in life as she laid her head back down on the exposed tree root. Her breaths were shallow and her thoughts fogged over. "Paul?" she mumbled in question. "I've missed you so much." She sobbed with relief.

Not this way, Erin, her husband said with a sad smile. It was too late; Erin's heart slowed further and then stopped. Her eyes shot open, frozen in surprise at her final resting spot.

***

"How much time do we have?" Gary asked, looking out the small road that led to the house.

"Well, they're on the access road for sure," Ron replied.

"So within three miles," Gary said aloud.

"Too close, brother. I know what you're thinking."

Gary was done thinking; he was heading for the front gate. Ron had dug out a pit in the middle of the access road; it was seven feet deep, twelve feet across, and the width of the road across about ten feet. They had built a makeshift bridge over the gap so that they could get in and out when needed. The aluminum structure was held in place with heavy metal rods which, if removed, would cause the bridge to collapse once anything of substantial weight bore down on it. The idea being that the defenses around the house were stout but would have great difficulty holding up to a tank or in this case tractor trailers ramming at full steam.

"Dad!" Ron said louder than he needed to.

"I'm covering...nothing yet," he said, looking through his scope.

Travis was back with his second ammo run. He had

just stood up and was turning to run back in. "Zombies!" he yelled, pointing into the woods about forty yards away. They had been heading towards the house, but changed direction when they spotted movement; Gary.

"There's dozens of them," Lyndsey said.

"Sis, get the kids down into the fallout shelter," Ron said, not taking his eyes off Gary. There were dozens in sight, but more kept coming. "Gary, it isn't worth it!" Ron shouted wrapping his hands around his mouth to project his voice. But that was a lie, it was worth it. One truck could smash through just about everything they had accomplished.

Gary was humming as he was running, then he started to sing softly, *"Risin' up, back on the street. Did my time, took my chances. Went the distance, now I'm back on my feet. Just a man and his will to survive..."* Gary reached the bridge just as he completed the first stanza. He saw the zombies but still figured he had enough time to pull the pin. His shoulders, arms, neck, and legs, strained as he pulled on the two foot around pin. Inch by blessed inch it scraped free.

"Gary, get out of there," Ron shouted.

Tony started shooting. Gary could hear zombies thudding to the ground.

"Still time," he said as the bodies hitting the ground still sounded far enough away.

Added to Tony's precision shots was Travis' cover fire. "Uncle Gary, you should really get your ass moving!" Travis shouted.

"No swearing," Tracy admonished him.

"This is as good a time as any," he answered his mother in between blasts.

She was too lost in twisting worry to give Travis any flack over his response as she watched zombies streaming through the woods like ghostly bearers of death.

Gary had both legs dug into the ground and was pulling with all his might, the pin yielding but on its own schedule, not caring in the least that Gary's timetable was running late. The majority of it was out, but now the bullets were of close enough proximity that he could hear them whining by like relentless deer flies. He pushed up and down until the heavy 'pin' dropped to the ground. He lifted it over his head and again broke out into song. "*It's the eye of the tiger, it's the thrill of the fight...*" Gary tossed it to the side and started running.

"Let's go, Rocky, get your ass back here!" Ron was motioning for him. "If he starts shadow boxing while he's running, I'm going to kill him."

BT was beside Travis, they were keeping the zombies to Gary's left from approaching any closer, but it was Tony's sniper rifle shooting that was keeping the ones that had gotten up behind him from being able to drag him down.

Cindy held the gate open for him as he ran through. She quickly closed it and latched it, heading back up to the deck as the first of the zombies crashed into it. Gary gave the zombies the finger, sang one more stanza and headed upstairs. "*Risin' up to the challenge of our rival, and the last known survivor...*"

"Are you nuts?" Ron yelled at his younger brother. "You did good." He gave Gary a hug. "Don't do it again."

Gary saw a trail of dead zombies where he had been. "Yeah, that's probably safe to say."

"It doesn't sound like they're coming any closer," Tracy said.

"Looks like they're just dropping their payload," Ron said, looking as zombies were coming by the score.

Nicole came up to Ron's side. "MJ wants to know if he should throw the switch."

"Now would be as good a time as any." Ron was still trying to bring his beating heart down to a manageable rate and not having much success.

The six-foot high chain link fence was swaying as more zombies walked into the impediment, the extra braces on the poles and the chain link section themselves would not be yielding anytime soon.

Perimeter lights flooded on just as the zombies

touching the gate and fence stood bolt upright, a decent current running through their frames, enough to kill a man or at the very least incapacitate him. The zombies' muscles were locked in place, and still more came pressing up against their stock still brethren only to join them in their rigidity.

"Is it killing them?" Tracy asked, hoping that was the case.

Ron grabbed his binoculars. "I can't tell for sure. Travis, can you go down and tell MJ to turn the fence off for a minute, then back on? Thanks," he added as Travis went by.

The first few zombies that had been the unfortunate first test zombies fell to the ground as the current let their muscles loose. More moved in to take their spot, but there were not yet enough that they blocked out the zombies on the ground as they stood and fought for access to the fence.

"Well that answers that question," Ron said more to himself. He walked inside and yelled down the stairs. "Turn the fence back on." Travis was already on his way back up and heading for the outside deck.

"Time to make them pay for their trespassing," Tony said as he sent a bullet through the forehead of the nearest zombie. A plume shot out the back of its skull. Travis, Gary, and BT joined in the shooting.

"Take your time," Tony told them. "One shot, at least one kill with them packing this closely. Bullets are going to get precious by the time this is all over."

The first quandary surfaced about twenty minutes into the firefight. The dead zombies up against the fence hadn't seen fit to fall away so that it would be easier targeting in on those behind.

Mad Jack had just come up from the basement to see how his handiwork was holding up.

"Going to need you to go back downstairs and turn it off," Ron told him.

Mad Jack's face fell. His face, which had a moment before been beaming, was now dejected.

"It works fine, MJ," Ron said, picking up on the man's feelings. "Probably too well. We can't get the extra dead ones off the fence. Listen, shut it off for about a solid minute, keep it on for ten and just keep repeating the cycle while the zombies change out."

Mad Jack had an extra swagger in his step as he headed back down.

Mrs. Deneaux was sitting on a lounger looking up at the sky as she enjoyed one of her cigarettes.

"You getting in on this?" Ron asked, preparing his rifle.

"When it counts I suppose I will," she said after exhaling.

Zombies still flowed. The fence which encased the entire grounds was now at least ten deep at the minimum; the only thing keeping them from going deeper where the trees. The accumulated weight—no matter how strong the supports—was beginning to fold the structure in on itself. They had to keep revolving weapons out as they got too hot to shoot without damaging the barrels and still it would not be enough.

"Truck coming!" Gary shouted over the blasts.

"Want me to take out the driver?" Travis asked. "I've got a clear shot."

"Let him come," Tony said. "He'll fill in the hole nicely." *And then I'll kill him when he tries to run*, Tony thought, trying to protect his grandson from the distaste of killing a man that would linger with him through his entire life like a rotten piece of food that would come back up for a second taste from time to time.

The truck started slowly down the dense, tree-lined path, then began to pick up speed. Tony thought that someone had surely drawn the short end of the stick as they barreled towards the fence line and ultimately the house. The trailer had been removed, giving the truck the ability to be more maneuverable and move faster. Tony could not see the driver as he sighted in. The straw had been short, but not short enough that they didn't try to protect that driver. He was hidden behind what looked like a piece of steel.

"Might as well have some fun," Tony said aloud as he pulled the trigger on his favorite weapon: a Remington 30-30, bolt-action hunting rifle with a Leupold 8-times scope. The bullet smashed easily through the safety glass of the windshield and hit the steel. The resulting gong could be heard over the roar of the engine. The truck swerved momentarily, nearly clipping a tree as the driver placed his hands over his ears. The steel was still vibrating when the front end of the truck began to dip down. The unsupported 'bridge' dropped out from under the truck, the front end smashing into the far side of the earthen embankment. The metal screeched as it took on its new form. Plastic and glass smashed, and once the truck engine seized, they could hear the driver moaning.

"Al, you alright?" someone yelled out from around a small curve in the road safely tucked away from any defender shots.

"My head, Kong, I'm bleeding...smashed myself on the plating. Get me out of here, man!" Al yelled frantically. He didn't want to tell Kong that he had also broken his vial; the man would probably leave him where he was.

"Go hook up some tow cables to the back end of the truck," Kong told the nearest driver. He though his name might be Scribner or Scrivener, he didn't really care.

"Why me, man?" the guy asked.

"Because I said. Get someone to cover your ass if you need to," Kong said

"Let's just leave the damn truck there. It ain't bothering anyone," Scribner replied.

"It's bothering me and fucking bad!" Kong yelled. "I want the damn thing removed so we can throw something over that hole and drive in if we want to. Plus, I sort of owe Al one. And if you don't, I'll kill you...enough reason?"

"Yeah, yeah, I get it." Scribner walked back up the road to the staging area, which was basically just a road with trucks parked up and down the length of it. He got a tow line from his rig and grabbed two men sitting on their fender. They were the only ones with rifles on and if he was going to get cover, he at least wanted men that were armed.

"What's going on?" the taller of the two asked. His name was Burkes, he had a moustache that made him look somewhat like a cowboy and he may have been able to pull it off, but instead of cowboy hat, he insisted on a golf visor, and instead of the signature leather boots, he wore Keds.

"The truck they sent in to bust down the fence got stuck and..." For a moment he thought about lying and telling the man that Kong had told him to get a man to hook it up, but Kong was still standing at the curve and would never let him get away with it. "...I have to hook this up to the rear end of it so we can pull it out." He held the hook up.

"I'm not going near that house," the shorter man replied. His name was Dobbs; he looked like a cross between an accountant and a construction worker. Small spectacles did little to re-shape his square head and jaw. Powerful arms were sheathed in a button-up shirt. Add to that the fact that he was wearing khakis and Hush Puppies, it seemed he was having great difficulty defining his cliché. "You hear all those shots? Sounds like a war up there."

"It is a war, dip wad," Scribner said. "And do you know what happens to soldiers that disobey orders?"

Dobbs' eyes widened. He hadn't really thought of it that way until just now. He checked his weapon.

"Three men heading towards the back of the truck, Pops," Travis told his grandfather. The three men approaching the truck were bent over so far, they looked like the trio were all vying for the part of Quasimodo in *The Bells of Notre Dame* at the local dinner theater.

"Do they think nobody can see them?" Mrs. Deneaux asked, finally getting up from her chair.

"Looks like they're going to try and pull the truck out," Ron said, clenching something tightly in his left hand.

"Did the hook one of them is carrying give it away?"

Deneaux asked.

"Ron?" Tony asked his oldest son.

Ron knew what he had to do, but theory was always easier than practice.

"Ron, once he lays that hook on, they're gone," Tony stated looking through his scope.

Ron was a devout anarchist…that was why his next words seemed to take on more meaning. "God forgive me," he said as he pressed down on the detonator. For the briefest of moments nothing happened, and Ron was relieved. Then the earth exploded, or at least that was what it looked like as two strategically placed Claymore mines went off—one on each side of the disabled truck. Ball bearings shredded the three men like a fork pulled along a slow roasted pork loin. Meat, bones, and blood…lots and lots of blood coated the trees on either side of the roadway.

The man still in the truck opened his door and fell to the ground, the sound and possibly some shrapnel injuring him further. He began to crawl back towards the truckers' encampment. Tony severed his spine, killing him instantly.

"It's good to see at least one Talbot not all wrapped up in morality," Mrs. Deneaux said as she turned to get back on her chair.

Tony let his head drop a bit, he had not wanted to kill the man, he *had* to.

"Well, they'll think twice before they come that route," Mrs. Deneaux said smiling, lighting another cigarette.

"Wish we had more of those," Ron said, putting the detonator down on a small table, absently wiping his hand on his shirt as if he could wipe off the death his thumb had just delivered.

"It's alright, son," Tony said. "Mrs. Deneaux is right. No one is going to come up that way."

***

Eliza's head whipped around as the explosion tore

through her men. "Kong," she said to the truck driver's leader.

"I'll find out," he told her.

"Seems the rest of the Talbot clan has just as many surprises as Michael," Tomas said smiling.

"Do not start!" she said, pointing her finger at her brother.

Kong came back a moment later. "We have a truck stuck in the only approach a vehicle can make. They had it booby-trapped so when three of my men went up to hook up a tow cable it went off. They were killed instantly...plus the original driver."

"Have my zombies made progress?" Eliza asked.

"Their fence is holding so far. Doesn't make much sense, it's only a chain link fence and it has extra supports, but still with as much push as the zombies should be giving it. It should have buckled by now. And what makes it weirder is the zombies up towards the front are not really doing anything, they just kind of stand there," Kong finished.

Tomas had an idea of what might be going on. His sister looked completely befuddled and he decided to not tell her.

"We can make it more difficult on these people," Kong stated.

"I'm listening," Eliza told him.

"We can station men in the woods and shoot back. Maybe we kill some of them...at the very least we can keep them off that wraparound deck. We have more options if they're not cutting down your zombies at the rate they are now. And a few of the driver's are prior military, we could probably assemble some sort of strike team when they're all huddled inside."

"I would like at least some of them taken alive," Eliza intoned.

"Of course," Kong said, leaving to get some planning done.

CHAPTER THIRTY-THREE

Mike Journal Entry 13

According to the mile markers, we had walked ten miles and where getting pretty close to the 495 and 95 interchange. Our traveling was getting slower and slower; Azilc was having great difficulty walking under such a heavy load. Every time she lagged behind, I would take more equipment from her even as she protested that she needed to do her part. By the time we hit ten miles, the only thing left to carry would have been her.

"Someone's coming," Azile said as she stood back up. She had been sitting by the side of the road with her shoes off tenderly rubbing around her sore spots. "Hide?" she asked me when she realized I wasn't moving.

Normally that would have been standard operating procedure, but we hadn't encountered so much as a scooter. We were traveling at a whopping ten miles per half day, and at this rate, we'd get to Maine and it'd be winter and I had no desire to revisit sled travel. "Hold still, but get ready to move."

"That's your plan?"

"Better than most," I told her. My heart thudded a little heavier when I saw that big rig crest over the top of a small rise.

"It's a truck, Mike," Azile said, looking over towards the trees.

"Hold steady," I told her, the trucker had already seen us. He flashed his lights, if we bolted now it would look mighty suspicious, although 'suspected' is better than dead. Now I was looking over at the tree line.

The truck was slowing as it approached. It stopped

about twenty feet away. "That rig back there yours?" he shouted, sticking his head out from the window.

"Hers!" I pointed to Azile. She did not look pleased that I had singled her out.

"Run into a bit of trouble?" the trucker asked.

"Flat tire," I told him.

"Is that right?" he asked back.

"We're running late for an appointment, is there any chance you could help us out?" Azile asked.

The driver switched his gaze from me to Azile, but keeping me in his periphery due to all the weaponry I was carrying. "That's funny 'cause I'm a little late, too…had some truck trouble and had to stop and get a quick fix on."

What were the odds? I thought. I was going to give it a shot. "Listen, we need to get to a particular thing in Maine, or we're going to be in a world of hurt."

I watched as recognition lit the man's face up. "Well fancy that, I have an engagement in Maine also. I just need to make sure we're playing for the same team, you can never be too careful."

"Never too careful," I reiterated when I saw the barrel of his rifle resting on his dashboard.

"We had a shipment of guns and food," Azile said. "Kong gave us directions to a place in Maine where we were supposed to deliver them. If I don't at least show up and tell him what happened he'll think I stole the stuff."

The man's face softened when he heard Kong's name. "Kong isn't the most forgiving man, are you sure you don't want to just start walking the other way?" The driver asked.

"I'm his niece," Azile said, "he might be mad but he'll understand."

"What about him?" the driver asked.

"He's my porter."

"Funny," I said under my breath.

"Come on, you both can tell me what happened when you get up here," the driver said as he reached over and opened his passenger door.

A large orange tabby was staring me straight in the face as I went to climb into the rig.

"Oh, don't mind him, I picked him up back in North Carolina. He was just wandering around. He climbed up into the truck and now he's convinced he owns the place," the driver said, smiling as he reached under and picked the cat up.

The cat hissed violently as he did so, but it was looking squarely at me. The cat remembered me. *Good*, I thought, *he'll know why I'm cutting off its air flow when I get the chance.*

"Take a little longer," Azile said as she brushed past.

"Can we put some of the rifles in the back?" I asked the driver.

He looked at me strangely. "You may have been carrying food and weapons, not me."

Then I realized it, his trailer was jammed full of zombies. "Yeah, I'll just hold on to them," I told him as I handed the weapons up to Azile, truly hoping that one would accidently discharge and take out the damn cat.

"My name is Jake Fitzgerald, most folks just call me Fritz," he said, extending his hand.

I nearly froze, remembering the last person I'd known with the same moniker. I recovered smoothly enough, I hoped. I wasn't an actor. "Mike, Mike Tal...isman." I was figuratively fist-palming my forehead. I had nearly given the man my true name.

I could see Azile's slight head shake as she realized what I had nearly done. Fritz hadn't seemed to catch my error as he was getting the truck rolling. "Nice to meet you, Mike, it'll be great to have some company. What happened to your rig?" Fritz asked, looking into the back where the sleeper was.

"Someone was shooting at us, must have hit a fuel line. They took off once we started returning fire," Azile replied, trying to be as least descriptive as possible.

"Man, looks more like a bomb went off," Fritzy laughed.

"You'd think," I half laughed, keeping an eye on him to see if he was fishing or not. He didn't seem to be.

"Have you tried this little vial thing out yet?" he asked as he pulled a small bottle wrapped in an ornate piece of silver jewelry out to show us.

I clutched my shirt as if I had one underneath. "Not yet. Not sure I want to, either," I told him.

"I get you, I mean the only way you could, would entail being face-to-face with a zombie and I don't want to do that. Already been close enough a few times, no desire to do it anymore and willingly. Besides, Kong said he tested it and it worked, his word is good enough for me. And if it does work it's worth what we're going to do."

"Do you even know?" I asked him.

"Well I know that Eliza woman has a personal vendetta to settle, that's about it."

"So you signed up with her not caring the consequences?" I asked.

"Why should I?" he shot back. "As long as I gain from it, that's all that really matters."

"Fuck everyone else?" I asked.

"Basically. I don't know why you're getting all judgmental on me, you signed up for the same damn mission," Fritzy said indignantly. "You know, I've known Kong a good many years now."

Shit. Alarms started going off in my mind's early warning detection system.

It must have for Azile, too, she pressed the barrel of an as yet unseen weapon—at least to me—up to Fritzy's head.

"Yup I figured, he never once did say anything about a niece. I'm getting hijacked by my own pistol," he said, looking over slightly at the revolver. "Well isn't that wonderful."

"Is it the name?" I asked aloud, but to no one in

particularly.

"Huh?" Azile and Fritzy asked.

"I haven't had much luck with people named Fritzy or similar sounding anyway," I told them. "Stop the truck."

"Pretty please," Azile said as she pulled the hammer of the pistol back.

"You gonna shoot me now?" he asked nervously as the big rig came to a halt.

"No, something much better," I told him.

By the time Azile was putting the truck in gear, Fritzy, his vial and that stupid fucking cat were neatly tucked away in the trailer with a few hundred zombies.

"Should have just shot him," Azile said. "It would have been more humane."

"He was going to wipe out my family just because. Fuck humane."

We could hear him screaming for mercy occasionally, then some heavy duty sobbing. A few times I thought I heard some serious hissings from a cat, but that just may have been wishful thinking on my part.

CHAPTER THIRTY-FOUR

The Deck

Tony was on the deck reassembling one of his rifles after a thorough cleaning when he heard the shot. He grabbed another rifle to go investigate. The rest of the family was trying to get some sleep as he did his watch. At first, he thought that perhaps someone was up and decided to take out a little frustration on the zombies, but when he turned the corner and saw that one of the spotlights was out he knew what was happening. The other side had decided to fire back.

He dipped down below the edge of the railing which had been lined with half-inch steel plating, trying to see if he could possibly figure out where the shots were coming from. Travis came running out when he heard the shots. Tony's cries of warning were intermingled with the sound of the rifle shot as Travis went down. Tony stood and peppered the location where he had seen the muzzle flash, then he ran back to his grandson.

"I've been shot, Pops," Travis said. "It hurts so bad." His teeth were chattering between words.

"What's happening?" Nancy asked, coming towards the door.

"Get down!" Tony yelled. "Help me get Travis back in."

Help was coming in droves now. BT was next, he quickly traversed the length of the room and grabbed Travis as Tony kept them covered.

Nancy swept everything off the kitchen table as BT placed him gently down.

"Hurts so bad, BT," Travis said, his eyes clenched shut, tears of pain attempting to push through.

"It'll be alright," BT said stroking the boy's head.

"Nancy, get some towels, water and a knife," Tony said as he put his rifle down. "And then get his mother."

BT looked over at Tony with concern.

"I...I'm so cold," Travis said. "I could use a shot of whiskey for the pain."

BT ran over to the liquor cabinet as Tony cut Travis' shirt off. "Well De Niro you're not," Tony told him. He grabbed the bottle from BT, popped the top off, and took a long pull. "That's for not being careful," he told his grandson, "and this...well this is for scaring the hell out of me." He poured a fair amount over Travis' wound. Now Travis' howls of pain were real.

"Jesus H. Christ, what the hell are you doing, Tony?" BT shouted, throwing his hands to his head, unsure what to do. "The more time I spend with the Talbots, the more I feel like I'm the sanest person in an insane asylum, but at that point what difference does it make?"

Tracy was now at the entry to the kitchen. "Tony?" she asked, her one word question turning her face ashen white.

"He'll be fine, bullet went in and out. I, on the other hand, probably suffered a heart attack." Tony sat down heavily on one of the kitchen chairs while taking another pull from the whiskey bottle.

"Mom, it hurts so bad," Travis said, reaching out with his arm from the undamaged side.

The bullet had caught him underneath the shoulder; it was a flesh wound that had already stopped bleeding for the most part.

"Oh, Travis," Tracy sobbed, grabbing her son.

Tony pressed the bottle up against his head. He hated the fiery liquid, but he thought it might be the only thing that would quell the panic of nearly seeing his grandson cut down. More shots had been going on as the rest of the clan gathered in and around the kitchen. Slowly but steadily, the compound was going dark as the spotlights were taken out.

Tony took one more pull. "Ron," he said as he stood, "they're getting ready for some sort of offensive, I can feel it, we're going to need a couple of more people out on duty. Everyone needs to make sure they stay below the lip of the railing. Shut off unessential lights in the house and get Travis down to the safe room at least until he gets patched up." He was trying his best to walk the fine line between allaying Tracy's fears and making sure the boy didn't feel like he was being left out.

Mrs. Deneaux was already on the deck sitting far enough back that the gunmen didn't have an angle on her. "How is the boy?" she asked Tony between cigarette puffs.

"He'll be fine, caught him under his shoulder."

"Fortunate. I don't believe Tracy could take another loss, she's like that candy that's all hard on the outside and soft on the inside."

"Better than hard and bitter all the way through," BT said as he was almost crawling to get his bulk through the doorway unseen.

"Debatable," Mrs. Deneaux said as she took humor from BT trying to make himself appear small. "You look like a bear trying to fit through a doggie door. Wake me before dawn, will you, Tony?" She asked before putting her cigarette out and closing her eyes.

"Why before dawn?" BT asked Tony as they settled in on the other side of the house.

"Any force that has wanted to catch its opponent at their least alert always attacks right before dawn," Tony told him, sitting with his back against the plating.

"And the old bat knew that?" BT asked sitting next to him.

"She's probably employed the tactic numerous times herself," Tony said smiling.

"Man I see so much of Mike in all of you," BT said sadly. "It's like he's not really gone."

"If only that were the case," Tony said.

CHAPTER THIRTY-FIVE

Mike Journal Entry 14

It was after three in the morning when we finally pulled into Searsport.

"Now what?" Azile asked.

"I'd rather just ditch the damn truck, but we're still ten miles out. However, if we get too close, they'll hear us coming and if we stop then and don't show up they'll get suspicious. How many of those driver's would recognize you?" I asked, the beginning of an idea forming in my head.

"Kong, Horatio, and maybe four or five others. Why?"

"I think we play the odds."

"Whose odds? Vegas odds? Because those are never good."

"So you have the potential of nine people knowing you including Tomas and Eliza, I only have two. When I tell you to pull over, do it, then I'll drive."

Azile's expression was dubious at best.

"It'll only be for a little way," I assured her.

"Kong will recognize you. I mean he'll recognize that you don't belong, I mean," Azile explained.

"That will have to be a problem we deal with later. First things first, there's a dry cleaner at the center of town, pull over when I tell you."

Between how ill-fitting and smelly my clothes were, Azile didn't have a comment about my wanting to change.

The sound of the idling truck barely masked the plate glass shattering as I threw an ashtray stand through it. It had been months since police had come to any crime scene and still I looked around guiltily, old habits die hard.

"Hurry up!" Azile said through the window. "And no suits."

"What are the odds they'll have jeans here?" I asked her.

"At a dry cleaners? Just hurry," she reiterated.

I stepped into the blackness of the store, the echoing engine vibrations were slightly disorienting. The long 'ess' of plastic wrapped clothes was directly in front of me as were every conceivable nightmare I could think of. I was convinced a horde of zombies laid in wait. I quickly moved behind the counter and scooped up a handful of clothes off the rack. I brushed anything that looked remotely like business wear off to the floor. I wasn't left with much to choose from.

"Who dry cleans a skull cap?" I asked the non-existent attendant. Someone was still in my corner as I grabbed the small bag off the line. It covered my Eliza blocker perfectly and gave me sort of a World War 2 James Dean look. Hey it's my mind I can live in any fantasy I want and this way I could get rid of the dreaded Yankees cap.

There was a long sleeved shirt that didn't look too bad; it had the name of a bar on it, Rollie's or something close to that. It was a little snug when I put it on, but nothing like my previous duds, and I knew this was clean. Now I needed some pants that didn't look like I shopped in the boys' department. This was proving a little more difficult. First off, most of the clothes were women's, I thought I should still be alright, Maine is known for its stout women. They were of the power suit variety though and then I came across not what I wanted but what I could use.

"They still make Chino's?" I asked holding the pants up to the near non-existent light. It was difficult to tell, but they looked brown from where I was standing. I turned so that I wasn't facing Azile and quickly stripped out of the old and into the new.

I ran back to the truck much more comfortable than when I had departed. The brightness of the dome light took some time to adjust as I got back in my seat.

"Well you look good," Azile laughed.

"My pants are purple," I said horrified.

Azile was laughing, but she didn't really let loose until she had me show her the back of my shirt.

"What?"

"It says you won a wet t-shirt contest."

"Are you kidding me?" I pulled the shirt over my head, and dammit if she wasn't right. For reasons known only to me, I looked at the care tag, 'dry clean only'. "Why the fuck would they make a wet t-shirt, shirt, dry clean only?"

"You want to get different clothes?" she asked.

I did and I didn't. Nothing happened and I didn't hear anything in there, but that dry cleaners just didn't feel right. Plus, being this close to my family, I just wanted to get there. "Let's go," I told Azile, taking one last look back.

"Last chance," she told me.

I sat steadfast. When we took the final road before my father's dirt road drive I had Azile pull over.

"It's not far is it?" she asked as I ground the gears into drive, forcing rather than allowing. The truck was bucking like a bull with his balls cinched tight—although, if my balls were cinched I'd probably just be crying in a corner.

"You should hide," I told her as I came up over a small rise. Trucks were lined up on both sides of the roadway, zombies were everywhere. Occasionally I would see a human, but for the most part, they were staying out of the way of the zombies. I eased the truck into the back of the last truck in the line. And by 'easing' I mean 'tapped' the bumper and by 'tapped' the bumper I mean did damage that would have entailed exchanging insurance papers in an earlier version of the world. The noise should not have gone unnoticed, but the sound of gunfire was prevalent. It didn't stop the owner of the truck from coming out of his cab to investigate.

"Hey, you fucking nimrod, what is your problem?" he

yelled as he hopped down, shying away as a couple of zombies checked him out, then moved on.

"I'm real sorry," I told him.

"Oh, you will be, dipshit," he said as he moved closer. "Get out here!" he shouted as he walked past the damage I had done to his rig.

"I'm trying...the seatbelt is stuck."

"Let me help you with that!" he said angrily as he opened my door and hopped on the running board.

The light glinted off the silver of the chain he wore around his neck. I snatched it before he could react, then I pushed him with my hand on his face off of the truck and onto the pavement. Zombies swept in before he could sound the alarm. It was gruesome being this close to a person being eaten, the sounds of lips smacking and teeth cracking into bone. I hoped no one else would notice the zombie congregation as they knelt at the altar of flesh.

A few zombies looked up at me as I came out of the truck. I put the vial around my neck and they went back to the business of orally eviscerating my accident victim. I hastily walked to the back of my truck and moved the latch. Fritz was no longer clutching the cat, for better or worse, the vermin had decided it was better off on its own, I'm sure the stringy thing hadn't tasted any good, but I won't lie and tell you I wasn't happy to see it gone.

"Oh thank God," Fritz said. He was huddled up against the doors, nearly falling out as I opened them, snot, tears and the drool of the closest zombies covered him from head to toe. I ripped the chain from his neck quickly closing the door to his screams. The trailer rocked a little as Fritz became a late night snack.

I climbed back into the truck and handed Azile a necklace. "Take this," I told her as I handed it into the back of the sleeper.

"Where'd you get it?"

"Do you really want to know?" I asked back. She accepted it without a response. "I'm going to see if I can find anything out."

"What about me?"

"I'll lock the doors. I should be right back, if I'm not, consider me lost."

Her eyes got big at that statement.

"Azile, if that's the case, unhitch the damn trailer and get out of here, just leave. If you do stay close enough to figure out what happened and you see Eliza leave, go west or north, just get out of here. If not, come back. Whoever is left standing will take you in."

"Mike, I came here to kill Eliza. I'm not leaving until that's done."

"Okay, let me see what I can find out," I told her as I got back out of the truck making sure to lock both sides up.

The zombies had pretty much stripped the truck driver clean. Most had left as he was down to about bone marrow; but a few of the more ravenous were even going after that. I pushed them away and I kicked what remained underneath his truck just to avoid any prying eyes. We were far enough from the action, but there wasn't any reason to take unnecessary risks. Unfortunately, it wasn't so much a kick as it was a push with my boot, because there just wasn't enough of him left for my sole to find purchase on.

"Fucking gross," I said looking at my boot that was now covered in what I was going to call 'goo'. I walked the rest of the way down Dowboin lane, then took the left down onto my father's lane. I was still about a quarter of a mile from the house but this was where all the activity was happening. The zombies were present but they were very sparse, those that I could see where heading towards the Talbot compound. I saw a knot of men and had to imagine that Eliza was in the middle of it.

I had my gun and I was weighing out the odds of success. If it were just zombies I had to deal with I might have taken a chance, and I still wasn't sure she was in the throng. I caught a glimpse of her as the group broke up. A large man was walking in my direction. Eliza went to wherever evil bitches go.

"I need prior military volunteers!" the large man was shouting.

"Fuck it," I muttered. At least I wasn't lying when I told him I was prior military. "Here." I raised my hand.

"Who the fuck are you?" he asked stopping right in front of me.

"I came in with Fritz. I helped him fix his truck, he told me what was going on and I wanted in. My name is... (what the fuck is my name?) Josh, Joshua Buker." *No clue where that came from but happy for the inspiration.*

"You all vialed up?" the man asked.

I showed him. He seemed to have completely missed my pause as I sought to name myself, understandable with how much was going on, add to that the repeated rifle shooting.

"Well, if he trusted you enough to give you his spare, then that's good enough for me."

He had a spare? I thought.

"Where's he at?"

"He's working on his trailer, told me to see what was going on."

"You're prior military?"

"Marines…Afghanistan and Iraq," I told him.

"Good enough for me, I've got a team with two Navy Seals, one Army Ranger and a Green Beret."

"Great," I said. *Why don't we just add in some fucking special forces ninjas to make it interesting?* I thought. The Army guys would be tough, but the Navy Seals would be brutal, I love my Marine Corps, but the SEALS were second to none, not only in the US, but the entire planet.

"My name is Kong." I stuck my hand out to shake, he looked at it and then at my face. I got the hint. "You take care of this…then I'll shake your hand."

I nodded. What I wanted to do was punch him in the head. Instead, I asked him where I could be briefed about what I had volunteered for.

Half an hour later I had an extra four magazines of ammo plus two grenades. Of the five men, I had come out of the service with the lowest rank, and now I was the oldest among them. My job was to bring up the rear, in this case, that was just fine. Someone had wrangled up a camouflage top for me which I was thankful to wear; the purple pants wouldn't be a problem in the impenetrable light. We melted into the woods and past the loose ring of men surrounding the house. There was a small sliver of moon to guide us by. I could see the now useless spotlights, shards of glass hanging precariously from them.

I waited until the two SEALS and the Green Beret entered into the ring of zombies before I made my move. I slung my rifle so that it was on my back and closed in.

"Watch it, fucking jarhead," the Ranger told me as I kicked the side of his boot. He turned I think to give me more shit, then, ironically, I shoved the knife he had given me into his Adam's apple. I thought the fibrous knot would resist more, but the knife cut the neck protrusion neatly in two. He gurgled as I drove it further in severing his spinal column.

His eyes pleaded for an answer, so I gave him one. "My name is Michael Talbot and that's my family you're trying to kill." He might have understood, but that wasn't making his passing any easier. I grabbed the chain off his neck and dropped him for the zombies, hurriedly catching up to the rest of *my squad.*

The fucking SEAL I think was prescient; he turned just as I was coming up on him. The set in my eye may have given it away, or the fresh blood still dripping from my Army combat knife. It had a nice feel to it, not quite as deadly as my beloved Ka-Bar but it would do in a pinch. A grin spread across his lips when he let his M-4 swing on its tactical harness as he pulled out what looked like a short sword from a leg sheath.

"Looks like you brought a butter knife to a sword fight," he said as he got down into a fighting stance, the zombies were not yielding much room. Our fighting circle wasn't going to be much more than two strides across. "I'm going to make a Popsicle out of you," he said, still grinning.

His smile may have faltered a little bit when he realized I wasn't dissuaded from my present course of action, although he may have just changed it to determination.

"Never much liked you fucking Marines, bullet catchers are all you're really good for." He said.

I got down into a fighting stance. "Are those really the last words you want to say?" I asked him earnestly. Before he could reply, I moved in. I've got to admit, he was fast. Unfortunately for him I was enhanced. I brought the blade up against his wrist severing as many arteries as I could.

"How...how did you do that?" he asked as blood welled then poured from his non-knife wielding arm. "I'm a Navy SEAL, you can't do this to me," he said.

"If you promise me that you'll leave now and never come back here, ever, I'll let you leave."

"Who the fuck are these people to you?" he asked, trying to staunch the flow. Zombies were beginning to jostle around him as fresh blood like ambrosia drew them tight.

"Does it matter?" I asked him back. "I'm giving you the opportunity to save yourself and be done with this madness. There's a short shelf life on your answer."

"I can't..."

I didn't let him finish the rest of his sentence, with his right hand desperately trying to hold his life fluid in, he was easy pickings. I cut his carotid artery and lifted the vial from his neck. The zombies were chewing flesh from him before he hit the ground.

The remaining two men were at the very edge of the compound, less than three or four zombies from the fence. They were looking back, waiting for the rest of the group to catch up, when I showed.

"Where's Able and Jericho?" the remaining SEAL asked.

"Hell I would imagine," I said as I leveled my rifle on them. "I wouldn't," I told the other Navy Seal who was trying to bring his rifle up. "Put your weapons on the ground," I told them.

"And if we don't?" the Ranger asked.

"I've killed four men tonight, do you think I've hit my limit?" I asked him. Slowly, with my right hand pulling the vials out of my pocket, I displayed them like trophies. I put them back in my pocket, then put my hand back up to brace the M-4.

"Why haven't you just killed us?" the Seal asked as he put his weapon down and was standing back up.

"Zombies are one thing, but killing men, that's completely another," I told him.

The Navy man nodded slightly in agreement.

"You both have one chance to save yourselves, leave and never come back. That's all you have to do."

"That's it? You're not going to shoot us in the back?" the Army man asked.

"I could have already done that. Listen, I'm not going to play this game much longer, either leave or die."

To his credit, the Army guy headed off to the left. I wasn't sure if he planned on keeping his word or not. More than likely he was going to get out of range, then head back to Kong and tell him what happened. That was actually alright. Let the man know that I had bested four of their best and maybe he would debate the operation in its entirety.

"Knives?" the Seal asked.

"I did knives with your partner," I told him. "I wish you'd left."

In one fluid motion I pushed my rifle onto my back and grabbed a grenade. I pulled the pin and ran to the Seal's location as I pulled on his waistband I deposited the grenade, then I quickly grabbed the chain around his neck. Zombies were vying for position around him as I pushed away. A mash of zombie and human parts burst under the assault of the grenade's shrapnel. Unluckily for me, I was in the midst of the fallout zone. Hot pieces of anatomy rained down. I was covered in the remains of multiple zombies and at least one man.

Some sporadic gunfire erupted from around me after the explosion, but nothing close. It seemed to be merely a reflexive action. Now that I was paying attention, I could hear the hum of the fence as electric current ran through it. *Had to be MJ*, I thought, *friggen brilliant*. I didn't think it was enough to kill a man if only because of the zombies' actions as they touched it, but I wasn't confident enough in their physiology to trust my own life to it. Who knows, maybe what only gave them a slight jolt would send me sprawling through the air like a circus clown shot from a cannon, fun to watch, sucky to live through.

The fence was six-feet high and there wasn't a tree anywhere near it. I began to rip shirts off the zombies nearest me, they didn't care and seemed happy to oblige. I wrapped my feet as best I could, hoping that I would have enough insulation, then I sought out a stout zombie which in this case appeared to be a woman of East German descent. She was only about five feet tall, mostly round and looked like she could bench a Beetle.

"Nice to make your acquaintance," I told her back. She wasn't properly couched in etiquette. "You'll do."

I pushed the back of her knees until she fell to them, then I climbed up. I was now getting quite possibly the first zombie piggy back ride. I wasn't thrilled with having my knees next to her mouth, but after one failed attempt with her thick arms to wave me away she completely forgot about me as she stood back up, my added weight not hampering or hindering her in the least. I thought this could be a boon for parents everywhere, I could make millions! How many times had we as parents been ridden into the ground from the insistent wishes of our offspring to give them rides, even when their age and weight had begun to exceed our limits? Now, I could sell zombies fitted with saddles that would take the kiddies for rides indefinitely. ZTI could become a global entity (Zombie Transportation Incorporated). Our dependence on foreign oil would be over. They'd have to invent a new monetary term for how rich I'd be.

I would have kept thinking along those lines if I wasn't receiving a tingling across my thighs and ass. Greta (that's what I was calling her) was now about two zombies away from the fence, her body was slowly taking on the rigidity of her peers in front of her. I placed my hand on the top of her dirt and oil laden head and balanced my weight so that I could stand. I was thankful the night was still mostly dark, dawn was approaching but still it would be difficult to pick me out of the rest of the crowd, the longer I stayed standing on her shoulders, the better my odds of getting shot at by either side though.

I didn't feel any electricity as I stood tall on her shoulders—only wavering once, luckily she seemed fairly rooted to the ground at this point. I stepped on the man in front of her—at this point I had a slight tingling—and then, as I stepped on the zombie actually touching the fence, I felt what seemed like pins and needles traversing up my calves. It was uncomfortable at the moment, but I could see it becoming debilitating if I stayed there long enough. My first thought was to place a foot on the fence and jump, but if the current increased and I lost motor function chances were I'd fall back into the zombie stew. The man's head was at most a foot away from the fence and my feet were less than six inches below the top of it. Even if I were drunk, the jump shouldn't be a problem.

I think the pressure as I pushed off broke the zombie's collar bone. He didn't yell in protest, so I took that as a good sign. I was happy the ground on the other side had been moved recently as it was softer than normal because I had hit it pretty hard. My knees were already suspect at best, and I was happy not to give them any more reason to fail me now. I was a couple of feet away from a ditch that was at least six feet across and peppered with all manner of spikes protruding from the ground; the stink of kerosene was heavy from where I stood. I won't lie, I was dismayed that my approach was going unnoticed.

The unit that I had dispatched of would have easily made it into my brother's home and then what? I decided not to dwell on it, nothing fruitful could be gained from it. Twenty years ago, I wouldn't have even paused at the gap I had to bridge, right now it may as well have been double its width. Eventually I was going to figure out I was far from an ordinary human…but that moment wasn't one of them.

"What are the odds there's a minefield?" I asked.

"Probably pretty damned good." Super deluxe model or not, I was confident that a bomb would send me on my way.

***

"Wait, you're saying this, what the hell was his name? Buker? Buker fellow took out the entire team?" Kong was asking the out-of-breath Army Ranger, Hank O'Reilly.

"He said he had dusted the other two, then told me and John that we could leave and never come back or die."

"So was the explosion this Buker guy or John?" Kong asked.

"Oh, I can assure you it was your Navy Seal," Tommy said, seemingly peering through the trees to the Talbot household.

"How can you be so sure?" Kong asked him.

"Because it was Michael Talbot," Eliza said, striding up to the circle. "And apparently nothing short of the Rapture is going to take him off this earth. It makes no difference, now at least I know where he is and the whole lot of them can die simultaneously."

"I just lost three well-trained men, some of my best," Kong said turning to Eliza, anger flushing his cheeks.

"Perhaps you should have had a better screening technique," Tomas said smiling. "Maybe asked each of them what side they were on. Michael most likely would have told you the truth."

Eliza nodded in agreement. "I imagine he would have…right before he killed you."

Kong didn't seem so convinced that the man that had called himself Buker would have been able to take him out, but he had just killed three Special Forces men and was still at large. *What did I get myself into?* "Eliza, I do not think you were forthcoming in our agreement."

"If you had doubts you should have voiced them before we left," Eliza told him. "Now organize another team."

I had my doubts when you ripped Randy's dick off, Kong thought as he clenched his fists.

"Ten this time…that should be sufficient," she said.

"Sufficient for what?" Kong asked, trying valiantly to keep his cool. He knew Eliza would have no qualms about eliminating him and putting someone else at the top. He didn't even consider himself a pawn; he was the board upon which the actual game was being played.

Hank hadn't left Kong's side since he got back and already he knew that legend of Buker or Talbot would be spreading across his men like wildfire. He had yet to figure out quite how that phenomenon worked, and something inside him told him he didn't have the time left to figure it out either.

***

"Can't stay here, sun is going to be up soon and I'll be stuck in dead man's land. And me being covered in gore like this, someone in that house is going to think I'm a zombie and that I somehow got past the fence."

Minefield or not, I had to leave the spot I was becoming rooted to. I guess it shouldn't have surprised me how easily I traversed the gap, but it did. Now I was just hoping I wasn't smack dab in the middle of a minefield and everything would be A-Okay. I was within fifteen feet of the deck which was a good ten feet off the ground. I was happy and slightly dismayed to see that the stairs had been removed. I did a once over around the bottom part of the house. There was no way in, it was completely shuttered off with steel plating. I looked up at the decking overhead.

"I should have brought Greta," I said. "Okay let's do the math, I'm almost six feet, give or take, mostly give...but whatever. Then if I outstretch my arms, add another three-ish feet, I really need to only jump up about a foot and I can grab the edge of the deck. Subtract from that, I'm a fortyish white guy and I'm still fucked. Wait...half-vamp trumps white. Let's give it a go."

I backed up a few feet, still not convinced that I had somehow miraculously crossed a minefield and I didn't want to throw that to chance again. I ran and jumped not taking into account my added abilities; I almost planted my face where I thought my hands were going to touch. That would have been awesome, me knocked out under the deck after smashing into it.

I grunted as I pulled myself up and over, but only because it felt like the right thing to do. "Why no guard?" The house appeared to be blacked out, but I could see some light spilling from around the blackout curtains. I walked to the back door and turned the unlocked knob. My heart lurched at how easy it could have been for the assassination team and then I entered.

CHAPTER THIRTY-SIX

Mike Journal Entry 15

"Miss me?" I asked a shocked room full of the people I loved the most in the whole world. Blood, gore, sinew and a fair amount of entrails hung from every exposed part of me. Henry was the first to react. I hadn't seen him leap since he was six months old and there was a particularly tasty shoe of Tracy's that he had enjoyed rending into bite-sized chunks. I had put it up on a coffee table thinking his little stubby legs would never allow him to regain his ill-gotten booty. He had proved me wrong and cost me two hundred bucks in the process (replacement fee of said shoes).

I stooped down a bit as he jumped into my outstretched arms, his stumped tail was going as fast as a hummingbird's wings after a Starbuck's double shot cappuccino. But even he had his standards; he would not lick my face.

"Talbot?" Tracy cried, barely able to contain her surprise or shock. "Is that really you?" She took a half step towards me.

"Of course it is!" BT said, barreling towards me. "Who the fuck else would wear a tin foil hat!" He swept me and Henry both up in his massive arms and twirled us around like we were in the Nutcracker ballet.

Apparently the explosion had ripped my knit cap off.

My father's legs gave out. "I...I couldn't stand to lose another child," he sobbed.

Nicole, who was visibly showing her pregnancy now, ran to me with a huge box of sani-wipes. "Oh, Dad, I missed you so much, but I don't know if I can hug you!" She sobbed and laughed at the same time.

Gary came running into the room. I would learn later that he had been pretty despondent about coming home without me. A massive case of survivor's guilt, compound that with the fact he had to tell our father he had lost his youngest son. And it wasn't such a great combination.

"I saw you die, Mike," Gary said, not quite yet ready to let go of the extra baggage he had been carrying around.

"Word of my death has been greatly exaggerated," I managed as I was twirled around like a record. "Any chance you could put me down now, BT? People are going to start to talk."

"Let them." He crushed me tighter to his chest. The added pressure pushing a little too much on Henry's midsection, we were rewarded with an air fouling mass of stench.

BT shuffled away from the stink as best he could, me and Henry still held captive.

"I missed you, too," I told him, "but I'd like to kiss my wife." BT finally put me down, but looked like he'd scoop me up in a moment's notice.

"You look like shit, Talbot," Tracy said stroking my cheek.

I grabbed the wipe proffered from my daughter and vigorously scrubbed my face. It burned and smelled like bleach—it was bliss. Tracy leaned in, we kissed, and the world around us dissolved, there was nothing but her tender lips upon mine. When we finally felt the accumulated gazes of all of those around us, we pulled away.

"I never thought I'd taste you again," she cried, dipping her head down.

"It's gonna take more than fire, rogue cats, vampires and zombies to kill me."

"Apparently." She kissed me quicker this time. "You will never leave without me again," she said with a force that made me know that this was no idle threat-slash-request; it was merely the truth. Where had I heard those words before?

Justin came up next; he was never a squeamish one.

He wasn't fond of public displays of affection, but just this one time he obviously figured he'd break his own rules as he hugged me tight. "It sucks being the man of the family," he smiled. "I'm glad you're here so you can take it back."

"Good to see you, too." I smiled.

Travis was on the verge of tears. He kept wiping his sleeve across his eyes in an attempt to keep up with the tears that were free flowing. As an eighteen-year-old boy, appearance is everything. "I knew you couldn't be dead," he said sniffing loudly, his head down. I watched as tears splashed down into the floor.

"Men cry, Travis," I told him.

He looked up. "Good thing," he said through the sobs as he wrapped one arm around me, the other looked stiff and I would learn later he had been winged by a bullet.

"What did I miss?" I asked.

Mad Jack and Ron began to tell me of their defenses and I gently reminded them about how easily I had got in.

"We didn't take into account humans," Mad Jack said with a frown.

"And I'm sure that's what Eliza's thoughts were, too. I took care of her first strike team, but I've got to believe she's going to send another one. I also have these," I said, holding up four zombie- repellant chains. I explained what they were to those who did not know and we would discuss a way to put them to better use.

Cindy kept looking at me and then the door expectantly. I think she thought that if I had come back from the dead, than quite possibly so had her Brian. I grabbed her hand and slightly shook my head. She *knew*, she fundamentally knew he wasn't ever coming back, but the human mind has a way of putting hope above reason. She brought my hand up to her face as she cried. It was long moments before her sobs gave way to a hitching cry, then finally stony silence punctuated by some sniffling. She released my hand and went into another room; I would imagine to be alone with her memories of happier times.

"Where's Erin?" I asked. Her above all others I owed an explanation.

"We don't know," Tracy told me. "She walked out and we haven't seen her since."

"She's out there?" I asked standing up.

"Mike, she wants to be," BT said, putting his hand on my shoulder. "She died when Paul did, she just didn't know it yet."

Now it was my time to bury my face in my hands. I dragged my hands down my face, then realized just how effen gross I was. "I'm going to get cleaned up. Post a guard, then we'll talk."

"It's good to have you back, brother," Ron said.

"It's good to be back," I told them all and I meant it. I left it up in the air if I meant physically *back* in the house or *back* from the dead. The clothes I stripped off and neatly deposited in the nearest trash receptacle. The drain was working overtime with the amount of dirt and human debris I was sending its way. I stared straight ahead at the stream of water, choosing, wisely I might add, to not look at what was swirling around my feet.

When I was sufficiently confident that I had stripped at least the top three layers of my skin off, I stopped the water and got out. It was invigorating to be alive, well alive and clean, and home. I stepped out of the bathroom and into the bedroom Ron had given Tracy and I for our stay.

I hastily covered up when I heard a slight cough. "Shit, woman, you scared me. Thought it might be one of the nieces or something."

"You look good, Mike, a little skinny…but good," Tracy said.

"I do, don't I," I said placing my hands on my abs. "I haven't seen those since the Marine Corps days."

"You should come over here."

"Let me just grab some clothes," I told her looking through the stack of stuff she had out for me.

"Those can wait," she said.

My head shot up (and then so did my other one). "Gotcha," I said, hastily moving over to the bed where she was already under the covers and I prayed naked. (And there was a prayer the big man had heard! Hallelujah! Praise the Lord! I would have raised my hands up in the air and shook them around like jazz hands if it were appropriate.)

"You going to keep that hat on?" she asked.

"You'll get used to it."

"It isn't just some random Mike phobia then, like the fear of using your cereal spoon more than once?"

"I thought we weren't going to talk about that anymore? And hey, who the hell knows where my mouth has been?"

"I know where I'd like it to be."

Conversation came to a lull at that point, and somehow it was right. We made love in the midst of a zombie apocalypse, surrounded on all sides by an enemy hell bent on our destruction and for at least a little bit of time we laid all of that on the bedroom floor. When we came to our blissful conclusion, Tracy spoke.

"Life without you was unimaginable," she said as her hand came up to the side of my face.

"I'll bet it was." I laughed as I kissed her palm. "Who wouldn't miss me?"

"Mike, no, I'm serious...and for once I wish you would be, too."

"I'm sorry. It wasn't too excellent on my end either. I lost a friend I've had for thirty years, I don't know if I'll ever get over that, and now his wife is missing. And we're still in one hell of a fuck-fest. Just because I'm back doesn't make that fact go away."

"Somehow it does," she said, laying her head on my shoulder."

"We don't have to cuddle now do we?" I asked. "I'd like get to get to work or something."

She smacked me upside the head. "I love you, Michael Talbot."

"I love you too, woman." I kissed her long and hard, and we could have rapidly found ourselves back in our earlier predicament (not that I was complaining), but it would have to wait.

Then I probably soured the mood anyway as I pulled away I asked the very last question anyone should ask while in bed with the one they love. "Where's Deneaux?"

"She was in the kitchen right before you got there. I really wasn't paying her all that much attention when you came in, why?"

"She's got some unanswered questions I like some further explanation for."

"About?"

"I'm pretty sure she has some culpability in Brian's death and possibly in Paul's," I told her as I got up and grabbed some clothes.

"Please tell me you're kidding?" Tracy asked, as she pulled off the covers and stood.

"Wow."

"What?" She was looking around.

"You look more beautiful than the day we met."

Tracy was slightly self-conscious, but even she had to admit that the apocalypse had done wonders for her body. "Thank you, Mike, but right now I just want to beat some answers out of that battle axe."

"I'm looking forward to it." I quickly dressed, as did Tracy.

CHAPTER THIRTY-SEVEN

Mrs. Deneaux

"Fuck me." Mrs. Deneaux said under her breath as Mike walked in the back door. She uncharacteristically panicked as the behemoth BT picked up Mike and twirled him around. She stayed in the shadows of the living room for a while listening, then quickly retired to her room so that she could make sure that her stories were all consistent.

She knew Mike might be saying all his greetings now, but that he would be trying to sniff around and under her many lies. He somehow knew she was lying, and it would only be a matter of time until he tripped her up.

And then what? she thought. "He'll probably kick me out."

She had her ear to the door and could hear the merriment down the hallway. She waited until it died down and mostly became celebration among those that were already at the house.

"...so good to see him."

"...thought he was dead."

Yadda yadda, blah blah, she thought. This was her worst case scenario. She exited her room just as she saw Tracy closing the door to her bedroom. She heard the soft hiss of the shower that Mike must be taking. She moved quickly down the hallway to see if he had possibly said anything to anyone else. Then her first chance at an alternate plan revealed itself as she looked down on the four silver chains that each had a small ornate vial filled with an amber colored fluid sitting on the kitchen table.

"Is this the zombie repellant?" she asked as she quickly snatched one off the table. "It just might be my ticket out of here." She thought about taking all of them, and just might have if Angel hadn't taken that most inopportune of times to walk in.

"You look guilty of something," Angel said pointing her finger at Mrs. Deneaux.

"It's that obvious is it?" Mrs. Deneaux asked. She wasn't playing with the girl, if her guilt was so apparent to the little rapscallion, then she would never be able to fool Mike who already had her tried and convicted in his mind.

"Ryan! The mean lady is up to no good!" Angel screamed into the other room.

"Well aren't you just a little darling," Mrs. Deneaux said through clenched teeth. "I would just love to squeeze the little life out of you."

"Ryan!" Angel screamed again, looking into the other room for her brother.

"I'm leaving and I'm going to make sure that you get what's coming to you," Mrs. Deneaux said as she placed her stolen chain and vial into her pocket.

Angel waited and watched as 'the Mean Lady' left the room. Then, when she was completely sure she was gone and not coming back, she stuck her tongue out at her.

Mrs. Deneaux went back to her room and grabbed her revolver and her bullets and quickly went down into the basement. It was cool, dark, and quiet down there. She paused long and hard, rationalizing out everything she was about to do. Mike still had no concrete evidence against her and never would. As for the vial, just because Mike had made it through that didn't mean it actually worked. It was mere minutes after she heard the whoosh of the shower turn off before she got moving. The man had changed significantly. He might not need proof to throw her outside, and he would make sure that she didn't have a vial. No, she would take her chances outside. *That way at least she would have one*, she thought.

She undid the heavy bar lock on the reinforced door and stole out into the night. She stayed hidden under the deck until she got to the back of the house. She waited patiently, listening to see if anyone was over her. When she was confident no one was watching from the deck, she walked purposefully across the yard. She was thankful that Mad Jack had been thoughtful enough to create a small draw bridge to get across the spike filled trench. She grabbed the handle and spun it counter-clockwise, the two foot wide beam eight feet long began to descend rapidly; within twenty seconds it spanned the death canal.

She keyed in a code to the electric fence, shutting off current to the gate which she hesitated to open. Zombies were now within an arm's length of her. She almost decided to turn around and try her luck with Michael. She hadn't done anything tonight that she could not recover from. Her foot turned in the loose soil as she looked back at the house. The girl Angel was on the deck watching her.

"Fucking brat," Mrs. Deneaux said as she opened the gate. Her eyes were closed as she waited expectantly for the bite of death. She opened her eyes as the first of the zombies that was doing its best to avoid her clipped her shoulder as it moved on past.

"Zombies!" Angel shouted.

Gunfire erupted, Mrs. Deneaux did not know from which side, and she didn't really care as she forced herself through the gate while zombies were pouring into the yard. Most were being forced into the pit, but a lucky few had found their way across the beam and into the Promised Land. Mrs. Deneaux did not look back as she cut a path through the horde.

She made it all the way through to almost be shot.

"Stop!" a nervous, gun-wielding man told her.

She put her hands up halfway. "You caught me," she said sardonically.

"Bernie, I've got a live one here!" he yelled to his left. "Barely," he added, looking back at her.

She flipped him the bird. Her pistol still safely tucked in her holster, she thought long and hard about pulling it out and killing the nervous little man, but there were more men in the woods and if she wanted to save her hide she would play the game by their rules for the time being.

"Bring her to the boss, dumbass," Bernie said as if he too could not stand the man.

"Right, let's go," Beans said to her as he motioned to his right with the rifle. "And keep your hands where I can see them."

"Why…are you afraid I'll do this?" she asked as she drew her pistol out and aimed it squarely at his chest.

Beans raised his hands up in the air, rifle included.

"Tell you what…you don't point your weapon at me, and I won't point mine at you. Sound fair?" she asked.

"Fair, very fair," Beans answered apprehensively.

"Now please kindly show me the way to your boss," Mrs. Deneaux said as she put her weapon away, a slight smile across her lips.

Mrs. Deneaux was led up to a small group. She noticed the idiot Tommy who was standing next to a big man she figured was 'the boss'. She began to think of a story that would position her in the best light and get her out of here. As she got closer, she noticed the slight woman that had been blocked from view. *Eliza*, she thought as she took in a sharp breath doing her best to remain calm.

Eliza looked past the big man to see Mrs. Deneaux's approach. Kong turned also when he saw Eliza looking. His eyebrows furrowed as he saw Beans leading the old woman towards him.

"Whoa…far enough," Kong said, putting one hand up and the other going for his hip.

"I caught her coming out of the house," Beans said excitedly.

"And you didn't think to take her sidearm? You dumbass," Kong told his subordinate.

"I…I she pulled it on me…we had an understanding,"

Beans stammered.

"Beans, you're an idiot. Ma'am, I'm going to need you to gently take that gun and put it on the ground."

"The name is Vivian," she said as she handed the gun to Beans. "Could you be a dear and place that on the ground for me? Bad hips," she told the group.

Eliza moved Kong over with her hand and stared intently at Mrs. Deneaux. "Is there a reason I should not immediately kill you?" she finally said.

"I want Mike dead as much as you," Mrs. Deneaux said as she struggled to find her reserves of courage.

"Is that so?" Eliza questioned.

"I killed two of his men that attacked you on the highway," Mrs. Deneaux said, now wishing that she had stayed with Michael. Nothing he could have done to her would have been equivalent to looking upon the embodiment of evil. She failed to mention that she was one of the bigger reasons for the success of the attack; that was better left unsaid. "I killed his childhood friend."

"Paul Ginson?" Tomas asked.

"Yes," Deneaux answered.

"You know of him?" Eliza asked her brother.

"Yes, they were very close, grew up together. I believe they considered themselves brothers," Tomas stated.

"Why?" Eliza asked. "Why would you kill him? Certainly not in preparation for meeting me."

"He had suspicions about the other man that I killed."

"Ah, self-preservation, I understand that all too well. None of this however has led me to any other conclusion except to kill you. We are not allies, you did not kill those men as a show of solidarity."

"I have allowed your zombies in past the fence," Mrs. Deneaux said, quickly running out of ways to save her skin.

"Is that true?" Kong asked Beans.

"I don't know," he answered.

"Find out, ass hat."

"How did you come across one of my vials?" Eliza

asked.

"I stole one of the ones Mike brought in with him," Mrs. Deneaux said as she licked her arid lips.

"How is Michael?" Eliza asked with a faraway look as if she was asking about a lover from long ago that she still harbored feelings for.

"He's different."

"How?" Eliza asked, snapping quickly back from her abstraction.

Mrs. Deneaux stood there for a few moments thinking about how to answer the question to her best benefit and could not think of anything more convincing than the truth. She was convinced Eliza would smell out any falsehoods like a hound dog on the trail of an escaped convict. "If I didn't believe Michael would exact revenge on me, I would have stayed in that house. He is...determined, and whereas he was sometimes non-committal or unwilling to do whatever it took, I think that has changed. I do not think that you can win here."

Eliza's full cruelty came to the fore. "You believe I can not destroy that pathetic man?" she roared.

Mrs. Deneaux put her head down waiting for Eliza to slash her open from neck to navel. "I am not always right," Mrs. Deneaux said weakly.

Beans came running back. He nearly handed Deneaux back her weapon. "The old bat was telling the truth, zombies are all over the yard."

"You will live long enough...if only to watch him die!" she yelled. "Kong, get her out of here."

"Beans, you screw this up and I'll personally kill you. Take the lady back to your truck and guard her," Kong told him.

Mrs. Deneaux once again found herself thrust onto Michael's side. She had to hope that he bested Eliza, or her death would immediately follow his. Beans opened up his passenger door and let her in. he walked around the front of the truck and got on his side.

"What are you doing here?" Mrs. Deneaux asked him as he closed the door. He looked infinitely happy that he was no longer in harm's way, although he quite possibly didn't realize he had allowed a pit viper in his cab.

"Just trying to stay alive," he answered ashamedly. "Why are you here?"

"Same reason." The wheels of survival began to spin in her head.

CHAPTER THIRTY-EIGHT

Mike Journal Entry 16

Angel's words hung in the air. Gary was the first one out there, he echoed her alarm. Mad Jack looked quickly over the railing and ran back into the house. Within a few moments, a fire spouted from the trench, the sizzle of burning zombies was the only sound. The footbridge burned also, at least a couple dozen zombies had made it into the yard and were now all underneath the deck.

"Well that's a slight design flaw," I told BT, looking over the rail trying to see the invaders. He shrugged his shoulders. "What's the plan for this scenario?" I asked Ron.

"We should get in. The gunmen are still out there," Ron said ushering us in.

"I'm not really thrilled with having zombies banging up against the house," I told him.

"Don't worry about it, Mad Jack has got it handled," Ron told me.

"Did you get laid?" BT asked in my ear.

"What are you, fifteen?" I asked him back.

"Sorry, man, even while you were looking at the zombies you've got this shit-eating grin on your face. I was just wondering if you were now shitting out gold pieces," he said referring to my failed love making attempt way back at the Big 5 sporting goods store.

"Even if I had gold pieces coming out of my ass, I wouldn't offer you any."

"I knew you did!" He smiled, pointing at me.

Tracy took that inopportune moment to show up at the doorway. "You get me in trouble and I'll toss you over this railing," I told the big man.

"We're cool, man, we're cool," he said as he smiled at Tracy and went in.

"What's that about?" Tracy asked as I went in.

"BT thinks I owe him some money," I told her.

"What would he do with it?" Tracy asked as she followed me into the room.

"Gloat…laugh…probably both."

"I don't understand what you're talking about?"

BT popped his head into the living room from the kitchen. "Ooh, Tracy you're hair is a mess do you need a brush?"

"Fuck," I mumbled.

Tracy spun on her heel. "You told him?" she accused me.

"He guessed," I said, throwing my hands up. Like what was I supposed to do?

"I hope you enjoyed it because that's the last apocalyptic sex you're going to have!" she said as she left the room.

"Man, that's why I've never dated redheads," BT laughed. "Don't sweat it she'll get over it."

"I didn't do anything for her to 'get over', that was you remember?"

"Oh yeah, sorry about that!"

"Hey, Mike, could you see if the zombies are moving away?" Ron's voice drifted down from the attic.

I went over to the window. "I'll be damned, they're walking into the fire."

"Mad Jack's magic box," BT said as he came up next to me. "He's been working on a giant one. We got it mounted on the roof."

"Holy crap, what's the range?"

"Just about the fire pit," BT said.

"Wow." I walked to the door leading up to the attic. "That's a roger on the zombies, they are now deep-fat fried."

"That's gross, Mike, but thanks," Ron said looking down from the top of the stairs.

"Was that gross?" I asked BT.

"A little bit." He held his finger and thumb close together.

"Huh, I didn't think so."

"You going to apologize to Tracy now?"

"What, are you fucking nuts? I'd rather go outside. Wait, why do I have to apologize? You're the one that did it."

"Admitting fault is the first step."

"One would think that someone who speaks the words would understand their meaning," I told him.

"Oh I see what you're doing there. It won't work, I'm smarter than you."

"Great, Joe IQ, got any ideas about our friends out there?" I asked him.

"Well, the magic box works great, but I can't imagine Miss Congeniality is just going to stand by and wait us out," BT said, getting serious for the moment.

"Miss Congeniality, that's some funny stuff, can you imagine Eliza in a beauty pageant?"

"I can't even imagine her trying to smile. Not enough Vaseline in the world to keep that upper lip from sticking to her blood-coated teeth, and God help the contestants if she didn't win."

"Stop, man, or I'm going to lose it, I keep picturing her in a sequined gown parade waving to the audience."

We might have gone on for a little while longer if not for the sound of an explosion outside. I ran to the sliding deck door, I had no sooner slid it open when a round lodged itself deep into the stucco next to my head. BT pulled me back with enough force that I could probably sue him for whiplash damages. Another couple of shots were taken, but without a target in sight they soon stopped. I scrambled over and grabbed my rifle.

I told BT thanks and crawled out the door, effectively hidden by the metal plating lining the railings. I wondered if, from the gunman's angle, he could put any rounds underneath me. There was no metal there. I looked through the gun slot cut into the metal. I could just see the section of fencing that had been shredded with a hand grenade. Zombies were pouring in—that was bad enough—most were stopping at the end of the pit of their own forced volition or were being involuntarily pushed into the spikes and fire by their brethren as they all fought for limited space. They, however, were not my first concern, I could see the hunched over forms of men trying to stealthily make their way, threading through the zombies.

The explosion had been to make an entry point and the rifle fire was to keep us from seeing their advance. Eliza was making her move. "Trouble," I told BT, who was on his hands and knees at the doorway to the deck.

"You don't say?"

"More than usual, okay, smartass?" I asked him back.

"Fine, what's going on?"

"I can't tell how many, but we definitely have men coming. Get everyone on alert, we got a few minutes—the number of zombies is actually working in our favor. They're having a hard time getting through." I watched a few moments longer. I had counted at least six—possibly seven—men coming our way. I crawled back inside and waited for the troops to rally.

It didn't take him long, the explosion had done most of the work. Absent were Ron and Mad Jack—who were still tweaking, the box, and sadly Erin, a kind-souled person who had not deserved the loss of her husband and my best friend. I shook my head; I could not afford to go down that dark path.

Then it hit me. "Where's Deneaux?" I couldn't stand the woman, but anyone that could shoot the balls off a moth was someone I didn't mind having in a firefight.

"Maybe God finally called her up," Nancy said in seriousness.

"No, that would imply he wanted her there," I told her truthfully.

"The mean lady left," Angel said right before BT was going to go down to her room and check.

"What?" I asked, spinning to look at the youngest amongst us.

"She stole one of these," Angel said, pulling a vial out of her pocket, "and then she said we were gonna get what was coming to us. She went downstairs, and then she crossed the yard and left."

My eyes grew wide. "The basement! BT, Gary...come on. Dad, get a couple of people on each entry point. Do not go outside, they have the exits covered." I was halfway downstairs by the time I had finished giving my orders.

The basement was how you figure most basements should be in a scary movie: pitch black and dank. I knew where the basement door was; not by sight, but by memory. I set up my defensive position behind a small knee wall that semi-hid a top loading freezer. I heard BT moving around, then Gary came down. The two seconds of blinding illumination as he turned on the lights almost had me in hysterical laughing, but first things first. "Gary, shut the damned light off," I told him.

"I can't see anything though," he said as he snapped the switch into the off position.

"Yeah, and now none of us can, except for the giant blob of yellow in front of my eyes," I told him.

"Sorry," he added as he 'oomphed' by his foot or shin striking the freezer hard.

"How many times have you been down here?" I asked.

"He keeps moving it." Gary found a spot behind a stack of MRE boxes.

I figured he should be safe; those meals would be dense enough to stop a tank round.

"I'm sure," I told him as he settled in. "That's a hell of a spot you found yourself there," I said to BT.

"It's all I could think of."

"Get over here, man, you hiding behind a lolly column is like an elephant hiding behind a street sign."

"I have no idea why I missed you," he said as he got in next to me.

"You think I should come over there, too?" Gary asked.

I was about to tell him 'sure', then we all froze when we heard the doorknob to the basement door moving.

"Bitch left it unlocked," BT growled.

"Someday she'll get hers. Let's just make sure her plan goes awry."

"Awry, funny word," BT said, and that was it.

Whoever was on the other side of the door was being cautious and I guess I couldn't really fault them that. The door cracked open an inch or two and light from a cracking dawn sliced a wedge into the basement.

"Lockner, Trent, you two to the left. Ranks, Hubner to the right. Remember…quiet," their leader said. In the soundless, holding-breath-stillness of the basement, we heard them clearly.

BT put his rifle up; I put my hand on his trigger hand, letting him know I wanted him to wait. Two figures came in and quickly went to the left where their biggest cover was a small file cabinet and lamp. The two heading to the right would actually have some cover as the bathroom was there. I was not going to give them the chance to get their foothold. As soon as they came in and began their deadly migration I opened fire, as did Gary and BT.

Only one of the men even got the chance to fire off a shot, which ended up in the ceiling as a round caught him flush in the kneecap and sent him crashing to the floor. The basement door slammed shut when whoever was on the other side figured out they had walked into an ambush.

We were bathed once again in darkness. At least one of the men I had been shooting at was down for eternity (or at least as long as it took to cycle through a reincarnation depending on your beliefs). I think the one still moaning—if the acoustics were correct in my brother's basement—was on my side. BT and Gary had been shooting to the left and I had seen multiple crimson blood sprays strike the wall.

"Gary, go upstairs and turn on the light," I told him.

"You sure, Mike?" he asked.

"You feel like puking?" I asked him.

"Not really."

"Then go upstairs and turn on the light."

He again smacked into the freezer as he went passed. "Damn thing," he said as he stopped to massage his shin.

"Do you think he's going to need help with that light?" BT asked me.

"BT, you can go, too. I won't think any less of you."

"What's that mean? That you already think so lowly of me that it can't sink any further?"

"Relax, big man, I'm in no rush to see our handiwork either."

"That obvious? It's just killing men…it doesn't sit right."

"I know, man," I told him as the light popped on. It didn't take long for my eyes to adjust to the carnage on the other side of the basement.

"Mike?" Ron asked, shouting down.

"Four down, three for good," I yelled. "At least three left, they are under the deck."

"You need help?" he asked.

"No." I swallowed. "I'll take care of it."

The wall looked like impressionistic art; red was splashed across it like an angry Jackson Pollack had flung the excess against his canvas. I had one headshot on my side, and rapidly graying pink matter was clumped on the wall. It looked like a handhold on those fake rock walls they have in some sporting goods stores. That was the thought I was planning on holding on to. BT had turned away. I cautiously approached; the man who had been knee-shot was still writhing in agony.

I kicked his gun away from him even though he was

paying it absolutely no attention. He was going into shock, his eyes pleaded with me for help. I quickly checked the other three for any signs of life. I needn't have wasted my time. I had drilled one in the eye, his one remaining blue eye gazed up at a Heaven I'm sure he would never see. The two on the left had taken primarily body shots, blood leaked out from at least five or six wounds on each.

"Please help me," the kneed man begged.

"BT, could you maybe get some bags and cleaning material?" I asked, turning back towards him.

"You sure, man? You have a funny look on your face."

"I'm good," I said as I turned back to the attempted usurper. I stepped over him and threw the heavy locking bar in place

I waited until BT was up the stairs, then got down on my haunches next to him. "How many of you were there? Just so you get your math correct, three are now dead."

"Please, I just need some help," he asked, licking his lips.

"If the roles were reversed, would you help me? Because I seriously doubt it, especially since you came into my brother's house and tried to kill us."

He flinched slightly. "Please."

"I value your life *less* than that of the zombies. They do what they do because they are compelled to do so. You did what you did out of self-interest. You purposely came here to murder my family. I will not so much as give you a fucking aspirin until you answer my questions."

"Five...there were five."

"I don't know why I would expect a potential murderer to tell the truth." I put my rifle down making sure the muzzle was pointing straight at his head. His eyes crossed as he stared down the bore. His hands were clamped against his shattered patella, which was fine, it wasn't my target anyway.

"What are you doing?" he asked as his eyes got big.

I clamped one of my hands over his mouth; he started to shake his head back and forth. "Stop," I told him through clenched teeth, "or I'm just going to blow a hole in your face and be done with it." He must have seen something in the set of my eyes because he did stop. "You see, there are kids upstairs, and whereas I know you don't give a shit because you were going to kill them, I care a lot. I don't want them to be exposed to what I am about to do." I clamped my hand harder over his face and quickly reached behind his damaged knee and started poking and prodding the wound, wiggling loose bone fragments and torn tendons around.

Tears streamed from his face as his screams were muffled in my hand. His breathing was hitching heavily he was in so much pain. His eyes started to close when, with a pop, I pulled two fingers from the back of his leg. I removed my mouth clamp and slapped him hard across the face.

"Don't pass out on me, champ," I told him.

"Please," he begged quietly.

"How many?"

"Ten...there were ten of us."

"How many truck drivers total?"

"I'm not sure...wait!" he said as I began to move my hand back in place over his mouth. "Over eighty...maybe a hundred."

"How many zombies?"

"Fifteen, sixteen thousand. I think I heard Kong tell the lady running all of this. She's...she's the one you need to watch out for."

"Yeah, I'm well aware of that."

"I told you everything, please can I get some help now."

I stood up and stepped over his body, I rapped on the steel reinforced door. "Hey, shitheads!" I yelled. "I know there's still six of you out there, want to know how I know." No response. "Because one is still alive, mostly. Not for long, though, I imagine. Shock alone will probably take him in the next twenty minutes or so."

Another long wait, I did not think they would respond. "Who is it?" one of the men asked.

"What's your name?" I asked the guy on the ground, I had to nudge him with my foot. It looked like he was going into pass out mode again.

"Adam," he rasped.

"Adam," I repeated.

"If you kill my brother, I'll gut you like a fish!" the man yelled through the door.

"Empty threat. First off, you were already going to kill me. *And* I'm the one in here with your rapidly dying brother. Funny you should say 'gutting' since I just happen to be holding a fillet knife," I lied.

I heard hammering blows on the door. "I'll fucking kill you!" Adam's brother screamed. His fist blows kept raining down. They eventually began to subside and were replaced by a quiet sobbing. "He's all I've got left."

I can't lie, I did have enough humanity in me to have that tug at me a bit. I just had to keep reminding myself of what they had initially come here for: the destruction of my family.

"You willing to trade?" I asked him.

"What do you want?" came his cautious reply.

"I want all of your weapons, then you can take his bleeding ass out of my basement."

"Fine," I heard him say quickly.

"Fuck no, Chaz, I'm not giving up my gun. Not here, not now," one of the attackers shouted. "That bitch will cut our throats if we go back with our tails between our—"

A shot rang out. I waited for the echo of it to die down before I spoke. "Chaz, you still there?"

"Anyone else got a problem with us giving up our weapons?"

I didn't hear any other dissention.

"Now what?" Chaz asked.

"After you've put down all your weapons, with your hands raised I want you to step back from the house so that someone on the deck will be able to see you," I told him.

"How do we know you're not going to kill us?" he asked.

"Simple, I'm not you. Better hurry up, Adam is looking mighty pale."

BT was at the bottom of the stairs with everything I had asked for. I looked over to him.

"Man, I just got down here," he told me.

"The exercise will do you good, it looks like you've been hitting the MRE oatmeal cookies a little hard lately."

"Fuck you, Mike." He turned and went back upstairs to check on the status of the gunmen.

"I love you too, man." I told him. "And stay low, the damn snipers are still out there."

"Yeah, mom," he told me.

"We're waiting!" Chaz yelled impatiently.

"You can wait another minute," I said under my breath. *Or maybe not*, I thought as I looked behind me at Adam. He was about as pale as I once figured vampires were; I now knew that wasn't the case, but just last year that was what I thought. Adam's breathing was shallow and anything less than a world class hospital wasn't going to do him much good.

"BT says everything is good to go," Angel yelled down the stairs. "He also said you were an asshole."

"Angel!" her brother Ryan shouted.

"Well that's what he said," she defended herself. It kept going, but the door upstairs closed and the rest was lost to me.

I grabbed my rifle and took a long look at Adam. I wasn't completely sure, but his dilated pupils gave me the impression he was no longer focusing on anything on this plane of existence. In fact, they were so wide, they looked like the last thing he had witnessed had scared the shit out of him. I wondered if that would be the last expression I would have when the Dark One came to claim me. Wait…could he claim me? I had no soul to lose? If I made it through the rest of the day I was going to grab some beers and think on that for a little while.

I made sure I was ready to fire and opened the door. Five men peered intently back at me, it was easy to determine who Chaz was by the worried expression on his face.

"All of you turn around," I told them.

"See! I fucking told you he was going to kill us!"

"I'm going to check for weapons, I've been burned by the *honor system* before," I told them.

BT was again in the basement. "Can you cover me?" I asked him.

"You want me to do anything else? Maybe get you a glass of water, shine your shoes, do a little tap dance?"

I looked over at him questioningly.

"Sorry, little amped up. Go ahead, I'll cover you."

"Gee thanks," I told him as I put my rifle up against the house. I checked Chaz first; except for a fingernail clipper he was clean as a whistle. The second man had an ankle pistol and a Bowie knife, the third had two grenades shoved in his front pants pockets, I was wondering if he thought I might think these were his balls and just leave them alone. The fourth was also clean, the fifth had a sawed off shotgun shoved down his pants.

"You're kidding right?" I asked. He shrugged. "Take it out nice and slow, please."

I jumped when his gun went off. Dumb ass had wrapped his hand around the trigger, when he pulled up he fired, neatly obliterating the front part of his right front from his body. He toppled face first not even attempting to break his own fall. I could hear Gary's retching from above us.

"Whatever you do, Gary, don't raise your head over the railing to puke!" I warned him. Brown bile began to leak through the floorboards above and slightly behind us.

"So fruggin gross," Gary said around a mouthful of semi-digested lunch; and it was. The man's boot had ripped in two at the top, tendons and muscles had curled up and over the exposed skin, blood drained out so quickly it was easy to see the delicate smashed white bones underneath it all.

"Don't worry, man, you can hold on to the gun," I told the fallen man.

He was grunting in misery. It was better than shrieks…but not by much.

"Can I get my brother now?" Chaz asked.

"One more thing," I said as I put the barrel of the second man's ankle pistol to his head. I ripped his chain off as I did all the rest excluding the now Shoeless Joe Jackson. "Get him," I said, stepping to the side. "Just you, though," I said when two of the others turned.

Chaz ran in to the house, his cry of agony came immediately. "He's dead!"

"He is?…now get him out of the house. And the other two, hell get them all out of here, including Stubby."

"What do you want us to do with them?" Steel Balls asked.

"Drag them over to the pit, I don't care."

"But…but you took our vials."

"I left Adam's and Stubby's on. You guys can fight for them, grab a body and get off my land."

"Mike?" BT asked.

"No room here for mercy, buddy."

"Mike?"

"BT, if we had a jail…maybe. Try to hold on to the reason why they were here."

"You're killing us," Steel Balls, said as he hefted the man Chaz had shot.

"I'm doing no more or no less than you would have done to us," I told him.

The other man went over and helped Stubby get up. Chaz was still in the basement rocking his brother back and forth in his lap.

The other men including one of their dead were heading across the yard. They were looking at the zombies that were eyeing them back. I wondered how large the sphere of influence for the vial would be. If they got into a tight enough huddle, it should protect the three of them.

I went into the house and dragged the other three dead men out of the house as BT covered me. Their blood had mostly stopped leaking, but I still left a trail a blind man could follow.

The man that had been shot through the head was the worst, dropping bits of brain matter of the floor. I tried to imagine it as something different, but I was staring straight at his head as I pulled him from his arms.

Two of the men were coming back to gather their dead, Stubby was sitting alone, the dead man was now burning in the kerosene at the bottom of the trench, black smoke was wafting up from his burning clothes and hair. The zombie congregation packed a little tighter where Stubby was sitting, either he looked delicious or they really liked smoked meat. A few were jostled into the trench below.

"Let's go," I told Chaz when I got the last man out.

His eyes were red-rimmed. "He's all I've got left."

"Yeah, and all those people you were going to kill upstairs, they're all I've got left. Get out."

He did without any further words, hefting his brother up over his shoulder. He brushed by as he left. Within a few more minutes all of the dead raiders were now permanent fixtures with the ground. The men were looking at the gap and the zombies, trying to figure out how they were going to get back across. BT and I watched as one of them actually turned and began to come back. I raised my rifle up and he turned back to the zombies.

Steel Balls and the man who had turned around began to talk rapidly, their voices rising to a peak. It looked like Steel Balls won. I could see Stubby begging, his hands were up in the air, he was shaking his head back and forth and trying to scoot back as fast as he could. Steel kicked Stubby in his bad foot. Stubby stopped moving immediately as his scream of pain pierced the silence. He paid no attention as Steel Balls moved and grabbed the chain off his neck.

"Help me, please!" Stubby begged.

I went back inside; BT stayed out a moment longer before joining me. I grabbed a bucket and some water out of the utility closet and had already started cleaning up stains that would never vanish.

"What happened out there, man?" BT asked me.

I looked up from my scrubbing. "What would you have done differently?"

"At least I would have left them the vials," BT said, rubbing his face with his hands like he was trying to scour away the grime of the event.

"I'm going to walk you through my thoughts."

"Go on," he said, pulling up a folding chair that I did not think was up to the task of holding him suspended in space.

"They weren't here to borrow sugar, BT."

"I get that, Mike, I do, but that's cold-blooded."

"I'm not done." BT motioned for me to continue. "I let them leave intact, they go right back to Eliza, regroup and try again. She's not just going to pat them on the shoulders and say, 'Nice try fellas'. Maybe we stop them again, maybe we don't. I'm not willing to gamble the lives of those people upstairs at all, no matter how good the odds may seem in our favor. Money is gambled, not lives. Now, as an added bonus, we have seven more vials of Eliza's brew that we can give to people upstairs. Because when our perimeter is overrun...which it will be..."

BT's eyes got wide.

"When the zombies get to the house, seven more people upstairs will now have a chance to blend in and maybe get the fuck away from this death house. Seven more of the people we love were just given an extra chance to hold on. And if the dip wads outside had played their cards right, I'm pretty sure the two vials would have been enough to protect all of them. Sure, they would have to know each other a little better than they may have wanted to, but they would have survived. And already they're turning on each other. I doubt two of them make it back. They're killing each other.

They would have had no problem killing us. I say fuck 'em, you should, too," I told him as I got back to scooping brain and scrubbing blood.

The folding chair sighed in relief as BT heaved himself to his feet. He squeezed my shoulder as he went by. "Is there another sponge?" he asked, pointing to the utility room.

"Enough to make it through the apocalypse."

"I hope so."

CHAPTER THIRTY-NINE

The Backyard

"What now?" Xander, the silent one of the remaining three live men said as they stared across the abyss.

"Well, near as I can tell," Steve, aka Steel Balls, began, "we have two vials and three people, and since I'm holding one and so is Chaz, it looks like you're odd man out."

"That's not right, man, if we stay together we can make it," Xander complained.

"Not a chance," Steve said as he jumped the gap. The zombies in the front row could not yield fast enough as Steve struck chest to chest. He bounced back, grabbing onto the zombie's tattered shirt pulling them both back into the pit.

He pulled the zombie to the side in a desperate attempt to avoid the deadly steel spikes. It worked to a point as a barb cleaved him on the left side of his abdomen. His hand clenching the vial opened to brace his body to stop any further damage. The zombie came straight down flush on the spike; it broke through his sternum and impaled him completely. The duo were locked head to foot, and without the vial to protect him, the zombie unaffected from the damage to his mid-section began to feed.

Steve started to pull frantically, his muscle and skin stretching violently as he tried to rip himself away sideways from the spike before the zombie could break through the denim pants he wore. "Xander, help me, man," Steve asked frantically.

He was crying out loud as he tried to sever through

three inches of his being. The zombie was making short work of the heavy material. Steve was kicking his leg so that the zombie could not seek purchase; he was losing the battle. Steve's skin split with a wet rip from the pole just as the zombie took a small ribbon of meat from his calf.

"Oh fuck, man!" he yelled as he scrambled to get away from the zombie. One hand was clenched over the wound in his side. The kerosene fire below was threatening to ignite his shoes and the zombies at the top, beginning to realize he was fair game, started to walk into the fire to get at him.

"Xander, Chaz, please help me," he begged.

Chaz was lost in the depths of his mourning and barely cognizant of the happenings in front of him. Xander had come to the conclusion that if Steve started to burn he wouldn't even piss on him.

"Come on," Xander said to Chaz as he led the brother away and to the other side of the yard where the steel framing to the foot bridge still remained. Steve screamed out four more times before either the fire or the zombies devoured him.

Xander made sure he had a handful of Chaz' shirt at all times as he led the man out of the zombies. The zombies pressed tightly as they passed, sometimes not yielding their spot even after Xander walked into them. He kept his head down thinking that somehow, by not making eye contact, he would not illicit a challenge. The zombies were within tongue range almost constantly and Xander had enough wet marks to prove that they were tasting the validity of the food. He was happy they weren't like sharks that bit first to determine taste.

Xander almost cried in relief when they made it through the brunt of the zombies and were stopped by a guard.

"Oh thank God," he said nearly collapsing.

"What happened to the rest of you guys?" the guard asked.

"Dead," was his one word reply.

"Holy shit, come on follow me. Kong gave us all orders that if any of you stumbled back to come and meet him personally without the woman." Nobody wanted to use Eliza's name, as if to speak it was to invoke her presence. And nobody wanted that cold beauty next to them. "Tell Kong I've got two coming," the guard said, speaking into a small two-way radio.

"Roger that, bring them out to Dowboin road and have them wait," the man on the other end said.

"Chaz, man, you alright?" the guard asked.

"I need to bury my brother," he answered through a mourning haze.

"We will, man, we will. You want some help carrying him?" the guard asked.

"It's just for a little while longer I can do it," Chaz said.

It was another ten minutes through their circuitous route that the men found themselves on the roadway that led into the Talbot compound.

Kong was waiting impatiently. "You can go back to your post," he told the guard. "What happened?" he asked when the guard was out of range.

"We never had a chance," Xander said. "They were waiting for us. Killed the first four through the door including Chaz' brother before we even knew what was going on."

"And the rest of you?" Kong asked.

"Chaz made us put down our weapons when the guy inside, Mike I think his name was, said that if he wanted to keep his brother alive that's what we had to do. Chaz shot Ned when he didn't want to. So when all of our guns were gone, he takes our vials except for Pete's and Adam's. Pete shot most of his foot off when he tried to hide his gun and Steve pushed him into the trench, so that he could take his vial."

"What a cluster fuck, where is Steve?"

"He fell into the pit, a few zombies ate him."

"Christ on a cracker! What the fuck am I going to tell Eliza? She'll want me to assemble another team. The men already think this Mike guy is supernatural."

"He is," Xander replied.

"What?" Kong asked.

"I'm telling you, man, there's something different about this guy, he's not normal. He was just in a gun battle and was as cool as a cucumber. Eliza is as mean as a rattlesnake, he *is* the rattlesnake. Why are we here Kong? What is it about this guy she hates so much? I think I deserve to know," Xander said.

"Deserve? You're better off not knowing," Kong told him.

"I think we earned the right to know," Chaz said, standing up from where he had laid his brother down. "Is the bitch even human?"

"I'm telling you, Chaz, you're better off just leaving it alone," Kong told him, trying to placate the other man.

"We've loaded trailers full of zombies and hauled them close to a thousand miles to fight a guy that has wiped out two insertion teams and killed my brother and you're telling me to mind my own business? Well fuck you, Kong!" Chaz shouted.

Kong punched the man so hard in the side of the temple, Chaz' legs locked up before he pitched over. "You got a problem with that?" Kong asked Xander.

Xander was backing up holding his hands in front of him. "No, man."

"Get him up and help him bury his brother," Kong said as he turned to relay the bad news to the one really in charge.

"There's something else, Kong," Xander said. "The zombies...they're acting weird. Yeah I know, but even weirder for zombies. There's a seven- or eight-foot deep trench, and it's lined with spikes and fire it's pretty nasty business. The zombies they won't even try to get over it.

They're just standing there."

"Are they looking down the trench?" Kong asked.

"No, that's the thing, I don't think they give two shits about the trench. They're every one of them looking up at the house like they're under a spell or something. It's fucking creepy. The ones outside the fence keep moving in, then they stop. I noticed it when we were going in, and especially when we were leaving, because we were trying to get around them."

***

"I expected to have Michael's head by now," Eliza said.

Most people would say that as a euphemism, Kong knew she meant it literally. "The team is back."

"And yet I see none of the Talbots," Eliza said, looking around with an exaggerated swing of her head.

"Only two of them made it back," he told her hopelessly, hoping that would appease her.

"Did they exact any type of revenge for their losses?" Eliza asked.

"No," Kong answered honestly.

"Perhaps some of the Talbots were mortally wounded?" Eliza asked.

"No, Eliza."

"So twelve of your finest men were slaughtered and it appears that Michael has not so much as suffered a stubbed toe?" she asked, more of a smile showing on her lips than her normal sneer.

"It would appear that way," he told her, wishing that right now he was anywhere except here. He would gladly even go back to 2005 and relive the worst day of his life over if it would help him escape this hell. He had been living in Connecticut with his wife of seven years—Madeline. He had just accepted a long distance haul to bring components to a Californian firm in Silicon Valley. The pay was something the couple could not refuse, although, being away from home for ten days was not sitting well with him. Leaves blew around his yard on the blustery fall day, his wife blew him a kiss and he pulled out of the driveway.

He had made it all the way to Colorado when he received word from his company that InTech had gone belly up and he was to bring the shipment of electronic components back to the distributor in Massachusetts. His pay would be cut, but it would save him two days away from his home and for that he was grateful.

The car in his driveway was not familiar and he parked his Chevy pick-up truck behind the late model BMW. He moved quickly to the front door, fumbling with his keys as he began to live the nightmare of so many other long distance haulers. He could hear his wife's first words, 'I have needs!' she would yell.

Fear adrenaline blasted through his veins making the delicate action of slipping a key into a lock exceedingly difficult. He heard her cries of passion as he opened the door. He looked to the kitchen and the butcher block knife holder. "Fuck that, I'll crush his throat with my hands," he said as he tore down the hallway.

The bedroom door was open. Why would it be closed? They had no children and he wasn't expected home for another forty-eight hours. It took him many heartbeats to reconcile the sight he saw in his bedroom with what he thought he was going to see. His wife was sitting up in her bed, tears were streaking down her face as an older gentleman sat on the bed next to her, he was holding her hands. A small satchel sat on her nightstand.

"What," he said loudly, "is going on, Madeline?" His words getting quieter with each progressive syllable.

The older gentleman turned.

Madeline struggled to look through her natural waterfall. "Kong," she sniffed. "What are you doing home?" Her words sounding guilty, but her actions belied that.

"What is going on?" Kong asked even quieter than

before. His mind noticing the twin snakes wrapped around the pole emblazoned on the satchel. At that moment he hoped—no, he prayed—they were *playing* doctor.

"My name is Dr. Corren," the elderly man said, standing up. He walked over to Kong extending his hand.

Kong knew that most men that had just fucked another's wife didn't generally shake the hand of the jilted. Kong reluctantly accepted the man's gesture. "Hi," Kong said, staring at the man's hand as if it contained the answers he sought.

"I'm a friend of Maddie's dad. I've been their family physician since she was in diapers," he said, smiling back at Madeline. "Maddie's mom, Gwen, asked me to stop by."

"Stop by? Maddie's from West Roxbury. You practice in this neighborhood now?"

"Not quite."

"Doc, you made a hundred mile house call?" Kong asked.

"For Maddie there would be no limits," the doctor answered.

Madeline was still crying.

"Maddie?" Kong asked, looking past the smaller man.

"I'm going to let you two be alone. Maddie, you call me if you need anything. Do you understand?" He waited until she answered. He walked over and kissed her forehead. The tenderness of the gesture made Kong realize that the doctor knew he would never have the opportunity to do that again.

Kong walked the doctor out, for a quick moment he thought about following him; irrationally thinking that if he waited the two days until when he was supposed to come home, that this waking nightmare would be over by then.

"Maddie?" Kong asked as he walked back into the room.

She broke out into fresh sobs as he approached.

"How bad is it?" he asked, sitting where the doc had been, a ghost of his body heat still present. For a moment,

Kong resented the man's presence in his bedroom.

"I have stage-three pancreatic cancer."

Kong's world spun sideways, he had heard about people having vertigo, but never experienced it himself until just that moment. Had he not been sitting on the edge of the bed, he knew that he would have toppled over. As it was he had to place both hands on the mattress to keep from tipping over onto his wife.

She started to talk rapidly as she was apt to do when she was nervous; something he usually found endearing, but he kept hearing words, like cancer, and chemotherapy, life-expectancy, treatment options. It was too much for him. He could not even begin to process what she was saying.

She had barely finished her first round of chemotherapy when she died. Small sparse flakes of snow lazily drifted to the ground as he laid his beloved to rest. The day he had found out about her disease and the culminating final few weeks had been the darkest period of his life. It had taken him years to once again find any joy, slim as it may be, in the world. And he decided that he would go back to that very moment she told him what she had rather than stand in front of the Shade Queen for one more moment.

"Kong, I suggest that when you stand before me that you do not let your mind drift elsewhere," Eliza said.

"Just remembering a happier time," he said sarcastically. "Is this one man worth it? Even now?"

"Especially now," she replied.

"Surely you have enough zombies here to take out one household."

"One would think," Eliza answered him.

"There's another problem."

"Do tell."

"They found a way to stop the zombies. They reach a point in the yard and will not go any further."

"Impossible!" she shouted. "Tomas, is this possible, does he possess the power to do such a thing?" she asked her brother.

"I do not know why you would doubt what he can and cannot do Eliza. I have begged you to stop the insanity of this quest."

"Kong you need to get me close to the house so that I can find out for myself," Eliza told the big man as she started to stride towards Ron's as if she were going on a power walk during a short lunch break.

"I don't think that's the best idea," he said catching up to her. He saw that he was not going to be able to dissuade her. "You two." Kong pointed to two men that were shuttling ammo and had the unfortunate stroke of luck to be crossing their path at that very moment, "you're both with me, put the cans down and let's go." He pushed both of the men in front of him, Eliza, and Tomas.

The zombies moved out of the way of the team as if they were repelled. Eliza was psychically pushing them away with her mind. The path she cut ahead of them closed neatly as they passed by, they were but a schooner in a sea of death.

CHAPTER FORTY

Mike Journal Entry 17

It took about an hour to make the basement somewhat presentable, although it would take a strong imagination to NOT see what had happened there.

"Need any help?" Gary asked, opening the basement door, I was three steps from the top.

"I think we're good," I told him.

BT was coming up the stairs slowly, his previous injury making his leg stiff from the awkward position he had been in while helping me clean.

"Sucks getting old," I told him from the top of the stairs.

"I hope I have the opportunity to find out, at least I have you to live vicariously through." He grabbed the handrail to help pull himself up.

"Great, I was going to help you the rest of the way up," I told him as I walked away, letting the basement door shut in his face.

"Anything?" I asked Travis going to the back of the house and talking through the window.

He was behind the protective metal barrier. He shook his head so that he wouldn't give his position away.

I walked across the house. "Anything, Dad?"

"Nothing. I'd be surprised if they tried that again."

"Probably right," I told him.

Mad Jack's box was still keeping the zombies at bay and I had to think Eliza was rethinking her strategy. We could possibly have a small lull.

The household was somewhat subdued. We were in the midst of a siege, and when nothing was happening, generally boredom became the biggest problem. Fear was too strong of an emotion to sustain for long periods of time. Everybody more or less was doing what I expected them to be doing: either busy work or lying about. I tracked back across the room. There was one notable exception to my previous statement. Justin looked like he was alternating between seeking comfort and finding some deep dark place to hide.

"Justin?" I asked, approaching him. He immediately shied away. I felt her the moment I pulled my hat off and placed it on his head. A genuine look of confusion, then elation spread across his features.

"This really works?" he asked incredulously.

I would have answered him but I ran out to the deck. Eliza might as well have had a stage light on her the way she stuck out from the crowd of zombies. She looked up immediately as she saw me. I had left my rifle in the living room; the only weapon I had was a 9 mm, and at fifty yards I'd have a better chance of throwing rocks at her. I did the next best thing—I flipped her the finger. I could hear and see Tomas laughing from here.

It was all fun and games until the two men leading the crusade started to open fire, then it got serious real quick.

At first I was outgunned two to none, within thirty seconds, I had Travis, Justin and my dad. I had run back in to snag my rifle. We got a few shots off, but Eliza and company had not advanced any further and the zombies had closed in around them like a protective barrier. I may have winged one of the men she was with…or he could have been dusting a fly off of himself. I ran to the kitchen and hastily fashioned my own hat, it wasn't done with the same level of expertise as Trip's but it did the job.

CHAPTER FORTY-ONE

Eliza

"That's him." Kong told Eliza as Michael came out onto the deck.

She nodded imperceptibly, her lips tightening at the sight of her adversary.

"Didn't seem like much when he said his name was Buker and doesn't seem like much now," he said a moment before Mike flipped Eliza off. Kong was both amused at the gesture and awed that someone had enough balls to do something like that to her.

Tomas burst out laughing, Kong had wanted to join him, but he didn't have a familiar relationship to fall back on like the boy did. He was certain she would cut his throat and let him bleed out where they were.

"Kill him," Eliza told her escort.

They hastily left the area as their firepower gave way to that of the defenders.

"Should we try a different approach?" Kong asked Eliza once they were in a safer area.

"No, I have found out what I need to know," she replied. "It is not Michael that keeps my zombies at bay."

"The trench then?" Kong asked, seeking clarification.

Eliza walked away looking more pissed then usual which Kong found hard to believe. He turned to Tomas.

"They are broadcasting a signal that interferes with the physiology of the zombies."

"Like the vials?" he asked.

"No, better," Tomas said with a hint of a smile.

"That's fucking brilliant," Kong said, turning back to the house he could no longer see due to the density of the woods. He wondered what other surprises they had in store. "You obviously care for your sister, I can see that, but you cannot hide the fact that you also care for the well-being of the Talbots. What's your story?" Kong asked.

"I do not think that either of us has enough life left in us for me to recount that," Tomas said sadly and walked to catch up with his sister.

Kong had two vampires, if he was to believe what Eliza told him—and he had no reason not to—around seventy men, and close to fifteen thousand zombies on his side against one house full of mostly women and children, and he thought that he had chosen poorly. "Well it's a shitty bed, but I made it. Might as well lie in it."

CHAPTER FORTY-TWO

Mike Journal Entry 18

"She's getting bold," BT said as I came back in the door.

"Our little girl is growing up," I told him, wiping a mock tear away from my eye.

"Should have put her over my knee a few more times," he said, following me into the room. "What's she doing?"

"I'm thinking trying to figure out why her zombies aren't eating us yet," I told him.

"I didn't know she cared."

"Don't worry, she doesn't."

"Any ideas?"

"Really?" Tracy asked BT. "You really want an unsolicited idea from Mike?"

"At least it's entertaining," BT told her.

I wanted to join in the reverie, but I could feel time slipping through our fingers. "She has us pretty buttoned up here with the zombies and the guards, but she's not going to wait us out. Eliza isn't much on patience."

"What are you thinking?" my dad asked.

"She has every tactical advantage right now. She's going to try and find a tank or rocket launchers or a damn Harrier Jet. We've got to stop her before that happens."

"You're kidding, right?" BT asked. "I merely asked you for an idea...not an overabundance of ways to get killed."

"BT, you should know better, man. All of my ideas are laced with an overabundance of ways to die."

"I know," he said, sitting down heavily. "When do we

go?"

"Are you serious? Are you that devoid of short-term memory that you cannot remember what happened the last time you went on the offensive against Eliza?" Tracy was shrieking.

If I thought Eliza was mad at me when I had given her the finger, I had yet to see Tracy's ire when I told her of my next great adventure. She definitely raised the anger bar. I think I was going to get my slogan trademarked: Michael Talbot, bringing hate and discontent to women everywhere for forty-plus years.

"I could crank up the outage on the frequency modulator," Mad Jack piped up.

"Okay." I answered, trying to figure out where he was going with it. Lord knew I'd had enough practice with John the Tripper I should have been able to figure him out, although that wasn't a fair comparison. MJ was logic based, John was acid based.

"Well that would mean more power was going out," he added.

"I get that, but to what end?" I asked.

"Mad Jack, you said that putting out too much power could fry the components," Ron said with concern.

"I did say that," Mad Jack pronounced.

"How could someone that snorted, inhaled or smoked enough drugs to finance a cartel sound as similar to someone that graduated the top of his class at MIT?" I demanded, throwing my hands in the air. "Ron? Help me out here, man. I don't speak genius."

"Relax, Mike, he usually has so much going on in his head, he doesn't know what he's told us or what he's thinking. He'll get there in a minute."

The cursory minute passed. We were all waiting for some more information that was not coming. Mad Jack was pacing the room, and it looked like he was about to leave before Ron stopped him.

"MJ?"

"I need some more transistors," Mad Jack told him as if that explained everything.

"Okay, we all get that you want to put more power through the modulator. The *Jeopardy* bonus round question is why?" Ron wanted to know.

"*Jeopardy* is for the uneducated," Mad Jack stated contemptuously. "The questions are so easy."

I had stopped watching *Jeopardy* years ago when I realized that I hardly ever knew the answers to even the easiest hundred dollar questions. Who needs to be reminded daily of their ignorance?

Ron tried Psych 101 on MJ. "The reason for increasing power to the frequency modulator that disrupts the thought patterns of the zombies is?"

"Nice...he phrased it as a question," Gary said, smacking my arm to make sure that I was watching the riveting action.

"To drive the zombies back, thus obscuring our vial-laden exit from the armed guards," Mad Jack retorted.

Now all of a sudden it was a riveting conversation. "That's brilliant," I said aloud.

"I know," Mad Jack said.

"But you're not thinking escape, are you, Mike?" Tracy asked.

"Where would we run to that she wouldn't find us? Where could we run that was more secure? Where could we run that was as well supplied? Where—"

"I get it," she lashed out.

"Plus I have someone waiting in a truck out there that I need to bring into the fold."

"What? Who?" came the myriad of questions.

I quickly explained where I had discovered Azile and how I had rescued her. I somehow failed to tell them that she had driven the majority of the way back because she was better at it than me, it must have slipped my mind.

"You just left her out there?" Tracy accused me.

"You know, I wasn't all that sure I was going to make

it back here. I figured she was safer in the truck," I said, defending myself.

"You need to go get her," Tracy said.

"I know that, dear. But it's not like I can just walk out the door and do that now, is it?"

"Don't you get condescending with me."

"Ooh look, the finger should be coming out any second," BT said to Gary.

"I don't know why you're so smug," Tracy said, turning her wrath to the big man. "You're going out there to help him."

"Me?" BT begged off. "I always have to pull his scrawny ass out of a scrape."

"And that's exactly why you and I are going with him."

"Oh no," BT and I said simultaneously.

"I'm used to saving his ass, I can't be looking out for you, too," BT shouted.

"BT, I'd been saving his ass for close to twenty-five years before you ever came in the picture. I think if anyone is qualified to do it, it's me."

"I hate when you two do this," I told them.

"You keep out of this," BT told me.

Tracy and BT were still arguing about who was better at keeping me alive when I turned my attention back to Mad Jack who had lost all interest with the ravings of the monkeys below the one-forty intelligence quotient level.

"How far back can you push the zombies?" I asked him.

"A couple of hundred feet at the most."

"Will it be fast?"

Mad Jack thought about it for a moment. "Yes, they'll want to get away from the signal as quickly as possible."

"Okay. Will it be like a fire drill where everyone leaves in an orderly fashion, or will it be like a real fire when everyone tramples over each other?"

"The latter I would imagine," Mad Jack replied,

looking up as he pondered the answer.

"Latter…that means last, right?"

He gave me the 'how have you survived this long' look.

I could have easily returned the gaze.

"There's one small problem with increasing the power output that much, though."

"Is there any chance you can just tell me what the problem is without me playing game show host?"

"It'll only last for sixty-four-and-a-half seconds."

"Exactly sixty-four-and-a-half seconds…or can we give or a take a second or two."

"Science doesn't lie," he stated vehemently.

"Alright sixty-four-and-one-half seconds it is, what happens after that?"

"No more signal."

"No more extended signal?" I asked hoping.

"No more signal, period, ever. I don't have the supplies here to recreate the box," Mad Jack told me in no uncertain terms.

"Wait so you know to the half second when the box is going to blow but you can only approximate the distance the zombies will be effected?" I asked, because I had to.

He shrugged his shoulders like I should leave the heavy thinking to the experts.

Now came the weighing out option. We would need the cover of the zombies to be able to get out of the house, but once the signal died, thousands of zombies would be pressed up against the structure like the skin of an apple.

"How long will it take for the modifications?" I asked him.

"You mean how long will it take to turn a knob?"

"Hilarious."

"I need to do some mods first, shouldn't take more than an hour, then it really is the turn of a knob."

Within a moment or two of Mad Jack going off to do whatever voodoo science he did to tweak his box, I was sitting at the kitchen table loading magazines.

"You're not really going to allow Tracy to go with you are you, Mike?" Ron asked, coming up to the table.

"Ron, you're married…when's the last time you told your wife she couldn't do something and she listened?" I asked him back. I gave him some credit; he actually spent a moment or two thinking about it. As if, he would have ever forgotten about a victory that significant.

"Listen, I know I don't have any military training," Ron began, "but I'd like to go out there with you."

"I don't think that's a great idea. The defense of this house falls squarely on your shoulders. And as soon as MJ's box fails, we'll be in full-press mode here. When we get Azile, and maybe take a swipe at Eliza, we're going to need someplace to come back to."

Ron looked equal parts relieved and distressed.

"You know I appreciate the offer. We'll be back before you know it," I told him as I loaded my fifth magazine. I wasn't going to die from lack of ammunition—of that fact I was certain.

I could hear Tracy and BT still going on with the merits of who was better equipped to save my ass when I got up from the table.

"We're leaving in fifteen minutes. You guys maybe want to load up?" I asked them.

"We're not done here," Tracy told BT.

"Not by a long shot," BT told her as he pulled on the waistband of his pants. "Thanks for saving me," he said quietly as he walked past.

I just laughed.

One more time I half-heartedly tried to convince Tracy not to come; almost immediately the finger of doom came out and I yielded.

We were huddled by the basement door waiting for Mad Jack to dial up some zombie despair. Beads of sweat were glistening on Tracy's forehead, BT had a look of consternation on his face, and I had just swallowed a live knot of garter snakes—at least that was what my belly felt like. I had not a lick of concern for myself, it was spread out for my two traveling companions.

"What some gum?" Gary asked, his mouth stuffed to near jaw-bursting proportions. He walked over to us extending a giant pack of bubble gum.

The idea of chewing anything that didn't start with Alka was making the writhing things in my stomach start a gymnastic routine. "I'm good," I told him.

"Oops, wait," Gary said as he listened to the crackling in his two way radio. "T-minus ten seconds until operation Zombie Nudge."

"Zombie Nudge?" BT lipped to me.

"Who knows," I told him back.

"Does anyone know what the 'T' stands for?" Gary asked.

Over the radio I could hear Mad Jack's explanation. "Ballistic equations begin with the variable 't' minus the rest of the algebraic equation which accounts for time and distance."

"Well now I can die in peace," BT said.

"Now?" Tracy asked. "This is the time you want to use that phrasing?"

"No shit," I told him. "Pretty fucking insensitive, BT." I chided him.

"Bullshit, Talbot, that's something you would normally say. I must have just been channeling you or something," BT snapped back. "And now I'm going into battle with a man with a tinfoil hat on and you're giving me shit? That's like the skunk calling the wet dog smelly!"

"What the fuck does that even mean, BT? Have you lost your damn mind?" I asked.

"I must have!" he shouted.

"Boys!" Tracy said.

"What?" we asked, turning on her.

Gary popped an over-sized bubble. "Mad Jack turned the dial."

That stopped us right quick. I opened the basement door to take a peek outside. Not much was happening; the zombies closest to us were trying their best to not become impaled in the trench from the push behind them of newcomers. Then I began to see a sudden change as they went from holding their spot to shuffling backwards, and within a matter of seconds, they were in a full on 'retreat' mode.

I had not a clue how we were going to get through the cluster fuck of zombies, all the closest ones were running to get out of range while the others behind were still forging forward and then there were the multitudes that were caught in the crossfire. Zombies by the dozens were being destroyed or irreparably damaged as they were caught within the vise like grips, of the outflow and influx as they in turn also tried to escape the invisible signal that was washing over them.

"Not going to get any better than this," I said as I swung the door open.

Tracy gasped at the scene before her, the screams that would be ensuing would have been deafening if they were still people, even so the cracking of bones and cartilage was disturbing maybe even more so because it was done in silence.

"Good luck, I'll save you some gum," Gary said as we ran to the right and towards the back of the house and the small footbridge. Gary closed the door and I could hear him engage the fortress-like steel bar across the door.

I couldn't see any of the guards from our vantage point, but I had to have confidence in the fact that they would be fleeing their posts. Vial or not, zombies running at you tends to loosen bladders and bowels. Our progress was hampered by the jumble of zombies strewn around the yard by the time we reached the trailing edge of the zombies still closest to the house we had in the neighborhood of fifteen seconds before the box fried itself.

The tree line was easily within distance with nothing in our way, fighting through the zombies was going to make it close. Once the box stopped broadcasting the zombies would again turn and head for the house, we would be caught and in a world of hurt, much like the plethora of zombies littering the ground.

"BT, we need to make a hole," I said pointing towards the nearest large oak. In all fairness by 'we' I meant him. He attacked the zombies with gusto, crushing over them like a fat mom does dieticians. I had no sooner touched bark on the tree when zombies in mid-stride changed their direction heading back from where we had come.

"Good luck Gary," BT said under his breath, his chest heaving from the exertion of zombie tackling as he leaned against the tree looking back at the house that was about to become besieged.

Zombies were within inches as they streamed past, a few took a quick glance at us as they ran by, but they seemed to be so used to the vials they wouldn't investigate any further.

I motioned to BT and Tracy that I was going to move around the tree. BT acknowledged me; Tracy I had to touch to get her to focus on me and not the shamble of zombies close by. I stayed tight to the trunk of the tree. I figured BT and Tracy were following. I don't know which of us was more surprised me or the guard when I came around the other side of the tree. He had been scratching his head, I would imagine at the peculiar behavior of the zombies when I showed up.

My rifle had been up against my chest, I would not be able to pull far enough away to use it anyway, the knife strapped to my thigh seemed the best course of action. That was up until BT came over the other side. I winced as BT's butt stock made bone crushing contact with the side of the man's skull. His eyes didn't even have enough time to roll back in his head as he fell over.

"Thanks, man," I told BT. "Hold Tracy back for a sec would you?" I asked as I leaned down. Blood was oozing from the side of the man's head as I reached down and yanked the vial off his neck. I stuck the chain in my pocket, then grabbed the man by the waistline and the back of his collar, when a slight break came in the zombie traffic I tossed him a few feet into the fray. He moaned for a few heartbeats as the zombies made short work of him.

BT gave Tracy the all clear sign when the zombies closed the gap around the man.

"Why the delay?" she asked, looking around.

"Mike ripped one, I waited until it cleared away."

"Thank you for that," Tracy said, placing her hand on BT's arm.

I flipped him off.

CHAPTER FORTY-THREE

The Bulkers

"Yes, Eliza, that's what my man reported. He said the zombies started running away from the house and then started running towards it and now they are right up against it. I bet whatever they were using had a power surge, then blew," Kong said to Eliza. He felt bad; he had hoped that the Talbots might make it through. If something as evil as Eliza wanted them destroyed then they must have walked strongly in the light. The world needed more people like them if it was ever going to recover, and now he was on the opposing force. If there ever was a history, how would he be remembered? *I'm the fucking Benedict Arnold of the zombie apocalypse*, he thought sourly.

"Release the contents of truck fifteen," Eliza said as Kong wrapped up.

He wanted to question the validity of her plan, but as long as it didn't involve his men, he thought discretion was the better part of valor. He might not be able to save the Talbots, but he would do all he could to save the people that he called his friends and co-workers.

He nodded to her. He noted the look of concern on Tomas' face; apparently the boy had the same reservations that he himself had. He walked away from the duo and back towards where the majority of trucks were parked. "Roy, radio the guards tell them to pull back to the fallback area."

"We getting out of here?" Roy asked, the hope clear in his voice.

"Just do what I said," Kong told him as he walked by.

"Walt!" Kong yelled motioning with his hand. Walt had been reading when he heard Kong's yell. He stepped down off the truck holding on to his book fearful he was going to lose his page. "What are you reading?" Kong asked, astonished that the man could concentrate enough to read in the midst of all that was going on.

"*BeSwitched* by Molly Snow, it's a paranormal romance, funny shit."

"Romance?" Kong asked.

"It takes me away from the horror of all this."

"Fair enough. In about ten minutes I'm going to need you to open up your trailer."

"You're really going to let them go?" Walt asked.

"*I'm* not doing anything Walt."

"Shit."

"Just make sure you get back in your truck as soon as you undo the latch."

"I appreciate the advice, but that's like telling me not to put my hand on a stove burner."

"I'm sorry for getting you into this, Walt."

"I'm a big boy, Kong, I should have taken one look at Eliza and left."

"Just get back in the truck as fast as you can," Kong said, clapping the man on the shoulder.

"Not a problem, even being in the cab knowing they're locked in the trailer is an uncomfortable feeling."

Kong wasn't sure where Eliza got the new breed of zombies, but they terrified him. There was rumor that she had a doctor that could genetically alter the zombies; some thought she had perhaps gone to a 'Fat Farm' and bitten the residents there. Though no matter where she got them from, the zombies in the back of Walt's truck were enormous; the smallest of the them tipping the scales at five hundred pounds, and they were meaner than the normal zombies, the vials were no guarantee against an attack. More than one of Eliza's helpers had been devoured while they were tasked with the unenviable job of strapping helmets on the brutes.

Eliza had armed herself with the zombie equivalent of a tank and she was about to unleash her armada. God help them all.

CHAPTER FORTY-FOUR

Mike Journal Entry 19

We were advancing slowly. The zombies were beginning to thin out as we got further from the house where rifle shots were starting to ring out. Thoughts of Little Turtle shot across my brain plate. I shook them out, that hadn't ended so well. Tracy kept looking back, worried about the kids. I was being cautious looking for guards. I knew that they must have sought safer ground for a moment as the zombies retreated, but that didn't explain the complete lack of them now. They were nowhere in sight. Normally that would have made me happy, except for that damn nagging pit in my stomach that told me all was not right in Oz.

"You feel that?" BT asked.

And I had. It was a slight tremor, then it began to build. I could feel the vibrations as they moved up my legs. We all were looking around trying to figure out what it was.

"Maybe hide?" Tracy asked the best question of the day.

We moved forward to get in and around some raspberry bushes. It wouldn't stop a bullet, but we were damn near invisible.

"Tanks?" BT asked.

"We have to go back!" Tracy said with alarm as she started to rise.

"It's not tanks," I told her, cocking my head to listen better.

"How do you know that? We have got to go back and protect them!" Tracy was on the verge of panic.

"Trace, hold on, it's not tanks. I'm not saying it's good, it's just not tanks," I told her, trying to get a bead on what was happening. The hanging raspberries in front of us were starting to dance on the vine.

"How do you know that, Mike?" BT asked looking around.

"Been in a few combat missions, tanks are noisy as fuck, so loud you can't hear yourself think." Now the bushes themselves were starting to sway. *It's fucking huge whatever it is*, I thought, keeping that little nugget of discord to myself. "Here goes nothing," I said as I slowly stood up so I could look over the hedge. At first I didn't see anything…and then I'd wished I hadn't seen anything. Amazing how quickly that change in thought set came about. I dropped down.

"Well?" BT asked.

"Tanks would have been better," I told them.

Tracy hazarded a look. "Oh my God."

BT popped up. Had anybody been watching, they would have thought they were catching an episode of *Mere Cat Manor* on NatGeo. "Are those helmets? Are those giant fucking zombies with helmets?" BT asked as he sat down hard in our makeshift hidey hole. Tracy had not yet come down. I pulled on her shirt.

"How can something that big be moving that fast?" she asked, looking off into a distance only in her field of vision.

"Now at least we know why all the guards are gone," I said.

"Now what?" BT asked.

"Eliza pulled her men back because of those things, so apparently they're as dangerous to her side as they are ours. We wait until they pass.

"The vials don't work?" BT asked, holding tighter on to his.

"I'm not sure maybe you should go check it out," I told him.

"Oh hell no. As the only black man surrounded by a bunch of whities, I've already bucked the trend by staying alive this long. I'm not going to do anything that would threaten that now."

"Fair enough," I told him. Wait it is.

CHAPTER FORTY-FIVE

Last Stand

Travis had been behind the steel curtain firing rounds at the advancing zombies. It was like killing mosquitoes; no matter how many you took out, there was always another one to take its place. Rifle fire was happening at various parts of the deck as the Talbots tried to keep the zombies at bay. The trench claimed a fair number, but was rapidly filling in as zombies literally fell 'on the sword' for their brethren.

"Should have dug it deeper," Ron said as he came in next to Travis. "Any return fire?"

"Nothing," Travis said, taking a moment to reload. "I don't think they're there anymore, but like my dad says, 'life isn't something you gamble with' so I haven't stuck my head up to really look around."

"Smart boy. They're going to have that trench filled in soon, and the fire won't last forever. The blood and gore from the zombies is going to clog the nozzles."

"You know that's pretty gross right?" Travis asked as he put his rifle back up to the firing slot.

"You feel that?" Ron asked as he watched a spent casing jump.

"You've got to see this," Travis said, pulling back and handing the scoped rifle to his uncle.

"What am I looking for?" Ron asked, looking through the scope.

"Look at the edge of the zombies."

"What...the...fuck?"

"Yeah that's pretty much what I thought." Travis

said.

"They moving in heavy machinery?" Gary asked, running around the corner of the house.

"I guess that settles the idea of guards still being out there," Travis said. Standing so he could get a better view of the oncoming nightmare.

"Cave trolls!" Gary yelled. "Where did they get cave trolls?" he asked, looking at his older brother who had just stood up.

"They're zombies, Gary," Ron told him.

"They have cave zombies?" he asked.

"There's no part of cave in it, I think," Ron said, doubt creeping into his voice.

"So we've got shufflers, speeders, headers, and now bulkers," Travis said, looking through the scope at the approaching horror.

"Headers?" Ron asked.

"The ones with the thicker foreheads. We didn't really prove it, though," Gary told him.

"They're running over the smaller zombies," Travis told them.

The smaller zombies that could not move out of the way in time found themselves melding into the ground as they were trampled underfoot.

***

The giant zombies had passed us by when I chanced another sneak peek. "They're just mowing the others down. It looks like a pro football team playing a pee wee team." BT and Tracy joined me.

"It does look like the other zombies are trying to get out of the way, though, doesn't it," Tracy asked as more of a statement.

"That's strange behavior in and of itself," BT said.

"Not entirely. I think they have a rudimentary self-preservation mode. It's pretty under-developed, but it's there.

Come on, this doesn't change our mission. If anything, it means we need to move faster.

***

The bulkers were at the edge of the trench. They traversed over the broken bodies of those that had gone before them, never once slowing their stride.

"Off the deck!" Ron yelled. "Everyone off the deck now!" he yelled louder.

He had just stepped into the living room when the first of the bulkers slammed into one of the support beams for the deck. The house shook from the contact—the unmistakable crack of pressure-treated wood cracking came next.

"That's a four by four support post," Gary said. "I should know, I'm the one that set it there."

"What the hell is that?" Tony asked coming across the room, he had been stationed on the other side of the house.

"Giant zombies." Ron told him.

"Will the basement door hold?" Travis asked, a hint of fear in his voice.

"It's a solid oak door with a two-inch thick piece of steel laid across it and the mounts are set with four inch concrete screws," Ron informed him. He seemed to be doing the math in his head, with the strength of the doorway with the force being applied. Although it was difficult to concentrate with the house shaking like the foundation was set on liquefied lard, and the deafening sound of splintering wood as the deck began to sag as its support posts were destroyed.

Planking rained down as it was torn free from the moorings to the house. The heavy decking crushed a few of the bulkers, but not enough to celebrate a victory.

"Holy shit," Cindy said as she gripped the couch. Dust hung thickly in the air as it poured in the open windows and doorways.

The bulkers surged back in following the brief lull, after the collapse, the house once again began to shake as they kept ramming into it apparently looking for the weak spot.

"We need to get everyone that isn't making the last stand into the bunker," Ron said.

"You don't think the door will hold up?" Cindy asked.

"It will for a little while," Ron said, looking a little lost in his thoughts. The zombies would destroy his house and that wasn't sitting well with him.

"Last stand?" Gary asked. "Is that literally or figuratively?"

"Figuratively," Ron clarified. "I'm not just going to give them the house...plus, we have got to give Mike, Tracy, BT, and Azile a chance to get back here. If we close up shop, they'll have nowhere to come back to."

"I'm in," Gary said.

"Me too," Tony said.

"So are we," Justin said putting his arm around his brother.

Everyone who was upstairs at that point volunteered. Ron pared it down to the Talbots; "his house...his rules" he had told them, and it seemed fitting anyway that they should be the ones to defend the homestead.

"Well at least let me figure out if there's a way to keep the door shut for a longer amount of time," Mad Jack said.

Ron waved him to go, Gary went with him.

"Alright, everyone else, grab what's important to you and get going, consider anything left out to be gone forever," Ron said having a hard time believing his own words.

"Better get moving, little brother," Ron said to the departed Mike as he walked around his house one last time.

***

"She's in that truck right over there," I said, pointing. We were a good ten or so feet within the trees.

"Oh, you mean the one on the other side of the road with all the men near it?" BT asked.

"Did you really think it was going to work out any differently?" I asked him.

"A boy can dream," BT said in seriousness.

"Hey at least they're not congregating around it." I told him.

"Is that her?" Tracy asked.

"Where?" I asked, looking up and down the road.

"She's looking out the window, it looks like she's going to try and make a run for it," Tracy said.

"I told her to stay put," I said.

"Talbot, how much luck have you had with telling any woman to do something?" BT said.

"Good point, BT."

"She can't see the one leaning up against the back of her truck."

"She's going to get caught. I do not want to get into a firefight right now," I told my band of travelers. I started waving frantically hoping she would see me, but all of her attention was to the front of the truck. The driver's side door started to ease open.

"Why doesn't she go out the passenger door and into the woods on that side?" Tracy asked.

***

"Shit," Azile said, peeking through the windshield. There was a man going down the line of trucks and looking in the cabs, she was far enough over on the shoulder that she'd been able to watch him go into the last five trucks. He didn't appear to be on alert, like he was looking for somebody, more likely something. But her cab was not big enough that she would be able to hide.

"Come on, find what you're looking for," she said through gritted teeth. She watched raptly as he stepped up on to the truck two spots ahead of her. He was in for about a minute, then jumped down, heading to the one right before hers.

"Shit, shit, shit." Azile couldn't take the chance that he actually found what he needed in that next truck. The view ahead and behind, from what she could tell, seemed mostly unobstructed, there were men about but they were mostly distracted talking with each other. She figured she could slip out the driver's side, cross the street and hide in the woods until that night when she would either get back in her cab and wait one more night for Mike or hunt down Eliza herself. Within moments, she was about to get to find both, although not on her terms and not even remotely how she would have planned it.

She opened the door as quietly as possible and climbed down, her left foot touching the pavement when she heard, "Well, well, what do we have here? A stowaway?"

She turned to see the trucker heading her way, his face split with a lascivious grin.

"Damn blind spot," she said softly. "I'm not a stowaway, this is my rig." She held herself high, trying to sound convincing over her fear.

The man faltered for a moment, but recovered. "There's no women on this haul."

"I was a last second addition, Kong needed someone to haul more zombies," Azile, said, sounding convincing even to herself.

"I'm still not convinced, there would have been talk of a woman…especially one that looked like you."

"Fine, let's go talk to Kong about it," she bluffed. *Take the bluff, take the bluff!*

He looked like he might walk away. "Fine, I needed to talk to him anyway."

Azile looked over to the tree line, wondering if she should make a run for it, that was when she saw Mike looking back at her. She didn't want to bring the fight to him. "Let's go." Azile waited until this man caught up so that he could lead. She saw the look of concern Mike displayed as he watched her walk down the roadway.

***

"Where are they going?" Tracy asked me.

"Brunch," BT said.

"Nice timing," I told him.

"Thanks, I've been working on it. Do we save her now?" he asked.

"That would be the wisest course of action," I told him.

"I forgot how much fun we have together," Tracy said sarcastically.

"Yeah just a barrel of fucking laughs, let's go," I said, pushing through the scrub brush. We were parallel to Azile, but we couldn't keep up with their unencumbered movement, add to that we had to have a factor of stealth in our travels. "Next place we live is not going to have bushes," I said, pissed off as I ripped through the barbs of another bush.

"Thorn or bullets?" BT asked, referring to how if we did not have cover we would be out in the open.

"Why are you spoiling my bitching session?" I asked.

The further Azile and the trucker walked down the road the more men they encountered. I was running out of ideas, although I guess that's not entirely accurate, running out of ideas would imply that I had some in the first place. The duo had stopped and the big man was moving quickly towards them talking animatedly. We were able to get alongside as they had as of yet not moved away, although it was easy to see that Azile's ruse had come to an abrupt end.

"This sucks," I said as I slowly stood from my crouching position, rifle at the ready. We would be able to do some serious damage before they knew what hit them. I could feel Tracy and BT rise next to me, next thing I knew I was forcibly put back into a crouch with the vise-like grip of BT's hand on my arm.

"I feel sorry for your penis," I told him, rubbing my arm after he let go.

Tracy and BT both looked at me. "What?" they asked.

"Nothing...sorry."

BT pointed down the road, my heart thudded in despair as I watched Eliza striding purposefully towards the burgeoning group with Azile at the center. The group parted quickly as Eliza stepped in, no one wanted to be that close to the devil, not even the ones that had struck a bargain with her. The slap and the resulting bright red spot on the side of Azile's face was easily visible from where we sat.

"How did you get him to find you?" Eliza asked coolly.

"I do not know what you are asking?" Azile said placing her hand to her sore face.

"That makes sense." I said aloud. I had been wondering how it had been possible, the chain of coincidences was entirely too great. I did find it funny though that I was willing to wipe all of that away and blame it on a spell cast by a witch. What a weird fucking world I was now living in.

"Are you a lunatic?" BT asked softly, not believing that I would say anything with Eliza that close.

"Probably," I told him, my feelings slightly bruised.

Tracy gave me the stink eye, meaning that if I spoke again, she was going to twist my ear off my head.

"It matters little what you say you don't know. You have accomplished what I needed anyway," Eliza said as she looked around her. "Michael, I can 'feel' you...muted somewhat, but I can feel you. If you do not come out now, I will rip out the throat of this pretty little thing that you risked your life to save. Making your actions all for naught." Eliza placed her hand around the front part of Azile's neck.

"Mike?" Tracy started.

"You know I have to. Eliza is not one for threats."

"Shit, let's do this," BT said as he stood up with me and Tracy.

"Oh look," Eliza said as she pushed Azile away. "It appears that the prodigal bastard has returned. Come out here and take off whatever that is on your head."

I did as she told me and nearly shattered my knee caps as I fell to the ground. Luckily for me I was still on the grass of the shoulder. Eliza was ripping though my mind like a seven-year-old spoiled brat high on Red Bull through a Toys R Us. She was pulling thoughts off the shelves and letting them cascade to the ground, not caring the damage she was wreaking.

***

"You dared to defy me?" Eliza asked coolly.

Mike didn't even have the mental capacity to reply, especially with any sort of wit.

"You're killing him!" Tracy screamed as blood was running from Mike's nose.

"Not yet, but soon," Eliza said releasing her psychic grip upon Mike's psyche.

"How could you let this happen?" Tracy asked of Tomas, who looked away.

"Excellent," Eliza said as BT emerged from the woods. "With the three of you destroyed, the rest will capitulate quickly."

"I think you overestimate our importance," Mike said with his head hanging down. "And underestimate theirs." He got up slowly, a river of red still flowing freely from him.

"I'm sorry, Michael," Tomas said.

Mike looked over at him, still not able to reconcile who stood before him as the boy Tommy he had known.

"Will your apology allow you to sleep at night?" BT asked.

"I do not sleep anymore," Tomas said honestly.

"Good, I hope it's torture for you," Tracy said. "We should have left you up on the WalMart roof to die."

Tomas flinched as if the words had been a physical entity hurled at him.

"Come here, Michael." Eliza said. "I had thought that I would like to stretch out your pain and misery longer, but now that you stand before me I only want your death which has eluded me for far too long."

Instead of running like his head wanted him too, Mike's legs betrayed him and brought him forward into the clutches of Eliza.

"NO!" Tracy screamed as she and BT rushed forward.

***

"NO!" Gary yelled as he stepped back.

The lag bolts sunk into the cement were moving as the heavy zombies repeatedly attacked the door.

"How is that possible?" Gary asked as he grabbed an aluminum chair and placed it up against the door as a prop.

"Force plus mass," Mad Jack said as he was thinking of how to delay the zombies, halting them at this point was an exercise in futility.

The best he could come up with on short notice and even shorter supplies was to wedge some two by fours against the door and the lolly column a few feet away.

Gary had put a couch parallel to the door and was laying magazines across it so he would have easy access.

"When you start to hear the support beams cracking you won't have much more than thirty seconds to get back to the shelter. You understand?" Mad Jack asked as he hurriedly went upstairs to tell Ron the status.

"Beams start to crack, thirty seconds to let everyone get back to the shelter. Got it," Gary said, making a clicking sound out of the side of his mouth.

Tony came down next followed by Justin and Travis.

They wordlessly took up spots behind the couch as the booming of the zombies became louder; perhaps realizing that a viable food source was near.

"Any room for me?" Ron asked as he got to the bottom step.

Gary scooted over.

"Five Talbots ought to be able to do it," Ron said as a lag bolt tinkled to the ground. There was one more round of magazine checks and making sure the weapons were off safe.

"I'll stop the world and melt with you..." Gary began to sing. "What?" he asked as Ron looked at him severely.

"Nothing, just wasn't ready for cheesy 80's songs," Ron replied.

"Cheesy 80's song!" Gary said aghast. "That's a classic!" He began anew. *"You've seen the difference and it's getting better all the time."*

"Getting better all the time," Travis mumbled. The second lag bolt on the support bracket tore free. The door was groaning—the two-by-fours were creaking.

"This might be important, but Mad Jack said that once the boards start to crack, you have thirty seconds to evacuate and get back to the shelter," Gary told the group.

"You?" Ron asked.

Gary shrugged, the two-by-fours were beginning to bend under the strain, and light was spilling all around the door as the seal was broken.

"For honor, for freedom, and most importantly...for family," Tony said as he rested the barrel of his rifle on the back of the couch.

The two-by-fours blew apart, the heavy cellar door slammed against the wall. A bulker that seemed surprised it had made it through took a step towards the rifles and came face to face with oblivion, the heavy metal helmet proving incompetent as the bullets entered its face and went into the brain cavity destroying the nerve center of the beast. He was pushed to the side; even as he thudded to the ground another took his place. Travis' next shot pushed the zombie's head back as the bullet struck the metal plating, it locked eye contact on the one that dared shoot at him and began its fifteen foot traversal, Tony's shot caught the zombie on the bridge of the nose, the cartilage erupted; white, wet, soft material sprayed against the far wall.

The light was blotted out every time a bulker entered the basement, as effectual as an eclipse. They grunted and groaned as they pushed through each almost wedging its enormous size in the doorframe. Rifle smoke filled the room quickly that and the blotted out light made finding targets difficult.

"Dad, we need to pull back!" Ron shouted.

"There is no 'pull back' its retreat from here, and we can't leave them out there," Tony said calmly to his son. "Get my grandsons to safety," Tony added with a resigned sigh. The bulkers had halved the distance to the couch.

"Dad?" Ron asked.

"Do it!" Tony uncharacteristically yelled. He said it as he fumbled in his jacket pocket, pulling out two grenades that Mike had brought back.

"What are you going to do with those?" Ron asked.

"What do you think? Get your brother and my grandsons to safety."

Rifle shots were now a continuous volley as aiming was not necessary. The cement rumbled from the weight of the bulkers as they pushed ever forward.

Even Ron had to admit the basement was lost, the next line of fallen bulkers would hit the couch and drive them into the wall where they would be pinned and helpless.

"Let's go!" Ron shouted, tapping Travis, Justin, and Gary.

"Pops?" Travis asked after they had traveled a few feet away and he realized his grandfather wasn't with them.

"Holding the line!" Ron told him as he urged his nephew on. A tear fell onto the floor.

The four had just rounded the corner and where within a few feet of Mad Jack who was urging them on when they lost their footing. The floor jumped up to meet them and all went silent as a giant explosion ripped through the house bringing some of it down upon itself.

***

Mike stood no more than a foot from Eliza, no more able to control his movements than he had been that fateful night so many months before when she had given him the kiss of death. For that is what it had truly been, everything else that had happened had merely been in preparation for this moment. Tracy was held back by one of the truckers as she tried to get to his side. BT had a small arsenal of weaponry pointed at him, no one dared leave him to his own devices.

"I do not know why this moment has eluded me. You are not supernatural…there is nothing extraordinary about you. You are merely flesh and bone, weak like all men. I do not see your God rushing in to help you. You are abandoned, and alone."

"Fuck you," Mike spat out, struggling to have at least that small victory as she held him tight within her mental grasp.

Kong watched fascinated, he knew that he would have been begging for her mercy were he in Michael's shoes, yet the man still fought. He hoped Mike's demise would be swift, but did not hold much stock on that assumption, Eliza held no ability for compassion.

"Would you rather I kill your pretty little wife before I dispose of you?" Eliza asked.

Mike was shaking with impotent rage. Eliza had his jaw clamped shut so that even a cutting remark could not be issued.

Kong almost made the fatal mistake of helping. The moment was beyond tense as three lives hung in the balance. Mike, with his arms pinned against his sides and his fists balled up, was still somehow able to unfurl his middle finger.

It was pointing downwards, but the message was not lost on Eliza.

"Is that for me? Let me get a closer look." Eliza said as she wrapped a small hand around Mike's neck. She picked him up as if he were no more than doll. Mike's legs began to buck as she cut off his air flow.

"Stop!" Tracy screamed, trying desperately to get through the guards.

"Your turn is coming, do not be in such a rush," Eliza said, turning a cruel smile Tracy's way. "Although I may allow my men a little fun first."

BT punched the guard nearest him in the temple. The man fell to his knees, BT pushed past the other two that had been watching Eliza between leers at Tracy. BT rushed at Eliza, she saw him coming and gripped tighter on Michael's neck in preparation for the attack. As BT came at her, Eliza let loose a back hand that sent the man sprawling, his legs lifted off the ground from the force of the blow. He struck the ground in a non-moving heap.

Michael's vision was tunneling, his legs twitching violently in their death throes, his knee struck against Eliza's chest a small tinkle as if a wine glass shattered could be heard over the din. Two spirits seemed to pull away from Eliza as she shrieked in horror.

One was her twin in looks only, not countenance; the other was a Native America Shaman. He gained stature as he stood tall. Eliza backed up, still holding Michael by the throat using him as a shield to keep the doppelganger away. The shaman took in the scene around him, his eyes finally resting on the surprised face of Azile, who was still on the ground. He took his old gnarled hands and meshed them together. At first Azile did not understand his message, then it dawned on her.

The truck drivers had moved back as the event unfolded.

Azile stood. "I bind you, lost soul, to the one that has forsaken you."

Eliza's head whipped around. "NO!" she screamed. "Kill her!"

Azile looked around and quickly repeated her words. "I bind you, lost soul, to the one that has forsaken you."

"Kong, kill her!" Eliza yelled, even as her soul began to merge within her.

One of Kong's men raced towards Azile, a club raised high, Kong who had been momentarily stunned by the events came out of his daze and shot the man in the chest, the club clattered to the ground as he shouted.

"Anyone else approaches and I'll kill them too!"

The shaman repeated the hand clasping gesture to Azile.

"I bind you, lost soul, to the one that has forsaken you!" Azile screamed.

Mike fell to the ground as the force and shock of the spell took hold within Eliza.

"She's mortal?" Tracy asked, never looking around to gather an answer.

She pulled free from the man that had been holding her and was now moving away. Mike's body was still and seemed devoid of life as she touched his face, he was so cold. In direct contrast, the anger within her was white hot. She reached down across his body and took his knife from the sheath attached to his leg; with one fluid movement she stood, spun and buried the Ka-Bar hilt deep into Eliza's breast.

"Till death do we part, bitch!" Tracy said as she twisted the knife.

The confusion and pain that were etched in Eliza's feature were quickly replaced by relief as she realized her unnaturally long life was coming to an end and then to sheer terror as Eliza glimpsed what her afterlife would entail.

"It appears that eternity is not quite as long as you would have believed." An evil voice said as it drifted up from and through the ground

Tomas fell to his knees, shrieks of pain and loss in his

voice. The shaman smiled sadly at Azile and walked towards a rhythmic drumming that only he could hear.

BT turned his sore and battered body over enough to witness the entire event, the first thing that came to his mind was to sing a line from one of his favorite childhood movies. "Ding Dong. The wicked witch is dead." He said before laying his aching head back down.

CHAPTER FORTY-SIX

Mike Journal Entry 20

I was shattered.

I felt like a mirror image of Humpty Dumpty, so when I fell, my eggshell and my reflection were destroyed. I felt arms around me, I could hear bedlam, men were screaming, shots were being fired and I was slowly rising to consciousness. I was in the arms of the trucker Kong who was rushing to get me to a rig. I could see zombies running towards us as we ran, or at least he ran. BT was cradled in Tommy's hands, parts of BT did not look to be moving, but I was having great difficulty focusing on anything as we bobbed.

I came up from the depths of unconsciousness, a killer headache worthy of a twelve-pack of cheap beer hangover thrumming through my temples. I saw Tracy and Azile in the sleeper behind me, they seemed to be constructing a makeshift sling for BT. Tommy had put my seat belt on as I kept finding myself pooling on the floor of the cab.

"Fucking zombies, now we'll show them!" Kong laughed as he pulled on his horn. Even the deep throated bass of his truck horn could do little more for me than allow me to make the pitchfork sign of rockers everywhere.

The truck bounced around as Kong did his best to make zombies an integral part of the roadway system. With the passing of Eliza, her vials and the safety they offered were removed. Truckers that were slow to recognize this often found themselves under the assault of multiple zombies. The zombies that had been single-mindedly attacking Ron's house relentlessly now pulled back when they saw no signs of food. Speeders and bulkers attacked the retreating truckers ferociously.

As I slowly came back to the world of air breathers, I got the sense that the only thing keeping the rest of the men from bolting was Kong and his threats of retribution if they ran.

The man was nuts, probably more so than me. The trucks were making short work of the zombies that dared come out, but they weren't quite as clueless as we hoped, more and more of them would wait by the edges of the road where the trucks could not get and would only attack when the truck had to slow down and turn around or open the windows to fire rounds. I witnessed at least one trucker get pulled from his truck, I would have sworn that the zombie pulled the door handle, yet I was holding out hope that my oxygen starved mind had maybe missed a detail or two. I still locked my door though.

"Shit," Kong said as he pulled his pistol in. "Out of rounds. I miss my wife," he said to no one in particular. "Do you think she still loves me?" he turned to asked Tracy. "I've done some things." Whether looking for forgiveness from my wife or a higher power I didn't know. "There's a duffel bag in the compartment over your head could you get that for me?"

With some effort she handed it past Tommy. Kong put the bag on his lap with a loud clang, he unzipped it, metal shone as he did so.

"Big ComiCon fan are you?" I asked him as I looked down at a satchel of swords and large knives.

"This isn't that reproduction shit, this stuff is real," Kong said, digging around through the contents.

"What are you going to do with them?" I had an idea I just didn't want to be right.

"I should've been a better man. When others around me were weak, I succumbed. Instead of helping, I made things worse…in most cases much worse. Well today that changes, today I go out a better man, hoping that God and my wife can find it in their hearts to..."

He didn't finish as he opened his door, a large two-handed broad sword slashing back and forth violently. Blood spray coated the windshield and driver's side door as he hacked off body parts with no more effort than a band saw would have going through balsa wood. Arms flopped to the ground, heads rolled away. Once or twice I saw him cut down zombies at the knees, but he was tiring and the zombies were just getting started.

"Help him," Tracy said in alarm.

"He *wants* to die, is that what you want me to help him do?" I asked her.

"He helped kill Eliza and he saved your life."

"Are we forgetting the little detail of why he was here to begin with?" I asked.

"Fine, I'll do it," she said, making a move to come up front. "In the end he did what was right."

And the truly fucking scary part is, for a moment, I almost told her 'go ahead, I won't stop you' and would have meant it. I reached over into the bag and grabbed two swords; they were smaller than the behemoth Kong was swinging.

"When the fuck did you become a Ninja?" BT asked as he sat up with a grimace of pain.

"Online correspondence classes," I told him as I opened my door.

"Be careful," Tracy threw out there at the last moment.

If you were about to immerse yourself among blood-thirsty zombies armed with only two swords, would you need the caveat to 'be careful' added in, or would that just be a given? Would we have needed to start telling electricians working on downed power lines while standing knee deep in flood water to 'be careful' or would they just get it?

I hopped down, zombies started to coalesce. I moved away from the truck so that I would have the ability to swing my swords. The steel jumped in my hands as it made bone jarring contact; I now understood the reasoning behind

Kong's heavier instrument of destruction. I felt diminished from Eliza's death, but I was still stronger than an average man. I was keeping the zombies at bay with a modicum of work. My efforts were for naught as I fought for inches to get over to Kong's side. I was halfway past the grill of the truck when I heard him fall; it was more of a cry of thanks than pain.

With the smell of blood, the zombies were momentarily pulled away from me. I hacked indiscriminately. Backs flayed open as I severed spinal columns, zombies hunched over as I cut through their powerful back muscles and they lost support. I almost dropped my swords when the powerful blatting of the truck horn sounded. I looked up to see Tracy frantically pointing behind me. Bulkers were bearing down, a herd of stampeding water buffalo would have been a more welcome sight. I would not make it back to my door, or Kong's for that matter, not unless I could cut through the swarm that was eating him in time.

I stepped up onto the bumper and onto the hood as the first of the big zombies rocked the rig. I nearly lost my balance until I dropped a sword and reached out to grab a windshield wiper. Bulker hands were reaching up and trying to seek purchase on any part of me so they could drag me down among them.

"Hold tight!" Azile screamed as she took over Kong's former seat.

Again with the superfluous cautions. I reluctantly let go of my remaining weapon and gripped the lip of the hood. The truck bucked as Azile put it in drive and was trying to pull away from the carnage. A bulker had somehow got up on the bumper and was chewing vigorously through the sole of my boot. My leg was whipping back and forth as the monster shook its mouth trying to get a tasty tidbit free. I repeatedly kicked at its head with my free foot; it couldn't have cared less as I slammed the side of its head.

My leg pulled free as the bulker ripped the tread of

my boot off. I pulled my legs up before he had a chance to start chewing on the bottom of my foot. The bulker didn't care that my shoe bottom wasn't food it tore through it and swallowed it as I watched over my shoulder. I turned back to look at the astonished faces of Azile and Tracy.

"It's climbing up the front isn't it?" I asked them without daring to look back.

Azile was nodding furiously.

"Shit."

"Mike, it's coming!" BT roared.

"Not sure what you'd have me do, BT!" I replied.

"Here goes nothing," Azile said. At least that's what the words looked like as she said them softly to Tracy.

I had pulled up my legs so far that I was nearly horizontal to the windshield. I could hear the top of the hood denting in as the bulker approached. The truck picked up speed as Azile cycled through her gears. I wanted to warn her that we were on a dead end, but it goes back to the superfluous, the truck had to be approaching sixty or seventy miles an hour as Azile slammed on the brakes at nearly the same time the bulker gripped around my ankle.

My fingers felt like they were going to snap off. I had them curled under the lip, my weight plus the bulkers and the drag of the braking was causing excruciating pain in my over-worked digits. The bulker had not been able to get as good a grip as I'm sure he would have wanted; the stuttering of the truck jumping and the inertia caused the zombie to slide down the front of the truck. And still the damned zombie nearly killed me as the truck went up and over the being, my entire body, save two fingers rose into the air from the force. Blood gore and half-digested body parts sprayed out from under the truck. I went to a place in my brain that said it was just the world's largest ketchup packet, sure filled with, blood, bile, body parts and bones—but ketchup nonetheless. Another forty feet or so and we came to a blissful stop.

It would be an hour before I could completely unfurl

my fingers and a few days until the dull ache would stop. I got down off the truck and walked to the passenger door with a noticeable limp due to my sole-less boot rather than any injury. Tracy had moved over so that I could get in.

"Thank you, Azile," I said as I cradled my hurt hands in my lap.

"I'm sorry, Mike. I wasn't thinking," Tracy said, gingerly rubbing my purpling digits.

"Is she talking about when she married him?" BT asked Tommy.

"You want some Ben-Gay Mr. T?" Tommy asked.

I could envision me wiping sweat off my brow while they were coated in the pungent concoction. "I'm good, thanks," I told him.

Zombies were getting scarce as were truckers, word of Kong's passing was making the rounds among the remaining men and with their leader and the threats removed they were more interested in saving themselves.

"Time to play the Pied Piper," I told Azile.

She got the rig turned around, and wasn't going more than five miles per hour, continually honking her horn, zombies fell in step (or got run over, which was just fine) as we drew them away from Ron's. Thousands had died over the last couple of days and still thousands remained. We had a few hundred with us, some would stay around the house and need to be dealt with, others would go into stasis and need to be dealt with at a later time, but for now the biggest threat to mankind was dead and I for one wouldn't miss her.

Azile drove over twenty miles away from the house until she picked up the speed to shake our entourage. I gave her an alternate way back to the house so that the zombies wouldn't merely turn around and come back.

"What now?" Tracy asked as we barreled down Route 1.

"Mop up duty," I hoped.

As we pulled on to the street before my father's I was (we were) wholly unprepared for the scene before us.

Hundreds if not thousands of zombies had been destroyed under the heavy wheels of tractor trailers. It was beyond putrid, there was nearly a six-inch layer of compressed zombies on the roadway, so thick I didn't think a snow plow would be able to sludge them off the roadway. Of all the smells I had encountered thus far during this apocalypse, this couldn't even be measured it was so far over the top.

I could go into gory detail about how much stomach butter was churned in that cab but I'll spare you the details. The truck at times slid sideways as we road over the crest of carnage, parts on occasion would be thrust out or particularly large blasts of air would pop as a vital organ was compressed past its limit much like those protective bubbles used for mail.

Zombies milled around Ron's house, unsure what to do now that they were not being directed or there wasn't a food supply available but that changed quickly when they saw us coming. I had Azile pull up to the wreckage of the first truck that had tried to make it in to the compound.

"Well shit…was kind of hoping they'd be gone. Let's play Piper again, then I know a back way we'll have to hoof it in by," I told everyone. They weren't listening much because I had just told them we were going to have to drive back over the horrid highway.

"You kind of suck, man," BT told me.

"Kind of?" Azile asked.

This time she only went about ten miles out. We got maybe another hundred or so of the slimy bastards to follow before we turned back around. I needed to get home, my stomach was cramping with worry, I had seen no signs of life from the house and I had seen some significant damage too. Everything could be fine and they were all hunkering down comfortably in Ron's prep shelter or…this was an apocalypse and I had to think of all possibilities.

Where I had Azile pull over was a two mile drive on roadways or about three quarters of a mile by crow flight. And that was about the only way someone should do this trek, was by air. There was a small field on this side but as we progressed onto Ron's land the foliage would become so thick that to get a sight line of more than five feet would be a rare occurrence, and we were now only armed with sharp pointy objects at the moment.

The field was covered in a low lying fog, of course it was, how else would it be. At least it was penetrable, that was of course until we entered the brush which seemed to grasp onto the ethereal mist like a lover to the blankets on a cold night. The five hoped for feet of range was halved, if anything came at us now we wouldn't have enough time to act surprised. We tried to keep our noise level to a minimum; mostly muttering as clothes were caught or thorns pushed through to rake against skin. The fog dampened noise and we stopped repeatedly to get our bearing and listen to anything else that might be in there with us.

More than once we heard things crashing through the trees, luckily heading away. The only zombie we stumbled across was one that had been run over through its midsection, its middle had been compressed to no thicker than a ream of paper and its spine must have been completely destroyed because it was bent over at the waist it's head dangling down uselessly by its knees. I felt a tremor of remorse as I cut through the zombie woman's neck that was at least until her pale blue eyes looked up from the ground at me with an accusatory glare. I pushed the sword into her mouth and flung the head away, that was not a sight that needed to infiltrate anyone else's dreams.

Ron's house was a mess. Smoke was issuing forth from his basement, not enough for me to think it was on fire, more like a swirling of dust settling after an explosion. I swear I could hear Tracy's heart pounding in unison to my own. Zombies were still around, but we had not been noticed as of yet. We moved further down the tree line so that we could see into the basement. That was not going to be a way of egress. I could see multiple bodies of dead bulkers, some wooden beams and nothing more, it was effectively sealed from outside intrusion. That left the deck which, at ten feet, wasn't insurmountable; but we still had to all get up it before the speeders noticed us and tried to eat us. That also involved getting to the other side of the house because the decking on this side was pretty much destroyed. I did not think that we would be able to cross over the cleared expanse without being seen.

"Okay I've got an idea," I said.

BT and Tracy groaned in unison.

"Mike, I need to see my babies," Tracy pleaded.

"I'm going to get on the deck." I started. "I'll get the zombies that are still here to follow me, then you guys just come up the other side of the house."

"That's not half bad," BT said, nodding his head.

"You going to be able to climb, big man?" I asked him, looking at his sling.

"More pain than damage, probably only a sprain," BT answered.

"No time for bravado, my friend. If you can't climb, we'll do something else, because nobody is going to be able to lift your ass that high," I told him.

I looked at him for a few moments, trying to see how good my 'bullshit detector' was calibrated. I didn't detect any deception. "Fine, Tommy, can you control the zombies?"

"No, I lost a lot with my sister's death. And there's more that I need to tell you," he replied.

"Can it wait?" I asked.

"It can, but not for long."

That sounded much more ominous than I was ready for. "Alright, give me a few minutes, I'm going to try to find a gun and make as much noise as possible to pull them my way. When you have an opening, go for it, because I'm sure any zombies that are in the woods will come back. I would imagine we'll be under siege again.

"Will it ever stop, Mike?" Tracy asked.

I shrugged my shoulders. "One minute at a time, my love, one minute at a time." I kissed her forehead, went about another twenty feet down the tree line in case there were any eagle-eyed zombies that saw my point of origin and my group. I made it to the fence before I was spotted. Fuck they were fast. I nearly lost my footing as I jumped over the nearly filled-in trench. The zombies were closing in fast, I was down to milliseconds with whether to stand and fight or drop the weapons and jump. If I miscalculated and slipped, it would be over before I hit the ground. Breath was coming out of me in great plumes as I fought for more speed, I felt a zombie's hand brush up against me as I launched forward and up, my right hand wrapped around a banister. I semi-missed with my left hand, ripping the fingernail of my middle finger clean off; the pain was significant but not a hindrance, not at that moment anyway. I'd had the good fortune to be alive for over four decades without ever losing a fingernail, now I'd lost two in less than a week, life is funny like that. I was just praying it didn't come in threes. I quickly pulled my legs up and onto the lip of the deck. Zombies began to pool under me. I had the strange urge to piss on their heads. Hey! I said it was strange, don't judge me.

I felt much better as I climbed over the railing and onto the relative safety of the structure. I entered the house quickly and quietly not sure what to expect. The house was as quiet as the woods had been, but this was worse because there should have been sound.

"Hello?" I asked expectantly. I felt mighty exposed at that moment with nothing in my hands. I approached the darkened kitchen and grabbed the first thing I came into contact with, a large cast iron frying pan, I felt like I was in the UK, no firearms and all. I grabbed a small pot when I realized that noting was up here with me, I would search for everyone else when I was sure, that Tracy, BT, Azile, and Tommy were safe.

I went out onto the deck and raised my pan laden hand high to the area in the trees where they were. I wanted to let them know I was alright, then I went to the far side of the house and banged the living shit out of them.

"Dinner assholes!" I shouted, oh and they came, in droves. My plan was working a little better than I had intended. I moved further back down the deck away from Tracy's approach.

I was torn between keeping the zombies attention on me, checking on Tracy's progress, and finding out the fate of the rest of my family. And still I banged pots over my head like a fucking loon. Then the real fun began as shots rang out. I tossed the pan and pot at the zombies and ducked back into the house (Nancy would later yell at me for tossing her cookware), and back out the French doors on the other side.

Ron, Gary, Travis, and Justin were giving cover fire for their running mother or sister-in-law as the case may be.

"Mom needs longer legs," Travis said as he chambered another round.

"Here!" Ron said, tossing me a Mossberg.

"How?" I asked.

"Closed-circuit TV. Shut up and start shooting," he said.

Tommy was following behind, the zombies had closed in behind him and unlike me he swung his swords like a ninja, a deadly assassin ninja. The death he was dealing was artistic in its fury and form. Our job on the deck was to keep the zombies from the sides and the front; our shots were getting closer and closer to Azile, Tracy, and BT. Soon we would be firing on their position.

"They're not going to make it," Ron said as he feverishly shoved new rounds in his magazine.

"Trav, trade me!" I yelled to him. He was putting a new magazine in the Armalite MP-4. There was no hesitation as he handed me the thirty round assault rifle for the five rounds of slugs the shotgun held. "Fuck, fuck, fuck," I said—or maybe thought—as I jumped down off the deck.

They were twenty feet away as I started to fire. I advanced a step or two, firing repeatedly.

"Dad!" Travis yelled. "Magazine!" he yelled down as

I heard it thud behind me. I silently thanked him as I continued to mow the zombies down trying to give my loved ones some running room. It was working but partly due to the fact that I was now on the menu and they were coming my way.

"...twenty-nine, thirty," I said as my breech stayed open, I quickly ejected the spent magazine and twirled to find the new one. I banged it against my leg to lose any dirty, and once I pulled and released the charging handle I was back in business. Good thing, too, because they were close enough to read the serial number on the barrel.

"Ron...gonna need some help!" I yelled as I started to back up. Getting onto the deck was not going to happen; we were going to be underneath it soon.

"Far side of the house! There's a barred window I can open up to get you in!" he shouted.

I quickly motioned for Tracy to come under the deck and towards the house. She looked longingly at the safety above her and ran to the house like it was a safe zone in a particularly rough game of Tag. Azile was next and a fighting retreating BT pulled up next to her. Tommy was still a one man Cuisinart but his setting was rapidly going from puree to chop.

"Around the house!" I shouted loudly, punctuating my words with rifle fire. I had lost count of my rounds, but I was at least halfway through my magazine and we now had no further support from above.

We were a moving bubble of death. Tommy was now to our side, holding the horde at bay. The swords looked like they were getting heavier by the second as his neck severing swipes were now becoming belly gutting strokes and soon would become soprano makers if you catch my meaning. BT was pushing ahead in front, hacking zombies as if they were wheat and he was a harvester. I was selectively shooting zombies as I brought up the rear. Occasionally, a glint of metal would fly by my face as Tracy felt the need to hack at a zombie.

"I like my nose where it is, woman," I told her.

Then my backpedaling feet walked into her. I stole a quick glance up ahead. We were stalled.

"BT?" I yelled.

"Stuck, man."

I heard splintering wood over my head. Travis and Justin were ripping up floorboards.

"Dad, you need ammo?" Justin asked.

"Like a fat kid needs a Twinkie. Tommy…need a little cover while I get this."

Tommy started to hack by my side along with the ever dangerous thrusts of Tracy. There was a good chance I was going to come out of this battle a eunuch.

Justin was reaching down to me while Travis kept ripping boards up with a crowbar. He got about three up when the barrel of his rifle came through.

Fuck yeah! I thought as he started blasting zombies to our front.

With a renewed vigor, I heard BT's war cry, zombies fell as his adrenaline surged. I drained the remainder of my magazine, giving us a little breathing room, although breathing was not on the top of favorite list right now, not with the smell that accompanied it anyway. Tommy focused his energy back to our side, as I replaced my magazine and began to fire.

"I'll have another one ready soon dad." Justin said as he was shoving 5.56 rounds into a fresh magazine.

I didn't have the heart to tell him that we didn't have another minute. If we didn't get into the house soon, we were done for.

We were again moving but slowly, the zombies were paying in buckets of blood for the precious inches we were gaining. I was on my twelfth round when massive rifle fire came from our front.

I couldn't see what was going on, but it was fast enough that I thought it was automatic gunfire. If Ron was holding out, I was going to be pissed, that was provided we made it.

"BT?" I screamed over the din.

"Gatling gun I think!" he yelled.

"Are you shitting me?" I asked softly. Now it was worth living just to see what the hell he was talking about.

The zombies were human once and they could not sustain the damage we were inflicting, Travis turned his attention to our backs as we passed his position above.

"You're uncle is going to be pissed when he sees this damage," I said as I went underneath him.

"I'll deal with that later." He smiled with a strain.

The Gatling gunfire stopped ahead as I imagined Ron was heading back into the basement. BT moved to the side as Azile and Tracy entered through the oversized window. Gary was holding the bars up.

"Go, man." I tapped BT.

"Go, Tommy!" I yelled.

I fired off the remainder of my rounds and ducked in. Gary let the bars clang down and locked them in place with first a pin and then a lock that I figure was first developed to hold an elephant in place.

Gary hugged me.

"Good to see you, man! Where's the Gatling gun?" I asked.

Ron was heading into the recesses of the basement.

"Whatcha got there, brother?" I called out.

"Nothing for you!" he said back.

I caught up to him, it was a thing of beauty—eight gun barrels shone brightly.

"It's a .22 caliber Gatling gun reproduction," he said defensively.

"You should have told me," I said, trying to place my hand on it.

"Mike, it cost me ten grand there's no fucking way I was going to tell you about it."

I was sort of hurt, but I wouldn't have told me about it either. "Is this what was in your trap door in your closet?" I asked, putting it all together. This was why he was so adamant about not letting me see it. I had wrongly figured it was porn, although this thing had me drooling as if it were.

Then Ron's next words doubled me over. "Dad didn't make it, Mike."

I staggered a step or two back, Tracy was there for support. I'm not ashamed to say that I cried like a five-year-old. I cried for the loss of my dad, my mom, my brother, my niece, Jed, Jen, Alex, Paul, Erin, Brian and at least a dozen other good souls we had lost along the way.

I stayed for a long time in that darkened basement, when Ron had told me how our father had died. I wanted to be as close to his final earthly spot as was possible. The battle raged on above me, but now it was more of a fish in the barrel scenario. We had position, ammo and security, I wasn't needed upstairs.

It would be another three days before the horde dwindled down to an unlucky few. I had joined in the fray if only to vent my misguided revenge. I wished desperately that they gave a shit for what they did. I had switched out my MP-4 for a Mosin-Nagant Russian WWII sniper rifle, a bit of overkill when the 7.62 by 4.42 round struck home. I watched each individual I hit as the back of its head blew out in a spray of white, crushed bone and diseased gray matter.

I drilled five hundred and twenty-six zombies into the ground that day, but whose counting. My fingers ached from jamming that many rounds through the old gun, my anger increased at each one, that they didn't care, that they didn't give a shit when the zombie next to them fell, that their sisters, brothers, fathers and friends were dying all around them. That was what stopped any war—when the killing just became too much, when neither side could stomach the mounting atrocities. The zombies would not stop, they would never stop, not until each and everyone one of them was dead.

AFTERWORD

Three days after the death of Eliza, the war at Camp Talbot was over. I could not do much more than shiver as I sat in a rocker, on the part of Ron's deck that was not on the blood steeped lawn. I watched, as he pushed piles of dead zombies into giant pyres with his tractor. The boys were keeping vigilance over him. Gary rode on the tractor as an added layer of protection.

"Will this ever get better?" I asked, my teeth chattering even in the seventy-degree heat of the day and two blankets wrapped around my legs.

"Not anytime soon, Mr. T," Tommy said as he sat beside me suffering through the same symptoms. "With Eliza, gone we've lost a piece of us."

I felt like a hard core heroin junkie who had gone cold turkey, my bones dripped in pain, if that makes any sense. I'd already taken a loss I did not figure I could absorb when I had lost my soul, but with the absence of whatever Eliza had filled the void in with, I was adrift in a sea of black. My innards ached as they seemed to move around in the shell that once housed me.

"It would be better to die," I told him with vacant eyes, "than to live like this."

He may have nodded in reply or it could have been my shivering that gave the illusion of movement on his part.

***

"Can you do anything?" Tracy asked Azile as she looked through the window and out at her husband who was so obviously suffering.

Azile shook her head, she also was trapped in her own misery.

***

"There's more," Tommy said.

I stood, hoping that my bones were not as hollow as I felt. "Do tell. I could use a bit of shitty news right about now."

"The order I put to halt the progress of BT's zombieism will unravel now that I no longer have as much power."

My legs weren't hollow, but they were having great difficulty supporting my weight at the moment. "How long?" I asked him.

With considerable effort, Tommy shrugged his shoulders.

"You once told me that you saw your sister get bitten, then she ultimately killed her sire. How did she survive? Did she walk all these years like this? Is that even possible? I feel hollow, Tommy. I can sense the pain I should be feeling, but I'm numb to it. With every beat of my heart I flip from my heart breaking at the death of my father to an absolute fathomless void, where nothing not even emotions can stem from. I know I should be concerned for my friend's health, sometimes I am and sometimes I'm not. I know I should be loving my family, and yet there are times when I can't even remember what the emotion entails. I felt more concern for a dead squirrel in the roadway when I was human than I do now."

***

Tracy shivered as she overheard words she wasn't supposed to.

***

"Eliza killed her sire. She was not diminished from his death, but rather enhanced by it. That was why she never let any of her charges live for very long, lest they try to take her power from her. The emptiness will go away, you'll fill it in with something, Mr. T. My sister filled hers in with hate and cruelty for everyone and everything. But that's not who you are, you have it, *we*," he stressed, "have it in us to fill it with something better."

"You're still a vampire right?" I asked him.

"I am." He let his head drop.

"Why now the change back to this 'Tommy' persona? How can I ever trust or believe you, if I ever even care again?"

"I took on a large part of my sister when she turned me. With her influence gone, I'm more the boy you remember."

"I wish I could believe that...I do...for my family."

I watched as zombies burned by the hundreds. With some effort, I was able to walk down towards one of the pyres. I should have been close enough for my skin to be melting, and still I quaked in the unoccupied recesses of my mind.

"You alright, Mike?" Ron asked a good fifteen feet behind me. I turned to see his hands shielding his face from the intense heat.

I waved him away, not because I was concerned for his safety, but rather, I wanted to be alone. I wondered if I would feel anything if I walked just a few more feet into the intense blaze.

Tommy stepped up beside me. "The shaman did it."

I didn't say anything. I realized that at one time I would have had an answer for him, something revolving around, 'Sure now all we need is some peyote, a shaman and sweat lodge and we'll be all set.'

"We have a witch," Tommy said, filling in the gaps in the conversation.

I turned and we walked back towards the house. Travis was watching me as I entered.

I went to BT's room. "Good news, buddy."

"They discovered a cure for sarcasm?" he answered.

"Better...road trip," I told him.

"You're kidding, right? You're not, are you? Fuck...why? This is about the Jeep isn't it? You want to go back and get your fucking Jeep! No, Mike I'm not traveling across the damn zombie infested country for a damn Jeep I won't do it!"

I'll admit that thought had crossed my mind, but even I wasn't that nuts, although if our travels brought us anywhere near Colorado I was going to snag it.

"No, my friend, we need to find Doc Baker," I told him.

"Oh, man, you know he's probably dead," BT said.

"I asked Tommy, he said he wasn't."

"And you believe the Edward wannabe?"

"Who?" I asked.

"Nothing, it was a character in a book I read before all this shit happened."

"We need the Doc, BT."

"Need? Why who's dying?"

I kept staring not saying anything.

"Oh shit, it's me isn't it? Dammit, I finally get to rest my damn body and now we got to go gallivanting all over the damn place again." BT put his shoes on.

I walked out in to the hallway. "Boys!"

"Not a chance, Talbot, not unless I'm coming with you," Tracy said.

"Are you friggen clairvoyant?" I asked her.

"No, you're just transparent."

"I would like to go to," Azile said, raising her hand slightly above her head.

"Fine...pack up. Travis, keep an eye on your uncle, I'm going to see if I can get in his closet trap door."

EPILOGUE

Mrs. Deneaux watched from the truck cab as Tracy plunged the knife into Eliza's chest. "Didn't see that coming." She said making sure to keep low and not attract any attention. She regretted her decision now to leave the Talbot household, once again she would be on her own. She wasn't overly concerned because she did what all survivors did, she survived. She waited for another three days in that cab, living off the stores the driver had left behind, it wasn't much but it was more than her and her boyfriend had when he had got them lost hiking the Ozark Mountains some forty years previous. At one point during the ordeal she had thought about killing him so she could feed. Luckily for Baxter he had redeemed himself the following morning by trapping a rabbit which they had shared over a small fire.

With no zombies in sight, Mrs. Deneaux left the confines of the truck cab, she stepped down onto the pavement, took care of some pressing matters. She then unhitched the trailer, got back in and started the rig up. Even she had to laugh at the irony of it all as she drove off into the sunset.

THE KISS

"Why me?" I begged. Her silence only confounded my bewilderment. "I can't."

The thin wisp of what some may construe as a smile vanished. As her arm came back down, I could feel the reneging of the offer. She approached slowly. I was going from freedom to food. My brain screamed for flight, the fight portion was nonexistent. This was no battle of wills, I was helpless, like a fear-frozen marmot I waited for the screaming eagle to descend and sink its claws deep into my flesh. I did not even have enough control to close my eyes. I watched in increasing horror as she approached; death would not be swift. My bladder burned to be released. I was denied even that last suffrage of indignity. A fly crawled into her nose. She paid it no more attention than the lice that swung freely from her dirty matted hair. A beetle plowed its way through a small hole in her neck holding a small nugget of meat, a trophy garnered from who knows where. The only thing still working was my olfactory sensors. This had to have been done on purpose. Gorge tried in vain to roar up and out of my stomach. The fetid odor was so palpable, I could see it, I could taste it. Like Campbell's soup, it was so thick I could eat it with a fork. Yeah, she hadn't cut off my sense of sarcasm either. Thin strips of flesh which used to be lips parted, revealing black cracked teeth from which strings of meat hung in decaying strands. Her charcoal gray tongue flicked over them, attempting to pull away some of the tastier morsels. She stood toe-to-toe with me, not six inches from my face. Sweat coursed down my body. I shook from impotence and then that stilled. I wouldn't die fighting, but at least I'd be standing, small consolation. It's like 'winning' a participation trophy in Little League baseball. Who gives a shit.

What would it feel like to have your face ripped open? Would she still my pain centers? Doubtful. I couldn't tell much from her near-frozen features, but still I sensed that she was taking some form of perverse satisfaction from these events. She moved in closer; I would have offered her a mint if I had one. My eyes still were not allowed to close. My vision of her blurred as she moved in even closer. A fly landed on my eyeball. It was singularly up to this point in my life, the most disgusting thing that had ever happened to me. Then my zombie girl topped it, she kissed me. My innards roiled in protest, my guts churned like a washing machine on spin cycle. If I wasn't allowed output through my intake or outlet valves this was going to blow a hole through my midsection *a la* Ripley's Alien. The kiss was not so surprisingly, very cold, but very surprisingly tender. It was literally the kiss of death from the dead. It doesn't get much more ironic than that, does it? A Brillo pad wrapped around coarse grit sandpaper applied at a hundred and ninety revolutions per minute under skin-scalding hot water would never allow me to feel clean again. I was tainted, for fuck's sake a zombie is kissing me. Didn't she get my bio? I'm a card-carrying germaphobe!

As she slowly pulled away, a dark viscous fluid kept us tenuously connected. The fly finally descended from my eye to land on this small bridge. Her tongue shot out, incredibly long, and pulled the fly into her canines. I swear I could hear the small crunching of its delicate exoskeleton. The spin cycle was in full throttle. A whoosh of haunted air escaped her lips. She was laughing, she had known exactly what she had done and she found humor in her dark actions. She pulled back another foot and let loose her controls. I fell to the ground, afflicted with crippling cramps. I rolled into a protective fetal position hugging my midsection. Mount Vesuvius erupted. Hot refuse steamed on the cold ground; the whoosh of air which accompanied her amusement persisted. Glad I could be her entertainment. For long minutes I alternated between evacuating my stomach and pulling in long, cold drags of air. How long this happened, I'm not sure. The pain lessened minutely—small fractions of degrees is the best way I can explain it. Each breath was better than the previous but only in infinitesimally small measures. It might have been minutes or days, all reference to time was lost, although my cheek touching the ground was rapidly becoming cold and my refused refuse was not steaming anymore.

"Mike?" I heard a tenuously thin voice try to break through the paralyzing grip of insanity that was beginning to blanket my mind.

"Mike?" There it was again, a disassociated voice speaking an incoherent word. "Grab his legs, I'll get his head."

I felt myself being lifted and then, mercifully, blackness sheathed my capacity for thought. I was floating in a white void, but I was not afraid, I was free; free from burden, free from sin, free from responsibility…and then I think I puked again. Not because I could 'feel' the sensation, but because I heard the disgust from one of the people carrying me. I found it funny the same way an insane person finds humor in slinging shit at walls. How different was this from that? I was close to the edge, maybe I had even taken that first perilous step over and gravity had finally worked its magic. I was being pulled down into the abyss. There wasn't a drug invented that would raise this sinking ship. I spiraled down. Whiteness faded to black, cognitive thought became an illusion.

***

Eventually, I will tell you what happened while I traveled the netherworlds, but that all hinges on what happens in the foreseeable future. I had come out from under my unnatural hibernation in remarkably good shape. There were no ill effects that I knew about; they would manifest later. I had lost weight and I was as thirsty as I had ever been, but after downing three huge glasses of water I felt right as rain, even more so. Now I know this sounds weird, but power is the word that comes foremost in my mind. Maybe healthy would be a better descriptive, but not as accurate, or as powerful. I just don't know, and I really don't have the time to dwell on it.

***

These are as near to the events as I can remember. Having lost the majority of my journals, I am thankful that I have found the power of an almost photographic memory with which to recreate the events. Some of them are indelible; it would take more than death itself to erase them from my mind. I should know.

A lot has happened since Little Turtle. I've lost a lot of friends, loved ones, and even a significant portion of myself. But we're the closest we have ever been to a victory. Okay, scratch that, we are the furthest from defeat that we have ever been. We've almost pulled into a stalemate. I consider that a huge improvement. Hey, we take what's given to us and do the best we can.

For three earth days I walked in Eliza's world, on her side it was significantly longer. My thoughts are that it had much more to do with the perceived passing of time rather than actual, but to*may*to, to*mah*to…who gives a shit when you're in hell. Okay, not literally, but it wasn't a walk in the park either. Henry just perked his ears up when he…what? Heard me think that? Is that possible? He was sitting with me doing his best to absorb the cold that flowed through me. He gave me a wide grin and laid his massive head back down on my lap.

"Son of a bitch," I said aloud. "You can read my thoughts." Henry's little tail wagged furiously, his eyes were shut. The economy of movement in this dog was a study in perfection; it was damn near an art form.

But I'm digressing and it's pretty much on purpose. I sat down here today with the express reason of relating all the events that happened while I was under Eliza's spell? Was that it? More like poison. But do people that go through traumatic events like a car crash really want to relive the whole damn thing, like when the safety glass shatters and chunks of sharpened fragments imbed themselves in the side of your face, rupturing your eye? Or how about when you're thrown violently sideways and the gearshift goes up and under your rib cage busting out your sternum, bone fragments cutting through the aorta, your life blood bleeding out inside of you. Are these things you want to revisit? I don't.

My wife says it will be cathartic, I say bullshit, she just wants me to get out from under her feet. I have not come out of this last battle as well as I went in. I know it and she knows it. I've been diminished, that's the best way I can put. I need to be around those I love CONSTANTLY and I think I'm driving Tracy a little nuts. But even in the best of times I had that effect on people. At least Henry doesn't seem to mind my constant ministrations.

"Damn, with the tail again, Henry? You're not even awake, I can hear you snoring." His tail didn't stop.

Fine, I'll corral my thoughts, kicking and screaming mind you and I'll probably lodge a formal protest when I'm done but let's see where this journey brings me. Back from the edge or over it, right now both are viable alternatives to the way I feel now.

The kiss…that damned kiss, it would have been more humanly (humanely?) of her to just rip my face off and be done with me, but cruelty is (was) Eliza's game. She survived the centuries with it as her guide, her driving force, and she was adept. She knew where I would end up, my guess is/was that she was hoping that I would never recover, that I would always be left to wander there, but she never took into account the power of love. How could she? She only ever had a taste of it, a morsel from her brother, whereas the Talbots basked in it like a Spring Break co-ed in coconut oil. (Good visual? Tracy probably won't appreciate that, but she's the one making me write this damn thing so she'll have to damn well live with it!) *Sorry, honey, if you read this*

The damned kiss, I felt myself slipping away the moment our lips parted. Black dots began to invade my vision. First they were barely bigger than a black fly (which I have since come to loathe here in Maine. Want to know the seasons in Maine? It goes, Summer, Fall, Winter, Mud and Black Fly, I shit you not!) I should have picked a better locale for my last stand or final resting spot. Sorry, I am avoiding this trip down memory lane like a fat kid avoids fourth period gym.

So the spots began to expand—black fly, mosquito, house fly, horse fly, fucking wasp, crow—then the sensation of my head bouncing off the frozen tundra. For a while there was nothing more than the sensation of pure and utter blackness. I was aware, but I was alone. It's hard to describe. I did not have the sensation of falling, but I also wasn't rooted to anything. I was afraid to move not knowing if I would fall into an abyss or into a wall. Terror began to mount; I had never felt so powerless in my life. There was nothing I could do. If she had just left me there, I would have been gone in a matter of hours, though the concept of time meant nothing there either.

By degrees the veil was unwrapped from my eyes, for time unimaginable there was a gauzy light that seeped into my vision, slowly that changed to a pre-dawn storm morning muted light. Then blissfully (at least at first) I was able to see, at least shapes, bathed in shadow but it was something. The human mind deprived of stimuli will begin to make its own nightmares up, like I needed any help in that department. The expanse that started to show itself could have been Mars as barren and rocky as it was. Or it could have been Eliza's parched, dry, dead heart, either would fit. I found myself standing on a significant sized boulder, had I moved I would have fallen a good two or three feet, not enough to die but maybe twist an ankle maybe bust a knee cap, who knows I'm getting up in there in years stuff doesn't work quite as well as when I used to take it for granted, like when I was a teenager.

I gingerly hopped down and tried to orientate myself, but the light did not come from a single source in the sky it was just an illumination across the entire expanse of my visage, that it was an ugly pea green did little to help with my discomfort.

"You ready for this, Talbot?" I asked myself. I even jumped a little it was the first sound I'd heard since this ordeal started and it startled me, God I hope nobody reads this. BT sees this and he's gonna call me a little girl. One direction seemed as good as the next so I took off for what I figured was north, but only because that was the direction I was headed, there wasn't a clue at all to let me know whether I had chosen wisely.

I whistled a little Zeppelin, *When the Levee Breaks* I think, maybe a bit of *In My time Of Dying*, followed by *In the Evening*, but my song choices started to sound a little ominous so I left it to the professionals. The light never changed in brightness as I trudged on through, at some points I could feel a 'shifting' in myself like I was being moved. And occasionally I swore I heard Tracy or the kids, maybe even a bark or two from Henry, but it was so far away it could have been brought along a non-existent breeze from a place that ceased to exist.

At times I felt that the ground I was on was sloped upward but the horizon never changed, odds were my dominant leg was pulling me just enough off course to lead me around in huge circles, learned this in the Marine Corps but without a compass or a point of reference there was no way for me to make any corrections, and I had a sneaking suspicion that even if I had a compass there would be no magnetic North anyway. No it would be much better to believe that I was still somehow on Earth.

If rocks were a life form I would have been inundated, with teeming abundant, prosperous life! But the world I was in was sterile, no sun, no water how could anything survive here. Then had I not stumbled over it I would have completely passed it by. As far as plants go, this would have been the one that the greenhouse threw out after the planting season was over. It would have been at the bottom of the large dumpster in the back of the building covered by the dried manure and broken bags of decorative rock. Right then that little runt of a twisted stick popping up from the soil was singularly the most beautiful thing I think I had ever seen.

I cried as I dropped to my knees to get a better look. No I didn't cry out, like 'Aha!' I actually cried. You know, the kind where moisture actually flows from the eyes…yeah that kind. A starving horse would have passed this thing over, yet, at this moment I would have staked my entire life on it. This represented a chance; if this was alive, there was more…that was for sure. Life is adaptable. Like a typical selfish human my first thought was to pull it up and take it with me, if I could have punched myself with enough force to make it worthwhile I would have.

It took me long moments before I could leave my new best friend behind. We had shared so much. I told him about my plight and he listened patiently. I knew it was a 'he' because he didn't interrupt me once. (I'm dead meat if Tracy sees this—WAY worth it though). I kept moving on, this was a *barely* habitable place. Although I wasn't sure if I was still trapped in my mind, or Eliza's for that matter (though I didn't know who she was at the time). It was another forty-seven days (or an hour) before I ran across the next plant, it was most assuredly a brother to the one I had met earlier, it was slightly more full-bodied, but it wasn't going to win any competitions at the Rose Off. I stopped briefly to acknowledge its existence and kept going.

Then I saw something in the far distance scurrying

off. 'Scurrying off' was just fine with me, that meant it wasn't coming my way, the best defense I would be able to muster would revolve around some rock throwing and in my High School hey days I hadn't been able to get a ball much over 65 miles per hour and I know my shoulder hadn't aged very well. Best I'd be able to do would be a nice bruising before whatever wanted to eat me slammed into my body with teeth a gnashing.

But whatever was going on, I was coming out of the abyss of sterility. The outer fringes of hardy life for sure, but who knows what I would begin to encounter as I kept moving steadily forward, but what were my options? Stay and languish waiting for death, but I wasn't sure if I could really die here. I'd been walking for hours and I wasn't tired, thirsty or hungry, I just *was.*

I was self-aware enough to realize that this woman (who I will now call Eliza going forward) hadn't physically teleported me to anywhere, but mentally I was on a trip for the ages. And not like any trip I had ever taken in my experimental drug days of college (shit forget Tracy finding this, I'm glad, in one sense, that my dad will never see this, he knew I wasn't the greatest student in school but he most likely didn't know why, even at this juncture in life I had no desire to spill the beans on what I used to do).

Mentally I was out to lunch. Was my body still in the ground across from Little Turtle or had Eliza hefted me over her shoulder and was even now bringing me back to her lair for whatever insidious reason she might have? I had no idea. More than likely, I was propped up in the corner of my home drooling excessively after finally having traveled into the deep end of psychosis. How long would Tracy change my diapers before she just put me out of all of our miseries?

I walked on because sitting and reflecting on what was or could be or may be, really just isn't my way. If you've read any of my journals I'm sure you've come to the realization that I act first and then have to figure out a way to get out of my newest predicament. Someday I'll learn not to do that, but my guess is that it will be my last (day).

The pea green color may have been steadily brightening it was difficult to say, if it was happening at all, it was in degrees so slow as to not be registerable. But I just got the feeling that was what was happening. Still didn't know if it even meant anything, although I would take any sort of light no matter the color over the pitch blackness I had been immersed in earlier. I would have feared any sort of movement in that environment. Looking back on all this now, I've got to wonder if Tommy's hand played in any of this. I can't imagine that Eliza would have given me any sort of handhold from which to pull myself out of the quagmire she had plunged me into.

The illumination had Tommy written all over it. In the short time that I got to know the boy he had stamped himself indelibly onto my life and the lives of all of those around me. It would have been just like him to risk everything to help a man he barely knew at the time. Although he was much more aware of the bigger picture than I was. I was under the very misguided thought process that I was only dealing with a zombie apocalypse, why and how could I have known any differently. Well like Alex's *meemaw* used to say, "When it rains, you get wet." No wiser words could have been uttered.

I miss Alex. My gut says he's dead, but I don't think I'll ever be able to confirm that until I meet him once again topside if the big man deems me worthy. Wow, I'm pretty easily distracted these days. I think a lot has to do with the injuries I've sustained. I think for necessity sake I will try harder to stay on task if only to finish this infernal story. Although it's hard not to miss the ones that have fallen along the way, it's when I write that the pain becomes acute, focused like the tip of a particularly sharp knife blade, it finds ways to cut and slice, deeply. Sorry. Where was I? Right, I didn't know it then, but it had to be Tommy's influence in this alien scape.

Fuck! (I yelled it, then wrote it, *that* was cathartic.)

The puke green light was getting brighter. *I think I've established that.* I was coming across increasing vegetation, nothing that could really even sustain a lone locust but there was a comfort of shared life here. I hadn't seen anything scurry off since that first time and was now beginning to wonder if I had even seen it or whether it was just my mind trying to establish some sort of normalcy to this void although a Wendy's or Subway would have been preferable (but not McDonald's, never them again.)

Still I wandered, much like Moses. (My blasphemy alone in these journals is probably enough to keep me exiled from THE epitome of gated communities.) My guess was I was meant to 'wait' in this place while my real self wasted away, would I know when that end came. Would I cease to exist here or would that mean I was now forever bound here. Did the zombie girl have that kind of sway? Could she parlay my soul? I wasn't much of a people person, but who the hell was I going to issue snide and sarcastic comments to if I was alone. I could always berate myself, it wouldn't be the first time, but that would get old quick.

I kept walking for what else was there, and then, in the hazy distance, there was an irregularity. At first I could not discern it and then it began to dawn on me that I was seeing objects not of nature. Man made? Could it be? My heart leapt, that of course was until I began to think of where I may or may not be, would I want to come across anything made by the sentient beings of this place, because that would mean the sentient beings were around also. Maybe that would be preferable, one quick death instead of this long drawn out crap.

Typical Talbot, jump headlong into the teeth of the tiger instead of gently skirting around. I guess I just work better with the gun pointing at my head rather than having to think my way out. Well when you have as little going on in your head as I do you could see why I tend to go with my strengths! As the day wore on I began to see wisps of smoke coming up from a variety of homes, I guess huts might be a more apt word. Well shit, if I want to get honest, more like earthen mounds with a thatch roof.

"Hello," I said, I wanted to yell it, but I still felt like a stranger in a strange land and until I knew the customs I wanted to be as discreet as possible. I began to peer inside of a hut when the flap of deer hide used as a door began to rustle. I stepped back as a heavyset man. No…that was the wrong terminology, he wasn't fat, he was thick as if he were hewn from one solid block of wood. There wasn't a curve on the man, he was all hard angles. I had height on him and that was it, his arms looked as thick as my legs. He walked right past me and I couldn't have been more than six inches from him. I wanted to shout at him to look at me, but the square set of his jaw outlined in a scowl made me think twice.

I could hear guttural talking inside, it sounded Germanic but the brutish words issuing softly made even the harsh modern day German language seem French. The only reason I dared peek in was the voices sounded young, I might be able to take the off spring of the thick man that had just passed me by. You'll notice I said 'maybe'. "Hello?" I asked as I walked in. I had a girlfriend back in college that was taking German as a second language. She used to speak it all the time around me. You'd think I would have at least retained the word 'hello' in German. Nope not me I was too busy staring at her tits, sue me. I'm sorry if what every male on the planet does offends you.

Listen, the planet right now is in the midst of a near extinction event, I can help with the repopulating of our home. It's VERY, VERY simple, because if you're a woman and a guy is next to you, he wants to have sex—except for the obvious exceptions, related, dead, or zombie. Other than that, if he's had a good sandwich today, humping is the only other thing on his mind. I mean now that sports have literally been wiped off the table, what else is there really?

I think I'm avoiding this next part; I've been sucker punched in the gut with less wind knocked out of me. The inside of the hut had a stone fireplace off to the side, a small table was in the center and a pile of filthy animal skins was in the far corner where I imagine the family, I use that word loosely, slept. A girl with long raven hair was leaning over a table, tears fell heavily from her face, her torn and worn skirt was draped around her shoulders, her skinny legs caked in dirt were shaking violently, an even younger boy was facing away from the scene he kept repeatedly banging his head against a stout branch, the sobbing and the hollow knocking were the only sounds in the small enclosure.

"Are you okay?" I asked. My heart was thumping wildly in my throat. I couldn't think of anything else to say. The girl had been raped and the young boy, I figured to be her brother, had not dealt with the violence very well. What kind of monster does this? I put my hands up in as non-threatening a posture as possible and approached. I had made up my mind, I was going to kill that man or die trying.

"Miss," I said trying to sound as comforting as possible. Her tears and mutterings kept up, the boy was now rocking back and forth crying heavily himself, he was saying something, but even in a foreign language I could tell it was gibberish by its tone and cadence. The girl had still not acknowledged my presence as I approached. She looked up wildly when she heard a noise behind me.

Zombie girl? Was the first thought that came through my head, she was a dead ringer for the thing that had kissed me albeit an earlier version, this girl couldn't have been more than twelve or thirteen, it was tough to tell with the amount of malnourishment she seemed to be sustaining. I stepped back as her intense, frightened gaze bore holes through me, then I realized she couldn't see me at all. She was reacting to the thick man who had come back from whatever errand asshole rapists do.

He yelled at the girl and she immediately stood up and placed her dress back into place. She stood there with her head down, looking completely beaten as the man kept berating her. This wasn't just some stranger. The longer I stayed and witnessed the interaction, such as it was, the more

I came to the realization that this thing that called himself a man was the father of the two children in the hut. He yelled until they began to do menial work around the house. The boy was fixing holes in the walls where light was spilling through and the girl took the pile of skins and brought them outside. She placed them on the branch of a small tree and began to beat the bugs and dirt out of them with a stick. Oh how I wished she would use that on the man.

I was a ghost here. I had no more influence than a flying piece of dust. No that wasn't true, dust could carry germs. Germs could be inhaled and the host could become infected and die. I shuddered at the thought (airborne germs I mean) not me being a ghost part. I watched as something in that girl was dying, she had lost whatever semblance of innocence she had possessed, it was early in her development but I thought I could see the foreshadowing of what she was to become. Abuse takes so much that is good from our children and replaces it with so much that is dark. Her scales had not yet been tipped but the process had begun.

Her brother came out and lay by her feet. He was still crying. The girl alternated between beating the skins and rubbing his head.

They began to utter that guttural language that I could not discern so I filled in what I thought they were saying merely by their tone and posture.

Tomas looked up at his sister, his tear-soaked face lined with muddy runnels. "Are you okay, Lizzie?"

A quick narrowing of the eyes, then a softening when she realized who she was talking to. She got down on her haunches and stroked his face. "Tomas, I have to leave this place."

Then and there I realized that Eliza had sacrificed all that she was and could have become to shield her brother from the man that they called 'father'. "He'll stop, Lizzie! Please don't leave," he begged, clutching onto her.

"Oh, Tomas," she cried. "He'll never stop." And in that she was right. But I think Eliza feared what would become of her brother if he was left behind to face the wrath of that sick bastard.

That was Eliza. She had been a small girl in a brutal world and she should have died after a pitiful existence. The dialog between the two siblings had no sooner finished when I felt a loud whooshing noise pass around my head, much like if you were crazy enough to stick your head out of a car moving at a hundred miles per hour down the Autobahn. I was at what looked like an alleyway abutting up to a small market; although I had not moved my feet so much as an inch. As I began to orientate myself, I noticed an older Eliza being dragged along by her father. He had one large meaty hand wrapped completely around her forearm and was pulling her towards the back of the alleyway.

My heart began to sink and gorge began to rise, if that was even possible in the embodiment that I was adorning. Eliza's head was whipping back and forth violently as she fought desperately to be released from her father's clutches. He turned and open palmed her so hard against the side of the face that she staggered. I impotently stepped forward. If I could have willed his death I would have done so. She recovered quickly and the look she directed at him more than adequately reflected the vampire she would become. I think even her father caught a glint of it for he pulled harder and faster to get her to her final destination and away from him.

A hook nosed man waited fervently in the corner, he may or may not have been rubbing his hands together, I honestly can't remember, I was so sickened from the events taking place I couldn't think clearly.

Asshole, I mean Eliza's father, pulled the girl flush with himself and then thrust her towards the other man. Eliza looked back defiantly at her father with eyes almost as black as coal. Hooknose pulled some coins out of his pocket and put them in the outstretched hand of Eliza's father. He eyed them greedily, then quickly put them in his own pocket. Eliza spit in her father's face and let loose with a litany I can only imagine was some of the most colorful commentary known up to that period in time.

Her father reared back and looked about to let loose with another vicious blow when Hooknose interceded. He waggled his finger and seemed to be saying that she was his property now and that the father no longer had claim. Eliza's father seemed happy to be rid of the girl, he 'pahed' as he turned and left, still looking at the money he clutched in his hand, never once turning to look at his daughter.

Hooknose was leering. It was not difficult to imagine what he was thinking. Eliza had a hint of fear in her, but she tried her best not to show it, weakness was not a virtue in this world. The scene again whooshed away, but was repeated often throughout the years. Eliza grew older, but there never seemed to be a shortage of lecherous men around. With each transfer of her body, I watched more of her soul become exposed and stripped bare. She looked beaten, worn down, possibly even disease-ravaged. Who knew what she could be carrying from her exposure to the worst of what the world had to offer.

I 'whooshed' again, this time into a market and at first I was unsure as to what I was hearing, then it dawned on me. I was hearing English. A cockney version for sure but it was English, I could understand at least a good two thirds of it through the thick accent. I won't even pretend to think that I could 'translate' the rest. I watched as Eliza was coming directly towards me, she looked both fiercely proud and sufficiently beat down it was a strange dichotomy. She looked much like the woman I would come to know as my mortal enemy Eliza, I'll be honest I was scared shitless to be this close to her even if she couldn't see me, even if this was only an echo of the past, didn't matter. Here was the woman that had the ways and means and, more importantly, the drive to kill all of those I loved.

I wished I could kill her here, right now, but I also felt a deep pity, her life had been nothing but a cesspool of slavery and deprivation. A man who I had not noticed earlier swept passed me on the left on an intercept course for her.

For a moment I wondered if he was also 'outside' of this time and knew that she had to be destroyed. He was a destroyer alright, but not just of bodies, souls were included.

I watched as he latched on to her arm much like her father had five maybe six years previous. Her eyes ratcheted up defiantly to look at him, then I watched as the will was sapped out of her and was replaced with rabid fear. She was petrified, but did not struggle as the stranger spoke.

His words were clear and of a higher origin than the rabble strewn around him, who I noticed tried their best to ignore him completely.

"I can give you the world," he promised her. "I can take you away from this filth of humanity. Do you want that?"

Eliza alternated between nodding and shaking her head back and forth. Who wouldn't want out of the shit hole she was in, but she was thinking the cost might be steeper than she was prepared to pay.

"Answer me correctly, girl," she stranger said angrily. "Either I will dine and you will die, or I will show you a world you never knew existed."

She was trapped. What were her options? I wonder now, if an Eliza with a soul was able to look back on her life if she would have stayed human. She had spent the last five hundred years making mankind pay for her rotten childhood, think of how many psychiatrists off-spring college tuitions she could have funded in that time. The thought of Eliza on a couch explaining all her problems brought a small smile to my face.

Eliza nodded as the stranger led her into an alleyway much like the one that had first enlisted her into the ranks of slavery, this was slavery but of another sort.

"I am going to feed on you slightly." Eliza's eyes grew wide. "If you live, you will be changed forever. You will be beautiful forever," he said, stroking some stray hair that had fallen across her eyes. Eliza winced but did not move. "When you are strong enough, I want you to meet me in London. There is a pub down by the docks called the Dragoon, I will be there tomorrow night only. If you do not show, it will be because the vampirism did not take." Eliza backed away at that word.

Vampire was still a scary word today. I can't imagine the connotations it held back in these dark ages.

"It would be a pity if you died," he said as he leaned in and bit deeply. Eliza's head tilted back as her eyes rolled up inside her head. Her ruddy cheeks began to drain of all color.

The stranger took his measure and seemed to take a cruel dose of pleasure when Tomas ran up to his sister. He moved swiftly and silently away as Tomas cradled his sister in his arms. I wept at the sight. I figured this was as about as safe as it was ever going to get for me to cry and nobody to actually witness it. What little part of her was still left when the vampire came was stripped away like rotten bark on a dead tree.

***

Her eye's fluttered open as Tomas cascaded her face with his tears. "Tomas? Is that really you, Tomas?" Eliza asked.

"It's me, Lizzie, it's me!" he cried. "We're finally together again! How I've missed you! Now we can be together again forever!"

"Tomas," Lizzie said sadly, stroking his face gently, "it's too late for me."

"What are you talking about, Lizzie? I'm here you're here, we're together." I wept even as Tomas uttered the words. He had been minutes from finding his sister still human. But she was not intact, her life thus far had twisted and gnarled her, she would be distrustful and bitter until the day she died, unfortunately the stranger had now extended that indefinitely.

Even as he wept for joy, it was not difficult to tell that

he sensed something else happening something evil beyond even his extraordinary sense of empathy.

"What is the matter Lizzie? You are burning up." Tomas asked the question but even from my vantage point I could see the snow around her melting at an alarming rate as if she were a mini sun going nova.

"You should go, Tomas," she said, closing her eyes.

"I can't leave you, Lizzie. We're all we have, you and me. You told me you would always look out for me. You were the only one that told me I didn't have witches living in my head."

I had no idea what the boy was referring to, but in these Middle Ages it was never good to be associated with witches. His life had most likely only been spared because he had left home to find his sister.

"I love you, Lizzie."

I wanted to turn away this was worse than watching the Hallmark channel.

"I love you too, Tomas. And that is why you should go."

"Why won't you open your eyes, Lizzie? Please, please look at me."

Tears pushed through her closed lids. "Please, Tomas, don't look at me this way. I'm not the sister you used to know. Unspeakable things have been done to me and I found a way to right those wrongs and I took it. I will exact my revenge."

"That's not how my Lizzie talks," Tomas said as he wiped at his blurring eyes.

"GO!" She pushed him away. Her eyes seemed to produce their own light as she looked at him menacingly. I backed up an extra step. This was more of the Eliza I knew, unbridled power and a deep wish to unleash it on all those around her.

"I will not!" he screamed, but to me it looked like he was tensing to spring away from her.

Eliza sat up. I could see Tomas' window of

opportunity to make a clean get away closing rapidly on exposed fingers. Tomas finally seemed to be getting it as he stood and started backing up, it would have been impossible to miss her cross over from love to predatory awareness. He kept shaking his head in denial but I knew that wasn't going to help him at all. The field mouse can continue to eat its seed even in the talons of the hawk, but that isn't going to change the outcome: flesh rending and bone crunching.

With an ungodly speed, Eliza wrapped her hand around Tomas' neck. He was at least six inches off the ground; I knew that feeling well enough.

"Lizzie, please," he begged.

Eliza didn't waste any time as she bit down hard on his neck. Tomas screamed in pain.

"Lizzie please, I love you!" His tears splashed down on her upturned face.

Some last remnant of Lizzie rose to the surface. She pulled her extended canines out of his neck. "GO!" she screamed again. "I won't be able to stop next time." She looked defeated, with her head bowed. Tomas dropped to the ground as she released her grip.

He scurried away. I would imagine scarcely believing the turn of events. "I love you, Lizzie. I will follow you until I find a way to fix whatever has happened here tonight."

I watched for a moment as Eliza hesitated, she looked like she had regretted her last decision. If I hadn't already met Tommie, I would have assumed she finished him off right there and then. She warred within herself for long minutes fighting the urge to hunt him down, the only thing that might have saved Tomas was an unfortunate boy who had just bought a loaf of bread and was most likely taking a short cut to get home. The bread soaked in the melting snow as Eliza drained the boy dry. She discarded his husk much like a smoker would a used cigarette, she flicked him away with no regard for who he was or had been.

He was a meal plain and simple. I mean, I guess it makes sense. Lions don't sit there and think about the gazelle's hopes and dreams as they rip chunks of meat from its hindquarters, why would she? We whooshed again, the journeys through the ripples of her mind were causing no small amounts of vertigo but since I was fairly certain I didn't have a stomach which to throw up with I should be fine.

Through a thick glassy haze I watched her meeting with The Stranger in the tavern in London, but her memory of it must have been skewed from the affects of the cross over, she was having a difficult time keeping her head up as long dirty stringy strands of her hair kept pooling up on the rough wooden table.

The Stranger smiled as Eliza staggered in, though she was the only female, lithe and beautiful in form and almost most assuredly drunk beyond awareness, the men in the tavern fell over themselves trying to get away from her. The Stranger did not stand to help her but merely smiled slightly as she fell into her seat.

"I did not think you would make the transition, and I'm still not so sure," he said as he tightly gripped her chin and thrust her face up so that he could look in her eyes. "You have eaten? Impressive, most die in these first few hours because they cannot overcome their human weaknesses. But you're a survivor aren't you? I think I chose wisely." He let go of her and her forehead almost bounced off the table.

"Come," he said, standing and whisking quickly towards the door. He did not help her or wait, she struggled to stand and lurched out into the murky light to try and keep pace. We whooshed quickly from scene to scene, most consisted of her severe beatings at the hands of her 'savior.' He had saved her from one hell only to be thrust into a different layer. The only time he seemed even remotely 'human' was when they would go on feeding frenzies in some of the more outlying areas of Britannia, if that was what it was even called back then. I got the sense we were still on English speaking soil, but mostly all I was hearing from the peasant populations was crying and screaming as the vampire duo tore through them like hyenas at an orphanage.

You get the imagery, right? It was that bad. I *wanted* to forget that this had ever happened. The human misery these two were doling out was without rival. They actually reveled in their kills, playing with children much like a cat does with a mouse. Even going so far as to toss one back and forth as they took small measures of blood, the mother screaming in horror as she would run from one vampire to the other in a desperate bid to get them to stop. If I could have stepped through the barrier of time to never return to my own era just to have the chance to stop them I would have. I was merely a voyeur to their disease.

This repeated to the point where I just stopped watching. She had each kill catalogued in her memory like a soccer mom stores dinner recipes on a little rolodex, although really, how many mom's still did that up until the end. Most likely all of that was either on a smart phone or a tablet, these days though it would be whatever was scavenged. It was only by mere chance that I caught what unfolded next, I was getting a crick in my non-existent neck and pulled my head back up from my penny finding pose.

The Stranger was completely old-school as far as vamps go, he was sleeping in a coffin, but where there should have been dirt I saw what looked like the finest of silks, apparently blood thirsty creatures of the night liked their comfort also. Eliza was staring down at him, she was on the far side of the coffin her hands guiltily behind her back, from this angle I could not tell what she was hiding. She was about as coy as a five year old with chocolate all over his face and a busted cookie jar on the kitchen floor, adamantly denying any knowledge to the events in said room.

She kept inching closer to him, peering intently at his face. It was impossible to figure out what she was doing but she looked to me like she was trying to find his soul.

"Good luck with that," I said aloud.

Eliza looked straight up and at me as I said the words,

she startled the shit out of me, I was pretty glad I was incorporeal at the moment or I would have had a hell of a mess to clean up. After my heart stopped trying to dislodge itself from my chest I realized she was looking through me and at the doorway where something heavy had scraped against stone, at least that's what it sounded like. When she looked back down at The Stranger, his eyes were open and he was eyeing Eliza curiously and I might add a little warily. It seems the same noise had disturbed his beauty rest.

"Up early, my dear?" he asked.

Her head moved back, but she did not. Eliza nodded once and I could tell she was wavering with whatever her plan had been.

He began to sit up; that was all the trigger Eliza needed as she pulled a large wooden stake from behind her back. What happened next was too fast to track with human eyes, but when I caught up, Eliza had plunged the stake at least 8 inches deep into The Stranger's chest. He in the mean time had wrapped his large hand around her slender throat, he was dying but he seemed very determined to take her with him. The world would have been a much brighter place had they both succeeded. Eliza finally wrenched free as the vampire's heart began to beat its final rhythm. Eliza stepped back and placed her hands to her bruised and blackened throat.

"You will never lay your hands on me again, Victor. No one will," she rasped heavily.

"I was wondering when you would turn. I knew I should have killed you weeks ago," Victor said as he placed both his hands around the stake.

I thought he was going to try and pull it out, but he seemed incapable of much more than lying there as his...what poured out? His death? Can death pour out? Nobody spills death. I'd let future theologians worry about it. I was glad beyond words that this monster was dying but he had bred one that would far surpass his mastery. Then Eliza hit me with words so hard I was knocked back into the reality of the

Zombie Apocalypse.

"I curse you, Victor Talbot, my hope is that you walk the world in eternal darkness. I will destroy every seed that you have ever sowed."

Check out these other titles by Mark Tufo

Zombie Fallout

It was a flu season like no other. With fears of contracting the H1N1 virus running rampant through the country, people lined up in droves to try and obtain one of the coveted vaccines. What was not known, was the effect this largely untested, rushed to market, inoculation was to have on the unsuspecting throngs.

Within days, feverish folk throughout the country, convulsed, collapsed and died, only to be re-born. With a taste for brains, blood and bodies, these modern day zombies scoured the lands for their next meal. Overnight the country became a killing ground for the hordes of zombies that ravaged the land.

This is the story of Michael Talbot, his family and his

friends. When disaster strikes, Mike a self-proclaimed survivalist, does his best to ensure the safety and security of those he cares for. Can brains beat brain eaters? It's a battle for survival, winner take all!

Zombie Fallout 2: A Plague Upon Your Family

Zombies have destroyed Little Turtle, the Talbot's find themselves on the run from a ruthless enemy that will stop at nothing to end their lineage. Here are the journal entries of Michael Talbot, his wife Tracy, their three kids Nicole, Justin and Travis. With them are Brendon, Nicole's fiancée and Tommy previously a Wal-Mart door greeter who may be more than he seems. Together they struggle against a relentless enemy that has singled them out above all others. As they travel across the war-torn country side they soon learn that there are more than just zombies to be fearful of, with law and order a long distant memory some humans have decided to take any and all matters into their own hands. Can the Talbots come through unscathed or will they suffer the fate of so many countless millions before them. It's not just brains versus brain-eaters anymore. And the stakes may be higher than merely life and death with eternal souls on the line.

Zombie Fallout 3: The End...

Continues Michael Talbot's quest to be rid of the evil named Eliza that hunts him and his family across the country. As the world spirals even further down into the abyss of apocalypse one man struggles to keep those around him safe. Side by side Michael stands with his wife, their children, his friends and the wonder Bulldog Henry along with the Wal-Mart greeter Tommy who is infinitely more than he appears and whether he is leading them to salvation or death is only a measure of degrees.

As Justin continues to slip further into the abyss he receives help from an unexpected ally all of which leads up to the biggest battle thus far.

Dr. Hugh Mann – A Zombie Fallout Prequel 3.5

Dr Hugh Mann delves deeper into what caused the zombie invasion. Early in the 1900's Dr. Mann discovers a parasite that brings man to the brink of an early extinction. Come along on the journey with Jonathan Talbot is bride to be Marissa and the occasional visitations from the boy with the incredible baklava. Could there be a cure somewhere here and what part does the blood locket play?

Zombie Fallout IV: The End...Has Come and Gone

The End...has come and gone. This is the new beginning, the new world order and it sucks. The end for humanity came the moment the U.S. government sent out the infected flu shots. My name is Michael Talbot and this is my journal. I'm writing this because no one's tomorrow is guaranteed, and I have to leave something behind to those who may follow.

So continues Mike's journey, will he give up all that he is in a desperate bid to save his family and friends? Eliza is coming, can anyone be prepared?

Zombie Fallout V: Alive In A Dead World

Michael Talbot has set up a plan to finally turn the tables on his bitter rival Eliza. Sick of being relentlessly hunted, Mike asks for volunteers in a pivotal move that could finally end their conflict. But like what always happens to the best laid plans, nothing goes as it was drawn up. Now they are once again struggling to survive and more than one will succumb to the evil that walks the world.

Indian Hill

This first story is about an ordinary boy, who grows up in relatively normal times to find himself thrust into an extra-ordinary position. Growing up in suburban Boston he enjoys the trials and tribulations that all adolescents go through. From the seemingly tyrannical mother, to girl problems to run-ins with the law. From there he escapes to college out in Colorado with his best friend, Paul, where they begin to forge new relationships with those around them. It is one girl in particular that has caught the eye of Michael and he alternately pines for her and then laments ever meeting her.

It is on their true 'first' date that things go strangely askew. Mike soon finds himself captive aboard an alien vessel, fighting for his very survival. The aliens have devised gladiator type games. The games are of two-fold importance for the aliens. One reason, being for the entertainment value, the other reason being that they want to see how combative humans are, what our weaknesses and strengths are.

Follow Mike as he battles for his life and Paul as he battles to try and keep main stream US safe.

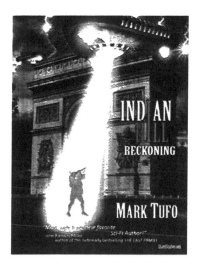

Indian Hill II: Reckoning

After escaping from the alien vessel with their Supreme Commander, Michael Talbot is now given the opportunity to hide in obscurity with the rest of the human race or rise to the occasion and once again he finds himself immersed in a battle that he wants nothing to do with.

Mike goes home and while reconnecting with a family that believed him dead, he decides to join whatever resistance force can be mustered to repel the oncoming invasion. As the world of man gets thrust towards the abyss of extinction, two women in love with the same man make a desperate bid to travel across the country to unite with him. Will mankind fall or will the tiny hu-mans thwart a takeover? Only time and bloodshed will tell.

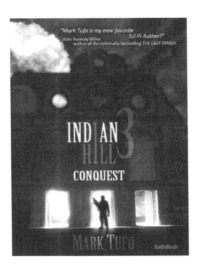

Indian Hill III: Conquest

The long awaited conclusion to man's very struggle to survive against overwhelming odds and an aggressive alien species hell-bent on enslaving the entire world.

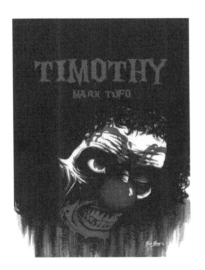

Timothy

Timothy was not a good man in life being undead did

little to improve his disposition. Find out what a man trapped in his own mind will do to survive when he wakes up to find himself a zombie controlled by a self-aware virus.

COMING SOON! - Part One in The Book of Riley series! - My Name is Riley

Follow the adventures of Riley an American Bulldog as she tries to keep her pack safe from a zombie invasion. Traveling with her are Ben-Ben the high strung Yorkie her favorite two-legger Jessie, Jessie's younger brother Zachary and Riley's arch-enemy Patches the Cat.

The Ravin
This is book one of the Indian Hill series in a more youth friendly version.

Coming Soon - The Prey! Book Two in the Youth Adventures of Michael Talbot.

The Spirit Clearing
Can love transcend even death?

Made in the USA
Lexington, KY
10 December 2012